Ask Alice

Fiction

Great Eastern Land
Real Life
English Settlement
After Bathing at Baxters: Stories
Trespass
The Comedy Man
Kept: A Victorian Mystery

Non-Fiction

A Vain Conceit: British Fiction in the 1980s
Other People: Portraits from the Nineties (with Marcus Berkmann)
After the War: The Novel and England since 1945
Thackeray
Orwell: The Life
On the Corinthian Spirit: The Decline of Amateurism in Sport
Bright Young People: The Rise and Fall of a Generation

Ask Alice

A NOVEL

D. J. TAYLOR

PEGASUS BOOKS
NEW YORK

ASK ALICE

Pegasus Books LLC
80 Broad Street, 5th Floor
New York, NY 10004

Copyright © 2009 by D. J. Taylor

First Pegasus Books edition April 2010

Library of Congress Cataloging-in-Publication Data is available.

ISBN: 978-1-60598-086-7

10 9 8 7 6 5 4 3 2 1

Printed in the United States of America
Distributed by W. W. Norton & Company

FOR ALISON SAMUEL

'Go ask Alice,
I think she'll know.'
JEFFERSON AIRPLANE – 'White Rabbit'

Contents

In the end only the photograph remained. Once there had been half a dozen mementoes of those ancient days — a piece of friendly blue calico from a dress that had hung over a chair in a bedroom in Kansas City, a pink keepsake book full of verses by girls whose faces she could not remember — but somehow they had disappeared, tumbled away into forgotten crannies with the other rubbish of her past, and all that was left was the picture of them grouped around the buggy in the yard, with the cherry trees hanging low over the picket fence and the hens roosting in the gaps between the piled-up straw bales. And yet even this was not a constant in her life. There were times when, for a week or even a month, the photograph would go missing, vanish unexpectedly from the drawers and workboxes where she kept such treasures. These absences distressed her, upset the life of her houses and tore apart the rigid timetables of her day, and she would sit for hours in her drawing room beneath the great mirror and the trays of glass until, finally, a footman sent to ransack some obscure cupboard would come running to her with it in his glove, or a maid ordered to search the library would find it pinned between the pages of a novel. And then she would brood over it like a fetish, turn it over in her fingers, wonder at the years that passed since it first came into her hand and shiver at the memories that it sent dancing into her head.

PART ONE

1904–1929

1

Behind Blue Eyes

1904

The travelling salesmen at the far end of the boxcar had constructed a kind of barricade made up of attaché cases, brown-paper parcels, string-tied packages, all the random paraphernalia of their trade. Fenced off by this embrasure, in low, enthused voices, they were exchanging professional small talk.

'At a time like this, Joe, it's the duty of sales specialists like you and me to sell confidence.'

'So I says to Mr Schenectady at the depot, when you've been selling this stuff as long as I have, chump, then you can tell me how to sell it.'

'Say, did you really call him a chump?'

'Didn't I just?'

Aunt Em, stirring in her seat with faint disapproval, saw the pale chipmunk faces hunched under the flaring gaslight and, smiling, said, 'Those fellows must think they're pretty smart,' but there was no conviction in her voice. In the course of her married life, Aunt Em had spent hundreds of dollars on patent suspender fasteners, on gadgets designed to prise lids from conserve jars, on factory-made pickling machines out of the East: a great pile of junk, some of it as much as fifteen years old, which lay in the lean-to, and over which Uncle Hi occasionally shook his head.

'Oh, I don't know,' Alice said. 'I guess it must be fun to go places.'

'Now your Uncle Kyle,' Aunt Em said, her mind drawn back to the business of the day. 'Whenever one of those salesmen walked in at the gate, didn't matter how polite he was, or touched his hat as nice as nice, he'd take a pitchfork to him. Said he'd sooner throw his money in the Ohio River.'

And Alice thought about Uncle Kyle, and his wife Aunt Docia, and her two cousins, Andy and Colin, and the farm out beyond Tupelo, and wondered about them all, how they talked over the dinner table, whether they went out driving on Sundays and half a dozen other things that gestured at the new life that lay before her. The train whistle blew and she sat up with a start, burdened by the loneliness that flared in her and the silence that seemed to press against the moving train once it had gone. Outside, the flat Kansas plains receded into twilight. A speeding automobile that had kept pace with them for the past half-mile veered off into scrub. The train passed rapidly through a village, full of long, low houses and empty streets, sped past a crossing where a cattle truck waited behind the barred gate and a knot of people – country people with bags and satchels in their hands – stood incuriously by, and she wondered where they lived, and about all the hidden towns out there beyond the horizon, while the last vestiges of sunlight faded to purple across the plain and the shadows lengthened towards the distant hills, and her own face stared back at her out of the gathering night.

The conductor, hurrying through the connecting door, stopped to consider the dozen or so passengers. He was a young man, not yet habituated to the work and still fascinated by the people who came beneath his vigilant eye. He was looking at them now as he stood beside the square poster advertising the Kansas Trade Fair, adjusting the peaked cap whose brim was irritating the back of his scalp, making tiny judgments and speculating about their livelihoods and destiny. The travelling salesmen he knew instantly for what they were and took no further interest in: he would tell them to move those parcels in a moment and give himself some fun. The two men seated further down he judged to be farmers on account of their denim overalls, weather-beaten faces and the curious faraway look that comes from staring across far-distant fields in the sun: he was a farm boy himself and he knew these things. The tall, smartly dressed man in the adjoining seat he could not quite place. The middle-aged-to-elderly woman and the girl at her side he judged to be related, but not intimately so, as there was no sympathy about their looks or gestures. The girl – and he was a connoisseur of such girls, he saw a dozen of them a day, talked with them and chaffed them as far as was consistent with the company's regulations – he thought striking, but he could not quite establish why this was so, whether it was in her auburn hair, her pale and, it seemed to him, almost stricken face, or in some odd combination of the two whose significance eluded him. The train rattled beneath his feet and he reached out a hand – it fell upon the poster of the Kansas Trade Fair – to steady himself, then moved off down the car, loudly intoning in a

4

high, sing-song voice, 'Ya ticket, sir. Thanking ya kindly . . . To Roswell, ma'am? And to Bellevue, miss? . . . Thanking ya . . . Now, see here, fellers. This ain't a postal department. Going to haveta ask ya to remove that contraption . . .' Then he was gone into the next car, taking the memory of the auburn-haired girl with him, thinking of his wife back in Independence and arranging the two of them together in a way that was somehow disagreeable and mutinous, like creek water blown back by the wind, while the white birds spiralled in the blue-black sky and the last streaks of light slid away over the dark horizon.

It was past twilight, now, and the train thundered on into darkness. The whistle blew again and Alice remembered how, even as a child, she had hidden her head beneath the pillow when she heard it, so desolate and mournful did it seem. The lights from the farms and homesteads out on the plain broke occasionally out of the shadow and she wondered how people could live as the farmers and their wives did, out in the silence of the Kansas flat, with no one but each other to talk to and the distant murmur of the freight trains in their ears. At her side, Aunt Em fiddled anxiously with the clasps of her big canvas bag, dipped into it and took out a folded square of paper, stamped with the crest of the train company, that Uncle Hi had brought home to her weeks ago. Aunt Em disliked paper. The receipts in the fat cookery book Uncle Hi had bought her one year jumped out and confounded her with their precision, and the stories in the *Kansas Chronicle*, with their square, solid print, had to be read to her aloud.

'Gracious, Aunt Em! As if you hadn't seen that schedule a dozen times. Why, everybody knows the next station is Silver Lake. And then after that Roswell.'

Roswell was where Aunt Em would leave the train, cross the platform and take the southern-bound express back to Kansas City.

'I declare,' Alice said, softening in her attitude to Aunt Em, who could not properly read and whose hens never laid, and whose own daughter was dead, and who would have travelled on to Bellevue with her had Uncle Hi not wanted her home, 'it's very good of you to see me all this way.'

'It's no trouble, child,' Aunt Em said, who used the word 'child' only at times of high emotion. There was something bothering her, altogether beyond the stations of the south-western Kansas line. She considered for a moment and then said, 'Be a good place for you, with Kyle and Docia. Don't doubt you'll fret. But it's a good place. Better than with me and Hi.'

'I like it with you and Uncle Hi.'

'And we like it. That's not what I'm saying. But with Kyle and Docia, why, you could marry a farmer, teach in a school, I don't know.'

'Catch me teach in a school.'

'Your ma would have wanted it,' Aunt Em said gravely and Alice thought of her mother, dead these ten years and no more than the memory of a face above a coverlet, and of whom Uncle Hi had remarked that she had not left enough behind her to clothe a skunk.

They were passing through flat, grey country, altogether gathered up into blackness but with an arterial road snaking alongside where occasional lights moved back and forth. Kansas City to Eudora is twenty-five miles. Eudora to Lawrence is fifteen, then Lawrence to Topeka makes another twenty. Topeka to Roswell is eight miles and Roswell by St Mary's to Bellevue another twelve. Ninety miles over the Kansas plain.

Still wanting to conciliate Aunt Em, who showed signs of becoming tearful, Alice said, 'Did you ever go any place yourself, Aunt Em?'

'Well, now,' Aunt Em said. 'I once went to the World's Fair.' But there was no revelation in this. The Chicago World's Fair had been the one bright, indisputable beacon of Aunt Em's life. It was there that she had ascended a clock tower two hundred feet high, heard a man speaking the language of France, purchased and brought home a souvenir plate that, even now, eleven years later, lay undefiled on the parlour sideboard. Now, curiously, such talk was comforting to her. So Alice listened to her discuss the white exhibition rooms and the perilous climb into the heavens above Illinois and M. de Brinvillier's exposition and Uncle Hi – a younger, imperturbable Uncle Hi of boundless gallantry – while around them the life of the car grew pale and subdued, and the farmers yawned in their sleep, the salesmen stowed away their parcels in battered carrying cases and the man in the dark suit took out an eyeglass and read the *Wilmington Plains Courier*, and the train bored on into pitch.

Drouett watched the girl with the auburn hair out of the corner of one eye. He was on his way west, to Denver, but not indifferent to anything that the journey might throw into his path. He, too, was a salesman, though of a rather superior sort: better dressed, better spoken, less forward in drawing attention to his trade. Just now he was travelling in veneers and inlays, samples of which could be found in the leather attaché case on the seat beside him. He was a year off his thirty-fifth birthday, good-looking in a florid way, with an easy, confident air about him, one of those men whom the modern age consistently breeds up: rootless, vagrant and rather admiring himself for this rootlessness and vagrancy, pretty much at home wherever he found himself. Eavesdropping on the two women, he fancied that he understood the relation between them and wondered idly how he might make it work to his advantage. He did this not out of any particular viciousness, but because that was how his mind operated, seizing on any opportunity or half-chance, pursuing it, but not regretting its passing. The girl had blue eyes – cornflower blue, he thought – and he watched them covertly from behind his newspaper, thinking they were certainly very fine eyes and that he should certainly like to get into conversation with their owner.

The grey, vestigial landscapes beyond the window continued to flash by, but he took no notice of them; the Kansas plain, to him, was simply the Kansas plain: its mystery and its pathos scarcely occurred to him; he was not that kind of man. When the train drew into Roswell and the older of the two women collected her bag and, with various expressions of regret and farewell, made her way to the car door, waving as she did so and then standing in the doorway for a moment with what seemed to him an intensely sorrowful look, he relaxed, for he knew that his assessment of the situation was accurate. The girl now sat on her own, her eyes fixed on some remote point in the distance. He looked at his watch – it was a giant repeater that lay in the pocket of his waistcoat – and saw that a good thirty minutes had to elapse before the train reached Bellevue. Emboldened, he picked up his newspaper once more and folded it out across his lap. One of the great maxims of his life was that there was always plenty of time.

She sat on the edge of the carriage seat and watched as the train pulled out of Roswell. Aunt Em had long disappeared, gathered up into a crowd of people and gesturing railway officials and porters manoeuvring cabin trunks, but still in the distance behind her she could see the uttermost extremity of the receding platform. The figures were now reduced to an ant-like insubstantiality, and the sight impressed her far more than Aunt Em's leave-taking. She was sorry to see Aunt Em gone, but she knew that she was excited by her absence and the pleasant feeling of possibility that it brought. When Roswell was gone – the travelling salesmen and the farmers had vanished too and the car was all but empty – her thoughts turned back to herself. The life she knew was changing: that much was certain. Uncle Kyle and Aunt Docia she had met but once, seven years ago. She could remember nothing about them, conceive no plan of how her days might be lived out among them. As for marrying a farmer, or teaching in a school, that might do for some of the girls she had known in Kansas, but it would not do for her. As for what might do, she was not entirely sure.

There was a newspaper lying on the seat beside her and she stared vaguely at it, leafed through its pages and found an account of a play at a theatre in Independence and the portrait of a young lady who had acted in it, and though the names 'Shakespeare' and *Romeo and Juliet* awoke only the faintest tremor of recognition, the report interested her and she thought she would have liked to be there. And, her mind moving on in this way, she remembered a morning at school, years ago, when she had recited 'The Ride of Paul Revere', and the teacher, Miss Etter, had praised her. She remembered sitting at her desk, with the sun streaming through the window, and Miss Etter regarding her from the slate blackboard, and children's voices sounding beyond the doorway. She was woken from this reverie by a faint movement somewhere close by and, raising her head, became aware that the red-faced man in the black cloth suit was transferring himself, by easy stages, on to the seat opposite her own. This done, he laid his travelling case across his knees, lifted his eyes and seemed to see her for the first time.

'Well, now,' he said. 'This is a nice, comfortable journey, is it not?'

She was not in the least put out by Drouett's attentions. In the course of her recent life – she was going on nineteen – she had met several other Drouetts – they stared at her from behind drugstore windows, from the flatbeds of wagons drawn up level with Uncle Hi's buggy – and she had learned, or so she thought, not to be intimidated by them. Part of her, noting Drouett's genteel suit and generally prosperous air, was merely gratified that he had selected her for his notice. There were some girls, she thought eagerly, to whom he would not have deigned to speak. But an equal part was, additionally, awed by his assumption of expertise, the talk of 'nice, comfortable journeys', all of which impressed her quite as much as the leather attaché case and the repeater watch that stuck out from his waistcoat pocket.

'Oh, I don't know,' she said humbly – not meaning to be humble, but somehow imparting to the words what to Drouett seemed a delightful air of meekness. 'It seems a very long way to me.'

'Surely not?' Drouett said genially. 'I suppose there are a good many journeys longer than this. Why, to travel from Chicago to Seattle you would have to stay a day and a night on the train.'

'Did you ever do that? Did you ever stay a day and a night on a train?'

There was a naivety in her tone that to Drouett was altogether charming. He felt like a man who has walked through dusty alleyways and trackless side streets feels when he glimpses the first green fields out beyond the city's boundary. Seeking to press home his advantage, he said, 'Well, I should say that I did. And longer, too. Why, it can take a week to get from Seattle to Rhode Island.' He held out his hand. 'I am George Drouett, by the by.'

'My name is Alice Alden.' Again there was something about her tone that captivated him. He was a womaniser in his way, but not a cynical one: his admiration for the girl was quite sincere and inwardly he cursed the fact that another fifteen or twenty minutes would see her quit the train at Bellevue.

'Delighted to meet you, Miss Alden.'

And then there occurred an act of pure chance, which for all its unexpectedness seemed calculated to work to his advantage. Drawing into St Mary's, the station on the south-western Kansas line that separates Roswell from Bellevue, the train juddered slightly in its approach and came to a premature halt with perhaps only eight of its dozen coaches drawn up alongside the platform. The driver and the brakeman joined each other on the concourse, and a short while later the conductor came hurrying through the car to announce that a mechanical fault had been detected in one of the pistons and that the progress of the train would be delayed for perhaps an hour.

Drouett saw that the situation required him to put on an act. Accordingly he rose to his feet, stretched his arms, yawned profoundly and strode out on to the platform on the pretext of consulting the brakeman. Returning after a moment or two he said, with apparent unconcern, 'Well, this is very annoying, isn't it? Quite a little delay. I don't know if I shall get where I'm going tonight. But never mind. I never was in St Mary's but twice in my life, but I recollect there is a hotel. What do you say that we have dinner while we wait for the engineer to be called?'

He pronounced this invitation very skilfully, contriving to imply, on the one hand, that nothing could be more ordinary than two travellers, becalmed in a defective train, dining together, and yet intruding into it, on the other, the faintest hint of irregularity. He thought, as he pronounced it, that the answer meant nothing to him, that whether the girl came or stayed mattered little in the general scheme of things.

'What do you say?' he repeated a little less blandly.

'Will the train wait for us?' she asked, somewhat uncertainly.

He made a small gesture with the fingers of his left hand and she knew that there was no question of the train not waiting for them. She understood that he was a man who knew about such things – about hotels and whether trains waited – and this pricked her curiosity. She thought that she liked the uncertainty, the postponement of her meeting with Uncle Kyle and Aunt Docia, and Drouett's frank, red-complexioned face.

'Is it far?' she said. 'To the hotel, I mean.'

'Not at all. Five minutes' walk, perhaps.' He could not remember in the least how far the hotel was from the station.

The conductor, who stood on the platform under the flaring gas jets with his hands plunged deep into the pockets of his tunic, watched them go. Must be cousins, he thought. Then the reality of the situation dawned on him and he chuckled. 'Who'd have thought it, eh?' he said to himself. 'Who'd have thought it?'

2

De Smet

1904
The first snow began to fall late in the afternoon, drifting in from Silver Lake and the Big Slough where a month or two before the farmers had harvested their winter hay. Drouett saw it as he came round the side of the barn, fresh from putting up the horses in their stable, and stood for a moment watching it gather on the rutted turf. He did this not because he had any interest in snow as a thing in itself, but because it allowed a break in the action of his day. Also it reminded him of some past event in his life: grey flakes, soiled a little by smoke rising from a distant chimney; a brazier glowing in the dawn; horses stamping their hoofs by the frozen surface of a river. Finding no clue in his mind as to where these images came from, and conscious that the ground beneath his feet was already frosting over, he hurried on up the path.

Out across the plain the grey afternoon sky was slowly receding into night. Under his gaze, perhaps a quarter of a mile distant from the low hill on which he now stood, the houses and cabins of De Smet extended in the shape of a long, irregular cross. Something in the low, formless solitude of the land drew his eye and he stared out vaguely to the north. Three hundred and fifty miles and you reached Canada. Another thousand and you came to the Arctic Circle itself. The thought of the Arctic, with its ice floes and high-masted ships emerging spectrally out of the frozen sea, impressed him disagreeably with a sense of his own insignificance. Hunching his shoulders further into the collar of his coat and clasping the parcel of bloody newsprint closer to his chest, he came up to the front of the house.

From the kitchen on the blind side of the house Alice heard but did not see him come into the lean-to. A month ago if she had heard these sounds she would perhaps have smoothed down her skirt and pushed her hair out of her eyes, but now she did not do these things. He came into the room by degrees, advancing his head beneath the low cross-beam of the doorway, placing his feet carefully on the uncertain timber floor.

'I got some steak,' he said, almost shyly. 'I thought maybe you could make a pie.'

'Did you? That was good of you.'

She had liked it better when he brought her presents. Just lately he had taken to bringing home food for the table.

'Seems to me steak's awfully expensive out here,' he offered. 'This was sixty cents the pound.'

It was one of his idiosyncrasies – not at all in keeping with her idea of what men should be like – to take an interest in such things as the price of steak.

'I suppose it's because they have so far to bring it,' she reasoned.

'Yes, I guess that's the explanation.'

'How did you get on?' she asked. There had been several days recently when he had come back empty-handed and this, too, had disturbed her. A man ought to be able to make a living, she thought, especially a man with as fine a collection of suits as Drouett.

'Oh, not so bad. There's a sawmill over in Andersonstown with a manufactory attached. Nothing much to speak of yet, but I dare say it will come to something.'

'All these people coming west are bound to want good furniture.'

She was still in awe of him, but not so much so that she did not care to ask questions of this kind. Appreciating this, and not altogether liking it, he took the coffee cup she offered him and moved into the main room where a fire had been lit and the snow could be seen falling beyond the blue-black window.

'It's snowing awful hard, George,' she said, coming into the room with certain items of clothing, which she began to dry on a stand next the fire. 'Do you think we shall be snowed in?'

'I shouldn't wonder.'

There was a copy of the *Dakota Free Pioneer*, a month old, lying on the rocking chair on which he now sat down and he gazed at it in a vague way, but he was a city man by birth and instinct, and the stories of stock prices and cattle rides did not interest him. Drouett realised that he was thinking furiously and that his thoughts were concentrated on things far removed from snow falling beyond his icy window and the distant lights rising to illuminate De Smet. Six months had elapsed since the evening he had stepped off the train at St Mary's and unusually for him – for he was a methodical and calculating man – he could not quite account for the time that had passed. His pocketbook, which he had now in his hand, with its list of transactions and connections, told him that they had moved slowly – desultorily even – through Nebraska and Minnesota to the Dakotas, but he could not quite establish why the trip had taken so long. At this time in the year he would customarily have been back in the east – his firm had offices in Pittsburgh – but somehow December had found him a thousand miles out of his usual orbit. He ran his fingers over the cover of the *Dakota Free Pioneer* again and thought about this curious interregnum in his life. As he did this his hand brushed against the trousers of his business suit and he noticed that a rent had appeared in the cloth that exposed an inch or two of his calf to view. This annoyed him and he resolved to go upstairs and change into another set of clothes, but the warmth of the fire and the thought of the chill staircase deterred him, and he sat and luxuriated in his chair, rocking himself slowly back and forth, and thinking again about the peculiarities of his situation.

'By the way,' she said, coming into the room once more with another armful of freshly laundered clothes, 'what do you think of this?'

She was wearing a new dress, he noticed, very daintily got up, with bunched sleeves and wide, hooped skirts.

'It's dandy,' he said. 'Neat.' And then, thinking that this might sound perfunctory: 'Did you have it made up?'

'I bought the material at Mrs Oleson's and sewed it myself.'

'That's neat,' he said again.

He got up from the chair and went over to the window once more to look at the snow. It certainly was coming down hard out there, he thought. A good job he had got the horses fed and watered. Something about this northern extremity – this was not something he would admit to Alice – scared and troubled him: it was so far from any of his known haunts. Someone had told him – one of the men in the town – that between here and Iroquois there was only a single tree, and this seemed unnatural to him. He was not an imaginative man – his imagination worked in small ways, in momentary strategies and bits of cunning – but he found his mind entirely absorbed by the landscape beyond the window, the low hills that encircled De Smet and the great, brooding plain beyond. He wondered about the settlers living out there in the wilds and the thought of the wide, implacable horizon rising before them and fading away at dusk. The wind blew in against the glass and rattled the door frame, and he returned to his chair and sat by the fire, feeling absently at the rent in his suit and thinking it certainly was very cold out there.

Presently they ate supper. The steak was not cooked quite the way he liked – not quite – but he found himself complimenting Alice. He could not understand why he was so solicitous to her, but – well, there it was.

'I declare,' she said at one point during the meal, 'I never was in such an out-of-the-way place with nothing to do.'

'Is that so?' The remark amused him. 'Why, what would you be doing if you were back at home in Kansas?'

'I don't know.' He could see her considering this. 'Sometimes I'd play checkers with Uncle Hi. Or read to Aunt Em out of the paper.'

'We'll be out of here soon,' he said.

'I guess so.'

Another grievance flared within her and she said, 'When I went to the store today Mrs O'Halloran made me wait in the line until she'd served half a dozen other folks.'

He looked at her curiously. 'Well,' he said, almost as if he were talking to himself. 'Why should she do a thing like that, I wonder?'

But he knew very well why Mrs O'Halloran had acted in this way. Still, the thought annoyed him and he wished that he could walk into O'Halloran's store and give Mrs O'Halloran a piece of his mind.

'I'll look into that,' he said absently, finding to his surprise that the thought of the land, its great empty snowdrifts and gathering ice, had somehow replaced Alice's humiliation at the grocery store in his mind. 'There must be some mistake, that's all.'

He went and sat by the fire again and listened to the sound of the boiling water being poured on to the supper things. His life was not quite satisfactory to him, he thought, but again he could not quite establish where the source of this dissatisfaction lay. He had a suspicion that Alice might be starting a baby, but he had been in situations like this before. Again, his hand fell to the rent in his suit and the thought of the lodging house he inhabited in Pittsburgh and the wardrobe of fine clothing he had left there. What was to stop him going back to Pittsburgh? The sound of boiling water had ceased, to be replaced by the chink of crockery being stacked on the dresser. He sat in the rocking chair for a further moment or so and then, wrapping an old horsehair blanket round him, climbed the wooden staircase to the upper part of the house. Here it was desperately cold – he could see from the light of the lantern he held in his left hand that ice had begun to form inside the window – but he stood irresolutely for a while listening to the noise from below. There was a chest of drawers a foot or so from the bedstead and he reached into the topmost drawer and brought out a second pocketbook, laid the banknotes that it contained out on the coverlet of the bed and counted them. Finding that there were five twenty-dollar bills and three tens, he reached into the drawer again and extracted a buff-coloured envelope, which had once contained a veneer sample and even now was not quite free of sawdust. Into this he carefully placed one of the twenty-dollar bills and one of the tens. Then, with the envelope in his hand, he sat on the bedstead, hearing the wind rush in against the timbers of the house and watching the lamp flare in its cylinder. 'I'd better get out of this, anyhow,' he said to himself once or twice. The envelope was still in his hand. He was surprised to find it there. Rising to his feet, he replaced it, together with the pocketbook, in the topmost drawer of the chest. Then, wrapping the horsehair blanket round himself again, he went downstairs.

That evening he was surprisingly gallant. 'This is what a fellow likes,' he said, as she poked up the fire and stood over it with a delightful scarlet flush on her cheek. She noticed the gallantry and wondered at it. Several times he made little remarks about the prospects for his business or her immediate comfort. There was fine, open driving land out beyond the lake where they sometimes went on a Sunday afternoon: should she like to see it when the weather cleared? A store in town was selling geese, shot on the lake shore: would she care to sample one? He had noticed a new style of bonnet in O'Halloran's: would she like him to buy it for her? To all these suggestions she graciously assented, not because the lakeside drive, or the goose, or the new bonnet especially attracted her, but because he seemed so eager to propose them.

It grew late and he went out to the stable to do the chores. The snow had stopped. But the ground was icy and the water in a pail he had left outside the stable door half frozen through.

'What'll you do tomorrow?' she asked.

'Oh, there's a new place opening up twenty miles south of here a fellow told me about I thought I might try.'

'That's good,' she said. There had been other new places opening up and she had grown cynical over their prospects. 'Shall you be leaving early?'

'I guess I might.'

Later he watched her standing in her nightgown brushing out her hair by the light of the lamp. Somehow this was very poignant to him. It reminded him of his sister standing by the window in Duluth, twenty years ago, waiting for a boy who took her out buggy riding.

'We'll get out of this,' he assured her.

He awoke just before the dawn began to break and lay with his breath rising in the frozen air like an orc's spout. She was lying beside him – so close that he could have reached out and touched her with the slightest movement of his finger – but he found that he could not bring himself to look at her, that the sound of her breathing was torture to him. In this mood – half fearful but strangely excited – he dressed himself hurriedly by the chest of drawers – the window was quite frozen and impenetrable – and hastened down the wooden staircase, taking care as he went to remove both envelope and pocketbook from the drawer, together with several other items, which he packed up noiselessly in a canvas satchel. In the kitchen there was still a faint warmth emanating from the stove and he bent over it as he ate his breakfast. Beyond the window the snow lay evenly along the hillside, turning candy-yellow in the pale sun: he watched it over his plate of sourdough biscuits and preserve. The brush of his hand against the lapel of his jacket reminded him of the envelope, and he drew it out of his pocket and ran it between the groove of his fingers. The envelope was a problem to him: this he acknowledged. First he laid it on the tiny kitchen table. Then, not liking the sight of it as he drank off his coffee, he took it into the main room and set it on the mantel next to the clock and an embroidered card purchased from one of the stores in town. He stood looking at it again for a moment, and at the other things that the room contained – the rocking chair, the parched embers of the fire, the attaché case with his samples – and then, in what he thought was a decisive gesture, pulled on his coat and scarf, picked up the case and the canvas satchel, took a key and placed it next to the envelope and stepped briskly out into the snow.

Here the cold leapt into his face like some living thing, but he fancied that he was used to cold now and busied himself by making his way to the stables and leading out his horses and the buggy. As he did this he turned and glanced occasionally at the house and at the low, level prairie beyond it, but nothing stirred. Looking at his watch, as he smoothed out the traces in his hand and examined the fastenings of the horses' bridles, he found that it was not yet seven. This encouraged him, for he knew that the scheme he was considering depended on time. 'I'm out of this, anyhow,' he said to himself again as he negotiated the rutted path that led from the stable door to the broken road along the hillside. The cold stung him again, and reaching into the satchel he added to his original covering of coat, gloves and scarf a second scarf, earmuffs and a travelling rug. He would be pretty snug up here, he thought, now that the snow was keeping off. In any case, he should be in Allington by mid-afternoon.

At the foot of the hill, where the path joined up with the main road into De Smet, he met a man he knew from the town – not driving like himself but out hunting for jackrabbits with an enormous wolf-dog – and was hailed by him.

'Is that you, Drouett? Not going out in this weather?'

'Well, now,' Drouett said a little uneasy. 'I've known colder.'

'It's twenty below and set to fall. But I suppose you know your own business.'

'Well – perhaps I do.'

The man strode on over the snow, with the great wolf-dog loping at his heels, and Drouett sat a little uncertainly in his buggy, the reins idle in his hand. These prairie old-timers always said such things, he told himself, but it certainly was very cold. He stared once more into the clear, pale sky, looked across the prairie – quite empty except for the receding figure of the hunter and his dog – and then stirred his horses into action, not southwards in the direction of the furniture manufactory – this was an invention – but east towards the town of Allington. Here, he knew, he could catch a train that would take him further east, to Chicago or even as far as Philadelphia. His spirits rose at the thought. He had a sudden vision of himself sitting in the foyer of O'Dowd's Hotel in Chicago greeting a friend – one of those chance acquaintances met on the road – and raising a glass as he did so, and the vision was very pleasant to him. Another thought welled in his mind and he gripped the reins a little tighter and said to himself, 'Well, I left her thirty dollars.' Still, he could not quite dismiss the thought of Alice from his imaginings. 'I got out of it, didn't I?' he said to himself. A jackrabbit came moving over the snow towards him, very fast and close to hand, so that the horses shied a little as it passed, and he watched it disappear, never slackening in its speed, until it was no more than a minute speck in the distance behind him.

It was now eight o'clock in the morning. Allington, he calculated, was a only thirty miles away – he had been there once before. Something in the movement of the buggy – some catch or hesitation – disturbed him and he thought that, seeing how cold it was, he should go easy on the horses. Accordingly he slowed his pace to a brisk trot. He became aware both of the noises of the buggy – the stamp of the horses' hoofs on the icy track, the jingle of the bridles, the creak of the transom beneath him – and also of the terrible silence beyond it. Once, when the team had slowed almost to a halt, he found himself rapping out a command and the sound of his voice seemed so feeble to him, so instantly gathered up in the enveloping air, that he wished he had stayed silent. It certainly was extraordinarily cold. He had a picture of himself as an ant, inching forward across the face of some cruelly exposed rock, clinging stubbornly to a surface from which the elements tried constantly to blast him away.

Nearly an hour passed. The pale northern sun rose in the sky before him and the horizon took on a roseate glow that fascinated him, so delicate was the arrangement of its colours set against the white foreground of the snow. It certainly was extraordinarily cold, though. Twice he fancied that he felt a numbness in the tips of his driving hand – he kept the other hand wedged into the breast pocket of his overcoat – and beat his gloved fingers against his chest in an effort to restore his circulation. Then again, there came a moment when one of the horses seemed to shuffle and sway slightly in its traces. This frightened him, but he was not such a novice in the ways of the prairie as to be ignorant of what had happened, so he brought the buggy to a halt, stepped down from the high seat and with the ends of his gloved fingers carefully removed the thin sheet of ice that had formed over the horse's nose and mouth. He clapped his arms briskly against his sides, shuffled his feet a little in their boots and peered determinedly in front of him, but the white arm of the land ran away in all directions. Never mind, he told himself. He had been gone an hour and a half. Another three would see him in Allington, smoking his cigar in the hotel foyer. As he thought about the Allington hotel the chill rose again in his hands and feet, and he wondered whether it would not be prudent to light a fire and warm himself and the horses before proceeding further. There were some lengths of sawn-off lumber and a bundle of kindling in the back of the buggy, stored for just such a need, and he dragged them down and began to arrange them to his satisfaction on a patch of ground from which he had scraped as much snow as was possible with the heel of his boot. This done, he struck a sulphur match, shielded it with his hands against the occasional gusts of wind that rose up from the prairie and set light to the kindling. The fire burned merrily and he pulled a packing case from the back of the buggy, upended it in the snow and sat on it to warm his feet at the fire, thinking that it might be pleasant to smoke a pipe and eat some of the bread and meat he had brought with him from De Smet. As he ate, a few flakes of snow began fitfully to descend, but he paid them no attention. The sky was still clear, and there was his pipe and his pieces of bread and meat to comfort him.

By the time he had finished the pipe and his pieces of bread and meat it was half past eleven: the morning was wearing on. Something told him that he would not reach Allington at the time he had imagined. The trail stretched on across the flat into nowhere. In the distance, the low, variegated hills looked down. Also – he noticed with a slight start – the sky had begun to darken over to the east. He had best get going, he told himself, indeed he had. The fire was still burning merrily and he was reluctant to leave it, but he could see the dark cloud moving nearer. Well, he would just have to see about it, that was all. As he climbed back on to the buggy, the chill struck at his hands and feet, and he shivered uncomfortably in his nest of travelling rugs. By now, seeing the dark cloud loom nearer still, he was seriously alarmed, for he had read in newspapers – the *Dakota Free Pioneer* was full of these stories – of prairie blizzards, of cattle frozen to death in the fields, farmers found stifled under a ton of snow. But then he told himself not to be a fool, that his team would see him through, that if necessary he could make a shelter for himself beneath the buggy. Thinking this he hunched his shoulders further down into the collar of his coat and pulled his hat down lower. The trail ran before him, a thin black line which the frost had even now not quite obliterated. The horses plodded on, their breath rising almost vertically in the dense air. Queerly, he found that his mind focused anywhere but on his predicament. He was in the bar of O'Dowd's in Chicago, with the bottles gleaming before the great glass surround and the pretty barmaids going about their work, and the people moving this way and that beneath the chandeliers. The snow came without warning. One moment he saw grey sky, the next a raging black cloud full of dense angry particles enveloped him. The horses shied and cowered. Head down, not knowing whether his hands still held the reins or not, he moved on into the eye of the storm.

*   *   *

Alice woke late out of a confused and troubling dream from which Aunt Em and Uncle Hi loomed so vividly that she imagined they were in the room with her. She opened her eyes with a start, but there was no one there, only the pale light seeping through the uncurtained window and the faint noise of the wind blowing against the slatted roof. Her first thought was that it was terribly cold. Stretching out her arms from the nest she had constructed for herself during the night, she discovered that the part of the blanket on which her breath had fallen was covered with a film of ice. As she dressed she cast her eye round the room seeking further evidence of the frost's encroachment. Moving downstairs, she found the marks of Drouett's departure – the coffee cup he had left on the kitchen table, the plate from which he had eaten his breakfast. Setting these to one side, she made her own meal, fetching logs from the pile in the lean-to to feed the stove, boiling a kettle, taking further logs into the main room, where a trace of last night's warmth still lingered, to build up the fire. She was aware, as she did this, that she existed in the middle of a great, enveloping silence, that the slightest noise – the rasp of a match, the clatter of a plate as it slipped from her fingers – instantly magnified itself into a paralysing clamour. She moved over to the window, looking for some sign of movement that might break the great disabling spell that surrounded her, but there was nothing there. In the near distance, smoke rose slowly from the few houses at the foot of the hill. Beyond, De Smet lay silent and inert, like a toy village that a child could despoil with a wave of its hand.

Taking her coffee cup to the main room, she established herself in the rocking chair and set her hands in her lap. There was nothing unusual in this. Most of her waking hours since leaving Kansas had been taken up in brooding: thoughts of Drouett, the old life that had come to an end that evening on the station platform at St Mary's, the things she had seen since it ended. Even now, she could form no fixed idea of Drouett. He was simply a part – the dominating part – of the new landscape she had fashioned around herself. She was flattered by his admiration, but she did not entirely trust him. She suspected, although she had no proof, that there might be a Mrs Drouett and a pack of little Drouetts somewhere in the east, perhaps in Pittsburgh, but even this did not greatly alarm her. Mrs Drouett, she thought, could look out for herself, just as she at some point, she imagined, would have to look out for her own interests. As for Drouett, she knew that the things she liked in him were the things that were most extraneous to their present life. Above all she liked to hear him talk of his travels, of his journeyings in the east, of theatres he had visited and hotels in which he had stayed – all the revolutions of the tumbling world, brought home to her in dribs and drabs of conversation – for they confirmed to her the existence of a universe she had only read about and wished very much to see for herself. Drouett's life, lived out in these distant thoroughfares, seemed to her a fabulous thing, almost beyond her power to comprehend.

There were little souvenirs that she kept of this – postcards of Boston and Washington, a copy of a New York newspaper, some stamped notepaper he had taken from a Galveston hotel – and she hoarded them, building up in her mind a series of ghostly pictures of the human traffic that flowed through them. Drouett was amused by her fixation. Though he was proud of the life he led and the world he moved in, he did not think them exceptional. New York was a fine big city. The Galveston hotel had been a swell place to stay in. His appreciation went no further than that. At the same time, aware of her intense absorption in these aspects of his life, he was careful to play upon this susceptibility, to instigate long, reminiscent conversations in which these elegant byways were brought out for her approval. For himself, taking the matter objectively, Drouett had thought Alice a fine, biddable girl, not excessive in her prettiness – he was mistrustful of beauty – but pleasant-minded. For her own part, Alice had noted the rent in his suit. Men who wore fine suits ought to keep them in good repair, she thought.

She was woken out of her reverie by a loud double rap at the door. Hastening up from the rocking chair, she discovered that the caller was a woman who lived in one of the houses at the foot of the hill and with whom she had some slight association.

'Coldest day I ever saw,' this lady remarked by way of preamble. She was a plump, middle-aged Irishwoman, wrapped up so ingeniously in a plaid shawl that only her forehead, eyes and mouth could be seen through the cloth. Once inside, she cast several shrewd looks around the interior, adjusted the shawl so that it sat back on her bony shoulders and said in a slyly conversational way, 'I seed your man set off three hours since. Out on the Allington road.'

'I'm sure you're mistaken,' Alice replied. 'Indeed, my husband' – she was conscious of the false note in her voice as she spoke the word – 'has business in Holywell.'

'Deed, then, he'll not find it in Allington. Never mind. I dare say it makes no odds, for there's snow coming. McElligot won't leave his fire, but I thought I'd come up and enquire after ye.'

'You are very kind,' Alice said, divining that, in spite of her slyness, the woman meant well. 'Won't you sit down?'

'It's you that should sit down, dear, with you being in a fambly way.' Something in the set of the younger woman's face caught her eye and she went on, 'Isn't that the truth of it?' Getting no answer, she continued, 'Well, either you are or you aren't. It's no concern of mine. There's no doctor here,' she added. 'But I hear there's one at Allington, so it's well your man knows the road.'

When she had gone Alice sat down once more on the rocking chair, but the placid mood of the early morning had left her. There was a copy of the *Ladies' Home Journal* by the fender, which Drouett had brought from the stationer's in town, but its accounts of the winter fashions and seasonal receipts were no salve. Outside the sky was darkening and she watched the shadows lengthening over the land. Something in the onrush of dark air moving beyond the low hills alarmed her and she told herself not to be foolish, that she sat in a stout, timber-frame house with a quarter-ton of coal piled up in its lean-to, that nothing could touch her, that she could stay here all winter if she chose. It was then, as her eye moved vaguely beyond the clock on the mantelpiece – this now stood at a little after ten – that she saw the envelope. Picking it up with her right hand and using her left hand to ward off the tongues of heat from the fire, she discovered that Drouett had written her name on it – not her Christian name, but a formal salutation: *Miss Alice Alden.* This struck her as intensely odd and she tore it open with a single, decisive movement of her fingers. The banknotes fell out into her hand. Even then she did not appreciate their significance. Why had Drouett left her thirty dollars in an envelope addressed to Miss Alice Alden?

The first fine flakes of snow blew in against the window and she watched them absently for a moment, thinking of other snows that had fallen long ago in Wichita when she was a girl, and Uncle Hi's shining red face as he cleared the path to the outhouse. Still she could not solve the mystery of the thirty dollars. Neither could she understand what Mrs McElligot had meant about seeing Drouett on the Allington road. Something occurred to her, a tiny stirring in the back of her mind, and she moved hurriedly up the wooden staircase. Here everything was just as normal. The coverlet lay drawn back upon the bed. The water was still frozen in the jug. But then something caught her eye, so small that it barely registered within her, and her mind searched desperately to establish what it was. It occurred to her that Drouett had owned a second pair of boots, in addition to the pair he habitually wore about his work, that these had lain next to the wall by the chest of drawers, but were now gone. She sat upon the bed, her breath rising in great clouds to the ceiling, with her arms clasped about her, considering this. A faint inkling of the truth prompted her to fling open a drawer and she discovered that the greater part of Drouett's clothing had disappeared. The snow beat against the window and she made her way back down the staircase and settled herself once more in the rocking chair.

She sat there for the rest of the day. Around noon the snow ceased for a moment before a second blanket of cloud rolled in from the west. She was thinking of Drouett and the life they had led during the six months she had known him. She knew that his desertion, if it was a desertion – and still a certain part of her would not admit that it was such a thing – profoundly angered her, not because she cared for him in the way she once had, but because she assumed that she had been judged and found wanting. Still, she could not put this anger into words. Had Drouett stood in the room before her she did not know what she would have said to him. There was a way in which he was not quite real to her, she thought. The clock inched forward and the snow continued to fall, but she sat there quite careless of her surroundings, thinking of the conversations she had had with him the night before and a drive they had once taken to Silver Lake. 'Anyhow,' she said to herself, 'he mayn't have gone.' The bare iron peg where his coat and hat had hung gleamed at her from across the room. As evening came she recollected that she had had nothing to eat since breakfast. It now occurred to her that she ought to conduct an inventory of what remained to her in the house. In the kitchen, casting her eye over the shelves, her face loomed up at her in the mirror that hung on the door frame and she wondered at its ghostly, frightened look. There was not, as she had predicted, a great deal – a loaf of bread and some dripping; half a stone of flour; a few odds and ends of vegetables – but she thought that at any rate she could see out the storm. She went to bed at seven with the wind tearing at the roof and the house shaking around her.

When she awoke the wind had dropped away to nothing and only the snow remained. It had snuffed out the familiar landmarks; the strew of houses further down the hill had become encircled and diminished by it. It occurred to her that she had no need to get out of bed, that her day would be better spent here beneath the covers. This thought was very seductive to her and she lay there a long time, drifting in and out of sleep, willing herself into movement but always failing in the attempt. Even now, though, her ears still strained for the sound of the team as they laboured on up the hill, the slam of the stable door and Drouett's hand fumbling with the latch. But nothing came and after a while she sat bolt upright in the bed, foolish and ashamed, dressed herself and hurried downstairs. Here it was dark and silent. Last night's fire had burned down to cinders and the ticking of the clock had an ominous sound. How she hated the ticking of that clock! There were occasions when it seemed to be perched on her shoulder. She wondered about Drouett and where he was – not hating him now, but merely curious – recollecting little things about him that she could not claim ever before to have noticed – a certain pin that he wore in his tie, a particular way he had of passing the back of his hand over his face as he talked – but she was aware that the wider image of Drouett was quickly fading from her, had become gathered up in the broader surround of the snow, the ticking of the clock and the silence beyond it.

Once, so terrified was she of the silence, she opened her mouth and sang a snatch of a song, but her voice cracked and flew away from her, up into the eaves of the house, and she sang no more. She was awake, she realised, but somehow detached from the things that lay around her – from the mantelpiece, with its ticking horror, the fireplace and the timber boards of the floor. The envelope with the thirty dollars was in her hand again. She wondered once more – the thought startling her as if it were newly minted – where Drouett was and why he did not come back to her, what she had done that had driven him away. She sat for a long time in this curious, disembodied state, hearing the soft footfalls beyond the window and the rapping at the knocker for what seemed like an eternity before deciding that they demanded a response. She got up from the chair, fastened her shawl more tightly round her shoulders and moved wonderingly to the door.

3

Loftholdingswood

1908–14

When, long years later – during the trial, it must have been – I tried to visualise the moment or two after it happened I could only see it as a reel of cine-film: the men carrying him along the hallway under the blanket, with stray arms and legs spilling out into view; the servant girl rushing out into the garden in hysterics; and the people running in from the terrace to see what was going on; and the white birds spiralling up from the dovecotes; and my uncle, sixty miles away in London, saying that he was b*****ed if he knew where this might lead, b*****ed if he did; while the smoke billowed from the cottage chimneys down in the valley; and the piles of telegrams from Atry lay accumulating on the brass tray by the bed; and that sinking feeling of things having gone too far, that you could never halt them or bring them back to how they ought to be. Even though I wasn't there, having left the scene twenty minutes before, I can see it. Hear it, too: the maid's pale face as she runs, the insufficient folds of the blanket, the car tyres grinding up the gravel in the drive, voices raised in uproar, heavy boots squeaking on the polished stone. But all this is advancing matters. For this is the end, rather than the beginning, and the beginning is more interesting to me, as it contains the seeds of everything that happened afterwards, and the first hint of the patterns that I've spent the rest of my life trying to trace out and ultimately, and unsuccessfully, subdue.

Ralph Bentley is my name – though how I came by it I do not know – and this is my story, and the story of my uncle, and of the finding of hogpen and how we became great people and moved in a world for which we were sadly unprepared: like arctic explorers, I sometimes used to think, condemned to travel the ice without benefit of husky dogs or tins of pemmican. It is also, if only incidentally, the story of how I met Lloyd George, shook hands with Montagu Norman in his great room at Threadneedle Street, saw Chaplin and even danced with Tallulah

Bankhead: none of which destinies could have been predicted from my early life, the company I kept or the figure I was expected to cut in the world. It was at a time when a tide of money ran through the City of London and out into the surrounding country, and the most unlikely people were allowed to dip their toe in its current. I remember going to London as a boy of eight in the summer before the war and no artist could ever have done it justice: the teeming traffic of the streets; the rumble of the lorries delivering newsprint to the ziggurats of Fleet Street; the extraordinary variety of the passers-by, all of them sustained and emboldened by the money tide, which flowed so hard that it gathered even my uncle and myself up in its wake and deposited us on a shore where I supposed – and continue to suppose – we had no right to be.

A tiny, outlying tributary of the money tide had even flowed as far as Loftholdingswood.

My overriding memory of the place where I spent my childhood is of the maids, Edna and Elsie, banging out the carpets in the nursery garden beyond the kitchen door. Edna was a big fat girl with a figure exactly like a bolster and arms like sausages, and when she hit the carpet a cloud of dust rose in the air like a swarm of midges. The carpets were laid over a thick washing line that hung between two apple trees and the girls took it in turns to flog them with old tennis rackets. Of the two it was Edna who was the more conscientious. She used to stand there with her mouth wide open and a vague, bovine look of concentration on her face, lips moving silently as she counted the strokes. When she'd done ten she'd sink down on her haunches with her maid's cap all awry on her thick, mouse-coloured hair and let Elsie have a go. Elsie, who was smaller and better-looking, frankly slacked, and most days Mrs Custance would bob up from her vantage point at the kitchen window to reprimand her and there'd be a row.

If I remember them so vividly it's because, together with the three or four adults on the premises, they represented the limit of my infant experience. I don't suppose that until I was seven I ever set foot outside Loftholdingswood, on the wide tarmacadam road that led in one direction to London and in the other to Brighton, and it wasn't until I came to leave the place that I had any real idea of its dimensions or the part that it played in the world that stretched out beyond it.

Even by the standards of the 1900s, Loftholdingswood was curiously detached from what you might call civilisation. It was a big, old, fifty-acre estate in one of those dense, wooded valleys on the border between Surrey and Sussex – the nearest town was Haslemere – with the weald running along the horizon and the footpaths disappearing into trackless wastes of furze and bracken, all horribly gone to seed with the grass grown up six feet high in the meadows and piles of long-cut timber gone mouldering in the beech woods. The house itself was a huge, overgrown pile, variously disposed around a cracked stone courtyard, but hopelessly run-down and decayed, with the state rooms all shut up and the west wing closed down entirely under sheeting and dust. In a bedroom on the east wing, under a cambric counterpane, with the Haslemere doctor coming to visit her twice a week, old Lady Delacave, its owner, lay quietly dying, but I only saw her once, when a cadaverous old woman with a yellow face and teeth like pegs was brought downstairs and wheeled about the place in a bath chair. According to Mrs Custance the Delacaves had owned Loftholdingswood for upwards of two hundred years, but the male line was extinct and on Lady Delacave's death – this had been first predicted at around the time of the Diamond Jubilee – a distant cousin would inherit, an eventuality which, as Mrs Custance put it, 'did not bear thinking about'.

As you can see, it was from Mrs Custance that I derived the greater part of my information. She was a tall, rather stooped woman of about forty, emphatically not my mother, as she every so often reminded me, but not for that reason any the less negligent in the care she took of me, and in possession of certain information, which she never communicated but that nevertheless lay like a bridge between us: she called me 'Ralph' with a decisive emphasis, as if I had only acquired the name by some recent accident of fate and needed to be constantly reminded of it. Mrs Custance was the housekeeper. Beyond her floated vaguer figures: Mr Montagu, the butler, Miss Mort, who had been governess to one of Lady Delacave's daughters, and Mrs Trotwood, the cook. Their vagueness comes from the fact that, although each possessed a sharp and distinctive personality, they tended to operate in unison. In fact, I can remember them only as a collective ellipse of old, white faces gathered round the table in the servants' dining hall. Miss Mort was a 'gentlewoman' – a word of enormous symbolic significance in the counsels of Loftholdingswood – fallen on hard times, an ancient, faded spinster of whom it was some-times pityingly said that she had seen 'better days'. Mr Montagu had first come to the house during the Crimean War, and Mrs Trotwood was famous in the neighbourhood for inventing a new kind of white sauce that you ate with pudding. I dare say the position in which they found themselves will seem ludicrous to you – six able-bodied people keeping up a gigantic country house for the benefit of a sick old lady – but if anyone had suggested to Mr Montagu that Lady Delacave would have been better off in the cottage hospital at Haslemere and her house converted into flats, he would have been genuinely shocked: it would have meant a throwing over of everything he believed in, far worse than the rumours of Socialists and Suffragettes that occasionally percolated into the depths of rural Sussex.

If all this makes Mrs Custance, Miss Mort and the others seem merely antediluvian and stupid, that isn't the case, for there was an ambiguity about their position which I think they themselves went halfway towards recognising. They were, of course – and even as a child I think I appreciated something of this – quite thoroughly and invincibly ignorant, but according to their lights, and in relation to the tiny, sequestered universe they inhabited, they were surprisingly well informed. They could not have told you with any certainty how to get from Canterbury to Leeds, but they could have given you Lady Desborough's London address. They conceived of the Kaiser only in the vaguest terms – 'that there German Emperor', 'that *Prooshan*' Mr Montagu called him – but they knew his precise relationship to the English Royal Family. It was the same in the schoolroom and Miss Mort, to which and to whom I proceeded at about the age of nine. Even today if you gave me a sheet of paper and a pencil I could write down without hesitation the names of the principal English county towns.

Lady Desborough! The Kaiser! These are the kind of names I remember from childhood, with Mr Montagu reading from the newspaper in his big chair at the end of the servants' hall and Miss Mort drowsing over embroidery by the fire with her shiny black hairpiece drifting to one side so you could see the grey curls underneath. They were packing the Channel with dreadnoughts just then, there was a military camp over on the downs whose soldiers could be seen marching along the roads, and everyone – even old Mr Montagu – knew there was war coming. The outside world didn't often intrude, but when it did it did so dramatically, with black borders that announced the old King's death or the screaming headlines when the *Titanic* went down. The old people at Loftholdingswood were very exercised by the *Titanic*. They were sorry for the passengers who'd died and the old lady found frozen to death on an ice floe by the rescue boats, but you could see that they thought it was a judgment, that mankind was being rebuked for its arrogance in trying to send people three thousand miles over the ocean in an outsize sardine can.

As for the life we led at Loftholdingswood, this was given pattern and design and in the end made tolerable by ritual. No meal was ever eaten without a gong being sounded in the hall – a gong whose reverberations echoed through the empty rooms while the seven people for whom it was intended hovered a few feet away. If I wanted a biscuit with my afternoon cup of cocoa, I had to knock at the pantry door, put my hands behind my back, bob my head and quaver, 'Please, Mrs Trotwood, is there anything for afters?' This courtesy was known as 'behaving like a little gentleman should': the wider question of whether I was a gentleman and from where my gentlemanliness derived stayed delicately in abeyance. Other bits of Loftholdingswood ritual advertised themselves by way of noise: the odd whirring sound of the butterfly keys on Saturday afternoons, which meant that Mr Montagu was winding the clocks (there were seventeen of them in all, ranging from the grandfather clock in the front hall to the silver fob watch that hung on Mr Montagu's waistcoat chain); the rattle of the solicitor's pony trap on Monday mornings when he came to confer with Mrs Custance over the housekeeping; the smash of cutlery thrown down on a tablecloth on Sunday evenings, which meant that somebody had dragooned Edna or Elsie – it was mostly Edna – into cleaning the silver – a ghastly job that took an hour and a half, as there were three full cases of knives and forks before you even got on to the plate.

Saturday nights were the high point of the Loftholdingswood calendar, for it was then that Mr Palmer came. More even than the newspapers, it was Mr Palmer who symbolised Loftholdingswood's links with the outside world, who could announce that a road was being built over the downs or that mange had broken out on one of the local farms. He was a grocer from Haslemere, which meant that he toadied the upper servants, Mrs Custance especially, with a deference that was almost painful to see. At the same time he'd been in service himself at some point, which meant that the others regarded him as an ally, not some tradesman who'd taken to soft-soaping them to guarantee his weekly order. As for the conversations they had, no salon at the court of Marie Antoinette was more exclusive. You might have thought that a group of middle-aged to elderly people gathered together in a country house in the foothills of the twentieth century might want to talk about Asquith's choice of ministers or

Mr Lloyd George and the Old Age Pension, but no, all they were interested in was bygone aristocratic life and who'd been First Lord of the Powder Closet back in 1869. Any argument would be settled by a shout of 'Look it up in the book. Fetch the book down, somebody, and we'll see for certain' and Edna, or Elsie, or whoever was to hand, would be sent off to bring back the ancient copy of *Debrett* or sometimes even *Burke's Peerage* from their resting places under the glass dome in Mr Montagu's pantry.

No doubt I've forgotten much of my time at Loftholdingswood, exaggerated its sequestration and its oddity. But there was no getting away from the queerness and detachment of the life I led, and no pretending that this queerness wasn't the thing that absorbed me most of all, for my position at Loftholdingswood was altogether anomalous and nobody quite knew what to do with me or how I should be treated. For myself, I was always on the lookout for some great revelation: of who I was, and where I came from, and who the Bentleys and my parents were, but it never arrived and I was forever on the edge of things, incubating hopes that always withered and waiting for words that never came. From time to time some inkling of this would pass over the adult community and there would be a shake of heads over the supper table and vague, inconclusive conversations about 'the boy'. Even Mrs Custance could see the dis-advantages of bringing up a child in the company of four grown-ups whose collective age amounted to two hundred and twenty-five, and sometimes another boy – one of the gamekeeper's sons or someone from the village – would be triumphantly produced for my recreation, but it never worked. The village children, I now realise, couldn't 'place' me. Their social antennae had no way of distinguishing whether I was an embryonic gentleman or an upper servant and they resented the puzzle I had set them.

Most of the time, consequently, when I wasn't running errands around the house for Mrs Custance or parsing sentences in the schoolroom with Miss Mort, I was placed in the care of Edna, she being the person in the house nearest to me in age and most capable of seeing that I didn't get into mischief. Edna was a good sort, who never minded fitting in with my schemes of entertainment, liked long, rambling walks around the estate and generally put herself out to be agreeable. She was one of those vague, confiding girls whose head was full of the most extraordinary nonsense, put there, I remember, by a weekly paper called *Bow Bells*, which ran serial stories about dashing young noblemen who rescued the lady passengers of carriages stuck on the edge of precipices and married servant girls against their parents' will. At the time I first knew her she would have been about seventeen, and her ignorance of the world beyond the Loftholdingswood gate was practically fathomless. But I liked Edna, liked her far more than Elsie, who came from London, shirked her work and was known to have 'admirers' in the village, and relished the walks we took through the woods to a kind of lost world on the estate's edge full of head-high bracken and sunken lakes, or the trips to the village to see a litter of foxhound puppies. Edna called me 'Master Ralph' and held my hand with the pride of responsibility, but apart from that she treated me as an equal and wasn't above retailing gossip from the servants' hall – it was from her that I heard that Mrs Trotwood 'drank' and that Mr Montagu had a wife and grown-up children living in Hove – and, I think, pitied me in a way that was agreeable to me while completely beyond my comprehension.

And so life went on, all through those dense, lost years before the war. I don't want you to think that I was unhappy, for I don't believe I was. It was the only life I knew, and like fish in a bowl or dogs in a yard I was habituated to it. Also, it was a good time to be a boy, there in the last years of Edwardian England. The pace of life in those days was extraordinarily slow. Cars hadn't yet come in much and you could wander for miles along the country roads without seeing a soul, except maybe one of the local squires on a horse or a farm labourer walking home in the twilight. Loftholdingswood, too, once I got to be about nine or ten, was a source of inexhaustible fascination to me: full of overgrown paths that led nowhere through the bracken, dense thickets from which pheasants would go tearing off into the treetops. I'm not sentimental about the countryside, but I do know that if you gave me the chance I should like to be nine years old again, idling through the cow parsley with Edna telling me about the latest serial where the baronet disguises himself as a grocer's assistant to win the heart of the laundrymaid, or on my own, breasting one of the ridges towards the weald and looking down on the rolling fields and the criss-crossing hedges going on for ever like the squares in a patchwork quilt, down to the sea and the English Channel and the rest of the tumbling world.

As for what went on in my head, I wasn't wholly without resource. The advice tendered to me by the griffins of the servants' hall was grimly aphoristic: 'Neither a borrower nor a lender be,' Miss Mort used to say with an absolutely awful gravity; or: 'Gambling only pays when you're winning.' But there were occasional newspapers left about the house that I took an interest in, and a room known as the 'library' in which, although it contained no books, there was a file of bound copies of *Punch* going back to the 1840s. There were days in the wet autumns, when the rain soaked the fields from dawn to dusk and the yard beyond the kitchen door turned into a quagmire, when I've spent entire afternoons under a fading gaslight brooding over the curious landscapes they offered up – that lost universe of lion-hunting hostesses and moustachioed majors of the Volunteers – and when I finally emerged into the world beyond Loftholdingswood it was rather a surprise to me to find that it didn't consist of heavy swells and 'hartists' and 'little coves' in tremendous frock-coats.

And yet I knew that the information that filled my head was of the wrong kind, that its value would be negligible beyond the immediate boundaries of my existence, that it solved none of the problems by which I was oppressed. I knew the names of Queen Victoria's surviving children, but I did not know who my parents were. I knew Lady Desborough's London address, but not what I was doing at Loftholdingswood or what lay in store for me beyond it. There was no certainty about my past and future, only occasional tantalising glances: an irregular letter, addressed to Mrs Custance, which caused her to stare over her spectacles at me in a faintly alarmed way; a ten-shilling note that was once presented to me – the implication being that it came from some remote third party – that I was told I might do what I wanted with; a mysterious summons to take tea in Haslemere with someone who did not come and whose absence alarmed Mrs Custance very much; a picture cut out of an illustrated paper of a woman's face, neatly surrounded by orange blossoms, that lay on the mantelpiece in the servants' hall for a month or so and which for some reason I associated with my predicament.

Meanwhile time was moving on: 1911, 1912 and on to 1913. Old Lady Delacave still lay insensible beneath the cambric counterpane and a foxy-faced man whom we assumed to be the distant cousin drove up in the solicitor's dog cart to inspect the estate. Mr Montagu ruptured himself carrying a case of claret up from the cellar and had to spend a fortnight in the hospital at Haslemere, and there was a terrific scandal when Elsie was discovered in one of the barns with the under-gardener. And yet while the armies massed across Europe and the grey ships steamed up and down the Channel – even the confraternity of the Loftholdingswood back kitchen had started to talk about the likelihood of war – that tide of late-Edwardian prosperity continued to flow through our veins. Loftholdingswood was a fairly primitive place on the big scale of things – there was no electricity, Lady Delacave 'didn't hold' with the telephone and the water had to be pumped up from the local spring – but even here, in darkest Sussex, you could still get some idea of the extraordinary blanket of wealth and security that covered England in the years before 1914. Mr Montagu and the others were living on board wages and their only employer was a bedridden old skeleton whose weekly meals could have been piled on a single dinner plate, but I've seen Mrs Trotwood throw out enough food to feed an entire family down in the village. 'Living as gentlefolks should' it was called, and if anyone had suggested to Mr Montagu that half the world was starving and he ought to have tightened his belt he'd have marked them down as a Bolshevik, an 'agitator', 'one of them radical fellers' he read about in the newspapers. The Loftholdingswood servants' hall had the proper *rentier* attitude towards Socialists: they were the shiftless, work-shy, rotten eggs that the factories wouldn't have, whom any decent working man would treat with the utmost contempt. 1912, 1913, 1914. There was even a plan for me by this time – God knows where it had been hatched – that I should join the Royal Naval College at Dartmouth – they took cadets at thirteen in those days – and go to sea. I'd read about Jackie Fisher and Admiral Jellicoe, and was very taken by the idea. I could already see myself in a midshipman's rig and a stiff collar standing on the quarterdeck of some destroyer as it sped out of the Thames into open water, with the ratings running out lengths of rope and the spray breaking across the rail.

And then, one morning in summer 1914 I came down to breakfast to find that everything had changed. For a start there was an undertaker's van out in the drive with a couple of horses stamping on the gravel, and Mr Montagu in a suit of rusty black wringing his hands in the porch. When I saw Elsie advancing from the servants' hall with a crêpe wreath, which she tied on to the door knocker with a twist of string, I finally twigged that old Lady Delacave was dead. The coffin came downstairs half an hour later – badly bumped by the undertaker's men as it reached the landing, I recall – with the servants following it out to the van. But what I really remember about that day is the whiteness of their faces under the July sun, like a lot of old ghosts back from a night's haunting, thoroughly bewildered by the turn their lives had taken.

After that things happened very quickly. Although there was a certain amount of talk about Lady Delacave's cousin coming to 'claim his inheritance', everyone knew that it was the end of Loftholdingswood. No sooner was the will proved than a surveyor arrived from Lewes to mark out the grounds on sheets of cartridge paper and an advert appeared in *Country Life*. I don't know if they got any takers, for the establishment was breaking up by then. Mr Montagu retired to Hove; Mrs Custance announced that she was going off to live with her widowed sister-in-law; Mrs Trotwood took a job in a pub-cum-restaurant in Haslemere; the girls were talking about a munitions factory that was starting up in Guildford. And so, eventually, on the very morning, I think, when the papers were carrying the news of the Archduke's assassination at Sarajevo, I found myself sitting in the library with Mrs Custance having a conversation that I can remember almost word for word and was, I suppose, one of the longest exchanges I ever had with that lady.

'Now, Ralph,' Mrs Custance said – she had a little hank of wool in her hand that she was teasing backwards and forwards between her fingers. 'I suppose you'd like to know what's to become of you.' She paused. 'Well, it's a difficult thing. A very difficult thing. Of course, there's no room for you at Mrs Rendall's – at my sister-in-law's, that is. And you can't stay where you are.'

'Won't anyone be living here?' I asked.

'Hm. Bailiff visiting once a month, I shouldn't wonder,' Mrs Custance sniffed. ''E' – she meant Lady Delacave's vulpine cousin – 'won't know how to keep up a house. It makes me sick to think of it.'

And I realised that the emotion Mrs Custance appeared to be suffering from had a great deal more to do with the house than the problem of myself. Perhaps she divined something of this, saw at least a little of the scale of moral values it implied, for she bobbed her head, gave another tug on the hank of wool and said, 'I'd love for you to come with me, Ralph, but it can't be done. There's six in the house already and Gladys wouldn't stand for it. No, I've made enquiries and you're to go to my brother in Norwich.'

This seemed such a dramatic step, so manifestly beyond my experience, that I sat silent, looking at the wool as it lapped back and forth in Mrs Custance's grasp.

'You know where Norwich is, don't you?' Mrs Custance went on.

'The principal city of Norfolk,' I confirmed, in tribute to Miss Mort.

'Well, then. My brother Alfred lives there. "E's a bachelor,' Mrs Custance announced rather doubtfully. 'Says he'd be glad to have a boy around the place. Why, you can go to school, you know, if you've a mind. Do all kinds of things if you've a mind to . . . It's what your mother would have wanted,' Mrs Custance said, with a kind of evasive finality.

Outside there were men routing out the ancient logs and carrying them on to the backs of wagons; their voices came haltingly through the window. Mrs Custance's words had shocked me, for they suggested that my mother was no longer there to do the wanting.

'. . . Sure you and he'll get on *famously*,' Mrs Custance said.

A week later, with the blinds of the house pulled down, and my suit-case lying packed in the hall, and the old servants shaking my hand, and Edna waving to me from an upstairs window, and the station fly waiting outside in the courtyard, I left Loftholdingswood for good.

4

Chicago

1905

It was late on a Sunday afternoon in the early autumn on the eastern side of Chicago, in a part of the city adjoining the Van Buren district – that time of the day when the faithful are accustomed to attend evening service. Here in the neighbourhood of Van Buren Street, a long grey thorough-fare crammed with stores and manufactories, three or four places of worship were opening their doors to greet the anticipated throng: a Presbyterian chapel, a Unitarian meeting house, a Catholic church fashioned in loud red brick with a cracked bell. Some of these congregations were so modestly established that, to the unknowing, they appeared to be ordinary street buildings: mere doors opening on to the pavement with an inky card announcing that the Rev. X or Brother Y would be preaching that night to reveal their true purpose. Outside one of these doors, in a rather quiet part of the street, a young woman – perhaps twenty years old, with soft red hair – stood looking out at the passers-by. She watched the street not as if she were waiting for somebody, but with a general curiosity: as if the sight of a busy thoroughfare with people moving briskly about it pleased her for no other reason than it was there. Occasionally she lifted her head to stare at the distant skyline – the factories and cranes that marked the line of the East River, the tall buildings of the financial district – only for her gaze to return, after a moment or so, to the life that seethed around her.

Presently a tall man in dark clothes, whose demeanour suggested that he might be a clergyman, came out of the door to call her: 'So there you are, Alice. It is nearly six o'clock.'

'Is that the time?' The late-afternoon sun was still streaming across the street and she raised her hand to shadow her eyes as she answered him. 'I did not know it was so late.'

'Well, everyone is here I think who will be.' He spoke in an oddly formal way that might have caused an eavesdropper to think that English did not come naturally to him. 'You had better come inside.'

With a last regretful look along Van Buren, where there was nothing more to see except a horse that had lost its legs on the cobbles and whose righting was being inspected by three or four passers-by, she followed him into the building. Within, an anteroom with a desk strewn with religious literature and pamphlets led into a dusty, low-ceilinged assembly hall, twenty feet square, in which stood a harmonium and several rows of chairs. On the wall at the farther end, and altogether dominating the room, hung a lithograph of the crucifixion. Here, perhaps two dozen people had assembled: the women seated, the men for the most part standing by the walls talking in low voices. They were inconspicuously but not poorly dressed: shopkeepers and their wives, an occasional brakeman from the railway. As the newcomers came into the room one or two of the men touched their hats – they wore these articles indoors – and said, 'Good evening, Pastor Hanson.' Remembering what was expected of her, Alice opened a small cupboard at the side of the harmonium and produced a stack of battered hymnals, which she proceeded to distribute. The light from the single window spilled in across the floor, making zebra patterns out of the chair backs and a dense blanket of shadow where the harmonium obstructed its path.

The service began with a hymn:

> Behold the lilies of the field,
> They toil not, neither spin.
> But yet our father gives to them
> The raiment they stand in.
>
> Behold the little birds in air,
> They care not for the morrow.
> And yet our heavenly father sees
> They have no need to borrow.
>
> So we will trust to God above,
> For we are better far
> Than lilies and the sparrows both;
> For his children we are.

There were dust-motes caught in the fading rays of the sun and she watched them suspended in the wall of light with an inexpressible melancholy. The doleful voices of the congregation – the gloom of the room in which they stood – seemed to her to mock any sentiment that the hymn might have conveyed. For a moment she remembered Aunt Em and Uncle Hi, and the tabernacle at Kansas and the Sunday School teacher Miss Ingalls.

Hanson stood by her side, not singing, a look of intense concentration on his face. When the hymn had finished he moved out into the centre of the room, fixed his gaze on a point slightly above the lithograph of the Crucifixion and said, 'The Good Lord is all around us. You may not think it, but he is. He is in this room with us as we go about our devotions. He will be with us again when we step outside it and return to our homes and our places of work. I have seen him. He is there. What does the Lord want from us? I do not know. Except that we should follow his instructions, which are set out in the book he left behind him to guide us. He is moving through this great city of ours. His arm guides the ships as they come down our great river. He is in our factories and our slaughterhouses. He sits down with us as we eat. He watches our children as they grow. How do I know this? Because he has told me and I am certain that it is so . . .'

Seated on the rough wooden chair, her hands moving restlessly in her lap, Alice reviewed the tasks that awaited her after the service. These included the preparation of supper, the putting to bed of the child and, she supposed, the entertainment of various parishioners whose custom it was to 'drop by' on the pastor on a Sunday evening. The prospect depressed her horribly, and she searched in it for an odd moment that she might call her own, where her mind was not bent on the mundane duties of housework. Hanson had finished his discourse and she became aware of the commencement of the second hymn:

There is a happy land, far, far away . . .

From the moment that he had knocked on her side door in the middle of the storm, Alice knew that she would marry Hanson. Fortunately, he had claimed to know it too. 'It is God's providence,' he said about the blizzard and the series of misjudgments that had brought him to the hills above De Smet rather than the road that curved round its southern flank. 'It is God himself who sent me to you.' He was a tall, pale-faced Swede, the son of an immigrant farmer, who sad 'yas' for 'yes' and 'tink' for 'think', and undertook missions for a Lutheran church in the east. He had no interest in Drouett, beyond establishing his unfittedness. 'He was a bad man,' he said. 'I am different. You shall see.' When he had been a week in the house – the blizzard ceased after two days – they went east by the railroad. De Smet had been a mistake, Hanson said: a preacher could do no good on the prairie. It was in the cities that the word of God needed to be heard. They had been married at the mission church in Duluth. The child – a boy – had been born seven months later. Again, Hanson had shown no interest in its parentage. 'It is God's blessing on us,' he had said. 'You shall see.' At first Alice had admired him for what seemed a conspicuous act of charity, had even been prepared to worship him for it, had he wanted worship, which he did not. At other times she thought him faintly inhuman. He was an intent, silent man, given to fits of brooding. These, too, she gathered, were examples of God's providence. And so, by degrees, they had come to Chicago and the mission house on Van Buren, where flakes of black soot fell from the factory chimneys on to the crowded pavements and the word of God needed to be heard.

When the service was over, Alice and Hanson passed through a second door at the back of the hall into the mission's living quarters: a small room containing a horsehair sofa, an armchair and a square deal table. A kitchen and two bedrooms on the upper floor completed the accommodation. As Alice set about fetching their supper, Hanson stood in the doorway and talked to her. This was his one moment of animation in the week when, spirits raised by his sermon, he would comment on the congregation and draw certain facts to her attention.

'Did you see that Stapleford was here tonight?' he now began. 'The grocer from two blocks down?'

'I didn't notice him. What does he look like?'

'The thin man with the grey beard. This is the second time that he has come. It is a good sign.'

There was a newspaper lying on the table. He picked it up restlessly, looked at its front page – he did not like newspapers as they reminded him of his uncertainties with language – and put it down again.

'And Mrs Connan has promised me five dollars for the fund. She is a good woman.'

The mission maintained a charitable fund, which was used to support the destitute during the winter months.

'A good woman,' Hanson said again, watching Alice set plates upon the table. 'If everyone was like her, there would be no poverty. No people sleeping in the street.'

'Folks ought not to come here when there's nothing for them to do,' ventured Alice, who had views on this subject.

They ate a frugal supper of food that Hanson had bought yesterday in the market: bread, cured herring, Swedish meatballs. As the meal proceeded the child, put down an hour before in his cot under the alcove, began to stir and she fetched him to the table and placed him on her lap. In this way several minutes passed, Alice alternately taking bites from her plate and feeding the child which, despite these attentions, continued to cry. Hanson's eye brightened. 'Here,' he said, taking him from her. 'That is not the way.' He held the child up between his great palms and began to rock it gently back and forth. 'No, that is not the way, is it now? It is not the way.'

Outside it was growing dark. In the distance came the rattle of a streetcar. 'Now then,' Hanson said again to the child, with an attempt at comedy. 'What are we to do with you? That is what I should like to know?' The child was called Asa, after Hanson's father. 'What are we to do with you?'

Not liking to break in on this idyll, but having a question that she burned to ask, Alice said suddenly, 'Sven. How long shall we be staying in Chicago?'

'Why? Do you not like Chicago?' He placed Asa, now silent and wide-eyed, on his knee and gave her his full attention.

'I like it well enough. But surely we won't stay here for ever?'

'It is God's will,' he said. 'Or that of the mission. Maybe they will call me back east. Who knows?'

Seeing that this was all he was prepared to say on the subject, she began to clear away the supper things. Again, she was struck by the dismal aspect of the room. The few books that Hanson owned – abstruse and theological – were cursorily arranged on the mantelpiece next to his pipe and a picture postcard of Lake Erie that she had bought in a corner store. Looking at the bare wall above them she said,

'We could paint this room and make it nice.'

'Paint it?' He looked up from his chair. 'Does it need painting?'

'No. But if we painted it, we could make it look nice.'

She saw that this suggestion had altogether bewildered him. He looked around the room once or twice and then said, rather shyly, 'Yas. That is a good idea. It would be a good thing to paint it. But we should need to ask permission of the secretary.'

'Could you do that?'

'It is a good idea,' he said again, but more vaguely. 'I could mention it in my next report.'

The second of the upstairs rooms served as a study. Here, each night after supper, Hanson went to write letters and conduct the mission's business. Hearing him climb the rickety staircase, Alice seated herself in the armchair. The child, returned to its cradle, had fallen asleep again. To the right of the hearth there was a foot-high stack of papers – old *Chicago-Sun-Tribunes*, mission gazettes with lists of attendances. Reaching into the very bottom of the stack, Alice sought for an item that, if not absolutely concealed there, was certainly well hidden from view, drew it out and began to read it.

Before long there was a noise of footsteps descending. As Hanson came into the room she saw that he had put on his hat.

'What is that you are reading?' he asked.

She showed him the cover: it was a Philadelphia theatre magazine, bought in Duluth at the time of their marriage and hoarded ever since.

'I don't like you to look at such things,' he said.

She considered this with the magazine held absently between her fingers. 'I don't see the harm in it.'

'I do not say there is harm. But they are . . .' – he searched for a word that would convey his disdain – 'low people.'

'If that is what you think then I shan't read it.'

'Very well.' He stood awkwardly by the fireplace, conscious that he had offended her. 'It would be a good idea to paint this room,' he said again. 'I shall write to the secretary about it.'

She acknowledged the concession with a nod. 'Will Mr Hurstwood and Elder Grice be coming this evening?'

'I don't think so. In any case, I have told them I am going out.' Seeing the look of enquiry on her face, he went on, 'There is a fellow who wishes to give money to our fund. A banker. I must see him and make a good . . .' – again he searched for the word – 'a good impression.'

'Shall you be late?'

'Yas. Perhaps eleven. He lives on Wabash Avenue.'

More than any other properties in Chicago, Alice admired the houses on Wabash Avenue. 'He must be very rich.'

'Yas,' Hanson said with faint irritation. 'I suppose he is what you would call rich. But let us hope he is like Mrs Connan.'

When he had gone she sat in the armchair by the hearth, listening to the rattle of the streetcars and the clatter of feet on the pavement. She wondered who the people were and what entertainment summoned them from their homes on a Sunday evening. The theatre magazine lay on the table at her side and she stared disloyally at the cover, which showed a gentleman in an evening suit raising his hat to a dashing young woman in a grey dress cut in the very latest fashion who would not meet his gaze but looked demurely at him out of the corner of her eye. HIS DEBT OF HONOUR ran the headline. MISS TOZER'S TRIUMPH. Everything about this scene fascinated her, from the gentleman's silver-topped cane to the little fringe of curls that ran down over the young woman's forehead and the backdrop of flunkies and mirrored glass – it was a photograph of the stage on which *His Debt of Honour* took place – and she considered it until, by an altogether unconscious process, she found that she was thinking about herself here in the missioner's parlour in Van Buren.

There was no resentment in her approach to this problem. Above all, she was struck by a profound sense of dislodgement and dislocation. Vast acres of time seemed to have passed since the afternoon when she had boarded the train at Kansas City with Aunt Em, but she saw now that it was little more than a year. The dress she now wore, she realised, was one that she had carried in her trunk. This continuity seemed to her very remarkable and she strove to find other mementoes of her past life, locating them eventually in the enamel pin that ornamented her dress and the ribbon that held back her hair at the neck. This comforted her, but she continued to brood about the pastor's lodgings and the dusty parlour room in which she sat, and Hanson. She took little interest in Hanson's work. She supposed, if she thought about it, that it was a good thing people should have the Gospel preached to them and that there were men to do the preaching, but she had no sympathy with the Van Buren congregation. The delight with which Hanson welcomed a contribution to the fund meant nothing to her. Occasionally some phrase from his sermons would settle in her head, but she was aware that she valued the words for the sensations they stirred in her mind – pictures of moving crowds, with herself among them – rather than any meaning they might have. As for Hanson, she did not quite know what she thought about him. He was not unkind to her – there were women in the congregation, she knew, who had to put up with far worse – and his pleasure in the child was a source of relief to her. Still, she thought, she would have liked to read her theatre magazine in peace.

It was by now about half past eight. She had not known that so much time had passed and, making this discovery, started up in her chair. Then, realising that there was nothing for her to do – that the chores were mostly completed and that the child still lay asleep in his cradle – she sank back again. The room had grown dark during her reverie and she lit the gas jet close to the hearth, filling the far wall with angular shadows. It occurred to her that there were various items that she might fetch from the bedroom – odd garments that needed darning, a piece of embroidery on which she was working – and so, moving softly so as not to disturb the child, she took a candle and went upstairs. Here there was a tiny landing, on which the two doors stood side by side. Customarily, the door of the bedroom lay open and that of Hanson's office stood closed. Now, for some reason, these positions had been reversed. As she stood with the fingers of her left hand reaching for the knob of the bedroom door, Alice found that the arc of light cast by the candle, which she held in her right hand, illuminated that small portion of the office that lay open to her gaze. It was not a room into which she usually went, indeed was regarded as Hanson's private fiefdom, but, her curiosity piqued, she held the candle out before her and pushed the door wide open. There was not a great deal to see: a small table, a chair, a brace of cabinets and a bookcase on which had been assembled a row of loose-leafed missionary tracts. Still, for reasons which she could not quite fathom, it amused her to linger there. She set the candle down on the table, caught deftly on her forefinger a drop of wax that came guttering down on to the polished surface, which Hanson would have noticed had it fallen there, and coaxed one of the tracts from the shelf. It told the story of a small boy who, by way of blacking his neighbours' shoes, managed to raise enough money to buy his widowed mother a winter shawl and would have seemed crude to a sensibility much less critical than hers: after a moment or so she put it back.

There was nothing more to keep her in the room, but as she was turning to leave she made what seemed to her quite a startling discovery. The fastening of the small safe that sat in the corner was slightly ajar. It was, she knew, a patent safe whose door, once opened, obeyed some hidden mechanical process and clicked shut. Clearly Hanson, in trying to secure it, had not closed the door with sufficient force: this had allowed it to spring back from its lock. The sight fascinated her. She knew that the safe was no more than a halfway house, in which the proceeds of collections and subscriptions to the fund were stored prior to their removal to the bank, but even so she began to speculate how much money there might be there. Might there be twenty dollars? Thirty, maybe? Thinking that she ought to shut the door of the safe – it was a squat metal box, a foot square, and as she now saw bolted to the floor – she moved towards it through the arc of candlelight, and began to examine the gap between door and jamb. Still, though, something stayed her hand. 'I shall stop this,' she said to herself, planting her fingers on the door of the safe. A noise from below caught her attention and she stood for a moment, stock still, until she established that it came from the street. 'Anyhow,' she said to herself again, 'he shan't tell me what I'm to read.'

She thought that it would do no harm to open the door of the safe a little before she closed it, so she bent down on one knee and rested her hand on the door. The inside of the safe consisted of two metal trays, one set on top of the other, on which lay folded banknotes and a number of loose coins in a small wooden box. Again she wondered how much money was left in the safe. Might there be thirty-five dollars? Forty, even? The most money she had ever seen in her life was the ninety dollars Uncle Hi had once for selling his team. Without being entirely conscious of her actions she found that she had taken out the upper drawer and was running her eye over the coins. Placing the tray on the table, she sat down on the chair and began to count the money, arranging it in small, symmetrical piles – so many quarters in this area of the table, so many dimes in another, nickels and pennies in a third and fourth. She did this without haste, for her mind, though absorbed in the task, seemed simultaneously to have carried her far away from the room in which she sat with its guttering candle and its arc of light. In her reverie she was sitting on the porch with her friend Lizzie Sparkes, the butcher's daughter, who with her long white face and mournful eyes looked uncomfortably like the oxen that her father slaughtered behind his store each Monday and Thursday, and laughing over the way they had teased out the hair on the front of their heads into what Aunt Em called a 'lunatic fringe', while the sun hung in an orange dish over the distant wheat fields and the geese wandered vigilantly through the yard, plundering it for bugs and corn ears. Then she remembered that she was a thousand miles away in a missioner's lodging in Van Buren with a pile of money from Hanson's safe ranged on the tabletop before her.

There was well over a hundred dollars, a hundred and thirty even, nearly a hundred and forty, and she wondered how Hanson had accumulated such a vast sum and why it should have been left in the house. Now that she knew its value the sight of it scared her, worried her in its immensity, and she felt that she wanted never to see it again, or even know that she had seen it.

Somehow, though, she did not place the notes and coins back in their metal trays and reposition these containers in the safe. Instead, she saw Hanson's face as he shaved in the morning, with the fingers of his right hand flicking the soap from his razor as he worked, and singing quietly in Swedish under his breath, and the journey back from the prairie, and passing through the potato fields in Iowa in a covered wagon, which seemed to her the most desolate place she had seen on earth, with the wind blowing the dust this way and that over the bare ground and the stooped figures of the potato pickers moving slowly over the rim of the low, flat hills, and Hanson saying that the Lord was with those people as he was with them all, and a tin kettle tied to the threads of the canvas wagon cover clinking with an indescribably melancholy sound as they trailed on into the twilight and the land running away into greyness and a great silence broken only by the far-off barking of dogs and the jingle of the horses' bridles and the creak of the wagon shafts.

The vision faded and she found she was staring at the rolls of notes and coins which, though she did not remember how she had arrived at the total, amounted to a hundred and thirty-seven dollars. Again she wondered how Hanson had come to be in possession of such a fabulous sum and why it had not been transferred to the bank. Then she recalled that on the previous Tuesday, which was Hanson's day for dealing with the financial affairs of the mission, he had been confined to bed with a cold. This meant that the proceeds from two Sunday evening services lay in the safe rather than one. With an explanation of the total, her mind relaxed. Still, a hundred and thirty-seven dollars was a lot of money. She tried to recall the most expensive thing she had ever seen in a store window, and decided it was a dress in one of the big emporia in Kansas, which had cost all of twenty-three dollars and which Aunt Em had described as 'sinful'. She reassembled the money in its original situation on the trays and looked closely at it, examining the banknotes – dusty and flecked with spots of grease – the milled edges of the coins, the faces of the presidents that stared out from them. She made a little gallery of those faces and cautiously inspected them, fascinated and also repelled by the row of long, lean jaws and sharp eyes. It occurred to her suddenly that it must be getting late, that Hanson would be returning soon, but a clock chiming some distance away down the street assured her that it was only nine o'clock, and she rearranged the little gallery and polished one or two of the faces with the hem of her apron.

For perhaps another five minutes she sat in this way, staring at the coins and the notes and the empty, open safe. Then suddenly a feeling of horror swept over her and she flung the money back on to the tray and hastily put both the containers back into the safe. This done, she sank back in her chair again with a feeling of intense relief. The door wanted only the briefest pressure from her hand to be secured, but somehow she did not shut it. Instead, picking up the candlestick and holding it carefully before her, she made her way down the staircase and stood in the parlour listening to the noises in the street and staring at the mantelpiece. The child still slept, but going to inspect its cradle she found that the coverlet was awry and she stood for a moment rearranging it, her ear cocked for the slightest sound that would indicate the unfastening of the outer door or the move-ment of feet through the hall. But there was nothing, and she bent over the cradle again, clasping her hands nervously together and occasionally retrieving a strand of hair that fell over her forehead. It was fine red hair and she curled it admiringly over her finger before pinning it back.

The clock on the mantelpiece now told her that it was a quarter past nine, and she supposed that she should light the fire, Hanson setting great store by the cheerfulness of his hearth when he returned home. But although she went so far as to sweep the previous night's ashes out of the grate, arrange a shovelful of coals in a small, conical pile and secure a firelighter at their base, she could not bring herself to strike the sulphur match she had ready in her hand. Her nervousness had reached such a point that she could not remain still. Sofa, chair and hearth alike were distasteful to her, and she roamed around the room, her eye falling on tiny discrepancies – a book fallen on to its side on Hanson's shelf, a piece of bread discarded beneath a chair – and her hand correcting them as she went. Again she was back in the fields in Iowa, with the dusk slowly descending and the figures of the potato pickers receding into the shadow, and herself enquiring of Hanson, 'Don't they stop when it's dark?' and Hanson gravely replying, 'It is important to them to earn money. No, they do not stop' and the moon rising suddenly above the low hills to flood the valley where the potato fields lay with livid, mournful light.

She looked up at the clock again to find that barely five minutes had passed. Half of her, she realised, wished that Hanson would come home instantly; the other half shrank from the sound of his key in the lock. She stood uncertainly in the centre of the room for another half-minute and then, seizing the candlestick with such force that the flame danced and almost went out, climbed rapidly up the stairs to the office. Here everything was just as she had left it: chair, table and metal cabinets in their normal positions, with the door of the safe an inch or two ajar. She bent down and flicked the door gently with her fingers so that it wavered slightly. Thinking that it would do no harm to confirm that her earlier calculation had been correct, she took out the metal trays again and began once more to count the money. To her surprise she found that the second tray contained a recess, built into its base, and that this harboured an unsealed envelope containing a further fifty dollars. That made one hundred and eighty-seven dollars! Hanson had said that the pickers in the Iowa potato fields earned two dollars a day. She smoothed the newly discovered notes between her fingers and replaced them in the envelope, took them out again and then, for a second time, put them back.

A dreadful feeling of anxiety passed through her, so unsettling that she dropped the bundle of notes on the floor and bent hurriedly to retrieve them. She knew that the only way to comfort herself was to put the trays back in the safe. Still, though, she hesitated. Balancing one tray on her right hand, she bent down, thinking that she could draw the door open with the fingers of her left. Her foot stumbled against the chair, hidden by the half-light and her hand fell against the door of the safe with greater force than she had intended. All at once the door snapped shut.

Curiously, the effect on her was not what she had foreseen. As the implications of what she had done dawned on her, she was horror-struck. Twice she tugged violently at the closed door, but it was to no avail: it would not reopen without Hanson's key in its lock. When the second attempt on the door was unsuccessful, she sank back into the chair, yet she discovered, to her surprise, that she was unexpectedly calm. A bridge had been crossed. When Hanson came back he would know that she had taken the money from the safe. Nothing that she did could disguise this fact. To excuse herself – and she did not know if he would excuse her – she would have to explain what she had done. The thought of this, although

47

the explanation seemed perfectly logical in her mind, revolted her. She half rose to her feet and then fell into the chair again, thinking hard. Whatever she said, she feared that Hanson would suspect her, would see the money set out upon the table in its trays and draw conclusions that would not be favourable to her. Once more she rose from the chair and tugged at the handle of the safe: it did not respond. What was to be done? She was conscious that she owed Hanson a great deal, that there were things he had given her which most of the world would have denied her, and she was grateful for this. Yet she was also conscious that there were things Hanson had not given her, which she had very much wanted, that certain pathways she had wished to wander had been summarily closed off. 'Anyway,' she said out loud, 'he'll not tell me what I'm to read.' She discovered that she had unthinkingly picked up the money and that it now lay in her hands, coins and paper all mixed together. The sight of it re-assured her. She told herself that it was not her fault it had come there, but a mischance of fate. It occurred to her that she might try the door one final time, but the impulse was waning fast in her. She imagined Hanson coming to the room and finding the safe empty, but somehow this did not seem as shocking to her as it had done a few moments before. Going gingerly downstairs in the dark – for she felt that it needed two hands to convey her burden – she found her purse on the corner of the kitchen table. There was an easiness about her movements now. Hastily she went upstairs to the bedroom and packed some clothes in a travelling case, took the child from its cradle and wrapped it in a shawl, which she secured in the crook of her left arm. With the travelling case in her right hand, she passed through the assembly hall – very dark and gloomy now, with the mice skittering away from beneath her feet – and opened the door into the street. The light from a street lamp fell suddenly on her face, but there was no one about. She set out westwards along Van Buren towards the heart of the city, where, she knew, there would be streetcars, railway stations, ways of escape.

All that night, and for most of the next day and the night following that, Alice travels. At first she does this in a state of extreme trepidation. Hanson will pursue her, she thinks. Some instinct will prompt him to follow the path she has taken. He is in some ways an astute man, who can divine weather conditions from the pattern of the clouds: maybe some of this skill can be applied to his absconding wife. Gradually, as the hours go by, this feeling passes. America is a big place. Hanson has no way of knowing where she has gone. She may safely disregard him, she decides. But there are other things that need urgent consideration. Where will she go? And what will she do when she gets there? At Chicago Central, to which she has proceeded by streetcar, she takes a cup of coffee at one of the trackside cafés and examines her situation. There are trains heading out everywhere: to Kansas, Indianapolis, Detroit, across the border to Canada, down into the South. A freight train full of livestock, bound for the stock-yards, lies drawn up in a siding and she listens to the cries of the animals, who seem to know where it is they are headed and what lies in store. Beasts can foretell their destinies, Hanson says, know if trouble is brewing, when death is at hand. Perhaps this is another part of God's plan: who knows? In the end, she buys a ticket to Indianapolis, which has a comforting sound to it and, in addition, lies in the east, to which, for some reason, she finds herself drawn. The train leaves at eleven, sliding out through the empty freight yards into the Chicago suburbs and beyond them into the Indiana wheat fields.

As she travels, she feels herself growing smaller, less noticeable. A woman journeying alone with a baby ought to be conspicuous, she feels, but somehow she is not. Nocturnal America turns out to be full of people like her: families going who knows where, with white-faced children staring anxiously out of blankets, solitary women with their belongings done up in canvas bags who lie awkwardly across the double seats chewing gum. There is a solidarity about them that she likes. They offer food and comment on the travelling conditions, fall asleep in mid-sentence and snap back into consciousness without noticing that the time has passed. The child looks on curiously, alternately sleeping and waking, blinking in the arti-ficial light. Sometimes she points things out to him in the great space beyond the window, but there is little to see: cornfields gathered up in gloom, the sleeping towns, grey horses moving silently through the dawn. What she remembers are odd fragments: a woman with a pale face streaked with dirt asking her if this is the right train for Louisville; waking at sunrise with mist from the fields rolling up to the carriage window; a child crying in its sleep away down the corridor and being shushed into silence.

At Indianapolis – greatly daring – she breakfasts in a restaurant beyond the station concourse. Still a small part of her fears that Hanson may be on her track, that the policeman guarding the station entrance might have been expressly ordered to seek her out and bring her back to Chicago.

But a glance at the street, in which, or so it seems, thousands of people are already on the move towards their places of business, reassures her. She is quite alone: no one will come. While this thought exhilarates her, it is also alarming. She figures that maybe she can do cleaning work, get a job in a hotel, where perhaps there may be someone who can look after Asa. An idea occurs to her and she crosses the road to a stationery store, buys a letter card with a picture of Indianapolis City Hall on the front, borrows a pencil from the owner of the restaurant, who has been observing her with a friendly interest, and writes *Dear Sven, I am sure you will want to know* . . . But what will Sven want to know? That she did not mean to take the money but, finding it within her grasp, took it anyway? That she does not intend to return it? That she is ashamed about the money, but not about the fact of her escape? In the end the task proves too much for her and she stows the letter card in the recesses of her bag, picks up her belongings, pays the proprietor his fifteen cents, balances the child on her hip and passes back into the mouth of the station, where the policeman, far from arresting her, directs her to a waiting room where, once again, she sits down and considers her situation.

It is here in the waiting room that she remembers something that may be useful to her. This is that she has kin living in the east: Aunt Patty, one of Aunt Em's younger sisters, and her daughters Carrie and Etta, who moved to New York ten years since. There is even an address, scrawled faintly in the pink keepsake book in her bag, and she takes it out and studies it. She wonders what they may know about her and what Aunt Em may have said, but somehow this is secondary to the fact of their existence, however many hundreds of miles away in the east. It is eight o'clock in the morning now, with autumn sun shining down on the heads of the passers-by and reflecting off the great girders of the station's superstructure, and she decides that she will go to New York and see if she can stay with Aunt Patty and Carrie and Etta while she looks about for something. The thought emboldens her and she attracts the attention of a porter and has her bag carried off to the ticket office. The porter, who is impressed by her appearance, asks, 'Travelling far today, ma'am?' and she answers 'New York City', and the porter smiles and says New York City is a mighty long way, but that he once went as far as Cincinnati. The ticket costs her twenty dollars, to add to the money already spent on her journey to Indianapolis and her breakfast, and she is aware that there are now only a hundred and fifty-seven dollars and some change in her purse, but this fact is somehow immaterial to her. She is going to New York City to stay with Aunt Patty and Carrie and Etta. There is bright sunshine falling on the track and the yards alongside it as the train steams out, and she shows it to the child as the car bumps and judders on the points beneath. 'There now,' she says, 'there now.' 'Anyhow,' she says to herself again, 'he shan't tell me what I'm to read.' Hanson, she discovers, is already a blur, the mission pastor's lodging a kind of dim cavern from which she is glad to have escaped. Perhaps her coming across the money and accidentally taking it – even now she cannot regard the taking as theft – is a part of God's plan. It is hard to tell.

There is a map of the north-eastern states on the wall of the car above her head, all the region that this train company runs, with the principal stations all indicated in red and the railroad routes moving along in black lines, and she uses it to trace the course of her journey. Indianapolis to Dayton is ninety miles and that's the end of Indiana. Dayton to Colombus is sixty-five miles, Columbus to Mingo Junction is another hundred and thirty and that's the end of Ohio. There are people joining and leaving the train at every station, all that outpouring of vagrant America, and she stops to examine them: businessmen in sober suits, farmers in denim overalls with shovel hats on the seats beside them; salesmen with their cases. The salesmen make her think of Drouett and what happened to him, where he is now or, as she half suspects, if he died in the storm. This probability does not disturb her, for the life that goes on around her seems full of such possibilities. Uncle Hi's cousin Wilbur was crushed to death under his own horse. A Kansas neighbour died of a hornet sting. Maybe this, too, is part of God's plan. One of the salesmen gives her what he calls a 'sample' out of his case, a blue packet with some kind of powder in it, which he says she can use when washing her clothes, and she tucks it in the lip of her bag, then falls asleep with Asa cradled in her arms as the train steams on over the Ohio River and through the glittering corn. A poem Miss Hoover read to her at grade school stirs in her mind, about long fields of barley and of rye, clothing the wolds and meeting the sky, and she tries to recite it to herself, but the words are all vanished into the past. When she wakes up at Pittsburgh it is late in the afternoon and the travelling salesmen are all gone, with only the blue packet to remind her that they were ever there, and she steps off the train to board the express that will take her to New York.

Pittsburgh to New York is all of two hundred and fifty miles. As she travels, the land around her changes. The cornfields are gone now, and in their place are little towns and factories, the hills and mountains that lead on to Harrisburg and the state line. Asa is restless, unused to the constant, monotonous shaking of the car, and she cradles him on her lap and sings to him in a low voice that barely carries above the juddering of the train. Scarcely a day has passed, she thinks, since she stood in Hanson's office, but already it seems a long way off, quite remote and detached from anything that concerns her now. They reach Grand Central Station an hour after midnight – too late, she knows, to begin her search for Aunt Patty and Carrie and Etta – and for a moment the high glass ceiling and the mill of people alarm and oppress her, but she is growing used to these places, summons another porter and has her bag carried to a hotel nearby where the charge is a dollar. In the morning, wondering at the wide streets and the dizzying skyline, she makes her way, by streetcar and on foot, to the address in Queen's written down in her pink keepsake book. The street is full of low terraced houses with porches and fenced-in yards, with cats staring out of windows, and looks nice, Alice thinks. She has a little speech prepared to say to Aunt Patty, but a strange woman opens the door and stares balefully out, and the words crackle and dissolve in the bright air around her and the dust motes that press against her skirt.

'Well, now,' the strange woman says and Alice asks, already knowing what the answer will be, if this is the right house for Mrs Whitear, and the strange woman shakes her head and says they left three, four years ago. 'Do you know, ma'am, where they went?' Alice wonders, and the strange woman inclines her head and says that it may have been to Rhode Island or maybe Vermont even. And so that is that. Aunt Patty and the girls are gone and she has a hundred and fifty-three dollars in her purse. There is a funeral going on at the next house with a pair of great horses with purple plumes stamping their feet before the hearse, and the coffin being solemnly loaded up by the undertaker's men, and she and the strange woman stand and watch it for a moment. But then the coffin disappears into the hearse, the door is shut and she wanders away along the wide, sand-strewn street into the unknown future.

5

Yare Valley Mud

1919–20
Snow, falling out of a grey sky, came slanting in across the birch trees.
Further up the bank, where the ground rose sharply towards the ridge,
an animal – a dog fox by the sound of it – barked twice and then fell
silent. Nearer at hand, where black water ran sluggishly away towards the
lock gate, the squat outlines of the mill house were already lost in shadow.
In the distance, towards Colney, a few lights showed palely through the
tangles of foliage and cramped inflexions of the river. It was growing
dark.

Living in this river valley, it was easy to believe that the forward march
of English life had simply ground to a halt. The antique barges that moved
slowly past two or three times a day, heavy horses labouring on the towpath
at their side, looked as if they had escaped from Tudor paintings of the
Thames. The characters who prowled their decks seemed no less ancient:
dense, muffled figures swathed in greatcoats and sacking, like medieval
lightermen. My uncle was always keen to push these continuities far beyond
their natural limit. 'Look at that old chap,' he would say, pointing to an
elderly man, well wrapped up in overcoat and gaiters, sou'wester pulled
down low over his head. 'Been making his livin' here half a century, I
shouldn't wonder. River folk! It's a grand old life.' The fisherman might
turn out to be a local solicitor out on a Saturday afternoon jaunt – the
Lord Mayor of Norwich, even, who lived in the big house beyond the mill.
My uncle never liked to have these identifications pointed out to him. It
suited him to be lost in a world that bore no relation to the actual
landscape he inhabited.

The snow was starting to come down quite heavily now: huge, shapeless flakes that clung to the peak of my school cap – royal blue with a
faint tracery of red, I remember – and lay, daintily, on the dirt track
beyond. The fox barked again, but further away, high up on the Colney
escarpment. It was late on a Sunday afternoon towards the end of the year

and we were coming back from one of those long walks along the river that my uncle liked so much: vagrant excursions that sometimes led into Norwich and sometimes led out of it, that sometimes fetched up at the big hall in Earlham, where occasionally a housekeeper would let us have tea, and sometimes did not, that sometimes incorporated odd bits of botanising or local culture ('Queer 'ow the gate latchings change, even in the same county,' my uncle would pronounce, as he unfastened the wicket between two fields) but were at other times dogged, moody trudges with no thought for the surrounding scenery.

'Hi, there!' my uncle shouted, much louder than was warranted by the ten-yard distance between us. 'Can't see you for all this blessed snow.'

I saw that he had moved from his usual beat by the river's edge and was marauding through the undergrowth, fossicking as he went. At the point where the hedgerow rejoined the towpath there was a giant beech tree. Here he stopped and began to grub away at the roots. Soon, I knew, he would find something, make some discovery that would give the day purpose and design. Sure enough, he came bouncing on to the path a few minutes later holding a small, shiny object in the palm of his gloved hand.

'Look at that,' he said, almost reverently. 'Been 'ere a fair few centuries. Worth a packet, I shouldn't wonder.'

I held the coin up to the fading light. It was a florin from the early part of Queen Victoria's reign and had quite probably been dropped there the previous week by one of the fishermen.

'Anyhow' – he sighed, when this had been pointed out to him – 'makes a change from one of those blessed cartridge cases, eh?'

The war had been over for a year, but there was still an army camp a mile away at Hethersett, whose officers were known to come this way in pursuit of the geese.

'And two shillings', he said vaguely, 'is two shillings.'

I had spent long enough in my uncle's company by now to know that afternoon that there was something worrying him, beyond the snow and the phantom treasure trove of the beech root, that he couldn't yet articulate. We walked home silently between dense hedgerows, behind which horses stamped and bickered, over ploughed fields where flints glinted in the fading light. Finally, drawing in his breath sharply before he spoke, he said, 'Just think what it would be like if you could find a bran'-new colour.'

'Find it? What do you mean? Dig it up in your garden or something?'

'Don't be so silly. I mean invent one. Something no one had ever seen before.'

I wasn't in the least surprised by this. It was exactly the kind of thing my uncle came out with: an expression of the intense, romantic yearning that lay just beneath the surface of his mind. I'd also studied enough organic chemistry at school to have a vague idea of how this might be accomplished.

'All very well inventing a new colour,' I said. 'The problem is synthesising it. You know, finding some way of mass-producing it without the original ingredients. That's how' – I searched for the relevant textbook phrase – 'they came up with those aniline dyes.'

'So they did,' my uncle said, who, as I suspected, already knew a great deal more about the subject than the innocence of his remarks suggested. 'Tons of coal melted down into tar, and then you set about *extractin'* . . .'

My uncle had a habit of letting his sentences trail off into vague, suggestive hinterlands where even I could rarely follow.

'But think of it,' he went on. 'I mean, for a start, how would you describe it? That chap who found mauve. When he saw it there for the first time, what did he think? Did he just say *mauve* and that was that? That's what worries me, writing it down . . .

'And then 'ow you'd sell it,' he wondered. 'Sell something that no one had ever seen before. It's quite a thought!'

And this, it struck me, if not until a good while later, when the river and its traffic and the silence of those winter afternoons beneath the Colney Ridge had faded into a remote and largely unvisited past, was the origin of hogpen and the things that followed in its wake. At the time, naturally, I simply marked it down as another example of my uncle's altogether monstrous gift for whimsy.

Having mused on these observations, my uncle cheered up. He tapped my shoulder in a playful manner, skipped over a fallen beech log, ran a little way down the path with his hands windmilling at his sides and then came to a halt, breathing heavily. Here, swollen by last week's rain, for a distance of ten or fifteen yards, the river had inundated the towpath to create a giant lagoon extending almost to the margin of the surrounding trees. I could see that it was impassable to anyone not wearing wading boots, but that, for reasons connected to the view that he took of the world and his place in it, my uncle intended to pass.

The snow had stopped: it was bitterly cold. Interested, despite the chill and the promise of fire and supper back at the cottage in the Intwood Road, I watched as he teetered by the edge of this watery slough and then, in a gesture that always seemed to me in some quaint way to incorporate most of the elements of his character, in which exasperation, foolhardiness, triumph and determination to do the right thing were uncomfortably mingled, he gave a dramatic shrug of his shoulders.

'Yare Valley mud,' he said, and ploughed on.

But all this is advancing matters.

It was a mark of the guilt that Mrs Custance felt over my enforced departure from Loftholdingswood that she volunteered, at considerable personal inconvenience, to escort me to Norwich. Guilt, too, had turned her affable, and as the train sped eastwards through the flaring Suffolk cornfields she became, for perhaps the only time in my experience of her, almost confiding, prepared to answer the questions I put to her about her brother and the kind of life I might lead in his care. From her I learned that he was middle-aged, had a 'temper' when crossed, had never married, was 'a great reader' and beguiled his free time with 'hobbies'. What these diversions were I didn't find out and I don't believe Mrs Custance knew herself: indeed, her whole attitude to her brother was one of mild consternation, not very far removed from patronage. All the same this conversation made her seem more human to me and I enjoyed our trip together in the railway carriage – a packed and uneasy railway carriage, with a suggestion of great events looming in the background – and was sorry when it came to an end.

At Norwich station we descended into ferment. There was a brass band playing the National Anthem at one end, dozens of men with tankards in their hands had spilled out of the station bar and a crowd of people stood over a boy in an apron who was ripping the binding from a pile of newspapers with a clasp knife. Instantly, with a kind of tearing sensation in my insides, I knew what had happened. A burly man flung down a coin on to the station platform, picked up one of the papers and danced off shouting 'We've come in! We've come in!' and there was a ragged cheer from the drinkers outside the bar. If I'd expected any enthusiasm from Mrs Custance I didn't get it, for she merely waited for me to pick up my suitcase, jammed her own valise under her arm and marched me off in the direction of the station forecourt, where she commandeered a cab from the rank and threw the cases in the back with an undisguised fury that, amid the thump and judder of the band and the arrival of a second gang of drinkers howling like dervishes, very much alarmed me.

'I had a cousin died in South Africa,' was all Mrs Custance would say of this rare irruption of spirit.

There was some difficulty in finding her brother's house, for he turned out not to live in Norwich itself but in an outlying village named Cringleford. As she consulted his letter, and the extraordinarily ill-drawn map that accompanied it, something of Mrs Custance's usual demeanour returned. 'He says "send a telegram from Liverpool Street",' she complained at one point. 'The *idea*!' And so we travelled on through the south-western end of the city – very pretty it was in the late-afternoon sun, with big, double-fronted houses set back from the road – with news of the war following us as we went and Union Jacks suddenly appearing in front gardens, and old men rushing to their gates to holloa at the traffic and shake their fists. In the end we came to a tiny stone bridge across a river that dropped into a foaming weir on its further side, turned left into what the street sign declared was the Intwood Road but the map had got down, apparently, as 'Tingorge', and came finally to a line of cottages, the first of them with a great wild garden and what looked like motor-bicycle parts lying over its lawn. 'That can't be it, surely,' Mrs Custance remarked, greatly scandalised, I could see, by this evidence of dirt and dereliction. Already, though, I'd formed an impression of her brother which this variegated spoor seemed to confirm and I wasn't in the least surprised when a short, fat man with wispy, brindled hair, holding what looked like the monstrously overwrought half of a sandwich, came rambling round the side of the cottage, looked at us curiously, took a bite out of the sandwich, looked at us again and then waved vigorously at Mrs Custance.

'Why, Jane. Didn't think you was coming until tomorrow afternoon for some reason.'

'Well, we're here,' said Mrs Custance, a touch snappishly. 'This is the boy.'

'The boy?' he wondered.

'You know very well it's the boy, Alfred, as I wrote and told you,' Mrs Custance went on, now thoroughly exasperated. 'Ralph, say good after-noon to Mr Rendall.'

I said hello at the exact moment that a fire engine, not come to attend a fire but with a flag draped over its water carrier and red, white and blue ribbons entangled in its traces, came tearing round the corner with half a dozen chaps huzzahing from the back.

'And a blessed war starting as well,' he conceded.

When the artists came to paint my uncle ten years later – I am thinking in particular of Isbister RA's portrait of him in oils from 1924 – they made him look commanding. Other qualities consistent with the image of the successful City man were also superimposed on his vague peasant's face, so that, in addition, he looked decisive, reflective, calm, charismatic. In reality my uncle's face possessed none of these features. Seen at his garden gate on the day war broke out, the half-eaten sandwich still dangling between his fingers, he looked harassed, put-upon, worried and faintly embarrassed.

It was Mrs Custance who took the initiative. 'Ent you going to invite us in, Alfred?'

And so we went indoors, with the fire-engine bell still ringing in our ears. Inside the cottage it was cool and dim, with vague outlines of furniture receding into the shadows, all fantastically dirty and disarranged, and full of odd little curiosities: a stuffed cat that sat on the kitchen table in a disturbingly lifelike attitude; a pile of stones painted in bright, primary colours that ran along the mantelpiece; a system of pulleys suspended from the low ceiling of the front room that made you drop your head instinctively as you came over the lintel.

At large in this mouldering labyrinth – there was a sensation of being far underground, despite the open windows – my uncle's spirits rose. Seeing my glance fall on the pulley system, he said, 'Useful piece of machinery, that is. Made it myself. Now, you just sit there and watch what happens.'

Here and there around the room butchers' hooks hung from the ceiling like inverted question marks. To one of these my uncle attached a small mug. Then, seizing a piece of rope that followed the line of the door frame, he gave several tugs. There was a thin, clanking noise and the machinery began to grind slowly into gear.

'Now,' my uncle said, perhaps a minute later, when the hook hung directly over my head. 'Just reach up, and there's your cup. See! Don't even have to get out of your blessed chair.'

Mrs Custance was unimpressed. 'It'd be quite as quick just to go and fetch it,' she said. 'Quicker.'

'Dare say it would,' my uncle retorted. 'But it's the *principle* of the thing, don't you see?'

Seated round the table in the kitchen, with the stuffed cat looking as if it were poised to sweep the food from our plates, we ate a frugal supper of sardines on toast and tinned tomatoes.

'Cosy place you got here, Alf,' Mrs Custance said encouragingly.

'Cosy? I dare say it is,' my uncle said, rather puzzled, as if cosiness was the last thing he would want to have associated with him. His eye moved slowly round the room, taking in the tower of crockery next to the sink, an enormous vat of what I took to be potato peelings, sheets of old newspaper tumbled over a chair – the top one, I saw, was three years old. 'Well, yes, I suppose you'd call it – cosy.'

'What's all them potato peelings for?' Mrs Custance asked.

'Pigs,' said my uncle. 'Thinking of going in for pigs. Good line to try, 'specially if there's a war starting.'

I had high hopes of that evening. Mrs Custance, I could see, was in a confiding mood and had even – unprecedentedly – accepted the offer of a bottle of stout. As they talked, I thought, I would learn things: about my situation, who I was, what was expected of me. In the end I was packed off to bed early and brother and sister retired to the front room. Lying awake in a tiny bedroom under the eaves, where pigeons clacked and summer rain dripped haltingly off the thatch, I could hear desultory snatches of conversation, quite impenetrable to me, interspersed with the whirr of the pulley as my uncle sent another object shuttling across the ceiling. When I woke up there was daylight flooding in across the counterpane and dew gleaming up off the fields, and I walked downstairs intending to accost Mrs Custance and ask her certain questions that she could not, in the nature of things, very well avoid, only to find the house empty, the front door half open and a large rat making a meal off a mouldy loaf of bread that lay on one of the kitchen chairs.

My uncle returned at eleven. Unlike the chaotic dishabille of the previous day, he was wearing a shabby linen suit, several sizes too small, and a straw hat. When he saw me sitting at the kitchen table he gave a start, as if the fact of my presence in his house had momentarily escaped him. 'Perishing 'ot day,' he said by way of explanation. 'Been seeing Jane – Mrs Custance – off at the station.'

'Good morning, Mr Rendall.'

'Mr Rendall, eh?' He laughed a bit at this. 'No, that won't do. That won't do at all. P'raps you'd better call me Uncle Alfred while we get to know each other.'

'Yes, Uncle Alfred.'

Still, though, there was something about me that he couldn't quite fathom, a human ingredient come to perplex a mind bent otherwise on vats of potato peelings and steel pulleys. He walked out of the room for a moment, came back into it and then stared at the table, scratching his head with one hand while the other jangled the change in his trouser pocket.

'If you were going to keep pigs,' he said finally, 'where would you keep them?'

The under-gardener at Loftholdingswood had kept pigs. It was a subject in which I had some faint expertise. 'In the garden,' I said. 'But downwind.'

'Else the neighbours might complain? Good point,' my uncle said.

And so, on a bright day in August, while the rest of the world was preparing for war, we went out into the rambling back garden of my uncle's cottage on the Intwood Road and discussed where you could put a pig and what the consequences might be if the wind were in the east.

So much has been written about my uncle and so much has been said on the subject of self-made men and home-taught titans that I think it only fair to offer some notion of how he appeared to me in the days of his obscurity, when we lived together cheek by jowl in the cottage at Cringleford, altogether removed from the world and subject to no authority except our own. For all the individuality of gesture and expression, there was something faintly familiar about my uncle. He was, I now realise, one of those men – very common they were in the first quarter of this century – with schemes in their heads. England in the years before the Great War was full of them: grocers' assistants absorbed in differential calculus, ground-down bank clerks convinced that they had stumbled upon a fail-safe way of playing the foreign exchanges. With my uncle the imaginative ferment that fuelled these enterprises became a kind of mania. His schemes were taken up and cast down in an instant; the relics of past activities littered his house like spent cartridge cases on a battlefield. The cottage was full of gadgets of his devising, ingenious little knick-knacks that you couldn't say there was a positive need for, but which reflected great credit on the ingenuity of the mind that had created them: an assemblage of wires that allowed you, mechanically, to strike a match against a matchbox; a glass dome which, when shaken, revealed Norwich Cathedral amid a whirling snowstorm; a model of Westminster Abbey made out of balsawood chips.

Just lately my uncle had abandoned gadgetry for more ambitious projects. With motor-bicycle construction practically given up, its only legacy the metal parts in the front garden, and pig-breeding pending, he was dividing his time between some kind of process for manufacturing leather aprons and a preparation that was supposed to enhance the glaze of earthenware pots. Where my uncle had picked up all this expertise was anyone's guess, for he seemed to have had almost no education and such reading as he did was done in self-help books of the kind in which Mr Carnegie divulges how he made his first million. Where he differed from the grocers' assistants and the ground-down bank clerks was not in the lowliness of his professional calling – he had some kind of job selling insurance, which occupied him for three mornings in a week – but in the altogether limitless boundaries of his ambition. Success, to my uncle, was not some vision of remote, abstracted glory but the fulfilment of a series of minutely itemised desires. My uncle wanted, in no particular order, to own a dress suit, to be accepted for membership of Norfolk County Cricket Club, to eat pâté de foie gras off a silver plate, to shake hands with their Royal Majesties, to stand for Parliament, to dine with the Lord Mayor of London and his Corporation at the Guildhall, to see his portrait printed in *The Times*, to write a book, to own a telephone, to travel to India, to ride on an elephant, to grow melons under glass, to employ a butler and to become a freemason. There were other ambitions, more obscure, which I have forgotten.

Taken together, it was an impressive list, all the more so because my uncle lacked nearly all the advantages by which such desires are usually realised. He had no money; he had no influence; above all, he had no poise. Lacking these advantages, my uncle would clearly have to get by on will alone and it was this quality, curiously enough – a certain inner steeliness, an understanding of how desperately hopeless his position was – that marked him out and made him distinctive. He was one of those people who look down their noses at the world around them in the absolute conviction that in ten years' time they will have triumphed over everything that fate has thrown in their way. 'When it's all come right', 'When I'm sitting pretty', 'When there's money in the bank'. My uncle really did use these phrases, and they were as necessary to him, as vital to his sense of self-preservation, as the air that blew in through the cottage windows.

They were his hedge against despair. At the same time his will led him inevitably to less concrete ambitions. He wanted, again in no particular order, to be pursued, to be admired, to dispense charity on a grand scale, to be written about in newspaper gossip columns, to be a source of mystery and fascination, to have his success drawn to the shocked and envious attention of people who had known him when young, to inspire others to do as he had done, to be spoken of with bated breath, to embolden, to inspire in his rivals a sense of their own unworthiness, to shame all those who had thought him incapable of the feats he had achieved.

He had, of course, no friends.

It was an odd kind of world we inhabited down here on the outskirts of Norwich, like a kind of cyst. The war rumbled on in the background – quite literally, as at Yarmouth you could actually hear the boom of the guns – but I don't think my uncle paid it much notice. He was lost some- where, roaming behind the thick, high hedge that encircled his mind and cut it off from the landscape beyond. You might think it a strange life I led, here in a dirty cottage on the Intwood Road with only my uncle and the rusting motor-bicycle parts and the vats of potato peelings for company, but in fact I was perfectly happy. For a start, my uncle was a source of inexhaustible fascination to me – absorbed, capricious, moody, humorous, quite unlike any other adult I had ever met. He was kind to me, in a rather abstract manner, and solicitous of my welfare in a way that Mrs Custance and the Loftholdingswood back kitchen had rather neglected, and all this, even if it did not solve the greater mystery of my upbringing, which I burned to decipher, was very comforting to me.

There were other ways, too, in which my uncle was conscious of his responsibilities. Norwich had a grammar school, of ancient foundation, with premises in the Cathedral Close, and it was here that I went one morning in the autumn to be interviewed by an old gentleman in a black stuff gown with white whiskers hanging down off his chin and, much to my surprise, welcomed into his establishment. This pleased me, too, for it seemed to shut a door on the old life of Sussex, the great house and Mr Mortimer's nutcracker face seen under the flaring gaslight. Loftholdingswood starts to fade from my mind now, turn very dim and remote. I could remember its essence – the smell of the courtyard in early morning, the springing orchard grass – but not its particularities. I was fourteen years old now, had a bright blue blazer that I wore to school and a second-hand bicycle, which my uncle had bought 'for a song' from an ironmonger's shop in Cringleford village and the past – that past – no longer interested me in the way it once had.

Meanwhile, there was another world reaching out to claim me – the world where my uncle wandered on weekend afternoons. Intwood! Hethersett! Colney! I don't suppose those names mean very much to you. I went back to Norwich a year or so ago and the bungalows and the little villas had spread out from the Newmarket Road like a rash, but in those days they were tiny villages out on the Norfolk flat, hidden behind forests of cow parsley and thickets of sedge, each with their row of cottages, their village green and the dull, incurious faces staring at you from behind garden gates. '*Peasant* faces,' my uncle used to say. It was through obliquities of this kind that I learned something of his history. I don't suppose he ever made a direct statement, but by piecing together what emerged I established that he'd been born in Essex but had lived for a time up north before coming to Norfolk and had worked, successively, as a railway porter, a printer's apprentice, a navvy, pot boy in a public house, assistant to a street photographer, undertaker, hirer-out of seaside deckchairs, sweet shop proprietor and the travelling representative of a cigarette firm. From each of these trades my uncle provided the liveliest reminiscences but there was something bitter about the way in which he regarded them, a sense of immortal spirit poured down the drain a pint at a time, parched, unfruitful soil in which his grand schemes would never germinate.

Like my uncle, I too had schemes in my head.

To begin with, I tried to tackle him on the subject of my parentage.

'About my mother,' I began one night as we sat over the fire in the parlour.

'The thing *is* . . .' my uncle said. Half-moon spectacles balanced on the bridge of his nose, he was brooding over a copy of the *Pig Breeder's Gazette*. Above his head the pulley system, in which he had unexpectedly lost interest, was turning to rust. 'Do we buy the stock in or start with a boar and a couple of sows and go on from there?'

'About my mother . . .'

'And then how are we going to get them to market? It's as well to get these things straight from the start.'

In the past four months the pig-breeding scheme had captured my uncle's mind entirely. There were lengths of timber lying against the back wall of the cottage out of which he proposed to construct a sty, and a bin, made out of corrugated iron, in which 'mashes' could be prepared.

Detached for a moment from the world of Black Devonshires and Gloucestershire Ridgebacks, he grew unexpectedly thoughtful and parenthetic. 'Sort of thing', he said, 'that you've a *right* to know about ...

'... Flesh and blood,' he suggested.

'... Jane would know,' he proposed. 'Jane would have it at her blessed fingertips.'

'... Best thing to do is to ask Jane,' he concluded.

And so a letter was written, in my uncle's wavering, uncertain hand, and sent off to Mrs Custance at her lodgings in Reigate. Thereafter our two schemes proceeded simultaneously: mine to discover the secret of my parentage; my uncle's to establish something that he called the Intwood Pork Repository. As a commercial undertaking, it displayed all the characteristics I had previously noted in his business dealings, which is to say that zeal, industry and ignorance came flagrantly combined. The pigs came not from the Norwich livestock market but from an old man in Hethersett who was retiring, ingloriously, from the trade. There were five of them and they sat in a hastily erected pen in the back garden, bawling piteously, while my uncle knocked up a sty out of the ends of lath and some chicken wire.

'Will they be all right?'

'Hardy animals, pigs,' said my uncle, banging a nail with such force that the joint he was sealing split beneath his hammer. 'If Shackleton'd taken a pig with him to the Pole he might have lived to tell the tale.'

'Will they mind being left out in the rain?'

'Hardy animals, pigs,' my uncle said again, with slightly less conviction.

From the surrounding cottages, our neighbours looked disapprovingly on.

For some reason the pigs did not thrive. They sat huddled in the sty ignoring the bins of mash that were laid out before them and regarded passers-by with dull, reproachful eyes. 'Putting on weight nicely,' my uncle commented, arriving home from work on the lunchtime of his second day as a pig breeder. Later, seeing the untouched bin, he demanded, 'What's wrong with that mash anyhow?'

'Maybe you should have used fresh potato peelings,' I suggested.

'It looked all right to me,' my uncle said. 'Perhaps they just need to settle in,' he proposed. 'Feel they're at 'ome.' To this end the water barrel was broached and a quantity of mud conjured up out of the garden's hard, dry earth.

Still the pigs continued to sit in their small, resentful huddle. 'I can't understand it,' my uncle said. But if the pigs declined to eat, their natural functions continued unabated. 'Terrible kind of *smell* out there,' my uncle acknowledged, a day or so later. 'Never knew anything like it . . .'

'You'd have thought', he said, not long after this, 'that pigs'd be *livelier*.' A vet, summoned from Norwich, diagnosed damp and suggested a mash made of oats. '*Oats*,' my uncle scoffed.

The neighbours tended to come at teatime, when they knew my uncle would be at home. They were polite, but insistent. Some, who had professional experience, made recommendations.

'We're doing this all wrong,' my uncle deposed, not long after this. 'What they need is *space*.'

Accordingly the sty was extended to half the length of the garden and some coils of corrugated iron introduced, which my uncle thought would do service as a dormitory. 'Known boarding houses as good as this,' he said reminiscently.

But the pigs showed little interest in their spacious new domain. They crawled under the cylinders of corrugated iron and lay there, or lingered by the food bin chewing morosely at the oats. The smell did not abate.

'They'll soon be fattening,' my uncle volunteered. But it was clear that his vision of the pig breeder's calling lacked some vital component. The vet, arriving affably on his bicycle, diagnosed liver fluke. My uncle took to leaning over the gate of the sty, arms folded across his chest, and making what he thought were encouraging noises. The pigs stared dully back. They were small, pale creatures with oddly shrivelled snouts, of uncertain ancestry, listless and bald.

Three months had passed now since my uncle had written to Mrs Custance. Coming home from school one afternoon at about the time of the Battle of the Somme, I found him sitting at the kitchen table with a look of quiet, exasperated fury on his face.

'How are the pigs?'

'Lloyd George ain't too well' – the pigs were named after members of the War Cabinet. 'Asquith's been off his food. Thing is, Ralph, you've 'ad a letter.'

'From Mrs Custance . . . ?'

'That's the problem,' said my uncle mournfully. 'Blessed if I can lay my hands on it. Came into the 'ouse this morning, I put it down on that tablecloth there and by three o'clock it's gone. I've gone and lost it, Ralph.'

Tea was postponed while we searched for it, and supper after that. From the garden the pigs moaned inconsolably, but no one went out to inspect them. At midnight, with the contents of the cottage yet more fantastically disarranged, we acknowledged defeat.

'You can write again,' I said.

'Oh yes,' said my uncle tragically. 'I can write again.'

So a second letter was dispatched to Mrs Custance at Reigate. But the enormity of this failure oppressed my uncle. Returning once more from school a week later, I found the sty empty and a puddle of blood oozing over the scullery steps. The body of Lloyd George hung from a hook by the door.

'You just missed the slaughterman,' my uncle said when I went inside. 'Five bob each. I thought we'd keep Lloyd George for ourselves.' I had not seen him so cheery for weeks.

Later that evening he took out a thick, forbidding textbook that had clearly come from the public library. 'Thinking of going in for chemistry,' he said.

Shortly after this we heard, in a roundabout way, that Mrs Custance had died of influenza.

6

Newman Street

1906
It was a damp autumn morning in Newman Street, that nondescript thoroughfare which connects Goodge Street and Oxford Street, and a young woman was making her way slowly along its western pavement. She was good-looking, with reddish hair and a somewhat delicate face, and two separate impediments dictated her slowness. The first was that she carried a small child lashed to her side by an arrangement of shawls. The second was that she appeared, among the range of house fronts and shop windows, to be searching for something, for she stopped several times and consulted a piece of paper, looking up a moment later to peer at the house numbers and the row of brass plates that lay beneath them. As for the woman herself, a sharp-eyed observer might have noticed that the clothing she wore – a print dress and a jacket, with a soft hat pinned to the back of her hair – was a shade too light for the time of the year and that the shoes were clearly about to fall apart.

Perhaps five minutes went by in this way. A print seller's, with its representations of Old Soho and other delights laid out on a little table beyond the window, had no charms for her, the tobacconist she did not even care to examine, but at the next set of premises she stopped, darted a look at the slip of paper, peered at the fourth of the four brass plates, which read *Alfd Boothby, Theatrical Agent*, and made her way inside. A staircase led sharply up into the interior of the house. Climbing its two flights and aware of voices conversing high above her, she came out on to a tiny landing and a chamber about the size of a drawing room. On the wall, immediately catching the eye, hung a profusion of framed photographs. Here women in evening dress wept over departing soldiers; exquisitely dressed gentlemen presented flowers to ladies in chiffon and white tulle with elaborate gestures; comedians stood with bowler hats tilted back from their foreheads, thumbs thrust into waistcoat pockets, as they prepared to deliver some unanswerable sally; 'character parts' – old washerwomen, villainous tramps, gauche footmen – abounded. In the corner of the room, behind a bare, unvarnished desk, a young woman with dyed yellow hair sat working a typewriter. Alice found that her courage had altogether failed her.

'I . . . That is, would it be possible to see Mr Boothby?'

She was given a chair and told that she could wait if she cared, but that Mr Boothby's attendance could not be guaranteed. Although one or two of the people gathered on the bench beside her cast sympathetic looks, no one spoke. Gradually, however, the atmosphere of the theatrical agent's waiting room relaxed itself slightly. An old gentleman at the end of the bench remarked as he rose to leave that if he waited any longer to see whether there was a part at the Sceptre, that theatre would probably have crumbled into dust: they heard the thump of his stick echoing behind him down the stairs. Two middle-aged ladies began an animated conversation as to whether Ravenscourt Park was more difficult to get home to from the West End than Brixton. The young woman with the dyed yellow hair finished her final letter with a furious pinging of her typewriter bell, ate a sandwich out of a paper bag and unbent sufficiently to ask: would she like a glass of water? Meanwhile, various people came in and out of Mr Boothby's door: a young man with a wing collar who stayed five minutes; an old lady with a rush basket who stayed thirty seconds; a man with a squint in one eye and a prematurely bald head whose appearance suggested that he was not an actor but a friend of Mr Boothby's, who stayed nearly half an hour.

The young man seated next to Alice, having made one or two attempts to engage Asa by waving his fingers at him or peering over the top of a newspaper, said suddenly, 'So what are you up for, then?'

The expression, however commonplace in Mr Boothby's office, was at any rate new to Alice. She shook her head and said simply, 'I do not know what you mean.'

'I beg your pardon.' She saw that the man, though not what she would have called a gentleman, intended to be friendly. 'I mean, what part is it you're trying for? The beggar maid in *King Cophetua* at the Empire? Or one of the seven princesses at the Globe?'

Seeing her look of bewilderment, he went on, 'I can see you're new to the game. Now, the beggar maid is one that all the girls are after. But if I were in your shoes, I should go for one of the seven princesses, indeed I should. But come now, have you got a line?'

Again, she could only repeat the words. 'A line?'

'Well, what is it that you do best? The quiet one who's always in the way when the heroine's waiting to mash with her young man, or the consumptive one who takes sick but rallies in act three?'

'Indeed, I shall be grateful for anything I can get.'

'You *are* a flat,' the young man pronounced, whether in exasperation or admiration she could not quite tell, and fell into silence. The young woman with the dyed yellow hair resumed her typewriting. Above their heads a few drops of rain beat melancholically upon the bleary skylight. The two middle-aged ladies began to talk, with great passion and contempt, of a third party who might, from the way in which they discussed her, have been some gorgon from the classical dictionary but was probably the keeper of a theatrical lodging house. In this way, with Alice jiggling Asa on her knee and feeding him small pieces of bread and butter from a handkerchief concealed in the sleeve of her dress, a further twenty minutes went by. Then, abruptly, there came a piece of drama quite worthy to be photographed and framed in the sepia gallery upon the wall. First, a whisper of conversation that had been going on for some time beyond Mr Boothby's door rose gradually to a crescendo. Then, with a dramatic rattle of its fastening and a momentous scuffle of departing feet, the door was flung open. Finally, the person who had been closeted with Mr Boothby for the past half-hour – a middle-aged man with black eyebrows that contrasted oddly with his brindled hair – danced out of the room, pulled the door savagely to behind him and beat upon its surface with a silver-knobbed cane he carried under his arm. He then turned dramatically on his heel – it was really quite beautiful to see him do this – brandished the cane as if some invisible enemy lurked a yard or two before him, and addressed himself to the young woman at the typewriter. 'I told you, Maisie, that it would come to this,' he declared, with perhaps more vigour than was warranted by the size of the room.

'Well, perhaps you did,' Maisie conceded.

'There are some slurs that a man cannot bear. Slurs that one gentleman ought not to pronounce upon another.'

'I expect Alf's temper just got the better of him.'

Conscious that all those seated on the benches and chairs were regarding him with the keenest interest, the man went on, 'You know, Maisie, that if I quit these premises I shall not return?'

'I suppose that's the long and short of it.'

'That, in doing so, I shall cast off some of the tenderest associations of a proud career?'

'We all have our ups and downs.'

At this, the man raised the cane above his head, as if he were about to pulverise an aspidistra that stood in a pot by the vestibule, thought better of it and plunged off down the stairs.

'Did you see him?' the young man seated next to Alice remarked, some-what superfluously. 'That was Prendergast. Used to be a real top-notcher. Played the heavy father and the rich uncle who's making a new will and those kind of parts. Twenty guineas a week Prendergast used to make five years ago. But he's never got over it and won't ever again, for my money.'

Once more, the volley of professional jargon reduced Alice to bewilderment. 'What is it that Mr Prendergast will not get over?'

'Why, the drink. He was Moriarty, the butler, in *Servants' Hall* – you know, the piece that made Miss Tulliver her reputation. Came on drunk in the third act, flunked his lines and has never been the same since. Boothby puts him up for a part now and then for old's sake, but bless you, that sort of thing don't pay. Why, Prendergast had a house in Wimbledon once, and a carriage and pair.'

After Mr Prendergast's departure, a chill fell upon the company. There was something about the mention of the house at Wimbledon and the carriage and pair that was both lowering and moral, and in which everyone who had heard it was implicated. Maisie doubtfully patted her hair once or twice as if to acknowledge its imposture. The two actresses at the far end of the bench fell into silence and the young man flung the racing page of the newspaper he had open on his lap away from him in disgust. It was in this atmosphere of stern Puritanism and implacable duty that Maisie, realising that Alice had now been waiting nearly an hour, suggested that she might enter Mr Boothby's sanctum. Grateful for the favour – she was aware that at least half the occupants of the bench had sat there longer than she – Alice got to her feet. Something – if not the look in Maisie's eye then a faint gesture that the young man made as he retrieved his newspaper from the floor – told her that she could not take the child with her. As she looked anxiously around, conscious of an opportunity that might now be denied her, a youngish woman said encouragingly, 'Won't you let me take care of him? I am supposed to be good with children.'

'It is very kind of you' Alice admitted. 'I suppose I cannot take him in with me?'

'I should think not!' The woman, Alice noted, was perhaps three or four years older than herself, neatly dressed but showing signs of comparative poverty, chief among which was a pair of badly soled boots and a hat whose trimming was about to part company with its brim. 'And have Mr Boothby blow cigar smoke over him? They say Mr Boothby never has a cigar out of his mouth.'

Embarrassed by the attention that seemed to surround her – the young man was looking at her sharply, the two middle-actresses were evincing the keenest interest in the child – she hastened through the door that Maisie now held open for her, her mind still turning over the events of the past few minutes, on Mr Prendergast, the girl to whom she had consigned her child and the child itself. She had formed no impression of what kind of a person Mr Boothby might be. The words 'theatrical agent' conveyed nothing to her other than their utility. Of the wealth, airs and protocols that might legitimately attach themselves to theatrical agents she had no conception, but she assumed that such people would be gentlemen, that they would consider her prospects objectively and that they would treat her with courtesy.

It was said of Mr Boothby – or rather, it was said by Mr Boothby – that if the dozens of theatrical ladies and gentlemen who owed their careers on the London and provincial stage to him wished to offer up a token of their gratitude, then 'they knew where to find him'. If this was the case, it was remarkable how few of this gratified horde ever availed themselves of the opportunity. Mr Boothby was a short, stout man of fifty, who wore his hat – silk hat though it was – indoors and drew in cigar smoke as regularly as he drew breath. Mr Pinero, whom he had known when younger and who was perhaps conscious of one or two debts that were owed, had been very civil to him, which had worked in his favour. Mr Shaw, with whom he had had one or two incidental dealings, had called him a 'block-head', which had worked in his favour as well, but he could not, here in the first decade of the twentieth century, be described as a leading light of his profession. He liked good old-fashioned melodrama and broad comedy, while the playgoing tendency now was for genteel conversation and drawing rooms. He had been heard to say that the race of English comic dramatists was almost extinct, and thought nothing of Mr Barrie. But still there was a living to be made by peopling the casts of suburban repertory theatres and provincial touring companies, and he gladly snatched at it. There was also, as he well knew, an income to be gained out of premiums. Just now he was sitting in his armchair, wearing a frock-coat from whose buttons the gilt had long since disappeared, with his hat tilted down over his eyes, smoking one of his cigars – the butts of half a dozen others lay in the ashtray on his desk – and barely looked up when she entered the room. When he saw that there was someone before him on the threadbare carpet, he said, 'Well, Miss – er. I'm afraid I haven't anything today. Things are very quiet just at the moment.'

Not knowing that this was the sentence Mr Boothby habitually pronounced over the head of anyone who arrived in his office whom he did not immediately recognise, Alice stared uncertainly back at him. Something in the stare, and the fact that Alice was a young woman – the young man would already have been sent packing – unnerved Mr Boothby, who cracked his cigar up to a yet more jaunty angle and continued, 'Delighted to see you. But there is nothing – nothing. Perhaps in a fortnight when the suburban theatres know their Christmas requirements, but until then . . .' He made an expansive gesture with his right hand that would have done credit to one of the gentlemen in evening dress in the stage portraits above his head.

'It is very good of you to see me,' Alice said. 'But I never came here before. My name is Alice Hanson.'

'You are from America, I take it?' Mr Boothby always said that he disliked Americans.

Alice nodded her head.

Although Mr Boothby continued to regard her discouragingly, his manner changed. Looking her up and down in the frankest manner – a groom inspecting a horse in the paddock at Newmarket could not have been more frank – and being favourably impressed by what he saw, he said eventually, 'Delighted to make your acquaintance, Miss Hanson. And how may I be of assistance to you?'

'I wish – that is, I should like to be considered for a part in a play.'

'Would you indeed? Well, you have come to the right place. Why' – his eye, roving around the wall of studio portraits, fell upon a gentleman in tights brandishing a cutlass – 'who made Billy Leigh? That man was nothing until I took him up and made something of him.'

Mr Boothby did not think it necessary to add that Billy Leigh currently resided in an inebriates' home on the south coast, where his principal concern was that the single glass of wine allowed him each day at dinner should not be diluted. He would have bragged more about his clients, but he was somewhat intrigued by the girl, whose face and comportment he admired very much, and still assuming her to be an actress in search of a new sponsor, he said suavely, 'But I don't believe I have had the pleasure of seeing you in anything, Miss Hanson. What parts have you undertaken recently?'

'Oh, I have never appeared in anything. At least not – in England. But I wondered . . .'

The spurt of annoyance that Mr Boothby felt on learning that his time was being squandered – that the woman before him was not a practised thespian but an absolute tyro throwing herself on his mercy – was mitigated, but only slightly mitigated, by the blush that spread over her face. She really was exceedingly pretty, Mr Boothby thought. But he had resolved at an early stage in his career, and to do him justice more or less kept to this resolve, that his opinion should not be swayed by prettiness.

'No experience? Dear me, that's bad. We can't have that, you know.' Seeing her face fall, he went on, 'We could put you on our books, of course, and charge you the premium in the usual way, if that would suit.'

'A premium? What does that mean?'

And so Mr Boothby, rather to his surprise, found himself explaining the highly equitable arrangement whereby a theatrical agent accepts a sum of money from an aspiring actor or actress on the understanding that this should be an incentive for him to secure engagements for his client.

'We could do it for twenty guineas,' he concluded.

He was struck by the expression on her face. Another woman would have attempted to brazen it out, to have used, albeit in a very subtle and dextrous manner, her beauty and self-possession as a tool by which to reduce the premium or do away with it altogether. Miss Hanson's look of resignation, on the other hand, was pitiable to see. 'I couldn't afford twenty guineas,' she said.

Still he could not bring himself to dismiss her from his office. He had no work for her, nor the prospect of any, but still, she really was extraordinarily pretty. He found himself, again rather to his surprise, becoming lofty and paternal. 'Let me give you some advice, Miss Hanson. I should give up the idea, I really should. I have never known the profession as crowded as it is now. Do you live in London?'

'I – that is, I have been here two months.'

'In lodgings, I suppose?'

'I have a room in Kennington.'

'Kennington. Brixton. Clapham. It doesn't signify. Take my advice, Miss Hanson, and give it up. You will be very lucky to make any money and what you make will soon be spent.' Still, in spite of his resolution, he found himself conceding territory. 'I could reduce the premium to fifteen guineas if you positively insisted.'

'I am afraid it's quite out of the question.'

'Very well, then.'

When she had gone, Mr Boothby sat silently in his armchair, puffing savagely at his cigar and unable for the life of him to decide where the source of his bad temper lay. It was unfortunate, in these circumstances, that his next supplicant should be the young man who had sat next to Alice on the bench outside. With the portrait of Billy Leigh staring down upon them, Mr Boothby revenged himself by remarking that there wasn't anything today, that things were very quiet at the moment and would he kindly get out of his sight.

'Well, he has given you more of his time than I was ever allowed,' remarked the young woman Alice had befriended on the bench. 'What did he say?'

'That I could pay a twenty-guinea premium, or should give the business up.' She took the child and clasped him in her arms. 'Oh, but now I have lost you your place and that young man has gone in.'

'He would have gone in anyway, as that Miss Engledow' – she shot a glance at the girl with the dyed yellow hair – 'has such a down on me. I declare I have waited a whole hour and shan't wait any longer. Goodbye, Miss Engledow' – this said in a slightly louder voice – 'goodbye, all. Do you know', she went on as they began to descend the rickety staircase, 'that Miss Engledow was of the profession herself? But she couldn't pronounce her aitches, poor girl. She was a parlourmaid who had to say "Sir Harry Hotspur of Humblethwaite has happened to call" and it came out as "Sir 'Arry 'Otspur of 'Umblethwaite 'as 'appened". She never lived it down.'

Something in the way that this was said suggested to Alice that it might not be strictly truthful and she said, 'Why, you are making fun of me.'

'Well, perhaps. But only a very little. My name is Edith Jeffries, but you should call me Edie. Here, you had better watch out for those boxes.'

It was by now some time after one in the afternoon – a clock two or three streets away was striking the quarter-hour – and Newman Street was at its most melancholy. The entrance to the building on whose top floor Mr Boothby had his lair was obstructed by a quantity of packing cases that had not been there before. Fine rain fell across the greasy pavement.

'As for the twenty-guinea premium,' Miss Jeffries went on, giving one of the packing cases a knock with her umbrella handle, 'I paid that two years since, and I might as well have kept it safe at the post office.'

'You mean you have had no work at all?'

'Oh, it has not been so bad as all that. Look, here is my card.' She reached into her handbag and produced a rectangle of off-white pasteboard on which were printed the words *Miss Edith M. Jeffries*. 'Why, I opened the door for Mr Elveson when he surprised the lovers in the study in *Leap Before You Look*, and I was in Mr de Havilland's melodrama at the Empire last summer, only it closed after a fortnight.' Smiling ruefully as she did so, she held her watch up to her face. 'I declare it is nearly twenty past one and I am almost faint with hunger. Will you have something to eat with me, dear?'

Newman Street was not overburdened with restaurants. Having spurned the upstairs room of the Newman Arms ('for the men will always look at one, I find') Miss Jeffries selected an eating house on the corner of Goodge Street. It was a poor place, with great black-backed pews that had been fashionable sixty years before and the menu scrawled with soap on a mirror, but Miss Jeffries, who gave the interior several knowing looks, pronounced that it would do.

'You see,' she said, when their food was before them, 'these faggots are really very nice, for all that no lady of refinement would go anywhere near them. But then I suppose I am not a lady of refinement.'

Before long they were confiding their histories to one another. Miss Jeffries established that Alice had been in England two months and was living in a room at Kennington, and that her baby was nearly a year old, while Alice learned that Miss Jeffries had been in the profession three years, lived in a boarding house in Fulham and subsisted on occasional remittances from her father, a country solicitor.

'He is terribly shocked,' she explained. 'But you see, I determined on a career on the stage and I told him I should certainly starve if he did not support me. Your little boy is a darling, is he not? What is his name?'

'You are very kind to say so. He is called Asa. But it's a sad life for him trailing across the city with me all day. I should like to have somewhere where I could leave him, but the woman at my lodgings would need money.'

'Hm. I have half a mind to give up Mr Boothby and go to the horse's mouth. Most of the touring companies advertise, you know. If we had a copy of the *Era*, we could find out directly. But it wants sixpence and I'm afraid I've only three.'

'I have a threepenny piece. Here.'

The newspaper having been procured from a tobacconist's over the way, Miss Jeffries sat down once more and began to criticise it in an extremely satirical manner: 'Why, here is that Mrs Crosland coming out again as Violet in *Married to a Marquis*. I never heard of such a thing.'

'Why should Mrs Crosland not play Violet?' Alice wondered.

'Why, because Violet is supposed to be a lady undergraduate at Oxford and Mrs Crosland is nearly forty. She has three girls herself at school. Wait, though, here is something.

'*WANTED. To rehearse next week.* Ada's No Chicken. *Full company (with exceptions). To reliable artistes, very long tour assured.*'

An address was named in Clapham, at which applicants were invited to call between the hours of three and six.

'Is it a good play?' Alice enquired.

'Oh, capital. As fine as *Hamlet*, I should think. But it has five – no, six – female parts. And that's not including the parlourmaid. Let me see, it is past two. We could be at Clapham within the hour, I think. Will you come too?'

'I should like to very much.'

In Goodge Street the rain had settled down into a continuous fine drizzle, so that the shopfronts, irradiated by flaring gaslights, seemed ghostly and indistinct. The air was turning cold. At the Tottenham Court Road, empty of people but thronged with tenantless costers' barrows, they boarded an omnibus at the stand and were carried away southwards in the direction of Trafalgar Square. On all sides the traffic of the streets flowed around them. A great ducal carriage with a coronet stamped on its door and a coachman in livery seated on its box came gliding out of an alleyway near the Strand and went off towards the Mall. A little further along a cab horse had come down on the wet tarmacadam and a knot of people stood by sympathising with the cabman as he attempted to coax the beast back into its traces. The boy stirred at her side and she rocked him gently back and forth as the seat jolted beneath her, the white-feather plume of a woman's hat gave way to a view of a German band, very mournful and weather-beaten, assembled in the shadow of one of the lions, and abruptly she was shaken out of her reverie. At her side, Miss Jeffries was discoursing on the subject of her family.

'Do you ever see your people? Mine are a great trial. My brother lives at Kettering and we spend Christmas there, but his wife is such a *hum*. We played bezique last holidays and you would have thought the devil himself was dealing out the cards.'

Alice thought of her own 'people', of Aunt Em and Uncle Hi and the sundry cousins dispersed across the Kansas flat. She realised with a start – an almost physical sensation, like the jolt of the seat beneath her – that two years had passed since she had seen any of them. The enormity of this distance in time alarmed her and she tried to reconstruct Aunt Em's face on the station platform, Uncle Hi pouring salt into an upturned pork barrel, but the effort was too much for her and she took refuge in incidentals: a particular floral dress that she wore once at a social, the taste of the lemonade at Schwab's store, bright sun streaming down into the yard as Uncle Hi's chickens ran crazily in and out of their coops. It seemed to her that none of these memories was quite real to her; they had faded away almost beyond the point of recall, were as nothing compared to other, more recent, experiences that burned steadily in her mind. 'And then,' continued Miss Jeffries, 'she has an old aunt, who has to be humoured, as she was once lady's maid to a duchess or some such, and quite what Robert sees in her I can't imagine.' And so the journey to Clapham passed.

The advertiser, who called himself Armitage, lived in a small terraced house in the region of Clapham Junction. There was no servant and Mr Armitage was compelled to open the door himself. He was a tall, lugubrious man, who wore a crumpled summer waistcoat above the trousers of a suit that perhaps had once been sold as tweed. On a table in the room to which he led them lay the remnants of a plate of sardines and some pickled cabbage that was evidently the remains of his lunch. There was no sign of anyone else on the premises, or indeed much in the way of furnishing. Mr Armitage excused these deficiencies on the grounds that he had taken the house as a base from which to assemble his company. This was to open at Bolton in three weeks' time. As to their own inclusion in this assembly, which according to the handbill that lay on the table next to the lunch plate represented one of the most startling arrays of talent ever congregated on a provincial stage, Mr Armitage could not exactly say. But he brightened up on learning that Miss Jeffries was a client of Mr Boothby, a gentleman whom he apparently held in high regard. He was yet more intrigued by Alice's accent, 'for such things are still a great novelty on the stage, and very welcome'. Her inexperience did not seem to alarm him. The 'money', on which subject Miss Jeffries immediately addressed him, was small but 'sure'.

'You'll have to give that up, you know, though,' he remarked, nodding at the child, who throughout the interview had been lodged in Alice's arms.

Alice prudently said nothing, resolving to take the matter up with Miss Jeffries, whom she now regarded as the fount of all knowledge and wisdom. It was finally established that the 'money', whose smallness Mr Armitage had not exaggerated, amounted to three pounds a week. Having taken their names and addresses, and promised that they might 'hear from him' in two or three days, he ushered them out into the darkling street.

'It doesn't seem up to much,' said Miss Jeffries uncertainly as they stood on the pavement corner. A muffin man with a cracked bell was making his rounds in the next street and the sound rose discordantly above them.

'Did you ever hear of him before?'

'Mr Armitage? No, I don't think I ever did. That means nothing, of course. There are companies formed every week. I suppose he is a speculator who thinks he is on to a good thing. But he is right in one regard.'

'What is that?'

'Asa. You cannot take him to Bolton. Or anywhere else for that matter.'

'Why not?'

'Why not? Whoever heard of a baby in theatrical lodgings? The landladies don't like it and the other women won't either. And there are people – you must not mind me saying this, dear – who will ask how he was come by.'

'They can ask what they like.'

'It is not as if you could take him on stage with you – no, I am serious. Mrs Crackanthwaite had her baby with her in *The Duke's Heir* and was paid five shillings a week extra. But when we hear from Mr Armitage you must make an arrangement, I'm afraid you must.' Seeing the look on

Alice's face, she softened her tone. 'It is a sacrifice, I know, but in a profession such as this one makes them all the time. Why' – and then, perhaps conscious that she had said too much, she stopped and took hold of the child's fingers where they extended from his wrapper. 'Look, you have my address. You had better write to me when we have heard from Mr Armitage.'

'You seem very sure that we shall get a part.'

'At three pounds a week there is no doubt of it,' Miss Jeffries said. And so they bade each other goodnight at the street corner.

It is four miles from Clapham to Kennington. Alice negotiated this distance by way of two further omnibuses and a walk of several hundred yards. She was now exhausted, having been on her feet since eight that morning. The baby had gone to sleep again against her shoulder; the warmth comforted her as she walked. Reaching the Kennington Road, she crossed over to the farther side and made her way through Walcott Square to a small street with only a very few houses in it, stopped at the farthermost of them, dipped into the pocket of her dress and produced a latch key. Making as little noise as possible, but stumbling in the darkness on the uneven flags, she slipped through the front door.

Inside it was pitch dark, with only a chink of light coming from beneath a door in the back part of the house to illuminate the passage in which she now stood. Crouching down, with the child balanced on her knee, she began silently to remove her jacket. If by taking these precautions she had hoped to avoid the attentions of her landlady she was mistaken, for Mrs Gaffney, who had heard the first turning of the key in the lock, came bustling along the corridor with a lighted candle in one hand and a rolling pin in the other.

'Did you get anything?' this lady asked. 'You have been out long enough.'

'There is a gentleman who may give me a part in his company. That is, he will write in a day or so.'

'Well, I suppose a letter is better than nothing at all.' Mrs Gaffney's features, which had been set hard on her emergence from the kitchen, now relaxed slightly. 'How much will he pay?'

'Three pounds a week.'

'Three pounds? Well, that is all very fine.' Something of the bleakness of this interrogation seemed to occur to her, for she put down the candle, raising a spurt of dust from the chair on which she set it, and said in what was intended to be a more ingratiating manner, 'Perhaps now you might like something nice for your supper. A rarebit, say, or a chop?'

'I shall do very well, thank you, Mrs Gaffney.'

'I dare say. Well, it is all the same to me.' There was a white envelope, Alice saw, clutched between the fingers of her left hand. 'Here, there is this letter come.'

Mrs Gaffney's fingers were blunt, the nails curiously ground down as if their owner had been digging somewhere in dry, unyielding soil. Alice accepted the envelope and, still holding the baby tightly to her side, carefully climbed the uncertain stair boards (Mrs Gaffney deplored such fripperies as stair carpets) and emerged on to the pitch-black landing (Mrs Gaffney regarded gas jets in the upper part of her house as an unconscionable expense). In her room, she placed Asa in a cradle that lay by the far window, took a candlestick from the table and lit it with a match and opened the letter. As she had half expected, this was from another theatrical agency to whom she had applied, informing her that no vacancies existed for persons without experience. Never mind! There was a part for her now, Miss Jeffries had assured her, and such slights could be disregarded. She put the envelope down among a pile of other litter that lay on the tabletop – evening newspapers, Mrs Gaffney's stamped receipts – and stood in the centre of the room looking vaguely about her. There was not a great deal to see: a brass bedstead, a chair, a chest of drawers, a second table on which reposed an ewer and a water jug, and an ancient, glass-fronted bookcase that contained a copy of *The Christian Year*, Sir Lewis Monk's *Epic of Hades*, an almost equally ancient copy of the *Strand Magazine* and other items judged by Mrs Gaffney as suitable light reading for her guests. A series of furious knocks advertised the fact that Mrs Gaffney, baulked in the matter of her lodger's supper, which could have been added to the bill, was now setting about making her own. It was bitterly cold. In the distance, beyond the uncurtained window, Mrs Gaffney's unkempt garden lay in shadow.

It occurred to Alice that she was extraordinarily hungry. From the chest she now fetched a half-loaf of bread and a pot of jam. A spirit kettle, kept wrapped in newspapers and concealed among the bedclothes (Mrs Gaffney was wary of hot water beyond the kitchen) and a packet of tea completed these preparations. With a blanket from the bed draped over her shoulders, she sat down to eat and think about her situation.

She had been at Mrs Gaffney's a month. Her landlady would probably have said that she was quiet in her habits, received few letters, had, apparently, no friends and rarely left the house, when she did taking her baby with her. All this might have suggested that Mrs Gaffney approved of her lodger, which she did not, having doubts about the strangeness of her accent and the provenance of her child. The wedding ring on the third finger of her left hand Mrs Gaffney regarded as the gravest subterfuge. Was her husband dead? Well, then, she should be attired in widow's weeds. Was he working in some distant part of the country? Well, there would be letters sent and money remitted. No, there was no husband, she was no better than she should be and the fifteen shillings that constituted her weekly rent was charity. So Mrs Gaffney, knocking the pots in her kitchen crossly about, reasoned.

Alice, drinking her tea and warming her hands on the surface of the spirit kettle a dozen feet away, wished the distance between herself and her landlady were a couple of streets. On the other hand Mrs Gaffney was better than – what lay beyond Mrs Gaffney and Kennington she did not care to pursue. The dollar bills she had brought with her across the Atlantic, which she had changed into English money on the day of her arrival at Southampton, had realised nearly forty pounds. Three-quarters of this still remained. Barring emergencies, and sticking to a regime of extreme frugality, she thought that she could survive for another six months should her circumstances demand it. A part of her was gratified by this calculation, for it extended her confidence in her ability to survive, to make her own way through the world in which she found herself, but another part of her was revolted by the privations in which she was forced to live. And now there came Mr Armitage and the promise, if that was what it was, of work. Soon, she thought – the tea had grown cold, so absorbed was she by thinking – she would stand on a stage, speak words that were not her own to an audience and be judged on the excellence, or otherwise, of her performance. The prospect did not alarm her, for her mind had been concentrated on it long before it was offered to her. She found herself speaking sentences from plays she had seen long ago, whose dialogue had stuck in her head. There was a particular jumble of words, now all but unintelligible to her, that she brought out and developed in this way, softly enunciating the syllables until the arrangement satisfied her. She beat her foot quietly against the leg of the chair and rattled the teacup on her lap in delight, until the incongruity of her position – the candlelit room, the child asleep in its cradle, the branches of the elm trees in Mrs Gaffney's desolate back garden – struck her and she fell silent. Whatever she did, she must make a success of Mr Armitage's offer and then the poltergeist of the back kitchen could go hang.

It was by now well past eight o'clock. The room grew colder still. Rising to her feet – how her bones ached after her omnibus rides and her march through the south London streets! – she picked up Asa from his cradle and held him in her arms. Much as she delighted in him, she was under no illusions as to his paternity. Asa was Drouett's. There was something about the set of his face that told her this, even had she not known it, and for a moment she remembered Drouett stepping down from the train with his attaché case under his arm. She told herself that she hated Drouett, but she knew that the presence of the child softened these feelings into a kind of neutrality. Asa, coming slowly awake, regarded her solemnly and she winked back. From the room below she could hear various small crashes and crepitations, as if Mrs Gaffney had suddenly decided to throw out the contents of the saucepan cupboard on to the kitchen floor. At her side the candle was beginning to gutter. Five minutes later and the room was in darkness.

The memories of her early days in London are horribly mundane. There is no pattern to them. Glassy-eyed rabbits that have lain two years on ice, supine on the trays of the Kennington street markets. Mrs Gaffney's false teeth, which she keeps conveniently to hand in a water glass. A china mug of King Edward's coronation. A gasometer which aggrandises over the Vauxhall rooftops. Horses' hoofs. A book of Tennyson's poems, bought for a shilling at a stationer's shop, on whose flyleaf some previous owner has written *Jas Stephens perlegi, 1863*. A steel buttonhook. Freezing dawns. Melancholy twilights. The London light intrigues her, its curious sheens and fiery sunsets, smoky tints fading away into the horizon. Often soot falls out of the sky: the dirt on Mrs Gaffney's sills is half an inch thick. Washing left out to dry goes grey in an hour. The house is sunk into decay. There are extraordinary cracks in the plaster, in which a human hand could be inserted without trouble. At night the rain cascades from defective guttering. Mrs Gaffney takes no notice. She is sixty years old, Alice discovers, a sea captain's widow who once saw the old Queen in her coach at Windsor, cannot read and can write only her signature on the stamped receipts that issue forth whenever the rent is paid.

The old life has gone, Alice thinks. It is made up – and the awareness startles her – of objects, not faces. Uncle Hi's buckle belt with the eagle head fastening. Aunt Em's calico dress. Kerosene lanterns hanging from the porch door. A blue shirtwaister laid out upon the ironing board. The urge to connect with these things, to jab at them before they recede entirely from view, is overwhelming. But they are five thousand miles away, she thinks, five thousand miles, and no longer quite real. The stationer's shop in which she found the book of Tennyson's poems has a rickety wooden spiral on which are stacked piles of illustrated letter cards. They are sepia coloured, but enticing. The cost is a penny. Having purchased one – a view of the approach to Victoria Station – she is confused, for there is no one to whom she can decently send it. In the end she remembers the name of a girl who lived three houses down the street at home and with whom she occasionally used to visit, and addresses the card to *Miss May Edwards, 73 Lincoln Terrace, Kansas City, Kansas.* On the other side, in between the scroll-work tracery and the wings of a pair of cupids there is space for a message, but Alice's courage has altogether failed her. She cannot think what to say to May Edwards, whose grandfather fought at Vicksburg and whose portrait sat on the mantelpiece next to the advertisements for seed drills and the copies of the *Kansas Free Citizen.* Eventually she prints the words *Your sincerely attached friend, Alice Hanson.* Even then, there is a problem. How will May know who 'Alice Hanson' is? In the end she abstracts a paring knife from Mrs Gaffney's kitchen drawer and carefully scrapes the second word away. The letter card is deposited in the post box at Walcott Square, a scarlet cylinder with the initials V&R gracefully intertwined beneath its mouth. Letters are her excitement, she thinks, and her terror.

7

Fog on the Wensum

1920–21

Receipt for hogpen

Take approximately 100 pounds of coal. From this it should be possible to derive perhaps 10 pounds 10 oz of coal tar, 8½ oz of coal tar naphtha and 2¼ oz of aniline. To the aniline add sulphuric acid and bicarbonate of potassium in equal measures and heat. The fine black solution that results may be filtered to produce a black powder able to be mistaken for soot. It will then be necessary to separate out the various products that this powder contains. The very troublesome brown resinous substance that is its greater part may be extracted by means of naphtha and methylated spirits. Place whatever remains in a still, to enable the distillation of the spirit. The remaining fluid can then be washed with caustic soda and water, and drained on a filter. A grain of the resulting dust placed in a carboy containing nine or ten gallons of water should illuminate the entire container within four to five seconds.

A. E. Rendall, 17 June 1921

Between three or four o'clock on those autumn afternoons, mist rapidly descended on the Cathedral Close and the river that bordered it on two sides, covering the nearby fields and meadows with vaporous trails the colour of cigarette smoke. The effect on the nondescript-looking buildings around them, some of them constructed of Caen stone, others in the local flint, was never less than uncanny. The gates of the playground vanished instantly into the fog. The cathedral itself metamorphosed into a Victorian aquatint, like a representation of *The Fighting Temeraire* – a reproduction of which hung on the wall at Intwood Road. The human voices that carried from this lost world – shouts from the playground, a porter at the far gate giving directions

– seemed faintly unreal: random, let in on sufferance, ripe to be extinguished.

On this particular afternoon the fog was patterned by soot: thick, dark flakes, blacker than the ash of the sky. It was increasing in volume as I hurried away from it, as the cathedral clock struck the quarter-hour. To walk through this part of Norwich, at whatever hour of the day or night, was to be oppressed by antiquity: architectural, ecclesiastical, moral. The statue of Nelson at the end of the green before the cathedral's west door; the discreet offices of clerical lawyers; gaitered clergymen as black as the rooks that soared above their heads: all this spoke of a distant past, far beyond the compass of the grocer's van that was delivering parcels by the Erpingham Gate or the policeman – scarlet-faced and looking like one of the comic policemen seen on the stages of variety halls – who stood talking to the gatekeeper. There was a minor canon living in Hook's Walk who remembered the church bells being rung for Balaclava. In my first year at the school I had been taught by a man who had seen the Prince Consort waving to the crowd at Windsor. The list of the names of the fifty-seven Old Boys who had died in France, which lay beneath a glass frame in the corner of the playground, pending a memorial stone, were no more than surface chatter failing to disturb the sombre utterances of the past.

It would have been the late autumn or early winter of 1920, and I would have been fifteen years old, well protected against the penetrating cold, with a pile of books under my arm, moving purposefully off in the direction of the river, over which so much fog now hung that the northernmost reaches of the city were altogether obscured. My uncle had – as I soon came to appreciate – little interest in the past. When Maradick the journalist wrote the first biography of him, he included some lines about 'a guardian of England's heritage, a mute, inglorious Milton allowed his own resonant voice'. This struck me as the purest nonsense. My uncle wandered through Norwich, a city of grave and thoroughgoing antiquity, in a state of supreme indifference. City walls, castle keeps, cobbled stones – they were all the same to him. As this indifference extended to his own past, unhappily, it also extended to mine.

Even my uncle was prepared to accept that, in the matter of Mrs Custance's letter, he had overstepped the mark and that reparation ought to be made. When repeated searches of the downstairs rooms failed to uncover it, he began on a momentous exercise, extending over an entire Bank Holiday weekend, that involved the transfer of every paper item that the cottage possessed into the garden beyond it. This yielded up some fascinating artefacts – share certificates in defunct companies, a signed photograph of Lord Roberts, to whom my uncle had capriciously written at the time of the South African war – but it did not produce Mrs Custance's letter. The search was conducted against a backdrop of roasting pork fat, washed plates and brown gravy, for we were hard at work consuming Lloyd George before the authorities, whom my uncle had kept in ignorance of the Intwood Pork Repository, found out about his existence. When it was over and the final bundle – a pile of picture postcards that my uncle had apparently sent himself from a holiday at Skegness – had been labelled and tied up with twine, he wrote a second letter to Mrs Custance's landlady, but I could tell that his heart wasn't in it. He wished me well, he was anxious to atone for his negligence, but there was something almost superstitious in the way that he accepted Mrs Custance's death as a fait accompli, a boulder flung across the trail, blocking the path for eternity.

'P'raps', he murmured about this time, 'it was *meant* to be.'

'What was?' I wondered.

'Oh, I don't know,' he said dismissively. 'A good woman, y'know,' he said vaguely, of the sister whose funeral he had not troubled to attend. 'Sorry to see her gone.'

'She was always kind to me,' I said loyally, which was not all that far from the truth.

'Someone's *bound* to know,' he said.

But this confidence was misplaced. The letter to Mrs Custance's landlady came back stamped 'Not Known at this Address'. A further letter, sent hopefully to the people at Loftholdingswood, vanished entirely. I saw how it was. All across England the tribes were in flight, the houses broken up and a great administrative chaos set in train. The whole thing was like a giant sorting office full of parcels that would never reach their destinations. The question of who I was, where I had come from, whether there were people in the world who wondered about me as I wondered about them, was curiously abstract to me. I had gone for so long without these vital pieces of information that I needed encouragement not to set them aside. My uncle was unsympathetic. 'Y'don't want to *brood*, Ralph,' he said, more than once, at about this juncture, and I saw him considering me in a thoughtful way, as if he had just seen me for the first time, wondered what he could make of me. The deep and secret recesses of his mind that were never fully revealed to me broke momentarily above the surface, like one of the Yare kingfishers seen hurtling in flight across the reed beds.

At the far end of the Close, beyond the deanery and the residences of the minor canons, the fog had receded a little. In the distance, beyond ancient stables and the outline of Pull's Ferry, the surface of the Wensum curved betweens banks of sedge. Turning into the passage that marked the precinct's north-eastern boundary, the fog of antiquity receded too. Here there were grim, grey little streets in the modern style, an equally grey and grim little park with an attendant routing out waste paper from the grass with a stick, and a line of small shops whose proprietors had all invested in the same brand of incandescent gas fittings, such was the uniformly bright orange façade that they presented to the world.

Outside the last of these shops a girl of about twenty in a long, ankle-length coat and a bell-shaped hat was buttoning up her gloves. 'You're a nice boy,' she said as I approached along the pavement. 'Does your mother know you're out?'

These were two of the three catchphrases current in Norwich at this time. The third, a variant on the second, was 'Has your mother sold her mangle?'

'You're a nice boy,' Marjorie said again, a bit more archly. 'Ent you pleased to see me?'

What do you say in such circumstances? I took hold of her hand and attempted to kiss the left side of her face, only to be repulsed by a determined shove in the ribs and the amusement of one of the shopkeepers on the pavement.

'Cheek,' she said indignantly. And then, seeing the look on my face, 'Gloomkins.'

It's odd that of the several faces I remember from those years, the years of my uncle's first boom and the rise of hogpen, hers should be the most vivid to me. She was a tall, cheerful, ungainly girl who lived in a cottage at the farther end of the Intwood Road and served in a tobacconist's shop near the station, and whom even my uncle – had he known of our association – would have vaguely disapproved of on class grounds. Her father worked as a post office clerk in the sorting office at Brigg Street, her mother was occasionally reduced to charring at the big houses on Cringleford Rise and there were six or seven other children, including a half-witted sister whose tongue was too big for her mouth and who lay around the house for days on end drawing pot-hooks on the backs of envelopes. Nowadays I suppose I'd be inclined to sympathise with Marjorie, for whom the job in the tobacconist's shop represented a Herculean leap up the social scale, but at the time I think I rather envied her for the hectic and indiscriminate quality of her life. Even the heaving cottage, with its terrible chaos of children crawling underfoot, damp washing drying in front of the fire and the stink of unwashed humanity failed to disturb the vision I had of her, for it was all quite alien to my own experience: the faded silence of Loftholdingswood and the six years in the company of a secretive and eccentric middle-aged bachelor who kept his secrets close to his chest.

This is not to say that I had any illusions about Marjorie. She was the kind of girl whom Mrs Custance, expert in these matters, would have called 'forward' and even by the standards of the farther end of the Intwood Road – not high – she had what was known in those days as 'a history'. There was even a story – something I never got to the bottom of – that the child represented as her youngest sister was actually her own daughter, its provenance hushed up by scandalised grandparents. All this necessarily gave our relationship a faint air of mutual bewilderment. We were always having conversations that petered out into inconsequentiality, neither of us quite understanding the other and never disguising the fact that each of us was rather frightened by the other's attentions.

'Do you like my 'at?' she said now, giving a little pat to the bonnet and setting her face at an angle.

'It's very nice.'

'Mother said it went with the rest.'

The post-war fashions – cylinder dresses, bead-string necklaces and cloche hats – hadn't yet got to Norwich.

'It's very nice,' I said again.

''Ere,' she said. 'You're a nice boy. Give us a ha'penny for the soldier.'

In the entrance to the tobacconist's, flanked by adverts for Abdulla cigarettes and Sahib smooth-cut Virginia, there was a life-size model of a grenadier holding out a box for some military charity. I gave her the halfpenny and watched her swing across the pavement to drop it in the slot. They were odd times, those years after the war, full of optimism on the surface, but with trouble brewing in the water below. The politicians' speeches were full of talk about homes for heroes, but nobody quite knew when the homes would be built or who was going to pay for them. There were ex-servicemen everywhere – selling matches on street corners, making their presence felt in bank queues with suits with one empty arm pinned up against the lapel – while the newspapers drivelled about 'youth' and 'new ideas' that 'forward-looking men' were going to manoeuvre into place.

It was in this final category that my uncle believed himself to reside.

The last months of the Great War had passed my uncle by. The Armistice. The flight of the Kaiser. Versailles. The peace treaty signed in a railway carriage. All these, I deduced, meant nothing to him. They were vague scufflings from the ocean floor that would never disturb the passage of the purposeful swimmer above their heads. You might wonder how a man living near a provincial city in the midst of the greatest conflagration in history could so thoroughly detach himself, but somehow my uncle managed it. He had a way of picking up papers that carried war news and somehow not seeing it, puzzling over them as if they were giant acrostics whose real meaning had somehow evaded his grasp. Only once had he grown animated. This was when a biplane – an RE8 from the RFC station at Coltishall – came down in a field up on the Colney escarpment. The pieces lay there for days, to be robbed by the souvenir hunters, among whom my uncle played a conspicuous role. A capstan. The greater part of an aileron. A wing tip. Half a machine-gun. All these items he brought home under cover of darkness and left lying around the cottage in varying states of disassembly until, like the pulley system or the cache of motor-cycle parts, they began to rust and were eventually taken away.

By this time I was thoroughly conversant with my uncle's moods. I knew when he was likely to take up one of his enthusiasms and when he was likely to put it aside. I knew when he was likely to be exalted by his prospects, and when he was likely to be cast down. I knew when he wanted to talk and when he wanted to be silent. All this may make it sound as if I understood my uncle's character, could diagnose his whims and account for the extraordinary detonations of temperament that made them pictur-esque, but this would be to exaggerate the hold he had on me, and I on him. If I've a memory from these times it's of him pondering, picking among the detritus of the cottage – piles of newspapers, boxes of ancient china, the canisters of tinned food laid down at the war's outbreak and then forgotten – with an odd, abstracted gleam in his eye. I found him furtive, ineffectual and self-deluding, and I believe that in his saner moments – I use these words carefully – he thought so too. There was always talk in those days – vague talk, but talk nonetheless – of betterment, of a house on the Newmarket Road, of new suits, of mysterious companies whose affairs my uncle would direct, but it never came to anything. My uncle, I imagined, got by on hope: a hope whose fulfilment would have profoundly unsettled him.

Here on the street corner it was turning cold. There would be frost tonight on what little grass of the cottage garden now remained, whitening the bars of the surviving pigpens and the long, low sheds that had lately supplanted them. The sheds were my uncle's latest enthusiasm and contained chemical apparatus. In fact, the aniline experiments had been going on for about a year now: secretive, intent, but like most of my uncle's hobbies not without entertainment. From somewhere, not without difficulty, for this was a time of shortage and deprivation, he had obtained a ton of coal, some distilling equipment, quite a lot of sulphur and some flagons of distilled water. The coal was kept in the first of the sheds, the second making do as a laboratory and a third as a repository for waste products prior to their removal. My uncle's plan, he had explained, was to use the coal as a means of extracting coal tar naphtha and use the chemical base that resulted to synthesise quinine. By this stage, having entered the school sixth form on the scientific side, I knew enough organic chemistry to be moderately sceptical of this procedure, or perhaps only of my uncle's ability to carry it out. But my uncle persisted. I've since learned – something I didn't know at the time – that the distilling process incorporated some genuine innovations. Maradick, supported by a man from the Royal Society, states that this was something to do with the heating apparatus: I don't know; in any case the original specifications are lost. Then, abruptly, the quinine scheme was abandoned for some experiments with aniline dyes. A shilling life of Sir William Perkins, the inventor of mauve, appeared in the house and was spoken of with what seemed to me an excessive reverence. Another ton of coal was ordered up, and quite a lot of potassium.

'Very interestin', this aniline business,' my uncle said once or twice.

Like the pig breeding before it, the attempt to manufacture aniline dye absorbed my uncle entirely. His insurance work declined to the point where it provided us with only the most basic wherewithal. Savage economies were imposed on the life of the cottage. The arrival of the second ton of coal coincided with the removal of all the furniture from the spare bedroom and the temporary disappearance of my uncle's watch and chain.

There were other difficulties attending the practice of organic chemistry in a cottage garden shed.

'What will you do with all the coal tar?' I wondered one morning, when an inch-high pile of soot lay on the downstairs windowsills.

'It don't signify,' my uncle said. He had been up until two in the morning: his face was white and ragged, and the back of one of his hands was entirely covered by a bright orange stain.

'You can't just leave it there. And I don't suppose anyone will come and take it away.'

But my uncle was lost in some private, rainbow-coloured world on whose kaleidoscopic surface the disposal of several hundred pounds of valueless black sludge scarcely registered.

'You've studied literature,' he said unexpectedly. 'Read poems and suchlike. Tell me some names for blue.'

'Royal. Cobalt. Cerulean. Cornflower. Aquamarine.'

'Now for red.'

'Scarlet. Carmine. Magenta. Crimson. Vermilion.'

'Always plenty of uses for coal tar,' said my uncle optimistically. 'Don't they make soap out of it?' he suggested.

In the end I think he buried the coal tar. Certainly, coming back from school a week or two later, I found a curious hummock of earth at the bottom of the garden where previously there had only been ragged lawn and on which no grass ever grew again.

As with the pigs, the neighbours came at teatime. It was then that the stench from the sulphur grew particularly bad. Somehow my uncle dealt with them.

More distilling apparatus arrived and some magnesium in a silver container. I began to find scraps of paper lying around the cottage with queer and, as it seemed to me, artificial words on them: *fluouroscene*; *diachrome*; *hispodyll*; *lilachrose*.

I realise that this is only a partial account of my uncle's voyage of discovery, but there can be no other, for my own part in it was limited to these incidental collaborations: a further request to name half a dozen variants on the colour yellow; to hold a test tube full of hydrogen between a pair of tongs while my uncle sulphuretted it; to put out a small fire that began in the corner of one of the sheds; to dispose, surreptitiously, of some bulky liquid in a tributary of the Yare that had the effect of turning the water bright purple. It was as if a giant tunnel were being constructed beneath the house by diggers who never appeared, using machinery that kept silent and whose only manifestations were a few handfuls of discarded earth.

It was about four o'clock in the afternoon. The fog, kept at bay on the outskirts of the Cathedral Close, was beginning to descend again over the nearby house tops. Eastwards, towards the Prince of Wales Road, lights were going on. From the middle distance came the odd, resonant sound which I knew to be the clanking together of the houseboats on the river. I wondered what my uncle was doing. Eight hours before I had left him installed in the second of the three sheds prodding morosely at the valve of a defunct Bunsen burner; the chances were that he was still there.

Marjorie came back from the tobacconist's doorway, fastening her hat more securely to the cottage-loaf arrangement of her hair. 'Here,' she said in a friendly way. ''Ave a cig.'

Marjorie was always having a cig or a cup of tea, or looking in the local paper to see if George Robey or Harry Tate was on the bill at the Norwich Hippodrome, or eyeing up the dress patterns in the outfitters' windows in Gentleman's Walk. She had a kind of genius for incidental pleasure, for extracting the maximum enjoyment from every situation she found herself in. I envied her this ease.

'No thanks.'

'Oh well, suit yourself.' She took a long, expert drag on the cigarette and blinked at me through the smoke. 'Ent you going to see me home then, Ralphie?'

And so, with occasional pauses at shop windows and detours into alleyways, we walked silently back through the city, as the twilight faded around us, south-west along the Prince of Wales Road and the cramped streets that bordered the ancient castle, whose rampart loomed bleakly out of the dusk. I say 'silently' as it was a peculiarity of our relationship that we had no conversation: in age, class and occupation the gap between us was too great. One of the telegraph boys who cycled past us every so often, bound for the Norwich Union Insurance Society offices in Surrey Street, would have known how to talk to Marjorie in a way I did not. She, on the other hand, though she asked occasional questions – what had I done at school? What was it like living with my uncle? – was merely puzzled by me and flattered by my interest. We were always, or so it seemed to me, taking up lines of enquiry and casting them aside, gazing at each other in an exasperation born of failure to communicate.

'I saw Him this morning,' she now ventured – 'Him' was my uncle, just as 'Her', for some reason, was her mother. 'Down near the bridge.'

'Oh yes?' This was an interesting piece of news, for it meant that he might not, in the end, have spent the day at home. 'What was he doing?'

'I don't know.' Marjorie had no descriptive powers. 'He looked A Sight. He wasn't wearing a coat. Reely. And he was walking around like he didn't know where he was going. It was Sorful,' Marjorie said.

Someone who didn't know my uncle might have been alarmed by this intelligence, but I was used to his vagaries.

'It must be difficult,' Marjorie said impenetrably, 'doing what he does.'

At St Stephen's we took a bus down the Newmarket Road. Here taxicabs plied to and fro under long shadows cast by the leafless horse chestnuts. A certain kind of semi-nocturnal life was moving incrementally into gear: children's faces seen fleetingly through windows; glimpses of bright drawing rooms; servants sent out on errands moving resourcefully through the murk. At one of the crossing places, under a flaring gaslight, a girl in an apron, a maid's cap and sleek lisle stockings stood chafing her hands against the cold.

'Catch me being a *servant*,' said Marjorie, who regarded the seventy-four hours spent weekly behind the tobacconist's counter as a very superior situation.

At some point during the journey home I took hold of her hand.

At Cringleford bridge, dark and remote beneath the elders, where a farmer's cart was blocking up the road ahead and the noise of water churned in the weir below, we left the bus and headed up the Intwood Road. Set back from the pavement, half concealed behind chest-high hedges, the cottages were gathered up in shadow. Here and there a light glowed. The effect was indescribably mournful: lowering sky, the scent of winter in the air, a breeze stirring in the reed beds beyond the mill, the immensity of the Norfolk plain stretching out beyond. Whatever plans I had for Marjorie – blissful, roseate visions, they were, in which the postal clerk's daughter metamorphosed into one of the Waterhouse portraits I had seen in the Castle Museum – perished on the instant. We had reached our gate by this time, through which could be glimpsed the desolate vista of scorched grass, the shadowy outline of the pens, where once Asquith and Churchill and Lloyd George had roamed, dark sheds to the rear, their impact increasingly heightened by a horrible smell of sulphur and creosote, with a faint aroma of benzine lurking at its edge.

'Here,' said my uncle's voice sharply, from a region somewhere beyond the hedge. 'Is that you, Ralph?'

I have a very clear memory of the next two moments, for they represented a turning point in both our lives. Marjorie took flight and soon became a shadow moving rapidly up the hill. Peering over the hedge, I found my uncle sitting on the grass with his hands drawn up under his chin and the light from the nearby street lamp gleaming off his shins. His spectacles were gone somewhere and he was wearing his idea of a laboratory coat, an old butcher's apron left over from the days of pig keeping, splashed with iridescent blues and greens. The breeze, whipping up now from the reed beds, had taken the grey curls on the side of his head and blown them up like a comb. When he saw me he rocked forward on his knees a little, raised his head, which without his spectacles gave him the appearance of an elderly tortoise, and said,

'I done it, Ralph. I always said I'd do it and I done it.'

'Done what? What have you done?'

'Kitchener couldn't do it,' my uncle went on. 'Lord Roberts couldn't do it and Asquith couldn't do it. But I done it.'

In his exaltation he had retreated so far into himself that he could not articulate the words he wished to say.

'What have you done?' I wondered again.

'You come over here,' my uncle said, with immense slyness, 'and I'll show you.'

By the time I passed through the gate he had clambered to his feet and stood waiting for me on the path. Without explanation, he plunged on into the cottage with the strings of his apron flapping behind him.

'Here,' he said, flinging out his arm in a dramatic gesture. 'Just you take a look at that and you'll see what I mean.'

Although in its customary state of chaos – the sofa almost lost under a tower of newsprint, a harrow that my uncle had bought at an agricultural show on the grounds that it 'might come in useful' sticking out of the fireplace – our sitting room had plainly undergone some major reconfiguration. In a space before the hearth, where formerly had lain a jumble of books and garden tools, he had placed a small occasional table, draped with what might have been a pillowcase. On this lay a china teacup half full of greyish powder.

'Go on,' said my uncle easily. 'Take a look, Ralph.'

I leant over the cup. Close up the powder seemed oddly friable, like Fuller's Earth. I took a pinch between finger and thumb, and felt individual grains crumble to dust. 'What is it?' I wondered.

But my uncle had gone to root around in the kitchen. I could hear the noise of cupboards being thrown open, the slap of liquid being ladled into a jug. I took another look at the powder on my thumb. It seemed horribly innocuous. When he came back into the room he was sweating beneath the weight of a monstrous glass container, like a fish tank, half full of water.

'See this?' my uncle said, carefully placing the tank on the floor between a jar containing a stuffed woodpecker and what looked like an embroidery sampler. 'Ten gallons in here. Well, nine and a half maybe, allowing for spillage.' He was breathing heavily. 'Anyway, I'd say six hundred thousand parts of water to a grain. Six hundred thousand parts, Ralphie! Just think of it. You could throw a bottle of ink in that tank and hardly know you'd done it. Now, watch.'

He took a pinch of the powder, stared at it – he had retrieved his spectacles from somewhere – selected a tiny fragment, rolled it with the finger and thumb of his left hand over the thumbnail of his right and flicked it over the rim of the tank.

'Should take four seconds,' my uncle said. 'Five, maybe.'

He may have been right. I think the standard reaction time was later set at 4.65 seconds, with an additional .12 second temperature variation, but to me it was instantaneous.

'What did I say, Ralph?' my uncle crowed. 'What did I tell you?'

As for the colour in the tank, I don't think I have the words to describe it even now. At first sight it was halfway between carmine and damask. Then, when you inspected it closely, you realised that beneath it lay what might have been a kind of blue, but a blue that could have been any one of half a dozen shades ranging from periwinkle to duck's-egg. Anstruther FRS, who conducted the first independent analysis, declared that in its purest form it was an amalgam of crimson and gentian, and he was the most eminent industrial chemist in western Europe, but that is to state it crudely. I have caught echoes of it in the military tunics of the mid nineteenth century, although it outshone any form of scarlet. In solution it sometimes seemed to have a greenish tint, yet this could disappear over time. Rex Whistler once suggested that the harsher elements could be removed or glossed over to produce an exceptionally delicate shade of purple.

'What did I tell you?' my uncle crowed again. He was taking in rapid, tiny breaths through his mouth like one of the pike hauled out of the Wensum on a fisherman's line. 'What did I say, Ralph?'

Later that night, when he grew rational once more and had recruited himself with a jug of stout from the Cringleford Red Lion, I made him explain exactly what he had done. As I'd half suspected, he had gone back to his original idea of synthesising quinine out of coal tar naphtha. But something had gone wrong and instead of quinine he'd ended up with a reddish powder. At this point, so he maintained, my uncle had been chiefly interested in understanding the chemical reaction that hadn't produced the quinine. Accordingly, he tried a more simply constructed aniline base. This time, though, he got a perfectly black solution. In a spirit of mild enquiry, my uncle purified and dried this solution, and digested it with some spirits of wine he happened to have lying about. The result was a fine powder capable of illuminating, in four seconds, water to the value of its six-hundredth dilute part.

'All very well finding a new colour,' I said – I, too, had read the account of Sir William Perkins's travails. 'Can you dye with it?'

'Already thought of that,' my uncle said. 'Put some of it on my hand-kerchief this forenoon and boiled it up in a saucepan. Did it half a dozen times and couldn't see it fade ... Of course,' he added, 'it'll probably need a mordant to get it to *stick*.'

I remembered the slips of paper found lying around the house: *Fluouroscene*; *Diachrome*; *Hispodyll*; *Lilachrose*. 'You'll need a name,' I said. 'A colour has to have a name.'

'Thought of that, too,' my uncle said. 'Don't like those fancy names. Do you know, when mauve was first invented, they called it mauveine? They did. When I sat there, with it in front of me – and I'm telling you, Ralph, it was the queerest thing in the world – I said to myself, I'll step outside and the first thing I see, that's what I'll call it.'

'So what is it?'

'Hogpen,' my uncle said shyly.

'I don't understand.'

'That's what I saw,' my uncle said. 'First thing I set eyes on when I came out of the shed – and I could barely see, Ralph, I'd been in the place so long – was the doosid pens we kept the pigs in. Hogpen, I thought. That'll make people sit up and take notice, you see if it doesn't.'

Later still, he began on a monologue of the kind I remembered from previous enthusiasms, in which the full range of his imaginative frenzy was allowed to free itself from all constraints of locale, economy and milieu.

'First thing is to get a *patent* ... Commercial laboratories're all very well, but we can do the job ourselves ... Need *capital*, Ralph ... A man who knows about the dyeing process to give us a hand ... How would it look, say, on cotton ...? Could get a kid to paint a picture with it for an advertisement maybe . . . Then there are food dyes. Imagine a *cake* that colour, Ralph, or a stick of rock . . . *Ooniform* even . . . Could we make sports togs out of it, d'you suppose . . . ? Wallpaper. Think if you c'd decorate your parlour in hogpen . . . Toothpaste . . . Toothpaste . . . City, of course. We shall have to go the City, talk to a bank . . . Need *a norfice*, with a manager . . . Then there's overseas, the empire, the empire . . . *Europe* . . . Carpets, Ralph! Think of it in the weave of a carpet . . .'

I have noted only a twentieth of what he said, but this is its essence.

And that is nearly all I have to say about the early days at Cringleford and the finding of hogpen. It seems very far away to me now, quite lost on the edge of the world that rose up to displace it, part of an older landscape that is altogether gone. When I went back there a year ago it was to find the depredations of the twentieth century savagely in train. The cottages had given way to tradesmen's villas, the Colney escarpment had been built up and the cubbyhole in which an old peasant woman had sat dispensing ginger beer and stale buns was a sub-post office counter. What happened to that old world, I wondered? Did it cease to exist or simply go elsewhere? Certainly I never found it again. Yet not everything was gone. My uncle's cottage had been plundered, and extended, and had its roof raised and a water fountain with a disreputable caryatid erected in its front garden, but the hedge was still there and an odd, irregular spasm in the arrangement of the lawn suggested that the coal tar still seethed beneath its surface. Further up the road the hovel where Marjorie's parents had raised their effervescing brood had disappeared: it was simply a square of flattened earth with a builder's man attaching little strings to a row of pegs, and half a ton of house bricks, sent from the kiln, lying ready nearby. No judgment could be made about this transformation, I saw. Something small and faintly stupid and fundamentally detached from the processes of life had been replaced by something else only marginally better able to cope with the situation in which it found itself. That was all. But I stared over the hedge, the hedge behind which my uncle had concealed himself on the night he discovered hogpen, for a long time, watching the play of light on the windows and the neatly tilled flower beds, until a woman in a floral dress, who I've no doubt imagined me to be a tout of some kind, came and asked me what I wanted. Well – I could have told her. Instead, I merely raised my hat, muttered something about a wrong address and walked back to the taxi I'd left ticking over at Cringleford bridge.

And so my uncle discovered hogpen and we became great people.

8

Mummer

Mr Armitage did not, as he had promised, write on the second or third day. This sent Alice into a panic. She fancied that Mrs Gaffney, whose interest in postal deliveries was surprising for one who could not read, mocked her in every glance that passed between them. Then, on the fourth morning, came a letter confirming the offer of a part in *Ada's No Chicken*, enclosing a script and bidding her to attend rehearsals in the following week. She plucked Asa out of his cot and hugged him to herself, and stared out at Mrs Gaffney's bleary garden as if it bordered an Elysian field rather than a couple of blackened house backs and a timber yard wreathed in creosote fumes. Miss Jeffries, instantly informed of Mr Armitage's decision, replied by return of post. *Dear Miss Hanson. I was delighted to hear your news. Happily, I too am engaged. I trust that we may see a great deal more of each other. Yours most truly, Edith Jeffries.* The handwriting, neat and italic, with Greek 'e's, confirmed Alice's good opinion of her new friend. She read it to Asa as the rain beat against the smeary window and the smell of a ham cooking in Mrs Gaffney's kitchen crept up through the floorboards beneath them.

The rehearsals took place in a room above a public house on Marylebone High Street, a few yards away from the Marylebone workhouse, into which, more than one member of the cast suggested – theatrical humour is of a very mordant kind – they might shortly be admitted. On a table lay several copies of a second handbill recommending *Ada's No Chicken* to provincial audiences by virtue of its run of three hundred and thirty-seven nights at a London theatre and insisting that the new cast 'constitutes an ensemble in no whit inferior to that which was so long the delight of the metropolis'. Alice heard footsteps on the stairs and looked up to find Miss Jeffries moving briskly into the room with the part of 'Laura' under her arm, very much scrawled about with red ink.

'I am delighted to see you. Truly. It would have been just luck if one of us had got the part and not the other. Wouldn't we have hated each other if that had been so? Isn't this a terrible room?'

'I think it is very nice,' Alice said.

'Well, you are very much mistaken if you think so,' Miss Jeffries went on, doing the public house's landlord, who stood nearby, the honour of lowering her voice. Her eye took in the eight or nine other men and women who stood in groups around the room. 'And the people! Dreadful old dugouts.' She looked Alice up and down once or twice. 'But where is baby?'

'He is with Miss Fotherington – Mrs Gaffney's lodger. I thought, just for an hour or two . . .'

'Something will have to be done about that. But look, here is Mr Armitage.'

If Mr Armitage had seemed unprepossessing in his Clapham parlour, he seemed yet more so in Marylebone High Street. He wore a blue frock-coat with a single remaining button and a made-up tie ornamented with a garnet tiepin, and seemed out of sorts. Once or twice Alice saw him dart sidelong glances at the door, as if he expected some further persons to enter. They were to run through the parts assigned to them, he explained to the circle of faces arranged around him, and he would criticise their diction. If Alice had feared that her inexperience would make her an object of derision, she soon found that this anxiety was misplaced and that most of the cast were as amateurish as she. The girl playing Ada stammered out her lines as if she had only just come upon them. One of the men pronounced the word 'menace' as 'men*ace*', an error in which Mr Armitage did not trouble to correct him.

In the intervals between reading, Miss Jeffries imparted such scraps of information as had come to her about the cast.

'The tall man with the waistcoat is Mr Lonsdale. They say he has paid a premium of fifty guineas to learn the trade. Why he should want to learn it here I can't imagine. The lady with the sour expression is Mrs Baker. I don't doubt that when you meet her she'll say she was Juliet once, but my dear it was forty years ago. Mr Thatcher by the door is famously improvident. If he asks you to lend him so much as a shilling you must refuse. They say there was an execution in the house yesterday and the bailiffs took away half the furniture, and his wife has gone with the children to her mother's at Cheam . . .'

Alice could only make a confused impression of these faces:

Mr Lonsdale's high, pink-cheeked and naive; Mrs Baker's red and resentful; Mr Thatcher's tremulous and ground down. The most conspicuous among them was a young man named Carmody, who from the gestures that he and Mr Armitage occasionally exchanged was supposed to exist in a more intimate relation to him than the rest of the cast. 'I declare', Miss Jeffries remarked, 'that that young man is Mr Armitage's *jackal*, for they wink at each other like a pair of schoolgirls and are always coming into the room together. You must make sure that you do not say anything disobliging about Mr Armitage to him.'

In this way Alice and Miss Jeffries became great friends. Miss Jeffries's stock of theatrical gossip was not very extensive, but it was certainly very entertaining. From her Alice heard tales of distinguished actresses who had played Shakespeare while confining their knowledge of the script entirely to their own part, of bitter professional enmities, of vials of prussic acid flung in the face of leading ladies by disappointed rivals, of unscrupulous managers absconding with the week's takings, of husbands and wives working in separate productions a hundred miles apart.

'For of all trades,' Miss Jeffries said, 'ours is the worst of all to be married in.'

'Do you think *Ada* will be a success?' Alice asked.

'Oh no. It couldn't be. But you see, provincial audiences have no taste. They will think that because a thing has succeeded in London it must be good. And they will see Mr Lonsdale' – Mr Lonsdale was a well-dressed young man whose wardrobe was thought to be the reason for his employment on the tour – 'and be quite won over. But you must not think me cynical, dear,' she said, seeing her companion's lowered face. 'It is just that . . . Why, I once saw Mr Evans and his wife, that the *Era* makes so much of, doting on each other in *We Two*, and within three minutes of coming off he had thrown an inkwell at her.'

'And where is Bolton?' Alice wondered.

'Oh, a dreadful place in the north. And filthy, too. Mark my words, London dirt is nothing to the dirt you will see in Lancashire.'

If these strictures were intended to curb Alice's enthusiasm, they had quite the opposite effect. For all her want of experience she could see that Miss Jeffries's complaints were accurate: that Mr Lonsdale had nothing to recommend him but his starched shirt-front, and that Mrs Baker was a sour old woman who could scarcely remember her lines. Still, though, there was something about the atmosphere that, to her, transcended these defects. At the final rehearsal Mr Carmody and a cabman dragged a trunk of ancient costumes up the stairs and they dressed themselves in character for the first time. Pulling the shabby gown assigned to her over her head, she felt an inexpressible thrill of satisfaction.

Something of this excitement conveyed itself to Mr Armitage. 'That will do very nicely, Miss Hanson,' he said affably. 'Very nicely indeed.'

It was by now the Wednesday of the week preceding the tour. The company would depart on the Sunday. Still she had made no arrangement for the child. For this oversight she was rebuked by Miss Jeffries and Mrs Gaffney. 'I'm sure he will come to no harm,' said Miss Jeffries. 'We shall be gone only four weeks. Bolton, and after that Manchester, Mr Armitage said, and possibly Liverpool.' Mrs Gaffney was more direct. 'You must put him out, mum, and look to yourself,' she advised – Mrs Gaffney had taken to calling Alice 'mum' after a payment of three pounds to secure the room during her absence. 'I can't see to him and that Miss Fotherington, though she means well, would drown him in the bath as soon as look at him, as you well know. No, you must put him out.'

This advice had its effect. Nothing could be easier, Alice was told, than the boarding out of a child. All over London maternally minded women stood ready to feed him, clothe him and attend to his wants. In the end, she set out late on the Friday afternoon. The address was in Wandsworth, a very poor part of Wandsworth to judge from its unswept pavements and the hordes of ragged children who swarmed over them. The house stood on its own, on the edge of a muddy 'green', in the shadow of a coal yard. A fat woman with a pendulous underlip opened the door.

'Are you Mrs Burgess?'

'That's so.' Her eye fell on the bundle at Alice's side. 'What can I do for you?'

Evidence of Mrs Burgess's professional calling lay everywhere to hand. Beside her, where the vestibule opened into a low-ceilinged parlour, two children sat silently in infant high chairs. A third crawled on the floor beneath them.

'I should like – that is, I wish to board out my baby.'

"Ow long?'

'Three weeks. Four weeks. It is not quite certain.'

'Well, you can leave him here, mum, if you've a mind.' She could see that Alice's gaze was fixed on the inner room, into which a bull-mastiff now ran snapping. 'This is a good 'ouse, mum, with every care taken. Where shall you be?'

'I am travelling in the north. That is, in a play. But you could write and tell me, if . . .'

'Usually, mum, I like my babbys' mothers to be in London. But I dare say an exception could be made. 'Ow much were you thinking of paying?'

'I was told – fifteen shillings.'

'Was you now? Well, I'm not one of the grasping ones. 'Ow much might you be earning in this play of yours? I usually takes half.'

'Thirty shillings a week,' Alice lied.

'Fifteen shillings it is, then. And extra if the doctor has to be called.'

And so the business was done and Alice looked out for herself.

She stood on the station platform, watching the people pass by around her. A dense gust of steam, sprung from one of the waiting engines, enveloped her head and shoulders; harsh, mechanical clanging sounded in her ears; a porter, hastening past with a loaded trolley, brushed roughly against her arm; yet none of these assaults broke the spell of her reverie. She was lost in the spectacle unfolding before her and its paraphernalia – a pile of cabin trunks, left haphazardly by the iron barrier, a file of schoolboys in scarlet caps and blazers in the care of a thin, uneasy man in a bowler hat, an old gentleman in an invalid's carriage with a quilt over his knees slowly perambulating the line of shops and refreshment booths. Beyond the tessellations of glass and metal, white birds soared into the pale air. Nearer at hand there were timetables painted on black boards bearing the names of places she remembered from a map pulled out from the litter of Mrs Gaffney's parlour: Derby and Birmingham, Chester and Holyhead, Liverpool and Manchester, and she spoke the words silently to herself, while another jet of steam rolled up from the waiting engine and noisily obliterated the scene around her, so that only the orange gaslights – fiery but somehow mournful – burned through the murk.

Alice stood there a few moments longer, travelling bag pushed up against her feet, with the people surging about her and the noise of the platform resounding in her ears, when a hand plucked insistently at her sleeve.

'My dear. There was a porter shouting at you just now to clear his way and I declare you did not hear him.'

Miss Jeffries was very nattily got up in a merino travelling jacket and a hat on to whose brim half a dozen red rosettes had been carefully stitched. Seeing Alice's glance, she said, 'I know what you are thinking, dear, but it is borrowed from my cousin, who is always pressing her cast-offs on me, and for once I did not trouble to decline. After all, it is not every day one goes on tour. But it is nearly a quarter to. We must find our train.'

The train was already drawn up alongside its platform. A slip of paper, stuck into the window of one of the third-class carriages, read: *Cast of Ada's No Chicken*. Here they found the remainder of Mr Armitage's company, very pale and silent, with their baggage drawn up under their feet or balanced precariously on the overhead racks. Mr Lonsdale, whose ankles were encased in a pair of spats, was reading the previous day's copy of the *Morning Post*. Mrs Baker was bidding farewell to her married daughter, who could not have been less than forty years of age. Mr Thatcher sat rather apart from the others, on the end of his bench, with the look of a man who does not care to explain the origins of the red welt that has appeared on the side of his face.

'Where is Mr Armitage?' Miss Jeffries wondered, her gaze roving around the carriage to take in both Mr Lonsdale's elegant cases, Mrs Baker's battered portmanteau and the fact that Mr Thatcher appeared to have no luggage at all. 'We cannot go without Mr Armitage.'

It transpired that Mr Armitage was making his own arrangements. Whereupon the atmosphere relaxed, people brought out flasks of tea and hot coffee or penny buns bought on the station concourse, and a certain amount of general conversation began.

Mr Lonsdale said that he had been instructed by Mr Armitage to take especial pains with his wardrobe and he had done his best. That he had brought a dress suit, a morning coat and a number of waistcoats, that he hoped that this would do and that he had an uncle living in Lancashire who hoped to attend one of the performances.

Mrs Baker said that this was the worst company by which she had ever been engaged. She meant no offence to anyone, but it was hard that a woman who had played Juliet, and been complimented by Mr Tree, should be reduced to this.

Mr Thatcher said that the Bolton lodgings, of which he had much experience, were the worst there were, and the most expensive, that he would see the week out, but after that he doubted if he could stand it.

'But my dear,' Mrs Baker said to Miss Jeffries, thinking perhaps that she had gone too far in her gloom, 'you must allow me to tell you that that is a very pretty hat.'

Alice sat by the door, watching the landscape change and unravel beneath her. Her mind hummed with excitement. Had Mr Thatcher suggested that the Bolton lodgings were alive with poisonous snakes, she would not have listened to him. The wide meadows and parks gave way to rough moorland, with high crags visible in the distance. From time to time they stopped at stations and she examined the white English faces drawn up on the platforms – men in Sunday suits with stiff collars and flat caps, women in shabby finery – but they were remote from her, altogether detached from the solitary inner world she now inhabited: the train lurching its way into the fog, her travelling bag rattling in the rack above her, steam blown sharply back by the wind beyond the window, and the sound, imperfectly concealed by whispering, of Mr Thatcher asking Mr Lonsdale if he could lend him a sovereign. Beyond the moors the light glinted off church spires dotted about a valley, then the land rose once more and it began to rain.

'November,' Mrs Baker pronounced. 'The worst month of all to take a touring company to a provincial town.'

The theatre was in a poor part of the town, set amid a maze of dismal streets, each with a public house on its farthermost corner. However, it was thought that the populace – these were millworkers and employees of a factory that belched smoke into the surrounding sky – might be susceptible to advertising, so a banner had been hung from the theatre's upper storey and a brass band hired to patrol the nearby thoroughfares. Mr Armitage, who had exchanged his blue frock-coat for a dark suit, stood in the foyer shaking hands with the manager, his operatives, the advertising agent, the cast and indeed anyone who wanted their hand to be shaken. There was a dissenting chapel thirty yards away, but it was not thought that this would substantially lessen their receipts.

Alice and Miss Jeffries had established themselves in lodgings a few streets away. These Miss Jeffries had unexpectedly approved, on the strength of a joint of meat which, taken from the supper table on the Sunday night, had reappeared almost unmolested at the Monday lunch hour. 'The professional landladies always steal, dear,' she explained. 'I dare say this one has taken pity on us.' The opening performance was at seven on the Monday night. 'My dear,' Miss Jeffries said, after they had lunched off the unmolested joint, 'I am terrible at times like these. Let us go for a walk.' And so they walked around Bolton, which was not very interesting, put their heads in at the door of the museum and took them out again, admired the spectacle of the mill girls returning from work and in this way arrived at the theatre at about a quarter to six. In the green room all was confusion. Mr Lonsdale sat whey-faced in his dress suit with his copy of the script open before him repeating lines of dialogue with a variety of intonations. Mrs Baker was recruiting herself with what she said was peppermint cordial. Mr Thatcher had taken a chair in the furthest corner of the room and was making calculations with a pencil on the back of an envelope. Alice found that the various elements of this tableau – stagehands running back and forth with pieces of scenery, the costumier mixing up a pot of rouge with a spoon, Mr Thatcher emerging from his cubicle with a pair of enormous false eyebrows, like black caterpillars – combined to produce a bewildering blur. The lines that she had to say – and there were a dozen of them – swam in her head, sometimes perfectly formed, at other times altogether beyond her grasp. There was an aperture in the green room's door, cunningly designed so that those inside it could view a portion of the stage and the tiers of seating beyond. Looking out, she saw that about half the theatre was full. In the front sat a few gentlefolk, smartly dressed and with programmes in their hands. Behind them the working men and their wives were congregated noisily in the cheaper seats. All this reduced her to a state of near-paralysis. What if she should lose her place, forget what she had to say and disgrace herself? It was here, by the spyhole, that Mrs Baker, her face carmined up like a pantomime dame's, found her as Mr Armitage, very confident now, with a white carnation stuck in the buttonhole of his inky suit, strode on to the stage to commend the evening's entertainment to the audience.

'Now, my dear, you must not take on,' Mrs Baker said. 'And be thankful this is not a London audience. You'll find that the people here want to be entertained. Why, I dare say if Mr Thatcher lost his lines and danced a jig they would find it funny.'

The play had begun: Mr Lonsdale and another man were amiably conversing in a representation of a suburban garden, while Mrs Baker, in the role of Ada's mother, sat roguishly on a reclining chair pretending to read a book. Alice saw that what Mrs Baker had said was true, that the majority of their audience had come merely to be amused and entertained. When Lonsdale pronounced a joke that did not seem to be funny, and so feebly that whatever humour remained in it was still further extinguished, he was met with a fusillade of laughter. This comforted her and she realised she would have to be very bad not to meet with the same treatment, but it also disappointed her, for a part of her had assumed that a theatregoer could tell good acting from bad. These thoughts were banished from her mind by the sight of Mr Armitage waving her to the doorway that led to the side of the stage and the sound of Lonsdale's voice speaking the words that she recognised as her cue, and in what seemed an instant she found herself on stage. Lonsdale flung her a line and she returned it, making sure as she did so that she moved to the back of the stage where, in a moment or two, there was a piece of business that required the deployment of some glasses and a water jug. Then Mrs Baker rose up with exaggerated movements from her chair and asked her a question: this she answered. Hers was a vestigial part – that of a governess, employed as go-between twixt Ada and her admirers – but it allowed for an amusing remark or two. One of these, now directed in the region of Mr Lonsdale's satin waistcoat, produced a ripple of laughter from the margin of the cheaper seats. Hearing it, her eyes gleamed. She was transfixed by the pleasure it gave her. It seemed to her that nothing could be so gratifying as that ripple. She tried another line, not comical in itself, but allowing for certain resonances in the manner of its delivery, and was disappointed when it fell flat, though Mr Lonsdale and Mrs Baker watched her in dumb approval.

By the final scene, in which she was only an interested spectator, Alice found that she had acquired a sense of perspective and was, as the closing speeches rose and fell, able to make certain judgments regarding the skill of her fellow actors. Lonsdale she thought mediocre in the extreme: not even his dress suit could redeem his missed cues and the manifest nervousness of his delivery. But what startled her was the feebleness of Miss Jeffries's performance. She spoke her lines woodenly and, in a scene expressly designed to allow Mrs Baker a volley of humorous sallies, irritated that lady by muddling the arrangement of her responses.

'That went very nicely, Miss Hanson,' Mr Armitage remarked to her as she returned to the dressing rooms after the performance, 'very nicely indeed', and she took the compliment – one that Mr Armitage would have offered to any member of his cast – and treasured it.

On the next morning the local newspaper printed a notice. As this organ was bound to support theatrical performances on account of the advertising revenue they produced, its effusiveness could perhaps be discounted.

But there was one genuine encomium. 'Among the minor parts,' Alice read, 'Miss Alice Hanson sustained the role of "Gretchen" the governess with admirable humour and spirit.'

'Well, that is very nice,' Miss Jeffries remarked, to whom this eulogy was read as they sat over breakfast. 'What does it say about me?'

'It does not say anything,' Alice said, who could not very well lie in such circumstances.

'How odd. Still,' said Miss Jeffries, with a faint note of asperity in her voice, 'it means nothing. I happen to know that Mr Anderson, the advertising manager, writes all the notices anyhow, and there is no merit in being praised by him.'

The opening performance was adjudged to have been a success. Not an unqualified success, perhaps, but – still. Two and hundred fifty tickets had apparently been sold and on the strength of this figure Mr Armitage treated the gentlemen of the cast to a glass of wine in a private room of his hotel.

Alas, how many times is a dramatic critic forced to insist that the second night of a performance in no way resembles the triumphant heights of the first? Tuesday was a decline. Mrs Baker had developed a streaming cold and coughed her way through her lines. Miss Jeffries missed an entrance and Mr Lonsdale, whose uncle occupied a seat in the dress circle, was in such a paroxysm of nervous fear that he stumbled headlong over Mrs Baker's reclining chair. All this, and other defects besides, Mr Armitage noted from his vantage point in the wings. 'Miss Hanson,' he enquired very suavely, meeting Alice at the green room door a few minutes after the performance had ended, 'I wonder if I might have a word with you?'

Fearing that the manager intended to upbraid her, Alice answered him with a look of deep misgiving. 'Pray don't be alarmed, Miss Hanson,' Mr Armitage went on. 'I have no fault to find. Quite the reverse. But the part of Laura Delane that Miss Jeffries plays. How long would it take you, do you imagine, to get the words?'

'An hour or two, I should think,' Alice said, mystified as to the purpose of the question. 'I all but know them.'

'Do you think that you could be word perfect by tomorrow's rehearsal?' Seeing her look of consternation, he went on, 'Naturally, I shall talk to Miss Jeffries.'

'I am sure that I could.'

'Well, let us consider it settled,' Mr Armitage said.

Miss Jeffries did not return to their lodging house until a late hour. When, finally, at about midnight she put her head in at the door of the attic bedroom – Mrs Baker was half asleep, and Alice lay gloomily awake beneath the half-extinguished lamp – she began immediately to abuse her. 'Alice, it is very ill-natured of you, taking another girl's part without so much as a by-your-leave. It is only that Mr Armitage has such a down on me. Why did you not tell him that you wouldn't do it?'

'Why should I do that?' Alice wondered. 'Mr Armitage is the manager. He can say what he likes.'

Miss Jeffries caught the note of remonstrance in her voice. 'Well, you are a nasty, sneaking thing. If this were a respectable company, no one would speak to you. You must go to Mr Armitage and tell him you have changed your mind.'

'I shall do no such thing,' Alice said. 'Indeed, I am very sorry, but why should I not do it if Mr Armitage says I can?'

'Why shouldn't she?' said Mrs Baker, rising up from the bedclothes and, in her unpainted state, presenting a very sorry sight to the world. 'As for you' – this to Miss Jeffries – 'leave her alone. It will be a pleasure to have a girl that can act as Laura Delane rather than a wooden-headed ninny.'

It was too much for Miss Jeffries, who burst into tears. 'It is all my fault,' she sobbed. 'Mr Armitage is quite right to ask you to change with me. I am so dreadful that Gretchen is all I am good for.'

'You are not dreadful,' Alice said. 'I wish this need not have happened.'

'I am very sorry,' said Miss Jeffries with awful humility. 'But it is hard on a girl.'

But Alice's triumph was short-lived. 'Oh dear,' Miss Jeffries whispered, as they met in the wings prior to the raising of the curtain, 'Mr Thatcher has taken more than is good for him. It is all he can do to rise from his chair. Mr Armitage thinks he may have to take the part himself.' It seemed Miss Jeffries spoke the truth. Mr Thatcher's role was fulfilled by Mr Armitage reading from a script, to the great amusement of the audience.

At Saturday lunchtime the cast were bidden to attend the theatre to prepare for the afternoon's matinée performance and collect their wages. 'And not before time,' observed Miss Jeffries, who had regained her old lightness of spirit, as they made their way through the windy streets, 'for I have but ninepence left in the world.' One o'clock came and then one-fifteen and one-thirty, but there was no sign of Mr Armitage. The actors stood about with long faces, discussing possible lines of enquiry – and discounting Mr Carmody's assurances that all would be well. The theatre manager confirmed that Mr Armitage's percentage of the profits had been remitted to him the evening before. Lonsdale, calling at his hotel, discovered what he feared – that the man had left Bolton on an early train. The matinée was cancelled and the banner taken down, and the members of the cast applied themselves to the question of how one settles a lodging-house bill with money that has vanished into the ether, and a pawnshop twenty yards down the street from the theatre, which had got wind of the event, opened its doors to receive the custom of a new clientele.

9

The Selling of Hogpen

1925
'D'you know who that chap there is?' my uncle asked.

'The one who just came in to bat?'

'No, not him. The one standing a bit to the right. Next to – next to the blessed umpire. With the I Zingari tie.'

I didn't like to admit that I could not identify an I Zingari tie. 'The tall one with the eyeglass?'

'That's the feller,' said my uncle a touch peevishly. 'Now, that is the Honourable Gerald Claridge, Viscount Parmenter's boy.'

Fifty yards away across the wide emerald lawn the cricketers were rearranging themselves. The two batsmen – one tall, the other disproportionately short – marched down the wicket to confer. The Honourable Gerald Claridge, Viscount Parmenter's boy, caught the ball that one of the other players had tossed to him and began picking deviously at its seam. Beyond the glare of sunlight burning off the surface of the lake, the towers and crenellations of the house stretched away into the distance. In a tent erected on the margin of the lawn a brass band was playing military music rather more loudly than was warranted by the languor of the afternoon.

'Dratted noise,' my uncle said, even more peevishly. He had been out of sorts since lunch (eaten in the tent amid a throng of Kentish gentry), delving into the wicker hamper to select delicacies he later rejected, striking up conversations with the other spectators – there were about fifty of us ranged around the ropes – making little excursions from the cane chairs only to turn disconsolately back.

'They do say,' said my uncle, taking up a pair of field glasses from his lap and training them on the Honourable Gerald Claridge as he came in to bowl, 'that he's booked to marry Lady Mersea's eldest, Lavinia – tall girl with spots that we met at Mrs Harry Brown's.'

There was something wonderfully unselfconscious about my uncle as he arranged these fragments of Mayfair lore, which the dinner table conversations of the past fortnight had steered into his grasp. It was a mark of his genius – and I do not use the term lightly – that he had been able to acclimatise himself so rapidly to the environment in which, for two or three years now and with varying degrees of acceleration, he had basked. There were plenty of people like my uncle in the world in which we now found ourselves – fat little men with unexpected fortunes made in the war – but they lacked his expertise, his self-assurance. Occasionally my uncle entertained his fellow arrivistes. 'Take young Sandilands,' he would say, 'that made such a packet selling butter to the navy. Nice feller, but he don't know a good suit from a bad 'un. Just goes to Savile Row and plonks his money down. And the worst of it is he don't realise these things matter.' My uncle's suits were made by a deferential Jew in Hoxton.

There was no sign of Sandilands, or of anyone remotely like him, here at Lytton Grange to watch the Gentlemen of Kent play – a 'parliamentary select'? An authors' XL? J. C. Squire's Invalids? Lytton Grange is gone now. It was all smashed up in the Slump and turned into a girls' school, but in those days it was the kind of place my uncle liked to be seen at. We were living at Richmond then, in the first of those big houses that my uncle bought near rivers or inland from the sea, but a part of him hankered after country estates, rolling parklands falling away into the Sussex forest, a terrace with views over the Hampshire downs. Here at Lytton Grange he took no interest in his host's possessions – the Dürer etching in the great hall, the diamond window with a royal signature scratched into the pane – his attitude was that of a surveyor measuring up the number of acres, the volume of the lake and the extent of the rose garden.

'Zinoviev,' he said now, unexpectedly. I saw that he had set down the field glasses and picked up a copy of the *Morning Post*. 'Never believed a word of it. Baldwin said the same. Lot of nonsense. *Noospaper* people . . .' he went on vaguely. I had spent enough time in my uncle's company – enough time, that is, in this new orbit of our lives – to know that a secret lay round the corner, that his decision – taken at breakfast that morning – to motor down to Kent had nothing to do with a charity cricket match or the splendours of Lytton Grange. I do not mean that he never confided in me, for he was always vouchsafing little pieces of information that he thought I might find amusing or instructive, merely that his way of making these confidences was essentially secretive, conducted by means of hints and incremental revelations whose ultimate design I could never see in advance.

'Here, Ralph,' he said now, taking up the field glasses and directing them not at the cricket square but in the region of the tent. 'S'pose you had a quarter of a million pounds. How would you lay it out?'

I was used to questions of this kind. They were rarely as fanciful as they sounded. 'I don't know. It would depend how the money was tied up.'

'Don't mean property or "'vestments",' my uncle said hastily. He was still peering into the field glasses. 'Cash in the bank.'

'That's different,' I said. 'I'd go in for bullion. There's a lot of money to be made in bullion.'

'American eagles. *Krooger*ands,' said my uncle. I could not tell whether he approved this sentiment or not. 'I know . . .' As I waited for him to explain his interest in what I might do with a quarter of a million pounds, in the Honourable Gerald Claridge and even in the I Zingari tie, my uncle raised himself up suddenly from the cane-bottomed chair, field glasses clutched in the outstretched fingers of his left hand, and executed a little dance of triumph. 'Now that's a sight to see,' he said, resuming his seat. 'Doosid sight more interestin' than a lot of chaps in white flannels playing . . . *cricket.*'

I glanced over in the direction of the tent. Towards us, picking her way determinedly through an obstacle course of guy-ropes and manservants bearing trays of glasses, came a girl of perhaps nineteen or twenty with very fair shingled hair wearing one of the new hogpen frocks. I immediately saw the point of my uncle's exultation. The first range of hogpen wear had sold very well, but it had not sold to the kind of people whose society my uncle frequented, who thought it mass-produced, lurid and vulgar.

'Look at that, will you?' my uncle shouted again. 'I told that chap at – that blessed magazine – *Vogue* he ought to think of it and I'll tell him again.'

A year ago, I knew, my uncle would have rushed over and engaged the girl in conversation, possibly even kissed her hand. Experience had made him wary. Now he was content to give her an encouraging wave as she came into view beyond the row of cane chairs, leaving me to drop my head over the wicker basket, for the girl, as I now saw, was Constance, whom I had no wish to meet just at this moment and certainly not with my uncle as he luxuriated in his triumph. As I searched among the parcels of game pie and bunched asparagus, I thought again about the quarter of a million pounds. Was he referring to his own fortune? It was quite possible. He had a habit at this time of leaving small pieces of paper around the house on which columns of figures were set down in his abstruse, untidy hand. I had found one only the other day.

Craven H	c.25,000
Secs	100,000
Braz Cons def	17,000
W.L.	30,000
Octs D.L.G.	2,500

Craven H was the place at Richmond. *Secs* must have meant securities. I had an idea that *Braz Cons def* stood for Brazilian Consolidated Deferred, an exotic South American stock predicated on the back of certain notional railway lines, in which my uncle was known to have dabbled. *W.L.*, a trawl through a stockbroker's directory suggested, was War Loans, but who, or what, was *Octs D.L.G.* and his, or its, 2,500 and was the figure a sum of money or a number of shares?

'That girl ought to mannequin,' my uncle pronounced. 'Why, I'd give her five guineas a day just to walk up and down Bond Street wearing that frock.'

Looking up from the hamper I saw that Constance was safely out of range.

'She might be glad of the money,' I said and my uncle laughed, not knowing that this was, in fact, the truth.

When I look back on the selling of hogpen, on which we were now wholeheartedly embarked, it is impossible for me not to appreciate the importance of that summer day in 1925 at Lytton Grange, with the Honourable Gerald Claridge stepping diffidently up to the wicket and the brass band playing 'Garryowen' in the billowing tent. Impossible, too, not to believe that the bridge which took us out of the old world that we had known in the Intwood Road and into the troubling landscapes beyond was long since crossed, that we had gone so far into this bright new horizon that there could be no hope of ever turning back, even had we wanted to. Not long before the first hogpen patent was proved – we were living in Southfields then, preparatory to our first great assault on the textile manufactories of the north-west – my uncle built a bonfire in the back garden and, not without ceremony, re-emerging every so often from the house with additional pieces of firewood, burned the contents of all but one of the six storage boxes that he had brought with him from Norwich. It was a kind of ritual transformation, like an animal sloughing off its skin and replacing it with another. Two years later it was as if the old hide had never existed. He knew Atry by this time, had attended conferences at Albion Towers, the big house outside Basingstoke, and taken a turn at the wheel of the *Peradventure* as she tacked up the Solent – all those names that are now so much a part of the folklore of our time but in those days went unknown and unreported.

As for hogpen itself, the romance of its first extraction rather escapes me, so emphatically was it bound up in the wider transformation of our lives. I confess now to a mild regret at this oversight, this absence from the laboratories at crucial points in the substance's application, and yet I see that even to my uncle, who had after all invented it, it was no more than a means to an end. I learn now from Maradick's *Hogpen: The Story of a Great Idea* that my uncle established his first laboratory at the Southfields site in the summer of 1922, and that the dye was first applied to cotton garments six months later and to silk and the more rarefied fabrics six months after that, that its first great taking up by the press came when the Duchess of Sutherland wore a dress patterned with it at a ball at her house in the winter of 1923, but all this is less concrete to me than the view of the Southfields house from the road, with its double-fronted windows and the laburnum hedge threatening altogether to shut it off from view, which seemed to me a very grand and forbidding place, and entirely redolent of the world into which we had miraculously been plunged.

It was mid-afternoon by now and the cricketers were trooping off to tea. High above the lake white birds sailed back and forth like scraps of paper flung by the wind. The noise of the brass band had been replaced by a gramophone playing 'Show Me the Way to Go Home'. Still clutching the field glasses in the fingers of his left hand, my uncle had begun to trample the breeze-blown pages of the *Morning Post* under his foot. 'Tired of all this,' he said. 'Tired of it.' The hint of wind raised his straw hat an inch or so on his head and he jerked it angrily back into place. 'Let's take a bit of a stroll.'

And so we set off around the margin of the empty cricket field, past an old gentleman being wheeled in an invalid carriage to whom my uncle rather knowingly tipped his hat, to the point at which the lakeside joined up with the outer limits of a shrubbery. Here, confirming my suspicion that he knew more about Lytton Grange than he had let on, had been here before and was engaged on some secret manoeuvre entirely beyond my understanding, my uncle made a sudden feint into the bushes and beckoned me to follow him along a hidden pathway. In those days, of which this particular day amid the brass bands and the promenading old gentlemen in invalid carriages was by no means an exception, I was always surveying my uncle as he went about his business, comparing him to the person he had been and trying to adduce morals from the comparison, but I don't think I gained very much from this prodigal expenditure of mental labour. Looking at him, as he foraged in the shrubbery, straw hat low down on his forehead, shirt cuffs descending on the backs of his pudgy hands, I saw now that his success – prosperity – celebrity – had exaggerated certain aspects of his character that had hitherto lain dormant, taken his irritability and turned it into bad temper, taken his preoccupied air and turned it into calculation, taken his caution and turned it into secretiveness. His schemes took deeper root in his imagination and grew more gargantuan still. In the past year he had been instrumental in a plan to construct the world's first jet engine, joined a consortium intending to pitch an electrical generator beneath Niagara, given a man money to perfect a patent cigar humidor and underwritten an excursion to the Matu Grosso in search of a lost Amazonian city.

'Nothing like keepin' your name before the public, Ralph,' he remarked once at about this time.

As for hogpen, one saw it everywhere. The new clothing dyes had been on the market six months. It was used for furnishings: house fronts had been painted in it: a fusilier regiment had adopted it for its dress uniforms. It had been synthesised into a food colouring, so that one saw hogpen water ices and hogpen boiled sweets. It was much admired by the labouring classes, with their love of cheap finery – passing back-to-back gardens in a poor district one grew used to washing lines in which profusions of hogpen aprons and hogpen handkerchiefs gaudily contended. Moralists rather deplored it – the stridency of its hues was thought to encourage licentiousness and there was something called a 'hogpen smile'.

Its total export value to the United Kingdom in the period 1923–5 had been estimated at two and three-quarter million pounds.

The path through the shrubbery led into a kitchen garden where rows of neatly tilled cabbages lay under netting, surveyed by a scarecrow in a suit of plus-fours. Beyond this, on the farther side of a screen of small trees, we came upon a lawn that descended gently towards the house. Here, dressed in linen suits appropriate to the season, three men were playing croquet. Knowing that my uncle had engineered this discovery, that it was part of some grander design he had not yet confided to me, I began to move downhill through the trees, but he seized my wrist. 'Hang on,' he said. 'Know who those chaps are?'

'Never seen them before.'

My uncle extracted a capacious bandana handkerchief from his trouser pocket and began to dab at his forehead with it. 'Thought you didn't. Hadn't come across them myself until a month since. Atry knows them, though.' At this stage Atry was the yardstick by which our commercial ventures were judged.

'What does Atry say about them, then?'

'What does Atry say?' My uncle was launched on another of his roles now, the *affairé* City man who sees all, knows everything and forgives nothing. Head bowed amid the bracken, the clack of the croquet balls resounding in his ears, my uncle relayed to me what Atry had said, together with a few inspired garnishes of his own devising. What he said has remained in my head as a sample of the epochal intelligence gathering of which he was capable.

'... The tall one with the moustache is Lord Parmenter. Owns that place up in Lincolnshire. There's no entail and he came a cropper on some railway shares not long back, so I don't suppose the Honourable Gerald'll inherit. Offered me a cigar once, he did, at a dinner. Lord, the airs those fellows give themselves, Ralph ... The little chap is Guy Keach. Made a mint of money out of the war, they say, something about selling old machinery he'd bought *off* the army in 1913 *back* to the army in 1915, I dunno ... Got a bad cough though, Ralph, *such* a bad cough. Went all the way to Madeira last winter thinking to cure it and came back with it just the same ... No point in owning three houses and a stable at Noomarket if you ain't well, Ralph. Always been civil to me, though, when we've 'ad dinner and such ... Lady Desborough speaks very 'ighly of him ... Other one is Sir Basil Ambrose. You've heard of him surely? Won the MC at Vimy Ridge and got in as a Unionist in 1918, though I hear he's a Liberal now ... Stood bail for Mrs Meyrick the other week, which his wife can't have liked, but fair play to him, I say ...'

I glanced beyond the trees to the croquet lawn, where the three middle-aged men strode back and forth. They seemed thoroughly innocuous to me, but I could see that for my uncle the scene was invested with an enormous emotional significance. We were through the trees now, my uncle's hand locked fast on my shoulder, and encroaching on the warm aromatic grass where the three croquet players, mallets raised – Sir Basil had one foot delicately poised on a hoop – waited to receive us, in a silence broken only by my uncle's low rumble of introduction.

'My Lord . . . Sir Basil . . . Mr Keach . . . Delighted . . . Agreeable day.'

And so began one of those conversations that were so characteristic of the world in which we now found ourselves, and of the first days of the selling of hogpen, in which little was said, but a great deal implied, and even more, perhaps, inferred, where a shaken head might signify agreement or a smile a flat refusal. My uncle complimented Lord Parmenter on his son's cricketing skills. Lord Parmenter's look of horror I diagnosed as faint amusement. Mr Keach coughed his cough – a cough such as you never heard, that nearly doubled him up with its ferocity. Sir Basil stood looking at the shining surface of his brown Oxfords as they rested on the croquet lawn. There was talk of Atry: terribly oblique and desultory talk it was. Lord Parmenter had seen him somewhere. Mr Keach hadn't seen him but had seen his wife (a gust of subdued laughter about Atry's wife!). Sir Basil, still inspecting the toecaps of his brown Oxfords, said that Atry had better get out of Amalgamated if he knew what was good for him. Lord Parmenter said that Atry was a Society man these days, wasn't he? (Another gust of subdued laughter about Atry the Society man!) And all the while my uncle making little interjections and whinnies of assent, at one moment seizing Lord Parmenter's croquet mallet the better to make some point or other, and standing solicitously by while Mr Keach coughed his cough and the great house loomed above us, and the white birds sailed past over the lofty terrace.

There was no place for memory in this world of bright sheens and incremental lustres, where everything merged into a single, flaring surface painted over with hogpen's authenticating gloss. The past – what there was of it – was altogether gathered up in the dazzling slipstream of the present. I was twenty then – sometimes charmed by my uncle, sometimes hugely irritated by him, and rather a dandy. I had a tailcoat from Lesley and Roberts in Hanover Square, a waistcoat by Messrs Hawes and Curtis of the Piccadilly Arcade, a silk hat that had come from Lock in St James's, a gold cigarette case bought at Asprey's in Bond Street and, or so I now think, not enough curiosity about the world around me. My uncle's vertiginous ascent into the world of commerce had mesmerised me to the point of stupor and the questions I should have asked him about the things he did stayed unspoken in my head. The rocket's arc, as it soared unhindered into the night sky, seemed limitless. That it might one day descend barely occurred to me.

Leaving the croquet lawn, and lured by the splash of colour slowly receding on the shrubbery's edge, I set off round the southern corner of the house, where an ornamental garden, dotted about with box firs and intricately patterned mosaics led down to a ha-ha, whose descent was marked by a couple of porphyry urns. Here, as I had expected, Constance lay in wait, leaning against one of the urns and smoking a cigarette. When she saw me she gave a little skip of mock surprise and sat down cross-legged on the grass.

'I didn't think you were coming.'

'I didn't think so either. But then Reggie said he'd motor me down.'

'I thought you said Reggie had gone back to Catterick.'

'Apparently the regiment isn't going to Burma for another month and they don't need him just yet. So of course the poor darling desperately needs cheering up.'

She was a sulky, languid girl of about my age, whose sulkiness and languor I found both irresistible and impossible to deal with. Reggie St Cloud, who so desperately needed cheering up, was a subaltern in a line regiment hitherto supposed to be safely out of the country.

Constance went on, 'Don't think I'm being *fantastically* mercenary, but there really is a *teeny* favour you could do for me.'

'What's that?'

'You always sound so *cross* whenever I mention Reggie and he's really just the sweetest pet . . . But you know this theatrical evening that Lavinia Sutherland's giving?'

It was a mark of Constance's upbringing that she said 'Lavinia' rather than giving the Duchess of Sutherland her full title.

'I think we had a card.'

'Yes, well, I thought you might rather like it if I came with you.'

'Doesn't Reggie want to go?'

'*Darling!* As if Lavinia would have him in the house . . . Apparently there's terribly bad blood over something his father said to her once . . . Normally, of course, one would just turn up, but they say Lavinia's got this thing about gatecrashers, and it's so tedious to arrive at a place and find that the servants won't let you in.'

I was always having conversations of this sort with Constance, who was, as she once put it, 'not such a tremendous gold-digger as some of them, darling', but, equally, made no bones about the fact that her interest in me stemmed from the position that my uncle occupied in the world. By birth she was an earl's granddaughter, but the particular branch of the family to which she belonged had lost its money. She lived in a flat in Chelsea and sometimes worked in a milliner's shop.

'I like your dress,' I said.

'Reggie said it reminded him of one of his charwoman's aprons.'

'My uncle said he'd pay you five guineas a week to walk up and down Bond Street in it.'

'Well, I wish he would, darling. After all, a girl's got to eat. No, you're *not* to do that, someone might come . . .' There was something else animating her, I saw, that had nothing to do with the possibility that we might be caught. 'I say,' she said, taking up a more secure vantage point behind one of the urns. 'Your uncle's awfully thick with Guy Keach and Basil Ambrose, isn't he?'

'They're all over on the croquet lawn just now. Why don't you come and say hello?'

'Basil Ambrose, darling? He once offered to stand me a weekend at Le Touquet and it was the most frightful disaster.' Constance smoothed down the hem of her dress with long, spatulate fingers. 'I've lived like a Quaker practically ever since. No, Reggie said he'd heard they were all madly keen on starting some kind of consortium – you know, so they could go about raising money in the City.'

I listened to this with interest. Constance was a shrewd girl, but you could never believe everything she told you.

'How would Reggie know anything about it?'

'Oh darling, he may not be terribly bright, but his brother Walter – you know that man with the Toc H tie and a face like a horse we met at the Huntercombes? – works at Grievesons, and someone told Walter and Walter told Reggie.'

In the distance, towards the lake, the brass band had started playing again. Somewhere above our heads, the drone of its rackety engine moving in counterpoint, a light aeroplane was passing above the uppermost turrets of the house with painful slowness. If it did not alter course, it would be in grave danger of hitting one of the chimney stacks. It was entirely characteristic of my uncle to have told me nothing about the consortium. That much was to be expected. He had a habit of procrastinating over business decisions until some rumour broke out from the City and put me on his trail. There had been several other revelations of this kind. But the news that my uncle might be combining with the confraternity of the croquet lawn stirred all kinds of uncertainties. Chief among them was the fact that although hogpen was doing very well, and although the export value of the dyes in the past two years amounted to two and three-quarter million pounds, the capital that had financed this progress was not, by and large, my uncle's. About three-quarters of the debt that he had accumulated over that time belonged to Atry, the financier. What would happen if, during the negotiations, Atry decided to call in that debt, use it to increase his stake in my uncle's operations or sell it on to someone else? And how much of this was known to the trio of croquet players? Several things clearly had to be done. The first was to get more information out of Constance, without alerting her to the seriousness of what lay at stake.

'Where's Reggie just at the moment?'

'Darling, I thought you simply loathed the sight of him . . . I think he said he was going over to Caterham to look up a chum at Staff College.'

Above our heads the light aeroplane continued to pass slowly by. There was a good chance now that it would not hit the chimney stack after all. It would be unwise to be too direct with Constance who, as she frequently put it, had been very strictly brought up.

'If I took you to the Duchess of Sutherland's,' I said, 'would you wear this dress?'

'I don't see why not . . . I could always ring up Walter, you know, if you wanted me to.'

The light aeroplane stalled violently, wavered a little in the air and then resumed its course.

'Are you staying here tonight?'

'I jolly well hope so . . . Reggie said he might show up a bit later too.'

'Well, I'll come and see how you get on with Walter, shall I?'

'This is frightfully exciting,' Constance said. She had curiously protu-berant eyes that sometimes looked like the North Sea on a good day and sometimes like the flint of a Norfolk church tower. 'But make sure you come up before midnight. A girl needs her beauty sleep, you know.'

Most of the cricketers had departed immediately after the match ended, but there were still enough guests present for thirty people to sit down to dinner round the big table in the dining hall at Lytton Grange. It was a meal that in its sumptuousness and its complexities, it banks of footmen, fans of cutlery and clumps of glassware, might have been expressly designed to confuse my uncle – I know that it unnerved me – to expose his social limitations, to erect a high, invisible barrier between him and the world he presumed to infiltrate. But here in the great hall at Lytton Grange, with Lady Lytton attentive at his side and the light from the candelabra shining off the glass and a portrait by Sisley a yard or two behind his shoulder, he was, I realised, in his element. He had a footman sent to the kitchen to find him a bottle of Worcester Sauce, which amused our hostess very much. He gave a little imitation of George Robey at which half the table laughed. Guy Keach sat a couple of places down from him, and coughed his cough and laughed very loudly at his imitation of George Robey. Outside the window the plum-coloured Kentish twilight melted into blackness and occasional cars crunched up the gravel in the drive.

All this, in its profusion and its faint hint of menace slowly uncoiling beneath a placid surface, was a formative experience for us both.

For myself, I sat next to Lady Llanstephan. This, too, was a formative experience. She was a formidable old lady with a great rhomboid face strung up in an assemblage of iron-grey curls, who had once sat in her parents' drawing room with Mr Disraeli while he read a newspaper, and I think, in case the record of our conversation sounds purely fantastic, that she knew who I was. A course and a half passed in silence before she swept her great old jowls towards me and said, 'Who is that man opposite with the terribly bad cough talking to Alicia Martingale?'

'He is called Mr Keach.'

'Oh, *that* Mr Keach. No – *not* marsala' – this to an inexperienced footman who misinterpreted her signal. 'Who married that American woman. Is she here?'

'I'm afraid I don't know Mrs Keach.'

'... But then everyone seems to be an American these days. They say that Mrs Keach used to be on the stage, and that Louisa Corrigan was a farmer's daughter from Wisconsin, or some such place.'

Not for the first time that day I experienced an odd little twist of disquiet. I looked down the table, but there was no sign of Constance. Guy Keach coughed his cough again and was helped to a glass of water by a footman. The light sparkled off the sea of glass, an old gentleman discreetly removed his false teeth behind a napkin and there was a distinct sensation of unease, averted faces shrinking from some sight that, mysteriously, should not have been seen, until Mr Keach and his bloody handkerchief were led away from the table, the level of chatter returned to its previous pitch and the moment passed.

The gentlemen – fifteen of them – were bidden to a small antechamber on the margin of the great hall, but I seized my uncle by the wrist and led him away into a billiard room, its curtains still undrawn, that looked out on to the lawn.

'Capital dinner that, Ralph,' he said expansively. 'Best bottle of wine I've drunk in a month, I shouldn't wonder.'

'Never mind about the dinner,' I told him. 'What about this consortium? With Guy Keach and Lord Parmenter and Sir Basil Ambrose?'

There was a kind of amorphousness about my uncle in those days, the sense of certain parts of his body vaguely dispersing into other parts without the customary checks of anatomical boundaries. His hair was mostly gone now, but what there was left of it had an odd perkiness, and the grey curls on the top of his scalp looked as if they had just sprung from beneath a cap. He seemed very hot. As I watched, a little rivulet of perspiration ran down his wrist along the cigar he held between his fingers and fizzed to extinction on its smoking tip.

'What consortium would that be, Ralph?' he said, quite mildly.

'The one you've been talking about with those three on the croquet lawn.'

My uncle looked a bit shamefaced at this: a strange look – half resentful, half confiding – that I remembered from the Intwood Road.

'Was goin' to tell you about that, Ralph,' he said. ''Deed I was. S'pose we sit down and I put you in the picture. There's two million those fellers can raise and with it we can . . .'

'Do they know about Atry?'

'Was Atry who put them in my way,' my uncle went on. 'Two million, which'll pay for the dye works rather than . . .'

'Do they know Atry's carrying three-quarters of the debt?' This was a superfluous question: they could hardly not have known. I tried again: 'What about if Atry called it in or sold it to them? Where would you be then?'

My uncle shot the cuffs of his evening shirt up beneath the sleeves of his dinner jacket, so that the pair of hogpen links glinted in the light. There was also a bright hogpen stud securing his collar.

'They're not the same tint,' I pointed out, gesturing from wrist to neck.

'Need to do more work on them enamel dyes,' my uncle agreed. 'Why, there was one I saw the other week someone wanted to paint a toy car with that came out nearly salmon . . . But Atry's on our side, Ralph. Leastways, that's what he told me.'

'How much are you letting Keach and the others in for?'

'Forty-nine per cent,' said my uncle proudly.

'So if he lets them buy the debt you've lost control of your own company?'

'But he won't, Ralph. That's the point, d'y'see? He won't.' My uncle had that exalted look on his face which I remembered from the very early days: the look with which he had canvassed the idea of the pig farm, the look he had worn on that fateful day on the Colney escarpment with the snowflakes falling over the Yare. 'Bin making a study of business methods, I have, bin looking into it, and you can't stay still. Not now. D'you know there's a feller in Stockholm just invented something he calls Mangazene? I seen samples of it. Not bad. Kind of greeny-blue with a yellowish tint. They'll be selling it here in the autumn, I shouldn't wonder. Competition, Ralph! Gambling only pays when you're winning. Well, we're ahead just now, so let's gamble, I say.'

Gambling only pays when you're winning. Miss Mort had said that a dozen years ago.

'Who's D.L.G.?' I wondered on the off-chance.

'No one you'd know,' said my uncle, his flight of exaltation descending instantly into shrewdness. 'Now, just trust me about Atry, will you?' Something seemed to strike him and he pulled his silver watch from a fold in his waistcoat and stared at it like a man in a pantomime. 'Gracious. Half past ten. And there's Lady Lytton promised to teach me bezique. Goo' night, Ralph.'

And so I left him hovering by the door of the drawing room and wandered back through the mass of serpentine corridors into the great hall, where trolleys full of smeared plates and empty glasses stood waiting for someone to take them back to the kitchen and two footmen, together with a patent lift apparatus, were trying to help Lady Llanstephan to her nightly ascent of the darkling stair.

* * *

'And then' – Constance giggled – 'Tallulah said that she didn't know why they were called private parts as hers weren't private in the least!'

'I don't think that's very original.'

'Don't you? I thought it was terribly witty.'

The bedroom window was half open and the hogpen dress, which had come to rest on the edge of the dressing table, stirred a little in the breeze. Outside, owls hooted through the murk. Somewhere in the middle distance a lamp in one of the estate cottages was slowly extinguished.

'Darling,' Constance said eventually, 'I'm getting just the tiniest bit *squashed*. If you could just move your . . . Anyway, I got hold of Walter in the end. It was rather dreadful, because I had to pretend I was his aunt, but he was frightfully sweet about it. He said he didn't know a great deal because it wasn't his firm who were acting, but he thought that Guy Keach was awfully clever and that your uncle ought to look out for himself.'

'Did he say anything about Atry?'

'Oh, he said he was the kind of man who could hide behind a corkscrew . . . Ralph, what *are* you doing?'

A bit later Constance said, 'I expect he thinks I'm a bit of a tart.'

'Who does?'

'Walter. He always sounds so terribly disapproving when he talks to me . . . You are going to take me to Lavinia Sutherland's, aren't you?'

'You know I said I would.'

'Because when I explained that I wasn't his aunt and I'd only done it because I wanted to speak to him, I think he was rather shocked . . . You couldn't just hand me those, could you? Over there on the carpet.'

'Here they are.'

'Thanks. Only he's terribly protective of Reggie, and I wouldn't want him to think I was corrupting the darling boy.'

The great hall, illuminated only by a single night-light, was dark and silent. Reggie St Cloud sat alone on a chair beneath the grandfather clock smoking a cigarette.

'Only just got here,' he said affably, in answer to my nod. 'I say, you haven't seen Constance anywhere, have you?'

He was a tall, pink-faced youth two or three years older than me, who bore no malice about this joint pursuit.

'I think she'll be in her room by now.'

'Yes, I suppose she will be. I'd have been here earlier only I was seeing a chum at Staff College.' A moth, floating suddenly out of the subfusc surround, landed on his shoulder and he flicked it off with his thumbnail. 'I say, you wouldn't know which room, would you? Only I've got her copy of *The Green Hat* I promised I'd give back.'

'I think she said it was the blue room on the west wing.'

'Did she? Well, that's jolly kind of you. Thanks very much. Ta-ta, then.' From the wall next to the grandfather clock, hemmed in between an umbrella stand and an engraving of the Battle of Sebastopol, a barometer gleamed out of the darkness. Rising cautiously from his chair, the remnant of the cigarette still clamped between his teeth, Reggie tapped it with his index finger. 'Falling fast,' he said, peering at the rubric. 'Could be a storm brewing.'

It had rained during the night and the wind had blown several of the terracotta pots on the terrace of Lytton Grange on to their sides. One of these had smashed in two and disgorged its contents, so that a spray of earth, in outline curiously reminiscent of the map of Norway, extended over the stone flags. Meanwhile the wind was getting up and a party of golfers was already coming back to the house. Standing at the window I watched their leader – a spindly old gentleman in plus-fours and enormous hobnail brogues – explaining something to a footman who stood holding an empty tray in front of him as if it contained several invisible objects that might crash to the ground if not watched. Constance, passing behind them with her arms folded across her chest, saw me and waved. She was wearing a bright blue mackintosh and had her hair tied up in a kind of wreath. Informed judges always said that Constance looked her best in the morning and it was only after lunch that she grew languid and sulky. In the sitting room my uncle sat blinking at a copy of *The Economic Consequences of the Peace*, while his secretary, Mr Gilmour, who had come down that morning by train, did the *Daily Mail* crossword.

'Cup-bearer,' he said. 'Six letters. Do you think that might be a classical clue?'

'Try "saucer",' said my uncle. He put the book down on the armrest of his chair and made a little excursion around the margins of the room to the bookcase, found nothing there that interested him, looked out of the window at the golfers as they drifted on to the terrace and resumed his seat. 'Anyone seen Keach this morning?' he wondered.

Nobody had seen Keach.

'Gilmour,' said my uncle. 'You better give me them papers. Not the Consolidated ones. You know, the ones that came up to the orfice before.'

Mr Gilmour folded up the copy of the *Daily Mail* into a parcel about the size of a banknote and, with an expression of considerable suffering, began to turn out the contents of a small briefcase on to the tabletop.

'That's the ticket,' my uncle said vaguely. Washed, scented and shaved – strangely enough, the prevailing tang was of Parma Violets – and crammed into a dark business suit, he looked oddly resentful, caught up in something that was not of his making, anxious to escape. There was a telephone standing on the table next to the wall and he examined it cautiously, picked it up briskly in one hand as if he intended to use it for some kind of physical jerks and put it down. 'Gilmour,' he said again. 'Just see if you can get through to Mr Atry, will you?'

With a look of infinite resignation – as if he did what he had to do with unimaginable reluctance – Mr Gilmour put down the pile of papers and spoke melancholically into the receiver, first to the operator, then to someone at Atry's office, then to a third person, possibly even to a fourth. The golfers had all disappeared and an ancient gardener, bent on one knee, had begun to sweep up the spilled earth. There was a noise of footsteps in the corridor.

'They say Mr Atry has gone to the Chelsea Flower Show, sir,' Mr Gilmour reported as the sitting-room door swung open.

'Well, leave a message then. *Urgent* message. Tell them . . . Morning, My Lord . . . Sir Basil . . . Move them blinkin' papers out of the way, will you, Gilmour.'

In the two years since we had embarked on the selling of hogpen my uncle had devised several plausible techniques for dealing with the business people he came up against: deferential without being positively obsequious, humble without being absolutely self-abasing, conciliating without being downright craven. He contrived to give the impression that he had stumbled on to the stage on which he now found himself almost by accident, that his success there faintly bewildered him, depended entirely on the goodwill of those around him, might disappear at a moment's notice. This air of vulnerability was my uncle's trump card, so to speak, for it encouraged people who failed to detect the inner steeliness beneath these soft exteriors to assume that he could be taken advantage of.

Another of my uncle's techniques was vagueness. 'Of course,' he said now to Sir Basil. 'Would be useful if you could come up to Perthshire and watch the dye being put in . . . Fascinatin' business.'

Sir Basil and Lord Parmenter, who must have known that the principal manufacturing plant was in Salford, exchanged glances.

'That three hundred thousand in the contingency fund . . .' Lord Parmenter now began.

'Three hundred thousand, is it?' my uncle said affably. 'I thought it was five.'

'And the renewal date for the European contracts . . .'

'Didn't know there *was* a renewal date.'

The trouble with this pose was that it could not be indefinitely sustained. Sooner or later hard information would be required. Not long after this Mr Gilmour, his face no longer cast down by suffering but alert and attentive, displayed sheets of figures from a second briefcase while my uncle smoked a cigar. Several times, I noticed, he glanced at the telephone. Punctuated by the rain, which was once more falling in cataracts on to the terrace, there began another of those conversations – horribly like the one that had been conducted on the croquet lawn the previous afternoon – in which little was said but a great deal implied. Atry's name was soon mentioned, who had picked a fine day to go the Chelsea Flower Show (my uncle). It was a great thing for Atry to be involved in such an enterprise (my uncle again). Mr Gilmour brought more figures and my uncle gave another uneasy glance at the telephone. And so, rather less desultorily, and with incremental pauses for cups of tea and further contributions from Mr Gilmour, a terrific air of tension began to invest the room. My uncle's interventions, I noticed, became even more bluff and more outlandish.

'. . . Of course, the cotton trade could be expanded by two hundred – three hundred – per cent.'

'. . . Afraid the statistics hardly support that kind of prediction.'

'. . . Thought of buying a row of houses in Oxford Street and painting them up as an advertisement.'

'. . . Feel that we ought to set our faces firmly against any kind of vulgar display.'

'. . . No reason why you couldn't dye a suit in it. No reason at all.'

There was something almost despairing about my uncle as he came out with this last projection, which of the various uses to which I had heard hogpen hypothetically put was perhaps the silliest of all. What would

Constance be doing now, I wondered? Sitting in the drawing room over *The Green Hat*, which she read continuously. Driving back to London with Reggie St Cloud? She had a figure like a boy's, with soft, pale breasts. Atry's name now began to appear in the conversation with ominous regularity, Atry and his underwriting of the debt, his interest in the anticipated expansion (Sir Basil), the possibility of the debt's transfer (Lord Parmenter). This was the closest anyone came to an outright statement of the threat that underlay the meeting – that it needed only Atry's say-so to take the control of my uncle's business out of his hands and give it to someone else – and even that was not very close, for the moment after it was said, quite unexpectedly, the telephone rang. There was some doubt as to who should answer it. Lord Parmenter, Sir Basil and my uncle all declined to act. Finally Mr Gilmour, speaking very precisely and sounding rather like a butler in a play, put the receiver to his ear.

'Mr Atry, sir.'

My uncle spoke only a few words before handing the receiver to Lord Parmenter and I knew from the way he did so that he had carried his point.

'That all seems to be very satisfactory,' Lord Parmenter said as he put the receiver back in its cradle. He looked deeply hurt.

'With Atry on board we can't go wrong,' said Sir Basil, who seemed less aware of the crisis that had passed.

'Flower show was a washout,' said my uncle inconsequently. 'Shame. Should have liked to be there myself.'

And so there came into being the agreement that created the Rendall Corporation and we became greater people, so great that Lytton Grange seems only a tiny and insignificant milestone on our path.

'A near-run thing that was, Ralph,' my uncle remarked a dozen hours later, as we plunged forward into the silent Kentish night. 'If that call hadn't come then – pop! – where would we be, eh? Anyhow, I'm going to buy them houses and have 'em painted, just for show.' All this, too, is very vivid to me, quite free of the intimations of disquiet that Atry's name brought subsequently to the margin of our lives: my uncle's face peering from the window of the speeding Daimler, Guy Keach coughing his cough – he was tubercular, it turned out, poor fellow, and didn't last the year – and the white birds soaring above the terrace.

Two weeks later Constance announced her engagement to an obscure Welsh peer – broken off a month later, I understood – and vanished altogether from my life.

10

Northern Lights

1908

Alice sat in the lodging-house sitting room, looking out over the wet streets.

It was a Saturday afternoon in the early part of the year and the pavements of the northern town twenty feet below her were full of people. She had arrived there only the previous evening and had no knowledge of the place other than that it resembled every other northern town she had ever seen: house fronts in dirty red brick; blackened warehouses following the trace of an oily river; trams and omnibuses thronging the cobbled squares. In the distance, beyond the factory chimneys and the metal turret of the railway station, low hills flanked the encircling moor. She glanced for a moment at the crowds beneath her – young men in flat caps with mufflers round their throats, mill girls with pale, slab-like faces – then turned back to the sitting room which, with the fire and a tray bearing tea things was of considerably more interest to her. In addition to the fire and the brimming coal scuttle that stood beside it there was a very large sofa, an excellent oil painting of some Pennine crag or other and some other furniture that, taken together, suggested a rent of not less than three guineas a week. The bedchamber, partly visible through an adjoining door, contained a double bed and a gentleman's shaving things were laid out on the table beyond it. Oblivious to the room, Alice was inspecting two letters recently delivered to her by the landlady. One of them, from the place in the country where Asa now lodged, was only a paragraph long and could be safely set aside. The contents of the second, which she examined in a rather agitated way, require some explanation.

A year had passed since Mr Armitage's flight from the Bolton theatre. The company had broken up the day after his departure. Of their present whereabouts, with the exception of Miss Jeffries, now returned to the bosom of her family, she knew scarcely anything. A paragraph in the *Era*, some time later, had told of Mr Armitage's arrest on an embezzlement charge somewhere on the south coast. It was a mark of her changed fortunes that she could read it with some amusement. Six months before, the mention of Mr Armitage would have had her cursing his name. The circumstances in which she read of his arraignment – the corner of a comfortable restaurant with a rich smell of cigar smoke pervading the air – allowed for a more circumspect attitude. 'Armitage,' her companion of the meal wondered, seeing the paragraph. 'Isn't that the fellow who levanted?' and she acknowledged with a smile that it was. 'Well, I dare say he will get his just desserts,' the companion replied, and with that Mr Armitage, his desertion and the sortie to the Bolton pawnshop were forgotten.

What had caused her to forget them? Returning to London and making immediate recourse to the columns of the *Era*, Alice and Miss Jeffries had been engaged – much to their relief – to join the chorus of a pantomime being staged at the Wimbledon Theatre. They would have been less gratified had they known that the engagement was quite fortuitous, the manager having been 'let down' on the day before rehearsals began. The manager's name was Fortescue and in theatrical terms he was the Alpha to Mr Armitage's Omega. Mr Shaw and Mr Barrie might not have wholly approved of him, but they treated him with respect. He was supposed to have made a small fortune out of a piece called *Daisy Get Your Hat*, whose copyright he had purchased off its author for ten guineas. Just now he was using the pantomime as a way of raising the capital needed to take one of his own melodramas out on the provincial circuit. He was a tall, heavy-set, good-looking man of forty or so who liked champagne, flat racing at Newmarket, lunch parties at the Trocadero – for which he did not mind in the least paying – and good-looking young women.

It should be said in Mr Fortescue's defence that his appreciation of the good-looking young women never blinded him to an honest estimate of their talents. His initial interest in Alice was entirely professional. The cast of the pantomime was by no means as extensive as it might have been, the small fortune that Mr Fortescue had made out of *Daisy Get Your Hat* being somewhat dissipated, and certain members of the chorus – Alice was one – were occasionally required to come to the front of the stage. On one of these occasions during rehearsal, Mr Fortescue happened to be lounging at the side of the stage smoking a cigar and talking to one of his assistants, and something in the way Alice produced the two or three lines allotted to her commended itself to him. 'What is the name of the girl with red hair?' he enquired of the assistant.

'I believe her name is Miss Hanson,' replied the assistant, who was nervous of Mr Fortescue. 'Why, is anything amiss?'

'Not at all. But you might see that she gets another line or two. Nothing to spoil the look of the piece, of course.'

There were several other theatrical matters clamouring for Mr Fortescue's attention besides his pantomime and it so happened that he did not return to the production until its opening night. Here again he was struck by the way in which Miss Hanson – that he only remembered her name with an effort showed how truly professional his interest was – delivered her lines. Her intonation – nasal and betraying foreign origins – he found irritating, but much may be done with an intonation. It is the ability to speak one's lines that counts. That she might also be good-looking stole up on him almost by accident. As the production went on, he found himself looking out for her as the chorus made its way on to the stage and regretting her absence when it departed. She had fine hair, he thought. Still, Mr Fortescue did not know what he might do with this deduction. The third week in January came, the pantomime, having raised a thousand pounds towards Mr Fortescue's spring tour, gave its final performance and the cast was released. Still Mr Fortescue hesitated. He did not think – still his professionalism endured – that she had the makings of a great actress, but for the role that he had in mind for her a great actress would have been superfluous, and even a moderately good actress might not have done. No, the melodrama Mr Fortescue proposed to bring to the provincial public that spring required of its leading lady someone who would do exactly what Mr Fortescue told her. Mr Fortescue wanted naturalness and, having failed to find it in the actresses who had so far auditioned for him, he was prepared to put up with an imitation of it. So he sent a note – it was by now early February – to Miss Hanson at her landlady's asking her to call on him at his office in the Strand.

'Well, now, Miss Hanson,' he said on her arrival. 'You are pretty new to this game, I take it?'

Seeing her nod of assent – a modest, downward glance in which she avoided looking at him altogether – he was struck once again by how good-looking she was. He would do something for her. Indeed he would.

'Well,' he went on. 'That need not be a bar to your succeeding, you know. Why, Miss Mangrove, that was such a hit in *Saints and Sinners*, had never been on a stage in her life before. Do you wish to succeed?'

'I should like to very much. Except that . . .'

'Except what?'

'Except that people say I don't talk as I should.'

'Do they, now? Well, let me tell you if that were a bar to performing on a stage, half the girls you see there would instantly exclude themselves. You have a very charming way of speaking' – he was not flattering her, he meant it – 'but that's not to say that something can't be done with it. Let me see, are you appearing in anything at present?'

'Miss Jeffries and I have auditions for *Jack Be Nimble* at the Imperial.'

'Well, I should give that up. I really should. From what I hear' – Mr Fortescue knew everything about every play that was to be produced in the West End – 'the capital will be insufficient. You would be much better sticking to the provinces at this stage in your career. That's where reputations can be made.'

If Mr Fortescue had expressly set out to make a good impression on Alice, he could not have done it better than this. First, there was the fact of his personal appearance – his elegant morning coat and his spotless collar – next to which Mr Armitage would scarcely have held his own against a Barbary ape from the zoo. But she fancied also that his interest in her was sincere. She had heard enough, too, from other members of the pantomime's cast to appreciate something of Mr Fortescue's position in the theatrical world and the kind of figure he cut. All this naturally predisposed her in his favour, while thoroughly alerting her to what he wanted in return.

'I could name a dozen ladies', Mr Fortescue went on, 'whose talents first came to public notice on a provincial tour. Take Miss Hardy, for example, and *The Duke's Dilemma*. Failed absolutely in the West End and then ran for a year beyond it.'

In this way he led her gradually to the question of his melodrama, the part he wished her to fill and the somewhat unusual circumstances in which it would be rehearsed. 'You'll find', he said, 'that I have a particular idea for this on which I'm very much set. You would have to promise to do exactly as you were told, down to the very last syllable, otherwise it won't work and the piece will be doomed.'

Saying this, he wondered if he should be so candid. On the other hand he had the advantage of dealing with inexperience. A young woman with two or three West End productions behind her would have taken umbrage at the thought that she was a clean sheet on which Mr Fortescue could scrawl suggestions at will. But Alice was not such a young woman. As the enormity of what he was proposing dawned on her, she grew fearful. It was all a joke. He could not possibly mean to give her such a part. But by the courtesy of his manner and his constant references to recent theatrical history, Mr Fortescue made it clear that it was not a joke and that he did mean it.

'Do you think I could do it?' she wondered.

'Certainly. I should not have asked you had I thought otherwise.'

'Would . . . Could there be something in it for Miss Jeffries?'

'Miss Jeffries?' He had to be reminded of the name before he could recollect her. A dull girl in the chorus who gabbled her lines. But perhaps it would be prudent to accommodate Miss Jeffries. 'Well, now,' he said, 'I have got no further in my preparations than this conversation, but if Miss Jeffries is a particular friend of yours, I have no doubt something could be found.'

The upshot was that Alice signed a piece of paper, which Mr Fortescue had witnessed by his clerk, and agreed to visit his home one evening in the week following to read through her part. Arriving at the address in Kensington, and conducted by a maid into the parlour lined with theatrical prints, she found that Mr Fortescue was as good as his word. Each line that she uttered provoked a volley of instructions. She should raise her chin when she spoke. She should look at him thus as she delivered the words (Mr Fortescue was to play the principal male part in the piece). She should emphasise that syllable but not the one that followed it. She should lower her eyes at this juncture, but not keep them lowered. All this, to one who had previously only spoken an occasional sentence, was intensely bewildering, and within half an hour she let the script fall upon the parlour table and said, almost tearfully, 'I cannot do it. You have no idea what it is like. You had better get somebody else who – who does not mind being shouted at.'

'I am very sorry if I have offended you' – he had taken off his coat and was standing in his shirtsleeves by the fire, the better to declaim a particularly violent passage – 'but, really, it is necessary to understand every word before we begin. Now, the line when you ask for the horses to be saddled. Say it again.' She did as she was bidden. 'And now, fling out your arm as if you meant it. Not as if you were waving a handkerchief to a friend.' After this she lost some of her awe of him and they got on better.

All this lasted for a fortnight, the play itself opening a month later at a theatre in Brighton. A part had indeed been found for Miss Jeffries, which that lady accepted in a spirit of great humility. It was, as Mr Fortescue had foreseen, a considerable success. The month at Brighton was followed by a month at Bournemouth and a further six weeks at Oxford. The piece had no great merit – it involved an abduction, the betrayal of the heroine by her delinquent brother, her defenestration from a castle window (very decorously done) by the malefactor and her rescue by Mr Fortescue – but there was something about the pathos of Alice's predicament that commended it to the public. 'Miss Hanson', one critic remarked, 'has an air of vulnerability, a delicate apprehension of the perils that surround her, that turns each male member of the audience into a Lancelot, anxious to do battle on her behalf.' When Mr Fortescue read this encomium, which he did with his feet planted squarely on the carpet of a hotel parlour somewhere in the English Midlands, he knew that he had succeeded in his task.

As for Alice, the incidental benefits of the situation in which she found herself were quite as wonderful as her nightly appearances before the provincial theatregoers. To earn twenty guineas a week (this was the salary at which Mr Fortescue had engaged her)! To stay in hotels and apartments of unimaginable luxury! To spend her leisure hours in the ceremonious comfort of a lodging-house parlour! Well! Knowing something of Mr Fortescue's reputation, which had been discussed by the ladies of the pantomime chorus, she had anticipated his advances. She liked Fortescue, thought him handsome and amusing. Next to Drouett and Hanson he was a demi-god, whose lustre shone over her imaginings to the point where these lesser lights were practically extinguished. Above all, she was conscious of her debt to him, knew that her destiny without him would have been Mrs Gaffney's first-floor back or another Mr Armitage. That there might be a moral dimension to this dilemma barely occurred to her. Such things happened in the world and the world did not cease to turn because they had happened. And so when there came an unignorable mark of Mr Fortescue's regard, she met it with one yet more unignorable still. All this had happened six months before, since which time they had lived together discreetly – Mr Fortescue was always discreet – as man and wife, she continuing to regard Mr Fortescue as handsome and amusing and her professional saviour, he regarding her in the spirit he regarded all the women with whom he became involved – affectionately yet realistically.

And now she was alone in a lodging-house sitting room awaiting his return, with two letters in her hand: one reassuring her as to the well-being of her son, the other from Mr Stanhope, the famous London theatrical manager, offering her a West End engagement.

She knew all about Mr Stanhope – six months in Mr Fortescue's company had taught her that. She knew, too, that an engagement procured for her by Mr Stanhope would be even loftier and better remunerated than anything Mr Fortescue could offer. What she did not know was how Mr Fortescue might react. She began to consider what she owed him and found, after a moment or two's reflection, that it amounted to a great deal. She was grateful to him for this – more grateful than she had ever been to anyone – but, still, she did not see that this placed her under any special obligation. Chance had brought her into Mr Fortescue's orbit and chance, she thought, might very likely take her away again. She knew, too, that had she not possessed the qualities Mr Fortescue had sought in her, he would very soon have dispensed with her: Mr Fortescue, in an intimate moment, had told her as much. This made her feel that the debt she owed him was possibly less great than she had first assumed. Still, she thought, she could not quite make up her mind how best to approach the business. This was not the first letter from Mr Stanhope, but should she fail to respond to it, it would probably be the last. Thinking of this, and of other things connected to Mr Fortescue – a diamond he had once given her, which she wore on a chain round her neck, the future destinations of the tour, which included Hull, Newcastle and other places besides – she moved back to the window and stared once again at the passing currents of humanity. It was in this attitude that Mr Fortescue found her as he came bouncing into the room, very red-cheeked from the cold air, throwing his silk hat upon the sofa and rapping his silver-knobbed cane against the sides of his boots.

'Well,' he said, seeing her by the window and beginning to warm his hands at the glowing fire, 'I have just been round to the theatre. Four hundred tickets sold and half as many again for tomorrow. I call that good business.'

'Very good, I should think,' she said, professionally interested in spite of her anxieties. 'What does the manager say?'

'Oh, he is delighted. Says it will be the making of them. Why, apparently they had *The Sailor's Return* here last week – you know, the piece in which Miss Tanqueray was supposed to be so remarkable – and not a box in the house could be disposed of. Oh, and there is this.' He held out a copy of a local newspaper, open at a page displaying an elaborate photograph of herself, and a paragraph to the effect that Miss Alice Hanson, the well-known actress, whose praises the theatre-going public had lately been singing, would shortly &c &c.

'People are very kind,' she said. She meant it, but she had also begun to think that this kind of thing was her due. As she handed back the newspaper, which he stuffed idly in the pocket of his coat, she looked at him closely. She thought that he was very handsome and vigorous, that he quite filled the room with his presence, standing before the fire with his cane still clutched in his hand, that he had possibly taken a drink and that she was grateful to him.

Not noting the stare, but still wrapped up in the four hundred tickets, he went on, 'We shall do very well here. Two weeks or even three. Tomkins was quite adamant about it.'

She decided to take the bull by the horns. 'I have had a letter from Mr Stanhope,' she said.

'Stanhope, eh?' The flush in his cheeks confirmed that he had taken a drink. 'Well I'll be d****d. What does it say?' he asked, with a lightness of tone that was clearly an effort to him. 'You are a dark horse. A letter from Stanhope. Will you let me see it?'

As it still lay in her hand, she could not very well refuse him. She gave it to him and went and sat by the fire as he read it, wondering what he might say and what she might say in return. Turning the piece of paper over in his fingers, Fortescue was thinking hard. The letter did not say a great deal, but what it did say was very definite. He was a sharp man and he understood, as he read it, that there had been other letters and that they had been answered. For all his sharpness, he did not know what to make of this. It seemed to him – and the realisation annoyed him – that the estimate of her character he had formed was all wrong, that there were elements in it that he had failed to appreciate and might now cost him dear. Still holding the letter between finger and thumb he said, with as much suavity as he could muster, 'Well, there has been quite a correspondence, has there not?'

She did not quite like the tone of this, for all its mildness, for it implied deceit and she was not conscious of having deceived him. 'I suppose', she said, perhaps more coldly than she intended, 'that I am allowed to receive letters?'

'From Lord Rosebery, if you like – or Mr Balfour. It is nothing to me.' He was smiling as he said this, but not perhaps very convincingly. 'What are you going to do about it?'

This was the question she had been dreading. Looking around the room, as if it might offer inspiration, her eye fell on the oil painting of the Pennine crag and she thought how much she would like to walk up to it, perch on its summit, in solitude, and inspect the land laid out below.

'What will you do about it?' he asked again.

'You have read the letter. There is an engagement offered. I can either take it or refuse it.'

'Well, that is one way of looking at it I suppose. We shall be three weeks here, you know. And then at Newcastle. Why only this morning I have had an offer from the people at Glasgow.' There was a faint note of asperity creeping into his voice. 'How does that fit in with your plans?'

'I have no plans. You know I do not.'

'And yet you have been writing letters to that Stanhope.' He was shrewd enough to realise that there would be no benefit in abusing his rival and continued more softly, 'What should we do here if you went?'

'There is Miss Wilkins, I suppose.' Miss Wilkins was the young lady who played the part of Alice's faithful companion and had the misfortune to suffer from eczema on her hands.

'Miss Wilkins can go hang!' He stalked a few paces up and down the carpet, swishing with his cane at the firedogs that sat mournfully on either side of the hearth. Still he did not know what to make of it. 'See here, Alice. West End engagements are all very well. I should be delighted for you, though I would rather it were not with Stanhope. But really it is out of the question.'

'Why is it out of the question?'

He was on the point of reminding her that she sat in a room he had paid for, wearing clothes that he had helped select for her from a ladies' outfitters in Regent Street and that the encomium in the paper that lay in his pocket had come about entirely through his agency, but then thought better of it. 'It is out of the question,' he said again. 'It would mean breaking agreements.'

'But I have not made any agreements.'

Again, he was astonished by her daring. He took another step along the carpet and swished so hard with his cane at the nearest of the fire-dogs that the creature shook a little against the flagstones of the hearth. 'Perhaps you haven't. But there are certain obligations.' By this he meant the room, the dress and the encomium in the newspaper. 'You must write to Stanhope and decline. Say you are delighted that he esteems your talents so highly and so forth, but that you are in the middle of a provincial tour.'

'Perhaps you are right.'

There was a meekness in her face as she said this that he found reassuring. She really was extraordinarily good-looking, he thought. The irritation that had come over him when he first read Stanhope's letter began to disappear. He started to think of little entertainments he might contrive for her, little excursions she might admire.

'Certainly I am right. And then there's the question of experience, you know. A West End audience is very different from, well' – he did not quite know how to convey this distinction without patronising her – 'the people here. You would need to prepare yourself.' What he meant by this was that she would need him to prepare her, but he did not care to say as much.

And so they lapsed into silence, she staring once again at the picture of the Pennine crag and hearing the noise of the people in the street below, he, thinking that he had carried his point, moving on to consider other matters necessary to a theatrical company that has just arrived in a provincial town where they are to open the following night.

'Would you like tea?' she enquired submissively. 'I can ring for the girl if you wish it.'

'Eh? No.' He was thinking of the percentage of the box office receipts that would be allotted him once a certain number of tickets had been sold. 'That is – I have to go out again. Those trunks may not have arrived from Worcester, you know, and there will be the deuce of a row if they haven't.'

The look in his eye said that he would be the originator of the row, and she saw it and smiled.

'When shall you be back, do you think?' she asked.

'What? An hour, I should say. Perhaps two.' He thought about the letter to Mr Stanhope: he assumed that it would be written, or at least meditated upon, while he was gone. 'Should you like to dine this evening?' he enquired. 'Not here, I mean, but in the town.'

'I should like that very much.'

He wondered whether to try another remark about Mr Stanhope, which would not have redounded very greatly to that impresario's credit, but thought better of it, swished with his cane at the second of the firedogs and bounced out of the room with very nearly all the vigour that he had entered it.

When he had gone – she looked out of the window to watch him striding briskly along the street, his silk hat contrasting oddly with the sea of flat caps and the bonnets of the mill girls – she sat once more upon the sofa, drank half a cup of the lukewarm tea that remained in the pot and, picking up Mr Stanhope's letter, considered it once more. As she did so she reflected dispassionately on the previous quarter-hour's conversation. She knew that not everything Fortescue said to her was self-interested. She knew, above all, that he believed she would obey his advice. It was this last point that irritated her – not that the advice was unreasonable, but that it came as a command. Thinking of this, and of one or two other remarks she had not quite liked, and reading the letter again, she saw that there was a railway timetable on the mantelpiece wedged up against the clock. She picked it up and sat considering it, as the afternoon passed into early evening and the noise from the street faded away, and white, vaporous fog crept up the sills and windowpanes of the room. Once she rang the bell and had a short conversation with the servant. After a little while she went into the bedroom and arranged her belongings. Then, later still, there came the sounds of hoofs on the cobbles and a cab halting at the lodging-house door.

Mr Fortescue, going jauntily about his business, stepping smartly on and off pavements to hasten his progress through the crowded streets, thought that he might delay the time of his return beyond the hour he had mentioned. He had won his victory, he thought, and he would be magnanimous. And in his absence she would have ample opportunity to reflect on what he had said. That was how he saw it, as he marched on through the streets, and an excellent strategy it seemed. Accordingly, he decided to amuse himself, insofar as amusement could be found on a wet Saturday afternoon in a northern provincial town. He bought himself a ticket for the municipal museum and admired its collection of stuffed birds. He smoked a cigar in the lea of the Angevin castle, with a newspaper held over his head against the rain. He went about looking keenly at the fragments of the town wall and a number of Methodist chapels. A little over two hours passed and, with the sky turning grey above his head and the streets gradually losing their traffic, he returned to the lodging house.

The initial thing that struck him was that the sitting room was icy cold. The fire had nearly gone out and the gas jet had been extinguished. His first thought was that Alice, tired by the previous day's journey, had gone to sleep in the bedroom, the door of which had been closed. Thinking that it would be churlish to wake her, he spent some time relaying the fire – he was not too proud to do this himself – relit the gas, seated himself in an armchair and read over a letter or two that he took from his pocket. After this he spent some time examining a line of Staffordshire figurines that ran along the mantelpiece. Finally, when all occupation failed him, he went and tapped lightly on the door of the bedroom. There was no answer and, tapping again, he pushed it an inch or two open. It was quite empty. Several explanations rose instantly in his head as to where she might be. He was moving back to the door when he noticed that her travelling case, which he remembered having left atop the mahogany chest of drawers, was no longer in the room. This frightened him. 'The deuce,' he said. There was a cupboard to the left of the chest of drawers in which he had seen her stow a hatbox and one or two other items. These, too, he found to have vanished.

'The deuce,' he said again. He sat on the bed – there was one of her handkerchiefs lying on it – and took stock of his situation. It was now about six o'clock and he knew that if she had left the town he would have no prospect of finding her. And if he did find her, what would he say? But still, he ought to assure himself of the details of her flight. The bell was answered not by the maidservant but by a young man whom he imagined to be the son of the people who owned the house. It now struck him that he was in a very awkward position, but still he persevered. Had the lady – had Mrs Fortescue – gone out, he wondered? Yes indeed, the young man volunteered, she had ordered a cab to the station an hour ago. And was there any message? No, there was no message. All this Mr Fortescue listened to with apparent good humour. But he was a resourceful man. When the young man had gone, he sat on the sitting-room sofa deep in thought. Once, but only once, he unravelled the newspaper photograph and looked at it. When half an hour had passed he rang the bell – it was the maidservant this time, which cheered him – ordered a plate of oysters, a pint of beer and pen and ink, with which he wrote a note to Miss Wilkins, sealed it up in an envelope, had it sent round to her lodgings and settled down to await her arrival.

11
A Case of Samples

1918

In those days in Pittsburgh the cheap hotels lay on the western side of the commercial district. Here there were wide, asphalted carriageways with tall buildings rising on either side – banking halls, warehouses, distilleries heavy with the stink of malt and barley, tinted smoke obscuring the view of the grey uplands beyond. All this Drouett saw from the window of his third-floor room, looking out over a succession of grey-stone frontages and plate-glass windows behind which clerks went about their business. He liked staying in the commercial districts for the sense they gave him of proximity to great events. A fellow went stale in the suburbs, he told himself, and the silence of the land beyond them was as deafening as the city's roar. Just now he was travelling in veneers and inlays again, for a firm in Philadelphia. There had been a little misunderstanding with his previous employers and a legal letter or two, but, well, Drouett was used to little misunderstandings, and Messrs Cowperwood could write as many legal letters as they chose and still not dislodge the two hundred dollars he had in his pocketbook. The memory of what he had said to Messrs Cowperwood's chief clerk on the occasion of their last meeting stirred in his mind and he gave a tug at the ends of the tie loosely fastened beneath his collar, which was intended to convey jauntiness and very nearly succeeded.

It was a bright, cold morning in the early part of the year – there was a rime of frost on the pillars of the banking halls – and he had been in Pittsburgh a week, making his way around the furniture manufactories and the finishing shops. He had a new kind of inlay – mother-of-pearl, they called it, though he fancied it was made of coloured glass – which his employer had insisted that he could do great things with if he tried. In his heart Drouett did not quite believe in the new inlay, but the knowledge was not enough to lessen his confidence in himself. With the ends of the tie still looped through his fingers, he looked at his reflection in the square of mirror that hung above the occasional table where he dressed. The heavy, placid face – gone to redness now, but, then, everyone's face turned red in the end, even those stuffed shirt bankers' – reassured him. He would just get a little breakfast – a glance at his watch told him that it was already past nine o'clock – and then he would keep the first of his appointments designed to sell that mother-of-pearl inlay, that was what he would do.

All this time, gazing from the high, third-floor window, seizing the ends of his tie, thinking about Messrs Cowperwood and their legal letters, he had been entirely self-absorbed. He was aware of this habit of his and occasionally rather puzzled by it. Six or seven times a day he would find himself pondering some incident in his past life, framing and reframing it in a way that would satisfy him. He knew that the habit was vital to him and that it constituted the greater part of his mental existence, but at the same time it alarmed him for it did not chime with the view he took of himself, which he imagined to be bold and decisive. Back in the immediate world of the hotel room, with its threadbare carpet, the faint crackings and contractions of the windows as the early sun caught them, the smell of sweat and powder – he felt faintly bewildered by it, could not establish how he came to be there, with an end of his tie grasped between each forefinger and thumb, the square attaché case packed with veneer samples and inlay cards a yard from his boot and the sound of the negro chambermaid clattering along the corridor. There was a softer, less insistent noise from the bed and he wondered if the girl – her name was Mae – had woken up, but no, she had merely thrown one arm out across the coverlet and groaned a little in her sleep. He stood for a moment at the end of the bedstead watching her, oddly uncertain in his movements. He was a realist about women, but there was something about Mae as she slept – red hair thrown back on the pillow, mouth half open – that offended him. He could not quite define the nature of this offence, but he knew that he was annoyed by it. She was a big, untidy girl of twenty-three or so who said that she had taught in a board school in Columbus, but Drouett knew better. For a moment he wondered whether to reach out and wake her – she was snoring loudly out of the side of her mouth, which annoyed him even more – but no, he would take his breakfast in solitude, he thought, with a newspaper to read, maybe, and a waitress to chaff, before stepping out on to the streets of Pittsburgh.

As he hurried downstairs he noticed further signs of the cheapness of the hotel. There was a rod out of the stair carpet, and the cut-off stationer's calendar on the wall of the second landing said 30 December, when he knew that it was a week into the New Year. All this, together with the sight of the waiter and a group of youngish men in shabby suits – clerks and lawyers' assistants, he thought – crowding out of the breakfast room, gave him a disagreeable sense of the figure he cut in the world, and he sat at his solitary table with its off-white cloth thinking that he must find a way of asserting his position. His coffee, when it came, was only luke-warm and he eagerly sent it back, thinking that this was as good a way as any of revenging himself on the defective stair carpet and the shabby clerks, but he regretted the command as soon as he had issued it. Why should the waiter care whether he sent his coffee back, eh? Still, as he sat over the second cup, alternately blowing off the steam and raising it to his lips, he felt his spirits rise and he looked around the room to see if there was anyone with whom he might share his good humour. But it was late for breakfast – the other salesmen had gone with the dawn – and he had the place to himself. Outside it had begun to snow – just a few flakes, drifting down over the porticos of the banking chambers to fall on the icy streets – and he watched it for a moment, with his coffee cup in his hand and a plate of eggs he had ordered growing cold at his elbow, cautious and sober, thinking, as he always did at these times, of the blizzard that had engulfed him in the Dakotas. By heavens, that had been a near-run thing! But he had got out of it, hadn't he? Crawled into that providential haystack and made himself secure until they dug him out two days later, and only a pair of frostbitten fingers to show for it! The memory cheered him, for he fancied that he had shown what he called 'pluck' or 'grit' – two more qualities that were highly important to his sense of himself and what the world owed him – and he ordered up another cup of coffee and sat drinking it while a few more snowflakes tumbled over the pediments of the banking chambers and the waiter shook out his cloth and slapped it against the sides of his wooden tray.

He had planned to go straight out into the business quarter – it was already nearly ten – but he found, to his immense annoyance, that he had left his attaché case in his room. Well, there was nothing to be done: he would have to go and fetch it. There were two men in dark suits who looked like undertakers standing talking to the manager on the stairs as he passed and he wondered if somebody had died. A regular frost that would be, he thought, managing a hotel where somebody died. As he came into the bedroom, pulling the door to behind him, Mae raised her head from the coverlet, half opened one eye and said sleepily, 'Is that you, George?'

'What's the matter?' he said absently. He had the attaché case in his hand now. 'Aren't you well?'

'Well enough. But I Have Got Such A Head.' She had a habit of saying her sentences as if each word had a capital letter. 'Such A Head,' she repeated stupidly.

As she raised herself up from the pillow he saw that she was not wearing any clothes and that one of her breasts was patterned with a bright red weal. For some reason this disgusted him and he changed his position in relation to the bed.

'Gracious, George,' she said, misinterpreting the gesture, 'but you have a look in your eye this morning.'

'What's that supposed to mean?'

'I didn't say that it meant anything, indeed I didn't. But seeing that you are here you may as well hand me those things.'

Her clothes lay folded on a chair by the bed, and he picked them up and handed them to her, garment by garment, with his eyes averted, scarcely able to bear the touch of the cotton on his hand. It was strange that he should be so fastidious, he thought, but – well, there it was.

'Will you go out, do you think?' he wondered.

'Well – maybe I shall try to see Mrs Elliot at her bureau.'

'That's a neat idea,' he said. 'Do you think she can give you something?'

'I should think she might . . . Say, George,' she went on – she was doing up her stockings now, head bent in concentration over a fat, dropsical knee. 'They're building some swell houses down on the East Side. You might go and see them if you wanted.'

'Well – maybe I will,' he said, not liking the way the conversation was tending.

'George, I shall need to take the streetcar to get to Mrs Elliot's.'

He gave her a dollar, descended the rickety stairs to the hotel lobby and went out into the street. He had a vague feeling that he had stirred up trouble for himself, let a genie out of its bottle that would have been better kept under glass. It was still snowing – not much, but enough to make him turn up the collar of his coat and pull the brim of his hat further down over his forehead. The attaché case banged against his knee.

He thought about the new houses down on the East Side. Maybe he would go down there when he had finished his appointments. A fellow could look at a house, after all. A flake of snow came whirling softly against his cheek and his mind went back to the Dakota storm. By jiminy, that had been a near-run thing. Another night in that haystack and he would have frozen. But he had got out of it, hadn't he? The memory comforted him and he forgot about the trouble that he had seemed to stir up for himself, and thought again about the new houses down on the East Side. He would sell fifty dollars' worth of the new inlays, he thought, have lunch in one of those restaurants where the stuffed-shirt bankers dined – and maybe see those houses.

Somehow, though, the morning did not go as he intended. At the first business house where he called the buyer was engaged and could not see him. At the second the man with whom he customarily dealt was away. Still he was not disheartened. He would go and see Messrs Dreiser and come away with his fifty-dollar order. But even at Messrs Dreiser, where the commissionaire nodded to him and a man in a frock-coat murmured 'How do, Drouett?' as he strode through the vestibule, all was not as it should have been. 'Why sure now, it's the latest thing,' he heard himself saying to the buyer as they stood together over his tray of samples, thinking that he had clinched the deal.

'I don't doubt that it's the latest thing,' said the buyer – he was smoking a fat cigar, which Drouett had prudently offered him – 'but see here, Drouett, we had a fellow from one of the Polish houses in here only the other day. They have some new process that cuts the price by twenty or thirty per cent.'

'Sure, I can fix that,' Drouett found himself saying.

'No doubt you can,' the buyer said and Drouett thought that he did not quite like the look in his eye. By proposing a twenty per cent discount he came away with a thirty-dollar order, but there was his commission gone and with it his lunch at the downtown restaurant. And really he had not quite liked the look in the other man's eye.

All this increased his sense of self-absorption. The attaché case bumped against his leg as he walked. A file of soldiers were marching along the street, led by an NCO on a grey horse and he watched them complacently. He wondered what he had done with his life. Not so very much, he thought. But there was three hundred dollars put aside in a Philadelphia bank. That wasn't so bad, was it? He pressed on into the commercial district looking for somewhere to eat his lunch, and found a bar full of bank clerks and typewriting girls and a sprinkling of college students, with steam rising from the big urns on the counter and people hurrying in from the street to buy telephone slugs. The snow had stopped, but somehow the memory of his days in Dakota stirred again in his head. All on account of that girl he had picked up on the train. It just went to show. He could see himself at the window of the timber-frame house with the wind tugging at the slates. Strange how one remembered things. The waitress came for his order and he gave it almost absently, lost in his recollections of the two of them together in that lonesome house, with the smoke rising over the low hills. He was not a man who ever regretted anything, but, well – there it was. Gosh, but wasn't this steam making him sweat and weren't those college boys snooting him with that bug-hunter's talk of theirs! He paid his bill and walked out into the street where the lunchtime crowds thronged the store windows and the taxicabs sailed by in the slush.

He was aware that the events of the morning – the snow, the sight of Mae snapping her suspenders, the interview with Messrs Dreiser's buyer – had disturbed him, that he seemed to be worth less in his estimation here in the middle of the day than he had been at its outset. Maybe he would go and inspect those houses they were building on the East Side. He had a vision of himself staring out of some upstairs window and solemnly appraising the view out over a yard where plane trees cast long shadows in the sunlight, running his eye over the fittings and the curve of the plaster. Well, no, he thought, remembering his bill at the hotel and the loss of his commission at Messrs Dreiser, perhaps he would not go and see the new houses today.

It was now about a quarter past one and the light, which had flashed over the grey, watery streets for the last half-hour, was turning in. Further off in the outer margin of the sky there were dark clouds gathering. He found, rather to his surprise, that he was a little tired after his morning's walk. Maybe he should rest up that afternoon, go through his book of contacts and figure out what the morning might bring. The thought cheered him and he imagined himself quitting one of those great manufactories on the East Side with a seventy-dollar order, a hundred-dollar order, and the commissionaire saluting him as he stepped out into the street. And then, just as he reached the block on which his hotel lay, he came upon an acquaintance – a traveller from one of the big Philadelphia concerns paying off a cabman who had just deposited him on the street corner.

'Is that you, Drouett?' remarked this gentleman, who was very taste-fully got up in a fur coat with an astrakhan collar and pulling on a pair of lavender-coloured gloves. 'I should have thought that Pittsburgh was too hot to hold you just now.'

'Now, why should that be?' Drouett wondered.

'Well, after that trick you played on Messrs Cowperwood. Don't worry, old fellow, I've as little love for them as you have, but that kind of thing gets you talked about, don't it?'

'I suppose that's so,' Drouett conceded, still not quite knowing what he meant.

'But I'm sure you know your business. Staying here long? That's right. I'm putting up at O'Neill's just now. You must come and look me up.'

'Well – maybe I will.'

They parted with every outward display of cordiality, but Drouett went on down the street with a heavy heart. He thought he knew now why the buyer at Messrs Dreiser had looked at him in the way he had. Maybe after all he should have heeded that letter from Messrs Cowperwood's attorney. Reaching the hotel – there was a chambermaid out sweeping the step with a wonderfully negligent air – he found that he was thinking of a drive he had once taken around Silver Lake and the look on Alice's face as he handed her down from the buggy. Queer how these things came back into your head, but – well, there it was. In the lobby of the hotel he found the manager lounging behind the reception desk with one eye on a copy of the *Sentinel*. A thought occurred to him.

'Is my wife – is Mrs Drouett – in the hotel?'

He had been keeping up the fiction of Mrs Drouett for nearly a week now. But no, Mrs Drouett had been out these two hours since.

'Well – make up my bill then, would you?' Drouett proposed.

If the manager thought that there was anything odd in a guest preparing to quit the premises while his wife was elsewhere, he did not think it necessary to say so. In two minutes the business was done and Drouett stood in his room stuffing clothes into a travelling case. But the feeling of urgency had left him and he found he was disposed to linger. If she came back he could find something to say to her, couldn't he just? The idea tickled him and he stood by the window smoking a cheroot, juggling the dimes in his trouser pockets and looking out at the pediments of the banking houses. Another thought struck him and he went over to the tallboy in the corner of the room where Mae had kept her things and turned out the contents on to the bed. Here, as he anticipated, he found a few little items of his own: a five-dollar bill he knew had come from his wallet, a little silver tie-clip that had gone missing a day or so before. 'Well, what do you know?' he said softly to himself. He sat on the bed for a long while, smoking his cheroot and thinking, until the light grew grey around him and the wind licked at the frail glass. One of the hotel servants came and knocked at the door but he shouted at the man not to disturb him. Perhaps half an hour passed in this way. Eventually he rose to his feet, cast a final look around the room, wrote something on a piece of paper and left it resting on the bedhead, stepped hastily out into the corridor and closed the door behind him. Five minutes later he might have been seen, travelling case in hand, disappearing round a street corner on the hotel's western side, just as Mae, who had not visited Mrs Elliot's bureau but spent the afternoon in various of the city's department stores, came toiling into view from the opposite direction.

12

Home Front

1918

They were cutting down timber in the beech copse that ran parallel to the lower lawn and the noise of the axes came up on the breeze to the open window. The sound struck her as somehow ominous – it reminded her of some incident in her past life she could not quite place – and she moved to the window to close it. Standing there with the fastening in her hand, and the birds that had gathered on the lawn fleeing at her approach, she saw a flash of sunlight catch on an axe head as it descended, and this, too, seemed to bring with it some sense of deep foreboding, quite out of kilter with the bright sunshine falling on to the grass and the sheep pastures beyond. There were people moving beneath the trees – an estate worker or two, the bailiff, a slighter figure that she recognised as her husband – and she stared at them for a moment before securing the window's catch and going back to her seat on the sofa, her teacup and the reflection of her face in the burnished copper pans that hung on the brickwork of the hearth.There was a copy of that week's *Bystander* on the table at her side, with a drawing – a humorous drawing – of a pair of human heads protruding above a trench as howitzer shells fell dangerously – but still humorously – around them, and she examined it for a moment, thinking that the heads looked like pineapples and that she did not see the joke.

She was tired of the war, which had already taken her from London to Northumberland, denied her Paris and promised Continental pleasures, and was now robbing the woods of their timber. It was not that she failed to appreciate its seriousness, or the incidental tragedies it had wrought – her brother-in-law had died in Flanders in the early months and they had worn black for a year – merely that she did not see how it concerned her. Like the sound of the axes, it burned on incessantly beyond her window, broke on to her consciousness in a way she did not like, awakened in the people she knew behaviour she could not understand, while constantly reminding her of the inexorability of its progress. Just as her brother-in-law's face would continue to gaze at her from its frame on the far wall of the dining room, so the whitened tree stumps stared up in permanent reproach.

It was now about eleven in the morning: the tree felling, which had begun just after dawn, would continue until dusk. She knew that unless she ordered up the car and had herself driven into Hexham (and what was there to do in Hexham?) or read *Mr Britling Sees It Through*, which somebody had put into her hand, she would have nothing to do until luncheon. She was also aware that she sat in a drawing room that was decorated to the highest point of ornamental *ton*, with little Sheraton desks and writing tables dotted about the carpet and a forest of antique mahogany dominating the further wall, and that this was some compensation for the choice between Hexham and Mr Britling. And then she reminded herself – she wondered how she could have forgotten it – that she had another scheme to ponder and that Hexham and Mr Britling meant nothing to her at all.

Nearly ten years had passed since the afternoon on which Alice had sat in the lodging-house parlour of the northern town reading Mr Stanhope's letter, and since that day a great deal had happened. By the time Mr Fortescue had returned to his eyrie and found the fire out and the gaslight extinguished she and her belongings were on the train to London, and by the time Miss Wilkins, with her hands done up in long white gloves to mask her eczema, made her first appearance as Carrie in *The Angel at the Hearth* (a trifle uncertain, but Mr Fortescue thought she would do) she was sitting in Mr Stanhope's office in Drury Lane. Mr Stanhope was pleased to see her – quite – and shook her hand very cordially. Not having previously encountered this colossus of the theatrical world, she had expected a superior, or at any rate contending version of Mr Fortescue, but in this she was disappointed. For Mr Stanhope was a slim, rather faded person with a cast in one eye who, unlike his rival, had plainly never stepped on a stage in his life. However, he was very affable, if somewhat condescending. He had seen Miss Hanson in that little thing of Fortescue's – what was its name? – in Brighton? – somewhere on the south coast, he could not remember – and found it – charming. A slight incompleteness about the drama, but – charming. Miss Hanson must understand that the sophistication of a West End audience was very different from the impressionable stupor of the provincial horde. But still, he confessed himself – charmed by the piece. A foppish secretary with his hair very low on the collar of his coat, on whom Mr Stanhope's good eye seemed to linger very favourably, then brought some papers for them to inspect. The rain beat upon the window and through the panelled wall they could hear the sound of Mr Stanhope's clerk dealing briskly with the morning's callers. He did not speak to such people himself, Mr Stanhope explained: indeed, it was really more than he could bear. He would have his secretary call a cab for her, and where should she be taken? Not to lodgings, surely? He would recommend that she stay at a hotel while the matter of her engagement was discussed: it was more convenient. Let the cab take her to Brown's Hotel. To all this Alice meekly acquiesced. The cab took her away through the rain to Brown's Hotel while Mr Stanhope stood at his window, as the foppish secretary rearranged the papers on his desk, watching her go.

Her association with Mr Stanhope lasted nearly two years. During this time she appeared in three West End productions, one of which lasted nine months and another four. From an early stage in these engagements she deduced that Mr Stanhope was a more successful impresario than Mr Fortescue and could understand something of the nature of his success: prudence, foresight and calculation. Mr Stanhope did not, she observed, go in for flamboyant gestures; he did not advertise the merits of his productions on every billboard in the West End; but it was rare for his theatres to stay unfilled. For her first engagement, the one that lasted nine months and of which the critics remarked that Mr Stanhope had brought off a clever stroke of business by securing Miss Hanson as his leading lady, he paid her a salary of eighty pounds a week. This seemed an unimaginable sum: enough to buy Uncle Hi and Aunt Em's house and practically everything in it; but the having of it did not greatly exalt her, for she knew – Mr Fortescue had told her this – that other ornaments of the profession earned even more, that Mr Kellaway, Mr Stanhope's great West End rival, had paid Miss Hislop a thousand a month out of the proceeds of *The Trojan Horse*. What intrigued and delighted her was the world on whose margins Mr Stanhope's clever stroke of business had now deposited her. She understood that for certain persons entry into this world was dependent on birth or hereditary association, but she knew that it could also be acquired by money, and within a short time the eighty pounds that Mr Stanhope's clerk handed to her in an envelope each Friday forenoon became very precious to her. She liked to dine in fashionable restaurants, not for the pleasure of eating but to see the people as they came and went, marvel at the exquisiteness of the women's dresses and the men's evening suits, to listen to the well-bred voices and to congratulate herself on her presence among them.

She was different from these people. She was very sure of this. She rather despised them for what she saw as their languor and complacency, but she enjoyed eavesdropping on them. A fortnight after accepting the first of Mr Stanhope's engagements she received an invitation to supper at a house in Bryanston Square. The invitation card, which had come through Mr Stanhope, terrified her. Her first thought was to refuse it. Gradually, though, the terror left her. She discovered that Mr Stanhope himself would be present and one or two other people connected with the production. Greatly daring, she spent ten guineas on a new dress – Mr Stanhope thought it – charming – and had her dresser order a cab to take her to Bryanston Square after the play was over. In the event she found the evening dull – her hosts were theatrical people and rather in awe of her – but Mr Stanhope, who detected something of her apprehension, was encouraging. 'Really, you know,' he explained, 'Newcome [this was the name of the host] is a very commonplace fellow. Started off behind a draper's counter, I believe, before he made his money. And Mrs Newcome was a drawing master's daughter from Kingly Street. You'll find social life a great bore, I dare say, but it's as well to see a little of it, for the people will like to talk to you.' She understood this to mean that she was as good as the people she met, that favours were to be extended as much as to be received, and was gratified by it. All of which Mr Stanhope, lighting his cigar from a spill at the drawing-room fire and yawning over his *entrées*, saw and silently approved.

And so life went on: a world of driving up in cabs to theatres where her name flared from billboards three feet high; of five nightly perform-ances and two matinées in the week; of sumptuous but solitary breakfasts in high rooms looking out over the London parks; of dressmakers' bills brought in at the stage door, trips to Windsor and carriage drives by the Serpentine. At first she lived in hotels until the impersonality of them became too much to bear and, on Mr Stanhope's advice, she took rooms in Thurloe Square. 'You'll find it very convenient,' Mr Stanhope confirmed. 'That is, no one who works in the West End should live there, I think.' Mr Stanhope lived at Clapham. Her loneliness did not oppress her, for she was entirely absorbed in her new life, could think of no finer destiny than the one allowed her. At the same time she made acquaintances among the professional people that chance threw in her way. There is always supposed to be something poignant about those actresses' tea parties, where no gentleman ever strays and the cabs stand waiting outside to take the guests off to evening engagements, but Alice did not find them so. She liked the clamour of female voices and the professional chit-chat and the overtures of friendship. There was also the great esteem in which, as one of Mr Stanhope's protégées, she was universally held. She was not (and this she very soon acknowledged to herself) a great actress – she wished sometimes that she still had Mr Fortescue to coach her – but she was a very skilful one. She had a way of turning her head to one side with her eyes lowered when the scene required pathos, which her audiences found irresistible, and a way of speaking her lines in a soft but curiously expressive tone that commended itself to dramatic critics.

And so her new life gathered pace. As for what took place in the world beyond, she could not have told you. The old King died and the newspapers came out in black borders, and the theatres closed for the day of the funeral. She watched the Coronation from a window in Whitehall, with a dozen theatrical people eating cold chicken in the room behind, but her mind was elsewhere, bent upon the part that Mr Stanhope had found for her in a new piece that was opening at the Drury Lane Theatre. There were other things pressing on her. Almost a year had passed since she had last set eyes on Asa. She could not believe it was a year. Twice at the onset of her dealings with Mr Stanhope she had had Asa brought up to London to see her, had taken him out to the park and made much of him. He was five years old now, with auburn hair like her own. On the second of these occasions they went to the Round Pound and it seemed to her as they walked over the grass at Kensington that they were the only people in the world. After an hour or so the woman who had brought him led him off, waving to her as he went. It was an afternoon in the early autumn with the sun burning off the distant rooftops and she watched the silhouettes fade away into nothing, and it pained her to see him go. Then, fearing that this arrangement was conspicuous she determined to visit Asa in the country. Somehow, though, she never went. She would set an afternoon aside to make her journey and then some professional obligation would rise up to turn her schemes into dust. This happened several times. And then a year had gone by and she had not seen him.

Sometimes this was a source of bitter reproach to her. She was with a group of professional friends once, at Maidenhead, very late at night, when one of the women grew suddenly confiding and began to tell her about her daughter, illegitimately born – her father was a well-known actor-manager – and at school somewhere in the west of England. She listened with sympathy, but also with a kind of self-condemning horror. Back at her rooms in Kensington she took out a photograph of Asa and a lock of his hair she had twisted into an envelope, and made various sober resolutions over them. On the very next day, she swore, she would go to Waterloo and set out in search of him. But the trip was never made. Mr Stanhope had some people with whom he wished her to lunch and a pressing journalist who could not be kept away. She supposed – and the revelation did not seem particularly shocking to her – that she was growing away from her old life. When she thought of Uncle Hi and Aunt Em she saw them as small, put-upon people. The very next week, she thought – she was between productions just now – she would go to Waterloo. But she never did and the twelve months grew into twenty-four. It was not, she hastened to assure herself, that she did not love him, merely that the circumstances of her life were as they were. There were two thousand pounds now in the bank account that Mr Stanhope had advised her to open, and she thought that a certain proportion of it could be used for Asa's education. She had a vision of his being educated at one of those great English schools, which she had heard about from Mr Stanhope, and of her visiting him there and the smile on his face and the sun on his red hair as he took her hand at the gate.

Then, quite unexpectedly, two things happened: she met Guy Keach and her association with Mr Stanhope came to an end. The ending of her association with Mr Stanhope was the more predictable. The third engagement that he had fixed for her in the West End had lasted only two months. The public did not perhaps admire it as much as the public might have done and the critics thought it – that terrible word – jejune. After this Mr Stanhope had engaged her in the friendliest conversation. There was a new secretary with long, hyacinthine locks who tidied away the papers on Mr Stanhope's desk as they spoke. He had found her performance in *Marchionesses and Milliners* – charming. But for his next production, for which that rising young playwright Mr Jouncer had written such a pretty script, he intended to give the part of the leading lady to Miss—— – and here he named a young woman of eighteen lately plucked from the obscurity of a provincial stage. She must understand that this was no reflection &c &c.

Alice listened to this without apparent emotion. She had seen enough of theatrical life, and of Mr Stanhope's companies, to be surprised by it, although she did think that Mr Stanhope might not have pronounced his sentence in front of the secretary with the hyacinthine locks. Six months later she had married Guy Keach. She knew that she had done this not on account of Mr Keach himself, but because of what he represented. No doubt this was very wrong of her. People did wrong things and couldn't help themselves. In her years in London she found that, almost unconsciously, she had made a study of the way in which the men she knew handed their hats to the servant on entering a private house. Mr Fortescue had performed this act brazenly and with a smirk; Mr Stanhope had done it studiously and ceremoniously; Guy Keach did it with a lack of concern which implied the gesture was habitual to him, that he was born, so to speak, to hand his coat to servants and have the butler bow to him as he stepped into his host's drawing room. This impressed her – impressed her far more, if the truth be known, than Guy Keach himself. He was a short, meagre and rather ungainly man, very correct in his attitudes and shrewd in his dealings, who had invested some money in one of Mr Stanhope's theatres. This, too, impressed her, for it confirmed that he belonged not to her own world but to a grander and more luxurious universe of which West End theatres and their impresarios were only a subsidiary part, that he could take Mr Stanhope or leave him. Next to him she knew that Mr Stanhope, who occasionally over-recruited himself with brandy and water, and was reputed to have an old mother still living in Hoxton, was nothing, and Mr Fortescue, with his pink face and his gold-topped cane, even less.

Still, though, she hesitated. She knew, with the realism that she brought to every relationship, that if she married him she would not be marrying the man himself, but an ideal, or rather a conduit to an ideal. She could not have put this ambition into words. It was made up not so much of material things but what material things brought with them: an atmosphere, not perhaps of outright luxury, but of very great comfort and security, composed of ancient houses and rolling fields, of long stretches of placid water seen from high windows. She knew also that in marrying Guy Keach she would have to give up Asa. There would be no place for Drouett's child in this new life she was forging for herself. She had not told Guy Keach about Drouett or Hanson and she did not intend to. He was a tolerant man in some ways, who knew that professional actresses did not live as nuns – he had said as much – but she knew that this tolerance would not extend to a child or to bigamy. There were pictures of ancestral Keaches in his house in Northumberland – bold-faced, dark-haired children in velvet suits and collars – but she knew that no picture of Asa could ever hang there. What should she do? She was appearing in a play at Richmond that would have been quite satisfactory to anyone who had not had to listen to Mr Stanhope's remarks about Miss———. But she was tired of the theatre. There would be no question of going on with all that should she marry Mr Keach. She considered it for several days, contriving elaborate futures for herself and then dispassionately rejecting them. That vision of ancient houses and rolling fields burned in her mind throughout. She knew – a part of her was constantly telling her – where her duty lay, but – well, there was a part of her still terrified of that old life where comfort and security had not been so readily to hand.

She made her decision very early one summer morning, a week before she was due to marry Guy Keach, in the rooms at Thurloe Square. The rooms were to be given up and she was going through her boxes. There were some baby clothes, a teething ring, a wooden toy she remembered Hanson buying from a shop in Van Buren, and she knew that she could not keep them. She reached out to touch the clothing: she had stitched it herself, she remembered. The world was very hard, she thought, to press these choices on her. There was a moment when she was almost prepared to give up Guy Keach. But then the moment passed. By the time the maid knocked on her door with the breakfast tray the parcel was all done up. 'Fine morning, ma'am,' the maid said, putting down the tray, and she nodded. There was a letter from Guy Keach's solicitor and she read as she drank her tea, with the parcel sitting on the table before her.

Two days later she sent three hundred pounds and an explanation – not a full explanation, but something that she knew to be sincere – to the place where Asa was lodged. She thought that by doing this she was merely temporising, that there would be a time in the future when these old threads could be picked up once more. Who could say how her life might turn out? Although she did not quite know how this might be effected, she determined that at some point he would be returned to her. *Say that I'm coming back to get him*, she wrote, *that I love him and will come back*. She cried over the letter and its enclosures, and the person who opened it wondered at the blots and the watery ink.

And so she married Guy Keach and was about as happy as anyone in such a marriage could reasonably expect to be. They went to Biarritz at first, and Menton – for the bridegroom's health, even then, was not good. And then the war came and they retreated to his estate in Northumberland, where the timber was being felled and an army camp had grown up in the fields beyond the wood, and the memory of the child and what she had done burned in her mind like the noise of the axe heads and the bugles sounding reveille through the summer dawns.

She was thinking of Asa now, as the noise of the axe heads faded away to be replaced by a shout or two and the sound of machinery grinding slowly into gear. Several years had passed since the despatch of the three hundred pounds. The finding of him had proved more difficult than she had expected. There was a letter lying in the drawer of the rosewood bureau by the window, beneath the photograph of Guy Keach in his Territorials uniform and a picture of a man in gaiters grimly regarding a prize sow at an agricultural fair, with a south London address on its envelope – an address that had needed a month's devious procuring. It had lain there a week now and she wondered why she had not yet sent it. Acting on impulse she went over to the bureau, took out the envelope – there was even a stamp on it, so great was her resolve – and held it between her fingers. There was a noise of footsteps approaching the door and she tossed the envelope hurriedly between one hand and the other, then placed it between the pages of the *Bystander* that lay beside her on the sofa, just as the door opened and Guy Keach came into the room.

He was a short, dark-haired, moustachioed man, so short that his lack of height obsessed him, to the point where he was sometimes unable to stand in a room with other men without casting jealous glances at them or bouncing up on the balls of his feet. At the start of the war he had gone with his yeomanry regiment to France, but this scheme had been quickly given up on grounds of bad health and he had stopped calling himself Major Keach. She saw that he was annoyed about something from the way he approached her, looking to right and left, and poking at the corners of the carpet with his stick. He was breathing rather heavily, and this increased his air of awkwardness and irritation.

'You have over-exerted yourself again,' she said, by way of a greeting.

'Maybe I have. It's that damned pull up from the wood. I always take it too fast.'

Knowing that he disliked questions about his health, she went on, 'How long will they be cutting down the trees, do you suppose?'

'A week will do it, I should think. Quite a lot of the timber is rotted, I'm afraid.'

There was something else annoying him, she could see, quite apart from his shortness of breath and a discrepancy in the set of the carpet, which he was restoring with his foot. 'Here, there is that fellow Baker come to lunch. He was riding back through the wood and I couldn't very well not ask him. Do you mind?'

'Not at all. I shall be very glad to see Captain Baker.'

'The fact is' – he was still manoeuvring the piece of carpet back into place with his boot toe – 'he has something he says he wants to ask you. I told him it was quite out of the question, but he wanted to hear it from you himself.'

'Gracious. You make it sound a terrible mystery.' She knew that he liked to be humoured in this way. 'What on earth can it be?'

'Well, here he is. He can tell you.'

A rustle of movement beyond the door indicated that Captain Baker was awaiting his host's introduction. As he came into the room, she could see immediately why Guy Keach might be irritated by his presence, for he was nearly six feet high and wore several campaign ribbons on the breast of his uniform. Seeing her he marched across the carpet, shook her hand in the frankest manner and said, 'This is a great honour, Mrs Keach. You see, I have always wanted to meet you.'

She felt herself laughing at his enthusiasm. 'Why should that be, Captain Baker?'

'Well, you'll scarcely credit it – perhaps it's something one ought not to admit to – but some years ago I had the very greatest pleasure in watching you on the stage of the Haymarket Theatre. I believe the piece was called *Mornings in Mayfair*. It wouldn't at all surprise me if I didn't have the programme still, somewhere in an old trunk.'

'Have a glass of sherry, Baker,' Guy Keach said, appearing between them with a decanter. There was a glint of fury in his eye. 'And tell me, are those beasts of yours getting enough fodder? I told Henshall that he could clear out the lower barn and give you half.'

'Plenty of fodder, thanks,' said Captain Baker, who had caught the tone in his host's voice but was clearly determined not to be ruffled by it. 'The thing is, Mrs Keach, I have a proposal to put to you.'

'You'll find the hay quite good around here,' Guy Keach went on, with faint menace, 'but that is more than can be said for the root crops.'

'You see' – for the first time in this exchange Captain Baker looked faintly embarrassed – 'we have determined on a theatrical evening to raise money for the battalion widows and orphans fund. And we'd consider it a great honour if you'd consent to appear. The colonel himself said what an excellent thing it would be.'

'Quite out of the question,' Guy Keach said, more genially now but still with a hint of sharpness. 'Why, I don't suppose my wife remembers what it was like to walk out on to a stage.'

'Oh, I don't know about that,' Captain Baker said, not looking at him. 'But we should most awfully appreciate it, Mrs Keach. Why, the VADs the adjutant has engaged for the minor parts would be absolutely thrilled. Come now, what do you say?'

Looking at the two of them as they stood before her – Guy Keach a full head shorter than his guest – she wondered if Captain Baker, who had clearly divined something of the air of tension in the room, was doing it on purpose; whether, to settle some private score, he had simply chosen the easiest way of infuriating his host. On the other hand there was something in his tone that suggested this was merely the way he behaved, that the presence of Field Marshal Haig and his retinue would have had him bouncing up to ask the Field Marshal how his batman got his buttons so bright. She knew – there had been occasional requests of this kind before – that nothing angered her husband more than breezy allusions to her professional life, yet the memories it stirred were so agreeable to her that she would not let the moment pass.

'Gracious, Baker,' Guy Keach went on, with altogether ghastly cordiality. 'I can't have my wife being made a spectacle of in this way. It really wouldn't do. Let me give you ten guineas for widows and orphans fund, if that would help.' He coughed slightly, with a little spasm in his throat – the cough made him angry, for it was the one thing he could not control – and she wondered if there would come a day when there was no Guy Keach standing on her drawing-room carpet to forbid her pleasures.

'Well, it's a great pity,' said Captain Baker, realising perhaps that he had gone too far. 'Why, with a little advertising we could have brought the whole village in, not to mention those nurses from the hospital at Hexham. Are you sure we can't persuade you to change your mind, Mrs Keach?' He meant Guy Keach's mind, but was too polite to say so.

'I fear it can't be done,' she said. But she knew that a part of her regretted it.

'My wife gets very tired in the evenings,' Guy Keach explained, which was an utter fabrication. 'I really couldn't countenance it. Tell me, how do you find the blacksmith over at Sowerby? I always say that he could crack a shoe simply by looking at it.'

Luncheon passed without incident. The noise of the axes had stopped, and Captain Baker talked about the local point-to-points and his sister, who was nursing at one of the Cambridge colleges. Afterwards she was sitting in the drawing room – the *Bystander* was open on her lap and the letter lay an inch or two beyond it – when her husband appeared unexpectedly in the doorway.

'Has Captain Baker gone back to camp?'

'I cannot have that man in the house,' Guy Keach said, in what was intended to be a satirical tone. 'Really, you know, his father is an agricultural salesman in Berkshire. I distinctly remember Colonel Fitzmaurice telling me.'

'You look better for your rest.'

'Do I? Well, that's good to know.' His gaze fell to the sofa. 'Who is that you are writing to?'

'It is only to Edie Jeffries.' She picked up the envelope and put it face down in her lap. 'You remember, you met her once.'

'The tall girl with the mousy hair who bragged about her uncle being a minor canon? I should say so. What does Miss Jeffries do with herself?'

'I don't think she does anything. I was going to send her twenty pounds.'

'Twenty pounds, eh? You should have her here as parlourmaid. She couldn't be any worse than Bassett. She absolutely dropped the teapot this morning.' His good humour was entirely restored. 'Would you like me to post it in the village?'

'No. There is something I wish to add to it.'

'Very well, then.'

He coughed his cough and it occurred to her again that there would come a time when he would not be there to read her letters and refuse her invitations, that she might look forward to a future in which she could do what she liked, write as many letters as she chose and have whoever she pleased to live with her. Shortly after this he went away, the sound of the axes rose up again from the distant wood and the letter Alice had thrown towards the fireplace burned itself to extinction against the glowing coals in the grate.

13

Araby

1928
And so we came to that altogether stupendous period in our lives, which the newspapers – who had followed our incandescent flight almost from the first – called the Hogpen Boom, that year or two when my uncle rose incontestably to dominate the affairs of the consortium that bore his name. In this, as I now realise, he had great luck. Guy Keach was gone. Sir Basil Ambrose's affairs had failed to prosper; he had quarrelled with Baldwin and lost his seat in Parliament. The men who came to take his place were in awe of my uncle. Nurtured on his myth, they found in him only what they expected to find, took his expostulations for tactics and his indecision for strategy. He was not quite real to them, and the fantasy of his appearance, background and sharp ascent bound them to him with an indissoluble knot.

My uncle was very great in those days. I have said that the mark of his genius was a willingness to adapt himself to whatever environment in which he happened to fetch up. He was as at home on the prow of Atry's yacht as it tacked desultorily across the Solent as he was slaughtering grouse on Lord Parmenter's Aberdeenshire estate, as happy dispensing seedcake to the Dowager Duchess of Sutherland in Pont Street as parading in the Ascot enclosure. I have a memory of him from this time at some reception on the House of Commons terrace, with a charged glass in his hand and Mrs Stanley Baldwin on his arm, and the look on his face was altogether euphoric. It was the look of an athlete who, having breasted the tape of some long and arduous race, glances over his shoulder at the flotsam of the finishing line straight behind him. He was, or so it seemed to me, like a great engine, forever roving forward, always seeking out new territory even as it colonised the ripped-up earth beneath its tread.

Between the spring of 1927 and the summer of 1929, I remember once calculating, his gross income exceeded two million pounds.

All this – my uncle, his personality, the face he presented to the world

– was very absorbing to me, as fascinating in its way as the affairs of hogpen on which I was – sometimes minutely – engaged. The big dyeing plant at Salford was well established by this time along with the 'Homeknit' manufactories that assembled garments for the retail trade. There was a household and domestic division – it was considered too bright for chintzes, but otherwise thought admirable for interior decoration – and a campaign in hand to encourage its use for sportswear. The 'hogpen bruin', that children's teddy bear given away in exchange for newspaper coupons, examples of which are still advertised by the memorabilia dealers, dates from this period. I remember that my uncle thought the bear gratuitous, for amid this prodigious spectacle of advertisement and solicitation he had – and this, I think, was another mark of his genius – a great feeling for the proprieties of the day. When a parliamentarian, for a joke, addressed the house in a hogpen waistcoat he deplored it as a 'stunt'. All this, curiously, seemed to increase the esteem in which he was held and to dispel the faint scent of trepidation that had followed him into the fashionable world. Amid these ominous prefigurations of social flux, he offered reassurance. He had a publicity photograph taken about this time, often reproduced in magazines that spoke of the accomplishments of self-made men, which showed him standing in a country lane, one arm flung over the upper rung of a five-barred gate, benevolently surveying a field of oilseed rape, which if it were bogus was no more inauthentic than any other of the myriad faces he presented to the world.

As all this may indicate, I do not think I quite understood my uncle then, appreciated the forces that drove him or saw what made him tick. The newspapers made much of his entertaining, those suppers for thirty in our house in Belgrave Square, of which, even now, occasional memories still linger – but I do not believe that, in the end, they were the recreations he would have chosen for himself. There were whole parts of his life, it seemed to me, that he had altogether extinguished, great fires of his inward existence expertly banked down, and chief among these was the past. The house at Southfields, with the tiny laboratory lost behind rhododendron bushes in its melancholy garden, seems very far away now, and the Intwood Road positively remote. Yet the zeal with which my uncle cultivated this new life of his was precisely the same. He could change his appearance, and his lodgings, but he could not, it seemed to me, counterfeit the larger matter of himself. I have another memory of him – very vivid and flagrant it is – lounging in the hallway of some Belgravia mansion preparatory to going in to dinner, together with Beverley Nichols, who was rather his crony, and thinking that the set of his forehead, the tortoise-like way that he blinked into the light that burned off the great chandeliers, was identical to the manner in which he had negotiated the Yare Valley mud. But even if I did not understand him, I do not believe that he was entirely self-interested. Once I remember, about this time, I found him in the vestibule of the house in Belgrave Square, rather flown with wine and with a pile of newspapers clasped uncertainly under his elbow.

'Bin lunchin' with that feller Drawbell,' he explained, as the butler fastened the door behind him.

'The man who edits the *Sunday Chronicle?*'

'That's the one.' He was expensively, but negligently dressed in a chalk-white pinstripe whose jacket buttons had mostly disappeared. 'Got a circulation of a quarter of a million, Ralph.'

As this information had clearly come from Drawbell, I did not contest it. There was a pause, during which the mingled scents of brandy, sweat and camphor contended with the vase of flowers by his elbow.

'Bin thinking of writing a column,' he said.

'A column?'

'A *column*.' He pronounced the word almost reverently, as if it were a hieroglyph in some oriental dictionary.

'What will you write about?'

I saw instantly that I had said the wrong thing. 'Spec I shall think of something, Ralph,' my uncle said stiffly.

Unexpectedly, the newspaper column was a great success. I have heard a rival editor maintain that it combined the advantages of business expertise with the common touch. My uncle furnished grave little exordia about the necessity of not living beyond your means and paying twenty shillings in the pound, mused on contemporary fads and bragged about his acquaintances. He did not, of course, write it himself – I suspect that Beverley Nichols may have had a hand in its composition – but its animating spirit was unquestionably his: shrewd, vainglorious, surprisingly well attuned to the lower-middle-class householders who were the *Chronicle*'s subscribers.

The column ran for a year until he lost interest in it, the highlights appearing in paper-covered booklets – *The Rendall Method*, they were called – occasional copies of which still survive on the shelves of stationers' shops.

All this necessarily extended my uncle's acquaintance. To politicians, business people, actors and actresses, he could now add press magnates, journalists, advertising agents. They came to dinner in Belgrave Square, could be seen on the lawn of the big house at Richmond and were alternately charmed, disillusioned or confirmed in their prejudices: bright, eager faces, framed by the emerald grass and the rolling river beyond. My uncle's attitude to them veered between a manifest gratitude for their presence and a sneaking disbelief that so much celebrity could fall so far short of the exacting standards he set for it. I saw him steal a glance at a Treasury minister once, who had offered some remark about the economic situation, with the look of one who calculates a bargain and fears that he has been sold short. For myself, I liked the variegated social experience any kind of proximity to my uncle entailed, while sharing his estimate of some of the people we knocked up against. I thought Tallulah Bankhead a noisy, rowdy girl, did not recognise Chaplin until he introduced himself and wondered why Queen Marie of Romania could not spoon her own sugar into the teacup. There was, too – as pervasive as the Philadelphus my uncle planted on the banks of our Richmond terrace – the scent of ulterior motive.

Perhaps this is a way of saying that my uncle had plans for me, in which the people assembled on the Richmond lawn were no doubt intended to play their part. Heiresses, chief whips, city moguls, regimental colonels: all passed through the Richmond caravanserai at one time or another in the not quite conscious thought that I could do business – social, emotional, commercial – with them and they with me. Lord Parmenter took me out into the rose garden once – I could see my uncle watching from the terrace with the sun glinting off his spectacles – and more or less proposed that I should marry his daughter. That was the kind of life we lived then, a world of slow, pompous dinners and antique ceremony, of liveried footman starting up in the corner of a room as we made our entrance, like a praetorian guard, and the hogpen advertisements – flaring and altogether unignorable – that greeted us wherever we went. The hogpen mania was at its height now: a Midlands municipality painted their fleet of buses in it; it was used for bunting; the decorative arts could not ignore it and the painting by Lysander Carey RA, *Studies in hogpen*, caused a sensation at the Summer Exhibition.

I remember above all a day in the summer of 1928 when the Richmond entertaining was at its zenith – less for its triumphant assertion of the particular social heights to which my uncle had clamorously ascended than for the first hint of the divide that lay between us and was, as I now suspect, to colour our remaining dealings with each other. The scene is very vivid to me, very charged and reconstitutable: the wide slope of grass sweeping down to the river, beyond which quaint suburban houses rose incrementally up the hill towards London, the pleasure craft drawn up under Richmond Bridge, the great swans nosing delicately at the reed beds. So, too, are the faces of the guests, a social matrix to which only my uncle possessed the key: Devonish, who managed his dye works, overdressed in a wing collar and dickie bow, casting agonised glances at other men who had come in summer suits; 'Young Mr Aberconway', Guy Keach's lawyer and his widow's representative; Mr Mortboy, the rationalist demagogue who had caused a furore by appearing on a public platform with the Bishop of Birmingham and denying the existence of God. So, too, is my uncle, who wandered through this curious assortment of people, sly and innocuous by turns, but somehow holding each person he met in thrall to his personality and the tenacity of his vision.

There was a string quartet playing selections from Scarlatti on the terrace's edge and he stopped to listen to it, an odd, perplexed expression on his face, as the sound of Devonish and Mortboy loudly arguing was borne up from the lawn.

'. . . When I walk into a room my activities are governed by a series of *physiological procedures*, not by the hand of God.'

'. . . That's what the atheist always says. Afraid to confront the mystery of the world around him.'

'. . . And where, my friend, is this soul that everyone talks about? Have you seen it? Show it to me.'

Of the two it was Devonish who was the more animated. Mr Mortboy was merely taking a professional interest. But Devonish was really cross.

My uncle regarded them benevolently. 'Should have got 'is Grace here,' he said. 'Then we should have had some fun.'

As with so many aspects of his inner life, I never really knew what my uncle thought about religion. He was rarely seen in a place of worship. On the other hand he had a superstitious side, which manifested itself in the touching of lamp posts and, in moments of commercial crisis, the conducting of *sortes Biblicae*. At the same time I knew that Mr Mortboy's presence on the Richmond lawn was purely ornamental, that the look of puzzlement that now returned to my uncle's brow had nothing to do with his views about God.

"Ad a telegram from that feller Archibald,' he began cautiously. '*Lord* Archibald. You'll remember him from the Worshipful Company of Dyers' dinner. Says he can't be here on account of it's the Eton-Harrow match.'

'No mystery about that,' I said. 'I dare say half the Cabinet's there.'

'What? Baldwin and Jix and the rest of 'em? Gone off to watch a lot of schoolboys play cricket?' I could see that what irked him was not Lord Archibald's desertion but the existence of a social code that he had failed to decipher. It was as if he had walked into a banqueting hall wearing a tailcoat, only to find everyone else in dinner jackets. Casting an eye across the terrace, where half a dozen gaudy girls in summer frocks were clustered around a pair of guards officers in scarlet tunics, and a parlour-maid was carrying iced hock cup to the people further down the lawn, he said, a touch peevishly, 'I know where *I'd* rather be.'

'It seems a nice afternoon,' I temporised.

'A nice afternoon? I should think that it *was* a nice afternoon,' said my uncle brusquely. 'There's young Tennant reading his poems in the conservatory – I don't understand 'em, but Mrs Keigwin says they're the latest thing – Tiarks has brought up a party from his place in Dorking – you'll have seen his car in the drive, I dare say – and that chap with the eyeglass' – he indicated a tall, fair-haired young man on the edge of the group of girls – 'is going to write it all up for the *Sketch*.'

Still, though, there was something preying on his mind. Tiarks and his party from Dorking? The *vers libre* experiments in the conservatory? Who could tell? The disputing voices from the lawn had grown louder.

'. . . A common misperception to think that a particular religious experience – *so-called* religious experience – can be translated into a universal truth.'

'. . . If you'd seen our Edie, laid out on her bed of pain, waiting to be took, you'd know the error of your ways, young man.'

'. . . Where is this spiritual dimension that everyone talks about? Have you been to it? Can you take me there?'

'. . . Disrespecting the clergy that are only trying to do their best in a wicked world is as big a sin as any, my dad used to say.'

As neither of the participants in this exchange was listening to the other, it was difficult to say which had the upper hand. Mr Mortboy was, on balance, louder in his expostulations but Devonish, it could be argued, was angrier. At this stage in the proceedings the smart money would have to have been on Devonish.

'Devonish is a Plymouth Brother I b'lieve,' my uncle said. 'Never heard him so sharp.'

When I look back on that afternoon at Richmond I see only a lost world, a vanished, paradisal Araby, never to be refashioned or revisited, but at the time I do not think that I enjoyed myself, for I was wary of my uncle's schemes, especially those that touched on my own immediate future. Just then, in addition to my subordinate position in the Hogpen Boom, I was making some little experiments with potassium, to which my uncle occasionally condescended. 'No money in that, Ralph,' he would say. 'No money at all. Why, you'd be much better tryin' to refine them dyes, or find a mordant that'd properly stick.' At the same time I distrusted what I can only call the showmanship of my uncle's approach to social life, its theatrical sheens and surfaces, the sense of deep, interior calculation. There had been a story in the newspapers recently about a tycoon so continuously occupied with his work that he kept a row of offices along a single corridor from which the doors had been removed, allowing him to conduct as many as half a dozen meetings at the same time. The afternoons at Richmond had something of the same air: half a dozen discrete objectives simultaneously pursued; half a dozen bargains waiting to be clinched.

'Why, there's Aberconway,' my uncle said now. 'Catch him going to the blessed Eton-Harrow match.'

This was the second or third time that we had seen 'Young Mr Aberconway', so called to distinguish him from other and yet more ancient Aberconways who featured on his firm's notepaper. He was a bald, obsequious but by no means spiritless man of fifty, with whom my uncle existed in a state of armed but not unfriendly neutrality. Guy Keach had been dead for over two years and the destiny of his stake in the consortium had absorbed my uncle for at least three-quarters of that time. Twice my uncle had offered to purchase it from his widow; twice this offer had been refused. 'Surprisin' a woman like that bothering herself with business,' my uncle more than once remarked.

The voices from the lawn were now threatening to get out of hand.

'. . . You may pity those South Sea islanders, my friend, bowing their heads to wood and stone, but is a man who contorts himself before a Christian altar any different?'

'. . . You turn up your nose at God, young man, and you'll find that one of these fine days God will punish you.'

There was a white-haired man with a fine, corrupt old face sitting not far from Aberconway's chair who caught my uncle's eye as he turned. My uncle signalled back with his forefinger. 'Now that', he said, 'is Sir Jocelyn Carbury. You'll have heard of him, Ralph. We 'ad his daughter to dinner, you'll recollect. Tall girl that fell off her horse at Badminton with her arm in a sling. Now that, Ralph, is a man I should like you to take the measure of.'

'Does he need a son-in-law?'

My uncle looked doubtful for a moment, then laughed. He would forgive almost anything in exchange for what he called 'gumption'. I tried to remember where I had heard of Sir Jocelyn Carbury and whether he conducted the City livery company that had recently welcomed my uncle into its hall or owned the moribund Leicestershire estate for which my uncle was supposed to be negotiating. The string quartet, which had been silent for a moment or two, now struck up again, but more forcefully so that the surrounding conversations were more or less extinguished. The look on Devonish's face, I saw, was almost apoplectic. There would be trouble about this. My uncle was always having difficulties with Devonish: this would add to them. There were other people – young people of about my own age, mostly – drifting across the terrace from the path that led to the conservatory. No doubt the poetry recitation was at an end. Instinctively I plunged off down the hill to where my uncle was deep in conversation with Mr Aberconway.

'Anxious to accommodate Mrs Keach's wishes,' I heard him say, as Mr Aberconway indulgently inclined his head.

In the past there had been talk of how much my uncle might offer for what now, with the passing of time and his own aggrandisement, amounted to a fifth share of the business. Such sums as I heard bandied about – the latest was half a million pounds – struck me as entirely fanciful.

Mr Aberconway said something about export markets: my uncle looked thoughtful. The heat of the garden, previously kept in check by a breeze blowing off the river, began to seem insupportable. There were dark clouds gathering beyond the bridge. Soon it would rain, and rain hard. Ten yards away, in the midst of a little circle of guests that had gathered to watch the dispute, Devonish was brandishing his fist in Mr Mortboy's face.

'I fear that a structured payment would not be in my client's best interests,' Mr Aberconway said.

'Maybe. Maybe not,' my uncle shot briskly back.

There was a tug at my elbow, at which Sir Jocelyn Carbury suddenly materialised. 'Do you suppose', he enquired, after we had exchanged a languid handshake, 'that we should do something about those two fellows? I really think there might be an altercation.'

'Perhaps I ought to tell my uncle.'

'Looks as if it might be about to rain, too. Makes me glad I decided not to go to the cricket.'

It was then that I remembered Sir Jocelyn's identity. He was responsible for the selection of Conservative candidates for the forthcoming election. Life suddenly seemed composed of a multitude of unwelcome choices. My uncle and Mr Aberconway continued to negotiate. The two guardsmen and their attendant sirens were coming back up the lawn, leaving a litter of teacups and empty glasses in their wake. Above their racket could be heard, quite clearly, the noise of Devonish and Mr Mortboy shouting at each other. The string quartet sawed mournfully on. Sir Jocelyn hovered in an uncertain attitude between these circling tribes of vagrant humanity. Then, suddenly, it began to rain, in a thin shower that, almost before anyone had become aware of its onset, swiftly developed into an absolute cataract. The effect on my uncle was unexpectedly galvanising. It was almost as if the rain had been a part of his strategy for the afternoon, a further contingency that he could bend to his will. He signalled to the string quartet to stop playing, patted Mr Aberconway on the back, approached Sir Jocelyn with a look of craven apology and regret, shooed away those of his guests who still remained on the terrace with an emphatic movement of his fingers, and finally made his way to Devonish and Mr Mortboy who, as the rain fell in torrents on their exposed heads, were still loudly disputing.

'Come along, Devonish. Come inside. You too, Mortboy.'

Mr Mortboy, to whom, as I had suspected, all this was nothing, merely a chance to exercise his debating skills, turned abruptly on his heel. Devonish, on the other hand, stood stock still as the rain continued to cascade over his forehead and over the glass of his rimless spectacles.

'I won't have it, sir.'

'What's that, Devonish?' My uncle paused to make some obscure signal to Mr Aberconway. 'What won't you 'ave?'

'I shan't stand by and have my religion insulted.'

'Don't be such an old woman.'

What Devonish said in return I failed to catch, but he was clearly profoundly put out, almost to the point of speechlessness. My uncle watched him for a moment with a certain puzzlement, then shrugged his shoulders. We became part of a generalised throng, hastily returning to the house. 'Here, Ralph,' he said confidingly, as the butler helped us ceremoniously over the lintel while attempting to hold an umbrella over Mr Aberconway's dripping head. 'Sir Jocelyn and me'll be taking our tea in the study, I b'lieve. Why don't you come along, eh?' The throng passed on inseparably into the vestibule and he was borne away.

Although nothing was said about my failure to wait upon Sir Jocelyn Carbury in the study I knew that my uncle did not like it. His rebuke, such as it was, was administered on the morning after the general election when I found, next to my breakfast plate, a copy of *The Times* with the result of a particular Home Counties constituency, won by a Conservative, marked with a pen stroke.

Not long after this Devonish resigned his post as manager of the dye works and went to work for a rival manufacturer. In the same week my uncle paid Mrs Keach three-quarters of a million pounds for her stake in the consortium. It was generally agreed that this was too much.

PART TWO

1929–1936

14

Returning

He saw her face again some time in the fall of 1929, as he sat in a little barber's shop on the south side of Chicago waiting to get his hair cut. It was the queerest thing. Usually on the small table at the rear of the shop there lay a pile of newspapers and magazines, and from among them he would mostly select, being interested in a mild way in baseball and ice hockey, an illustrated sports paper. Only this particular day there was nothing of that sort, only a New York Society sheet of a kind he frankly disliked, but took up now as there was nothing else. And there, on the first page that he came to, was an account of a dinner some New York notable – 'Fifty-Second Streeters' he called them satirically – vacationing in London had given to a dozen or so of his fellow countrymen, and here, set in a little frame to one side of the letterpress, was a portrait of 'the well-known hostess, Mrs Alice Keach'. Mrs Alice Keach. For a moment Drouett did not recognise her. He merely glanced at the portrait before continuing with the account of the furnishings of Mr Vanderbilt's suite at Claridge's Hotel. But then something in the line of her jaw, some curve in the tendril of hair that fell over her ear, drew him back and he laid the paper open on his knee the better to examine it. The realisation, when it came to him, did not seem so very remarkable. 'That's her all right,' he said to himself, and he sat for a second or two staring beyond the line of barbers' chairs and the low, tilted awning into the busy street beyond.

In a moment or two a chair became free, and he sat there talking languidly to the barber about business and pleasure, Lindbergh and Calvin Coolidge quite as if there had been nothing in the paper to stir the recollections that were now passing through his mind. But when he had paid the barber his forty cents and was standing at the back of the shop searching for his hat, there lay the paper again, open at that page, with her face – much more familiar and welcoming now, he thought – looking out at him. 'Say,' he said to the barber, whom he had known for a year or so, 'you mind if I take this paper?'

'Why sure,' the barber said, only briefly glancing up, but managing to suggest in his answer that Drouett was a dark horse and that something secret now lay between them. 'Be my guest.' And so, not quite knowing why he did so, Drouett folded up the paper quarter-size, placed it in the attaché case that he carried with him and walked out into the street.

He was nearly sixty now, but much the same as he had always been: not so very prosperous, but not, as he frequently assured himself, just scraping a living. A little investment he had made the previous spring had gone slightly awry. Just now he was travelling in whiskey – to Illinois mainly, but with occasional excursions east and west.

It struck him, as he looked once more at the paper, that this was not the end of the matter, that in picking it up he had started something he did not quite know how to finish. Throughout the ensuing days and months, he began unconsciously to assemble the fragments he recollected of their life together. He remembered her stepping out of bed once, with a lighted candle in her hand, and the light reflecting glorious tints and hues in her hair, another time when they had gone out driving in a buggy at Silver Lake, and each time the solidity of the memory comforted him. He found that he could recall a particular morning in the wooden house at De Smet – how the wind had rattled through that house! – with her standing at the open door and smiling at him. 'Well,' he said to himself, 'that was a fine time we had, anyhow.' These memories did not inspire in him, as they might have done in another person, any sense of wistfulness or regret, but he knew that he was glad to have them. Several times, waiting in the back room of some saloon to see a customer or out on the railroad to Detroit or Michigan, he found himself remembering details of this kind and luxuriating in them. She would be forty-four, he told himself, looking at his fat, red face in the window of the train car, or forty-five.

He was not an imaginative man, but he had his resources. One of these was a journalist friend who worked on the *Chicago Times Herald*. A fortnight after he had begun to think about this episode in his past life he sought out this man and, after several hesitations and the offering of several drinks, enquired: if a fellow wanted to find out about people who lived in England, grand people, not in the ordinary run of humanity, there would be books that might tell him, might there not? Certainly there might be books, the friend assured him – amused, but not exaggeratedly so, for he gathered that there was something intent and serious about the enquiry – in fact, nothing could be easier than finding the information he wanted.

And so, a fortnight after this, again not without several hesitations and misgivings, Drouett found himself striding into the city's central public library – not a place he had ever been before and whose corridors of stacked literature frankly intimidated him – to consult a copy of *Who's Who*. It was two years old, but the red gilt binding and the thick heavy feel of it in his hands consoled him. Such things were reliable, he told himself, would tell him what he wanted to know.

The paragraph about her was not more than a few lines long. It said merely that she was the widow of a Mr Guy Keach and lived at an address in Lowndes Square, London SW1. Who had Mr Guy Keach been, he wondered? Some stuffed shirt with a pile of money, no doubt. The incongruity of his situation – standing in the corridor of Chicago Central Library with the wind blowing in off the lake to rattle the panes and reading about Mrs Keach in her house at Lowndes Square – quickly occurred to him, and he put the book back on its shelf and walked away. All the same, the seeds of something had been sown. A week later, having talked once more to his acquaintance on the *Chicago Times Herald*, he was back at the library – very boldly he walked into it now – to examine the cartography section. Here he found a map of central London and a description of Lowndes Square, which interested him very much. As to why he accumulated this information – where it might lead him, what satisfaction he derived from it – he could not have said, but there – maps were fascinating things, were they not? He made a tracing of the London map on a piece of fine paper bought from a stationer's store and fixed it to the wall of his room.

Around this time there came a crisis in Drouett's business affairs. The distillery for whom he travelled had offices in the financial district. He was accustomed to call there once a month to confer with the manager. On one of these visits the manager, a sharp-featured man rather younger than himself, said with every appearance of cordiality, 'Well, now, Drouett. How do you find the trade these days?'

'I guess things are a little slow at the moment,' Drouett conceded, quite as affably as the manager.

'You don't say? Here. You had better take a look at these returns.'

Drouett accepted the proffered sheets of paper, which he knew related to his own area of territory. They certainly were a long way down, he reflected. Maybe he had been letting things slide.

Noting his silence, the manager went on, 'Mr Banahan and I' – Mr Banahan was one of the firm's directors – 'were thinking that it might be best to introduce a quota system.'

'Oh indeed?' said Drouett, who knew that a quota system meant death to the kind of licence he had hitherto enjoyed. 'I shouldn't be in too much of a hurry to do that, you know, if I were you.'

'Oh, wouldn't you?' the manager said.

Drouett missed the note of impatience. 'Well, no. I guess you'd find that some of us here would have to consider our positions.'

'You must do as you think fit,' the manager said.

Taking the streetcar home through the slush of the Chicago winter, Drouett knew that he had made a mistake. 'I'll fix this,' he said to himself. And so, when he returned home he immediately sat down and wrote a letter to his employers apologising for what he believed was his hastiness, allowing certain of the merits of the quota system, hoping that Mr Banahan &c. The reply, which reached him a day or so later, was everything that he might have expected. Messrs Shaughnessy had read his letter with interest. In the light of the sentiments previously expressed, they did not quite see their way to extending his employment beyond the month's end. They would reflect upon the matter and perhaps communicate with him again &c. Pondering the letter in his room at the lodging house, Drouett was not downcast. 'Sure, I'll fix something,' he said to himself, thinking of his thirty years in the trade. He decided that he would work out the end of his month: it would give him an opportunity to see how the land lay and look up a few old friends. Buoyed up by this decision, he went out that night and picked a little whore girl out of the line in a place on Van Buren that he knew. Standing on the street corner half an hour later, smelling the girl's scent on his shirt-front, he realised that this, too, had been a mistake. 'Sure, I'm getting too old for this,' he said to himself. The mission house where Alice had once lived with Hanson lay only a block or two away, had he but known it. Going back to his room at the lodging house he discovered that the smell of the scent disgusted him, and he took off his shirt and threw it on to the floor.

And all the time the thought of what he had discovered in the Society magazine burned in his mind. A week later he found himself at Sioux Falls, the outermost limit of his professional beat. Finishing his business early, and telling himself that it was nothing to his employers what he did with his time now, he did not immediately return to Chicago but instead bought a ticket for one of the western expresses and had himself carried away to De Smet. It was the first time he had been there since his adventure of twenty-five years before, and as the train sped over the long, empty prairie the recollection of it oppressed him horribly. He had been lucky, he supposed. Fate had been on his side. The thought cheered him and he came into De Smet almost light-headed, took a room in an inn near the station yard and sent down for a bottle of brandy. The next morning he got up early, walked out beyond the houses and the storage shacks, and stood on one of the low bluffs surveying the town. It was twice the size it had been, with a couple of large manufactories dominating the main street, but by no means unrecognisable. He found the slope where the old house had stood – it was gone now and the land turned into a lumber yard – and the walk up to its peak thoroughly disturbed him. Making enquiries back in town – he represented himself as a relative in search of a lost cousin – he turned up, at the end of a day's persistent search, an old woman who remembered a Lutheran preacher named Hanson and how he had departed the town, not without all scandal, with a girl who lived in one of the houses on the hill. This, the woman thought, might have happened twenty-five or even thirty years ago.

All this Drouett carefully remembered and afterwards, secretly exulting, wrote down in a pocketbook. He knew, or thought he knew, that there is no person quite so traceable as a minister of the church. He knew, too, that Mr Pinkerton had established an office in Chicago and that such work would be meat and drink to him. Still, he did not quite know why he wanted the information or what he would do with it when he found it; he knew only that the finding of it wholly absorbed him. Accordingly he presented himself at the office in Chicago, again using the fiction that he desired to re-acquaint himself with a long-lost cousin, and paid twenty dollars to Mr Pinkerton's representative to supply details of a Lutheran minister named Hanson, last heard of in the Dakotas in the early years of the century. The information came back in a week. There was a Lutheran pastor named Hanson fitting his description, who now directed the church's mission in Duluth. This Reverend Hanson, the Pinkerton man further confirmed, was in his late forties with a wife and two children. This information intrigued Drouett greatly. Yet more intriguing was the fact that Hanson now lived in Duluth, only a day's journey from Chicago. The job with Messrs Shaughnessy had reached its appointed end and he was travelling for a firm of carpet manufacturers on the lower east side and elsewhere. Never mind! He would find a way of going to Duluth! And so the early spring of 1930 found him in a train heading north-east in the direction of the Great Lakes with a slip of paper in his pocketbook on which the Pinkerton man had inscribed Pastor Hanson's address.

He was not quite sure how he was going to proceed – not quite. His first idea had been to pass himself off as an official representative – the Revenue Service, some government body – but he knew that if he did this he would very probably be asked for some proof of his identity, which he could not, in the nature of things, supply. Thinking the matter over, as the train pulled into the Duluth freight yards, he decided that he would stick to his original scheme: that he was a relative seeking to locate a long-vanished cousin. He fancied, too, that a minister of the church, hearing what he had to say, would not suspect him of any deception. Besides he had spent a lifetime, professionally, wheedling himself into the affections of people who had every cause to mistrust him and he thought that he could deal with the Rev. Hanson.

The Lutheran mission was in a poor part of Duluth, beyond the orbit of the streetcars, and he wandered along several grimy thoroughfares littered with garbage and road sweepings before he found it. Drouett knew little of the workings of church missions, but he did not imagine that he had stumbled upon a very flourishing enterprise. The premises consisted of a largish shack with a couple of outbuildings, the latter adjoining an unswept yard fenced off from the street, where a whey-faced woman stood feeding grain from a bucket to half a dozen chickens. Drouett walked round to the side door of the main building.

Here a tall, spare man with greying hair stood fixing a bill advertising next Sunday's service behind a glass display board. Seeing Drouett, he straightened up. 'Yas?'

Emboldened by the poverty around him and the odd note of deference in his voice, Drouett said suavely, 'Do I have the honour of speaking to the Reverend Hanson?'

'Hanson? Yas, that is me. What do you want? Is it about the homeless fund?'

Amused in spite of his anxieties by the man's obtuseness, Drouett shook his head. 'My name is Newhouse,' he said. 'From Kansas. I am sorry to intrude on you here at your work' – he made a little gesture at the display case – 'but I should like very much to speak to Mrs Hanson.'

Hanson stared at him uncomprehendingly. 'Elsa? She is in the yard. What do you wish to say to her?'

Drouett hesitated. Seeing Hanson outside his church, hearing the blunt-ness of his response and understanding something of the circumstances in which he lived, he realised that he was not certain of his man. One wrong word, he thought, and Hanson would retreat inside his shack, shut-ting the door behind him. From the yard he could hear the sound of the chickens squabbling over their food and children's voices drawing nearer.

'I'll be perfectly frank with you, Mr Hanson,' he said now, with consum-mate affability. 'It is not your wife that I wish to speak to. At least not this wife.' Seeing the glint in Hanson's eye he paused for a moment or two and then continued, 'You were married before, I think.'

The effect on Hanson was instantaneous. All the colour drained from his face. His hand, still lingering over the surface of the display case, shook against the glass. 'Who says so?' he demanded. 'What is it to you?'

'Well, I'm sorry that the subject is painful to you,' Drouett went on, quite as affably as before. 'As I say, my name is Newhouse. From Kansas. I have a cousin' – and here he thought a little blow might not come amiss – 'who was certainly Alice Hanson. There is money due to her – a legacy, you understand – and now I – that is, the family – want news of her.'

'News!' Hanson's face as he said this was deathly pale, the movement of his hand against the glass so purposeful that Drouett stepped back a pace. 'Well, I can give you news. You had better come with me.'

Drouett followed him through the half-open door of the house into a small, dingy room furnished as an office, with one or two poorly uphol-stered chairs and a table on which lay piles of pamphlets, a bible and other religious literature. From the window the view gave out on to the dusty street.

'Well, now,' Drouett said. 'This seems a very poor area.'

'It is a very poor area,' Hanson corrected him. He was in the act of retrieving a cardboard box from a desk drawer. 'On one night last week thirty-seven men in this district were forced to sleep out of doors. Yas, it is a very poor area. We have a homeless fund. But it is such a poor area that even the tradesmen – the shopkeepers – cannot support it, and so people sleep in the streets.'

'I should be delighted to make a contribution to that fund,' Drouett said easily. He was surer of himself now and regarded the cardboard box in the certainty that it contained useful information.

'You say you want news?' Hanson said suddenly. 'How is it you know who I am? And where to find me?'

'There was a letter written twenty years or more ago,' Drouett impro-
vised, 'in which she said that she was married to a Lutheran minister named
Hanson. I take it you're the fellow.'

Hanson put the box down on the table, moving the bible slightly to one
side as if he feared that the one might contaminate the other. 'It was God's
will that she came to me,' he said. 'It was God's will also that she should
leave me. Look.'

If Drouett had hoped that the box would contain anything startling,
he was disappointed. There was an old necklace, thick with dust, a keepsake card of a rosebowl, one or two scraps of paper. 'Here,' Hanson said,
delving among them. 'See this.'

It was no more than a paragraph long, cut out of the *Chicago-Sun-
Tribune* over twenty years ago, stating merely that a Mrs Alice Hanson,
formerly of the Lutheran mission, Van Buren, had absconded with a sum
of one hundred and eighty-seven dollars, the property of the church, and
that any information as to her whereabouts would be gratefully received.

'I most earnestly begged,' Hanson said, not looking at him but out of
the window at the street. 'I went down on my knees – on my knees – and
begged that this should not be said in a newspaper. In a place where people
could see.' There was a vein pulsing in his forehead, Drouett saw, like a
little valve switching on and off. 'I offered to work to repay the money,
all of it. But it was no good and no one would listen to me.'

'And what happened?' Drouett wondered.

'Nothing. Nothing happened. Somebody said they had seen her on a
train. At Indianapolis. I used to believe that she would return to me. Then
I stopped believing it.'

'Where do you think she went?'

'How should I know? Well, maybe I do. Yas, maybe I do. It is my belief
she went east. To New York. She had read in a magazine . . . evil things . . .
of stage plays and suchlike – and she thought she would like to be where
such things took place. That is why she took the child and left me.'

'So there was a child, was there?' Drouett said. He was surprised by
the news, so much so that he almost lost his composure.

'There was a child,' Hanson retorted. 'My son. Twenty-five years old
he would be. I keep his birthday. Always I remember it. But I have not
seen him since she left. Listen, Mr Newhouse, I do not care to talk now.
You have heard all there is to hear. Look!' He flicked the scrap from the
newspaper across the tabletop, where a ray of sunlight from the window

caught it suddenly and held it in a fast-fading glow. 'You may take this if you wish. There is your news.'

'Well, I'm obliged to you, Mr Hanson,' Drouett said. He placed the scrap of newsprint gingerly in his wallet. 'Truly.' Now he had got what he had come for he could not quite keep an exultant note out of his voice.

Hanson looked at him strangely. 'You say you are her cousin from Kansas. What did she look like?'

'A tall girl,' Drouett said. 'With blue eyes and red hair.'

'That is right, yas. Red hair.'

A ribbon of dust from the street blew violently against the glass. The wind was getting up. Drouett put the wallet in his pocket.

Back in Chicago Drouett marshalled his resources. He discovered, to his satisfaction, that he possessed nearly two thousand dollars – fifteen hundred in an account at the city's First Central Bank, a further five hundred held in public utility shares. This seemed to him ample for the plan he had in mind. But what was that plan exactly? In truth, he did not quite know. As to the value of the information he had accumulated, it could not be estimated. He was like the historian of some Indian tribe, he thought, busily constructing maps of the ancient hunting grounds, when the tribe itself was long quartered on a reservation.

Just now Drouett was 'keeping company' – an absurd phrase, but somehow descriptive of their association – with a widowed lady who kept a boarding house on Dearborn Street. 'I guess I shall be off soon on a little trip abroad,' he ventured during the course of one of these visits. 'To England, maybe.'

'You don't say?' said the widowed lady, who was under no illusions about Drouett. 'Well, perhaps you'll oblige me, George, now that I have a man in the house for a moment, by stepping up to Mr Culpepper on the second floor and telling him that if there's none of that twenty dollars he owes to hand he don't get no tea.'

Drouett accepted the rebuke. Things were changing, he thought. All around him life was shifting into new patterns and allegiances. He went and saw Mr Culpepper on the second floor and came back with ten dollars and a promissory note for ten more, but he thought as he did so that this was probably the last that the boarding house in Dearborn Street would see of him. That night he wrote a letter to the carpet company in his most professional style, saying that his circumstances had unexpectedly changed, that he found the work was not suited to him &c. A week later he took the train to New York, put up in a cheap hotel on the edge of the Bowery, for he knew he ought not to squander his capital, and purchased a ticket for one of the ten-day boats. The ship was full of wealthy Manhattanites going over to 'see the sights' and he kept out of their way, but in one of the Society magazines that lay in heaps in the tenantless library he discovered a second picture of Alice on the terrace of some country house, raptly conversing with an elderly man with side whiskers identified as the Duke of Northumberland. He cut out the picture and kept it carefully in his cabin. It was a good omen, he thought. At night he lay half dressed on his bunk smoking cheroots as the wild waves raged against the portholes and the electric lights danced in their sockets, hearing the noise of the ship's screw revolving in the distance and willing it on.

15

Henderson Nights

'Good evening?'

'So-so.'

'Go anywhere interesting?'

'Just the usual places . . . Brenda was at the Bat. She said to say hello.'

'Stout girl, Brenda. Was she with Harry?'

'I didn't see him. He may have been there . . . Patrick, if you're going to wear that suit to the office you really ought to know there's a swizzle stick hanging out of the pocket.'

'Is there?'

'Would I say so if there weren't?'

The Hendersons lived in Cleveland Square. The traffic roared round the corner from Paddington and the people coming out of the pub at closing time sometimes made a noise, but apart from that it was a convenient location and the taxi rank was said to be the friendliest in Bayswater. It was a raw November morning – the trees in the square dripped steadily from last night's rain – and Constance, well wrapped up in her angora dressing gown, was mixing a sachet of Bromo into a tumbler. She was twenty-six now, still with that delightfully washed-out look that men liked so much, but it was some years since anyone had suggested that she ought to mannequin. Somewhere in the middle distance a clock struck the hour.

'Darling, it's gone ten. You're going to be late again.'

'Am I? Well, there's rather a cachet about being late, if you can carry it off.'

'And can you? Carry it off, I mean?'

The Hendersons had been married for several years. They had had some private money, which had come to them through Patrick's aunt, but in general contrived to give an impression of being quite wonderfully classless and democratic, and Constance had once been seen in full view of half a dozen lunch guests making her charlady a cup of tea. Of the two, Patrick was thought by competent judges to have marginally the more distinctive personality.

'Well, tell me about your evening.'

'Not very amusing. Just bridge at the Pellys . . . Tell you what, darling, ring me up at lunchtime and tell me the news.'

After he had gone, Constance ran a bath, took off her angora dressing gown and lay in the scalding water for twenty minutes, staring at her face as it reflected back at her from the mirror on the wall. Sometimes people said she reminded them of Clara Bow and sometimes they did not. By the time she got out of the bath the post had come and she stood in the drawing room slitting open the envelopes with a paperknife. There were three bills, two invitations and a letter from Peter Jones telling her that her account had reached a total of £22.14s. Outside it had begun to rain again and she poked discontentedly around the flat for an umbrella before setting off for the dress shop in Mayfair where she worked, whose notional hours were from ten to five but where eleven to four was often countenanced, Sophie, as she often remarked to Patrick, being a perfect poppet and not constrained, as so many people were these days, by the tyranny of time.

Once he had left the flat, Patrick walked across the square and took the Underground to Chancery Lane. On the way he picked up a copy of the *Daily Sketch* that someone had left on the adjoining seat and read 'Mr Gossip's' account of a supper party at the Dorchester, so that the time passed satisfactorily. Tender and Mainprice had offices in Cursitor Street, although some people maintained that the melancholy nature of the area was mitigated by a surprising number of cheap sandwich bars. As he approached the front steps it was striking the half-hour, and the commissionaire with the purplish birthmark, looking out from his wire cage, said cheerfully, 'You're quite a stranger here.'

'I wouldn't say that.'

'I expect you've been enjoying yourself out on the town with the other young gentlemen.'

'That's the idea.'

In general the staff of Tender and Mainprice were proud of Patrick. As one of the firm's partners had remarked to another, it was not every day that they employed a man whose picture had appeared in the *Bystander*. On the morning on which his name had appeared in a newspaper account of a raid on a nightclub his stock soared to extravagant heights. Secure in this knowledge, he made his way to his desk and began to enter figures into a ledger with what he hoped was an air of suitable gravity.

The morning passed. At intervals men in subfusc jackets, some of them wholly unknown to him, brought sheets of paper for his inspection. They said things like 'Well, old boy, here are the United and Consolidated six monthlies', or 'Now, old boy, we shall want a deferred profit forecast on this'. At three-minute intervals the phone on his desk rang briskly.

'Is that Mr Patrick Henderson?'

'Don't be silly, darling, you know it's me . . . How are things?'

'Very quiet . . . Sophie's gone out to lunch with that madly attractive blackamoor we met at Elizabeth's wedding. What are you doing?'

'Loan consolidations for Rendall's.'

'Isn't that Ralph Bentley's uncle?'

'You know, I sometimes wish you wouldn't go on about all the glamorous men you've known.'

'I never mind it when you talk about Beryl Harcourt.'

'Perhaps not . . . Anyway, your Mr Bentley had better look out for himself.'

'Had he? Poor old Ralph. Listen! You'll never guess who's invited us for tonight. Mrs Keach!'

'I shouldn't get too excited. It's bound to be because a lot of people have chucked at the last minute.'

'Even so, darling. Mrs Keach!'

They luxuriated silently for a moment in this unlooked-for dispensation.

'You'll have to get your evening suit from the dry-cleaners,' Constance said, turning suddenly practical. 'And we shall need a taxi.'

'Goodness, what an extraordinary dress.'

'Do you like it? I got it out of the shop.'

'Will Sophie mind, do you think?'

'I can't see why. She's always taking things out of the shop herself. She says it's good advertising.'

As they had been raised by the generation that believed that if you were invited for somewhere for eight-thirty you should arrive at between twenty and twenty-three minutes to nine, they were standing on the further side of Lowndes Square watching the first of the evening's taxis delivering their occupants to Plantagenet House. Patrick, who was looking, Constance thought, particularly tired and charming, said, 'You'd better give me the form.'

'She's frightfully rich. With red hair. We met at that party at the Fairfaxes. American. Like Mrs Corrigan. And that other woman whose name I can never remember.'

'Mrs Keigwin?'

'No, not Mrs Keigwin.'

'Will people like Bryan and Diana be there?'

'I shouldn't think so.'

'But they're frightfully rich.'

'Beerage, darling, not peerage. Look, isn't that Harry Melville going in?'

'Who?'

'The old boy with the white hair and the mackintosh.'

'I don't think so.'

'Darling, I'm really getting fearfully cold, and this dress has holes in places I couldn't begin to tell you about.'

And so, hand in hand, nimbly evading the circling traffic of the square, they made their way to the further side, where a small crowd had gathered by the railings and a press photographer with a bulb camera was saying something to a footman against a backdrop of high, lit windows and behind them the glimpse of coruscating chandeliers, and were swallowed up into the wide, gaping maw of Plantagenet House.

'What a terrible party,' 'Mr Gossip' of the *Daily Sketch* said to 'The Dragoman' of the *Daily Express*, meeting him unexpectedly in a corridor. 'What are you going to say about it?'

Five yards in front of them a footman, his face wearing an expression of grim resignation, was carrying away an entire iced swan whose head had begun to part company with its neck.

'I don't know. I never met anybody here in my life before. Does your editor like Mrs Keach? Mine does. He says she epitomises the democratising spirit of our new post-war age.'

'How funny. My editor says he prefers her to Lady Cunard for pushing less. Is HRH coming?'

'No.'

'No?'

'No.'

'Well, then, is there a telephone?'

'Butler's pantry to the right of the hall,' 'The Dragoman' advised. 'But he's rather cross, because three other people have been in there already.'

Mrs Keach's party at Plantagenet House yesterday evening was one of the most elegant entertainments associated with that indefatigable hostess ['Mr Gossip' dictated]. *Although the rumour of a royal personage was, alas, unfounded, a sparkling assemblage of guests drawn from every quarter of her lustrous acquaintance could be seen gathered in rooms lately refurbished to the height of ton by Lady Colefax. The Hon. Mrs Pelly looked very fetching in green tulle and the Hon. Constance Henderson, the highly accomplished wife of Mr Patrick Henderson, was the cynosure of all eyes. The contrast between the inclement weather and the magnificence of some of the feminine apparel on display was more than once commented on, and the Hon. Billy Champing, who is a very amusing young man, remarked that it never rained but it Diored. At midnight, a spirited attempt was made by some of the younger guests to stage a handicap race round the square . . .*

'What an extraordinary party,' Constance said, four hours later.

'I should rather say that it was. Who on earth was that old chap with the side whiskers? You should have seen the look on Mrs K's face when he opened his mouth.'

'Oh, I thought he was quite sweet.'

'And Mr Schmiegelow. Who on earth can he have been?'

'He asked me if I was a Bright Young Person.'

'Well, whoever he is, he asked me if I wanted a job in his business. Look, here's his card.'

Later, when the excitement of discussing the party had exhausted them, Constance said, 'Damn! I seem to have torn the hem of that dress of Sophie's.'

'Couldn't you sew it up with something?'

'It's *chiffon*, darling. Even Sophie would notice something like that.'

'Hm. Darling?'

'Yes?'

'*Darling.*'

'Actually, I'm just the teeniest bit tired.'

This rebuff notwithstanding, it had, Patrick was forced to concede, as he lay in the wide double bed listening to the traffic and the smell of

Constance's face cream stealthily pervaded the room, been a memorable night.

'Gracious,' Constance said in the morning. 'It says here that I'm highly accomplished and the cynosure of all eyes.'

'That sounds pretty good. What does it say about me?'

'Nothing really. Only that I'm married to you.'

'What are you going to do about the dress?'

'Do you think Sophie would believe me if I told her a customer did it while she was trying it on?'

Well wrapped up in her angora dressing gown, Constance was mixing a sachet of Bromo into a tumbler. Somewhere in the middle distance a clock struck the hour.

'Darling, it's gone ten. You're going to be late again.'

'Am I? Oh well. Why don't you ring me up at lunchtime and tell me the news?'

It was generally agreed by the people who took an interest in these things that the Hendersons' social rise dated from their attendance at Mrs Keach's party. Several young married women who remembered her from debutante dances flocked to renew their acquaintance with 'that charming Constance Henderson'. Half a dozen young men who had known Patrick at Oxford looked out his address in the telephone book and asked him to lunch at their clubs, and in the space of a fortnight the Hendersons found themselves invited to a charity matinée in Grosvenor Square, an ultra-smart evening party in Kensington and a fancy-dress ball at which, greatly daring, Constance borrowed one of Patrick's school ties and a singlet, and appeared as part of an Harrovian ladies' rowing eight, coxed by an old gentleman who had once been Mr Gladstone's Under-Secretary for Ireland.

While all this was undoubtedly gratifying, it also led to mischief.

'Don't think I'm not delighted for you, darling,' said Sophie one morning in South Audley Street, 'but that Ancaster woman comes into the shop two mornings out of three, turns every hat in the place out of its box and never spends a cent.'

Then, two days after this, 'Mr Chatterbox' of the *Graphic*, in the course of a lavish description of a 'Second Childhood Party' held at the Gargoyle Club, made the fatal mistake of referring to Patrick as a 'part-time accountant'.

'It's not as if the poor thing's *trained* for anything else,' Constance complained to her married sister Marjorie. They were having lunch in one of those little restaurants in the King's Road Marjorie was always reading about in the *Evening News*. This one seemed not too bad, provided one avoided the salad and stuck to gin-and-Italian instead of wine.

'Couldn't he go in for politics?' Marjorie wondered. She was a fattish, vaguely discontented woman, who was said to try very hard in life and whose husband had just been adopted for a Conservative constituency. 'Alan says they're getting a very nice type of young man at the BBC.'

'My dear, I believe there's something *alive* on that plate. Do put it on the floor or something . . . No, he says he always liked it at Tender and Mainprice and if they don't want him now he hasn't the heart to go anywhere else.'

'Alan said the same when he got chucked from chambers . . . But Patrick's really quite clever. I'm sure he could find something.'

'Yes, he is, isn't he? I'm sure he can. Oh God! Is that the time? I must run to the shop or Sophie will be beastly to me again.'

'How was your sister?' Alan enquired, later that afternoon.

'Constance? Oh, she's been quite impossible since she took up with that Keach woman . . .'

'Good day?'

'Beastly. Sophie brought the blackamoor back to the shop after lunch and simply *drooled* at him over the counter all afternoon . . . Did you get any lunch?'

'I had a sandwich with Harry at the club. He says he's definitely leaving Brenda. And then those debt consolidations took all afternoon. I really do feel sorry for your Mr Bentley . . . Where are you going tonight?'

'Just supper at the Pellys . . . Patrick, darling, we need to talk.'

'Do you know there are no cigarettes in this box again..?'

'We haven't got any money, you know.'

'None at all? Couldn't you ask Sophie for some more?'

'She says what with the Slump she can barely pay her expenses . . . Did you ask Alan about his office?'

'He says they're not even taking unqualified people . . . What's this?'

'It's that nasty letter from Peter Jones. I left it on the cocktail cabinet so we'd be sure to remember it . . . Well, what about that man you met at Alice Keach's?'

'Mr Schmiegelow? Didn't you think he was just the tiniest bit bogus?'

'Beggars can't be choosers, darling.'

'I suppose not. Are you sure you couldn't ask Sophie for some more?'

'Quite sure, darling.'

So Patrick went to see Mr Schmiegelow at his subterranean office in the City Road, answered one or two perfunctory questions and, rather to his surprise, was offered a job in Mr Schmiegelow's newly opened gramophone shop in High Holborn at four pounds a week starting on the following Monday.

'Has your brother-in-law found anything to do yet?' Alan asked Marjorie.

'He's got a job with that climbing Mr Schmiegelow, who sells bracelets to Alice Keach.'

'Glad to hear it,' said Alan, who never allowed it to rankle that he had been to a slightly inferior school to Patrick's. 'All that thinking the world owes you a living just because your wife has a handle to her name is on the way out, if you want my opinion.'

16

Life from a Window

Drouett sits in his hotel bedroom looking out over the windy streets. The hotel is in one of the Bloomsbury squares, secluded yet carrying pleasant intimations of the clamour beyond. The Euston Road is within earshot: taxis tear round an exposed south-western flank. All this Drouett approves. He has chosen the hotel not only on account of its cheapness – he is husbanding his resources just now – but for the locale's faint resemblance to certain American cities he has lived in. It is something to do with the colour of the stone, the islet of plane trees set behind locked iron railings in the square gardens; he cannot quite make it out. All the same, the resemblance rather startles him. He had never thought there would come a time when he could feel homesick for Philadelphia, but there it is. Travel, he thinks, wreaks havoc not only on your sense of who you are but on the memory of the places you come from.

The hotel room is on the small side, but not for that reason uncomfortable. There is a high iron bedstead, a tallboy, a pair of armchairs, a writing desk and, on the far wall, a reproduction of a painting called *When Did You Last See Your Father*. This, too, Drouett approves. He likes the boy's curly hair and the look – half stern, half indulgent – on the face of his interrogators. The greater part of his life has been spent in hotel bedrooms: his valuation of them is usually correct. To the particular amenities available here he has added a coffee kettle, a milk jug and a patent Frigidaire. His travelling cases are stuffed under the bed. Sometimes, clambering out on to the threadbare carpet in the grim London dawn, his feet bang awkwardly against them. Along the mantelpiece runs a line of picture postcards: mounted guardsmen; the spires of St Paul's; a Beefeater looming from the shadow of the Tower. Alone in the room, Drouett feels his eye constantly returning to them. He finds them bizarre, altogether beyond his experience, faintly unreal. There are other parts of London in which he has foraged that have no souvenirs.

Just now Drouett is not alone: not quite. In the corner of the room, hard up against the wainscot and within striking distance of the bed, on a travelling rug Drouett has carefully folded out, sits a tiny dog. It is some kind of terrier – Scottish or Irish, perhaps; he is not quite certain of the breed – with wiry hair, not more than nine inches long, restless and neurotic. There are two or three biscuits lying on a plate on the arm of Drouett's chair, and he crumbles one up, drops the fragments into the palm of his outstretched hand and watches the dog nervously approach. Even now, he notices, a week into their relationship, the creature trembles with fear. Drouett is used to bold, sociable dogs: hounds bred up in the Illinois cornfields, wolfish huskies brought down from the frozen north. Still, though, he has made these overtures of friendship. He exercises it in the square gardens, where it chases small rodents into the herbaceous borders, takes fright at pigeons preening themselves on the oily grass. The gardens are horribly overgrown. There is an old gardener who sits in a shed brewing cups of tea and occasionally ventures out to rake the leaves: a self-absorbed manikin in moleskin trousers with a parched face who, Drouett thinks, should be tilling a field a hundred miles away, not idling in a half-acre of urban greenery. London is full of these incongruities: an extraordinary motorised carriage he once saw in the West End, like a moving bow window, which enquiry revealed to be an electric brougham; a footman with a cockade in his hat opening the door of a Rolls-Royce somewhere in Mayfair. It is as if, Drouett thinks, the place does not quite know what age it inhabits.

Coaxed out of its lair amid the blankets, the dog is licking up the biscuit crumbs out of Drouett's palm. Its manner, as it does this, turns suddenly aggressive: as if, by butting Drouett's fingers, it can somehow cause the hand to be withdrawn while allowing the biscuit to remain tantalisingly in mid-air. Later, Drouett thinks, he will take it for a walk around the square, better still to Coram Fields, where there is a café and he can get a cup of coffee. His landlady, whose pet the dog is, approves of this interest. She is a faded middle-aged woman with a voice so strangulated that it sometimes sounds as if she is barking. Drouett is not disconcerted by this: he knows by now that it is how certain English people talk. Still, there are whole conversations in which he strains to register exactly what is being said, nuances that he altogether misses. This is the price you pay for a Bloomsbury square and a garden choked with efflorescing autumnal verdure, Drouett supposes. Just now, as the dog hoovers up the last of the crumbs from the tip of his finger, Drouett is thinking. Small things and large things mixed: the grey bulk of the city at dawn, with the lamp-lights gently extinguishing themselves and all the colour draining out of the streets; the money in his pocketbook, which he knows is not in-exhaustible; Lowndes Square, which he has visited twice and stood each time in the rain looking up at the great high windows and the pillared door; the old King's portrait on the coins in his pocket, curiously melancholy and ground-down.

He has been here three weeks. England, he suspects, is not quite as he imagined. It seems smaller, grainier, less distinct. But London fascinates him. The fascination lies not in its symbolism – the picture postcard world of his mantelpiece is mostly beyond him – but its incidentals. He likes the Lyons cafés, with the steam rising from the row of urns, the prices chalked on blackboards and the bustling waitresses – 'nippies' they are called – banging down trays on the cramped surfaces. He likes the West End and the crazy little streets that lead out of it into the less sumptuous land-scapes beyond. He likes the little tobacconists' shops and the imploring blind boys with their charity boxes huddled in their porches. The tobacco is foul but, Drouett thinks, this is the price you pay for a lodgement in the old world, that right to hunker down here in civilisation's cradle. There is a private school in one of the big houses on the farther side of the square from which, at intervals during the day, crowds of boys emerge. They wear scarlet blazers and corduroy knee breeches, and have remorse-less basin haircuts. Even the older ones, Drouett notices, are denied long pants. He is charmed by their deference – the way in which the slightest rebuke from one of their teachers brings an apologetic smile or a bobbed head – but also by their assurance. They step along the street as confi-dently as their older selves will step into a gentlemen's club or on to a battlefield. The world, Drouett thinks, half enviously, half approvingly, is theirs to command, their private fiefdom. If he had a son, he believes, he would send him to this school and stand, concealed by the passing auto-mobiles on the corner of the sidewalk, to watch the crocodiles go by.

The dog has retired to its nest among the blankets. It is rooting around after the two or three toys Drouett has lately purchased for it: a rubber bone, nearly the length of its own spine; a piece of rope that it occa-sionally worries. Despite the biscuits and the bowl of water that lies nearby, its eyes have a resentful glare. Drouett thinks that instead of goading it around Coram Fields – the dog is an erratic walker – he will return it to the shoebox-sized kennel on the ground floor. If he does this he can also take the opportunity to ask after his landlady's rheumatism. Experience tells him that such enquiries are gratefully received. Like London, and the daily procession of crop-haired schoolboys, Drouett finds that the hotel's atmosphere suits him. He likes the big dining room, with its reek of gravy and the little forest of sauce and cruet bottles bunched in the middle of the snowy tablecloth. He likes the grandfather clock in the hall and the square yard of pigeonholes lined with green baize in which the guests' mail is lodged. Some of the letters have been there for years: he can tell by the franks. He wonders whether the people will ever come back to claim them. Another man, Drouett thinks, would not be able to acclimatise himself so successfully to this new milieu, would perhaps take fright at its exacting protocols. Thirty years on the road have cemented the salesman's instinct in him, that urge to find out what is wanted and supply it, to conciliate, temporise and triumph. Already, Drouett believes, he feels at home here. He can read the Underground map to his satisfaction. The money no longer confuses him. He has even found a woman.

The woman is called Joyce and works as a typist for a big legal firm in Holborn. One of the first things she told Drouett was that 'Holborn' is in fact pronounced 'Hoburn'. Drouett is used to these linguistic vagaries – 'Cheyne' as 'Chey-nee', 'Cholmondeley' as 'Chumley' and so on. He accepted the rebuke. Joyce is about thirty or thirty-five – nearer to thirty-five, Drouett thinks – with elaborate, marcelled hair and a slight impediment in the motion of her left foot. She has a way of saying 'I will admit' with reference to almost any eventuality that Drouett finds charming. She will admit that she is going to Minehead on holiday next year; that she might drink a cup of tea; that Victor McLaglen is her favourite movie actor. So far their relationship has been confined to a couple of meetings in a Lyons and a cinema visit, but Drouett is working on it. He has an idea that his landlady – Mrs Hook her name is – will probably not care much for Joyce's presence here on the premises in Bloomsbury and that the women's hostel in Kensington where Joyce resides will probably not care much for him. Joyce, Drouett suspects, is inexperienced with men. She has a way of looking at him across a table that is faintly timorous, but also expectant. From Joyce Drouett learns things about London that a six-month root through its guidebooks might never tell him: that second-hand automobiles are traded in the area south of Euston station; that jewellery is made in Hoxton and sold in Leather Lane; that Chelsea has a reputation for brazen bohemian laxity. Joyce is not a London girl – she comes from

Hampshire – but she will admit to having been here ten years. Long enough to know her way around, Drouett thinks.

Outside the wind has stopped and there is fine rain falling against the window, mixed with yellowy-grey light: the street lamps are going on. The dog has gone to sleep. Even when unconscious, its neuroses persist. There is a faint tremor of alarm pulsing from its hindquarters. Silent for the past two hours, the hotel is now emitting its own faint tremors. There are footsteps on the stairs, a gust of conversation: in the distance a door creaks. Drouett has had little contact with the other guests. They come and go. Often the language spoken at the dining table will not be English. A military-looking man with an extravagant moustache who sits each night at dinner before a solitary poached egg is the only permanency. Looking at his watch, Drouett sees that it is a quarter to six. There is a newspaper lying on the bed, a copy of the *Daily Sketch*, and he stands up to retrieve it. Drouett has tried the *Mail* and the *Express* – *The Times* is full of stuffed shirts and bug hunters – but the *Sketch* is the one he prefers. Like London, the English newspapers fascinate him. In Chicago the news is all of Hoover and Al Smith and the negroes down in the black belt. Over here an aristocratic youngster found drunk in charge of an automobile in Oxford Street merits half a page. Already Drouett is familiar with the names with which the newspapers deal: Mr Macdonald and Mr Lloyd George, Mrs Corrigan, the Hon. Mrs Guinness, Mrs Meyrick. Joyce, he realises, looks a little like Mrs Meyrick. The irony is not lost on him, for he knows that Mrs Meyrick is the proprietress of a speakeasy. Above all he likes the columns in which readers write in to ask advice. There is one here in the *Sketch*. A young man, introduced to a girl at a bridge club of which both are members, wonders how he may honourably insinuate himself into her affections. The pundit is encouraging but firm. The young man should mingle unobtrusively with the girl's set. On no account should he press his attentions if they are not wanted.

Drouett wonders how his own problem would look if couched in the language of the problem page: *A gentleman who many years ago was acquainted with a young lady, but whose association with her was broken off, now finds himself residing in the same town. In the interval the lady has acquired a substantial fortune. How should the gentleman take steps to renew the acquaintance?* Lowndes Square, when he saw it, terrified him. It was altogether beyond his comprehension: vast, remote, intimidating. Even now the object of his journey, on which he has lavished several hundred dollars, escapes him. Why is he here? What does he want? His dreams are so inchoate that he cannot quantify them. Does he write her a letter? Does he find some way in which he can unobtrusively insinuate himself into her company? What would she say if she saw him? What would he say if he saw her? There is no way of knowing, Drouett thinks. What is needed is some decisive step. The hotel is a modest establishment, but it runs to sheets of headed notepaper. Putting down the copy of the *Sketch*, he picks up one of them, takes a pen and scratches a few words, then softly excises them. In this way several hours pass. The dog wakes up and whines quietly for its supper. Down below in the dining room the evening meal Drouett has ordered and forgotten about is taken back to the kitchen and surreptitiously recycled. The military-looking gentleman eats his solitary poached egg. In Kensington Joyce, whom Drouett has half promised to telephone, gives up her vigil by the receiver in the hostel's cramped vestibule and creeps out instead to the Astoria cinema in the Fulham Palace Road to watch Edward G. Robinson in *A Country to Lose*. The traffic in the square reduces itself to an occasional cab. But still Drouett scribbles on in the orange light. He thinks of Joyce's lisle stockings, the spire of St Paul's Cathedral, the butter-coloured hair of the small boys in their crocodile, smoke rising in the pale Dakota sky, the dense waters of the Atlantic effervescing around the liner's dark, advancing prow, Alice in her great mansion, another child – a quarter of a century old he would be now, Drouett calculates, that he has never seen.

17

An Afternoon in Knightsbridge

She sat in the great grey drawing room with its view out over Lowndes
Square. Beyond the window the life of the Knightsbridge afternoon was
picturesquely unfurling – there were black horses stamping their feet on
the square's farther side in readiness for a funeral, and a girls' school
busily disgorging its pupils – but there was nothing there to interest her.
Alice's mind was concentrated on the slip of pasteboard just brought to
her by the butler, which now lay on the table before her. It was an
innocuous-looking thing, containing no more than a printed name and a
pencilled suggestion that its bearer would be glad of a moment of her
time, but she knew that both the name and the pencilling burned into her
consciousness like acid. The funeral horses were rattling off in the direction of the park, and the mob outside the school gates had reduced itself
to a solitary mistress in gaunt pince-nez casting vigilant glances along the
pavement, but still she sat there with the *carte de visite* in her hand and
her tea growing cold at her elbow.

Alice began to move around the room, effecting nervous little improve-
ments and adjustments to its fabric, restoring the symmetry of the sofa
cushions, manoeuvring the fan of invitations on the mantelpiece into a
single, unwavering line. Some people thought that Mrs Keach's drawing
room was too cold and too chastely decorated, and that the convex mirror
above the fireplace did odd things to its perspective, but it had been
designed by Lady Colefax and a civil young man in the *Architectural Review*
had praised its classic neo-Georgian simplicity. There were numberless
little occasional tables extending almost to the back of the room, a bureau
on which the weekly magazines were laid out in rows, vast amounts of
Lalique glass tastefully displayed on sideboards and writing desks, and a
tiger-skin rug which loomed up very fierily in the mirror. By the fireplace sat another table on which lay that week's *Bystander* and a copy of
Angel Pavement, which Mrs Keach had not read but had ordered up on
the grounds that everyone was talking about it. All of these things – glass,

mirror, book, invitation cards, neo-Georgian simplicity – she saw as she moved around the room, but none of them reassured her. Looking at the clock, on its stand among the ducal coronets, she saw that it was now a quarter to four and that she had been alone in her drawing room for nearly half an hour, and once again the card burned in her hand.

There was a faint rustling noise and Miss Jeffries slipped into the room. 'My dear,' she said – Miss Jeffries always called her employer 'my dear' – 'it is nearly four o'clock and they want to know if the car should be brought round. Shall you be going to Mrs Antrobus's this evening?'

'I don't like those Jewish people.'

'Well, no, perhaps not . . . I did hear', said Miss Jeffries loyally, 'that Mr Antrobus asked to see all the receipts for the theatrical party, as it cost such a tremendous amount of money, and he is only a bill broker, they say.'

But Mrs Keach was not interested in Mrs Antrobus. She had the card, still, in her hand. 'Edie' she said. 'Will you do something for me?'

Miss Jeffries caught the note in her voice and looked at her wonderingly. 'What is it?'

'There is a man downstairs, wanting to see me. I suppose they will have put him in the dining room. Just run down, will you – go in there as if you didn't expect to find him – as if you were just looking for something – and then come back here.'

If Miss Jeffries thought this instruction odd, she was too discreet a woman to say so. While she was gone, Alice went over to the armchair, picked up the *Bystander*, stared at the portrait on its frontispiece, which showed the Hon. Mrs Guinness relaxing at the Lido, and put it down, looked at the piece of pasteboard again and then hid it between the pages of Mr Priestley's novel. Her initial terror had subsided, borne gently away by Miss Jeffries and her talk of chauffeurs and Mrs Antrobus's party. She brought to mind – something that had almost escaped her when the card came into her hand – that she lived in a fine house in Knightsbridge, with other fine houses around the country to supplement its lustre, and that if anyone called on her whom she did not like, she could have them denied admittance by the butler. As for any sense of obligation that the person in the dining hall might try to kindle in her, she did not think that the kindling would have any effect. All this was very comforting to her. It left her more angry than alarmed. She would hear what he had to say, she thought, then reflect on it in a houseful of servants and with the bell rope a yard from her hand.

'Well, I have seen him,' Miss Jeffries said, gliding back into the room and breathing heavily with the excitement of this subterfuge. 'He was in the dining room and I pretended to search for a book.'

'What is he like?'

'Sixty, perhaps. And rather bald. Oh – and American. I heard him talking to Maslin' – Maslin was the butler – 'as I passed. He had on rather a bad suit, I thought.'

There was a pause, while Alice thought about the balding head and the bad suit.

'He seemed to be getting on frightfully well with Maslin,' Miss Jeffries went on, rather conscious of some secret lurking in the room to which she had not been made party.

Alice knew she could not have her there while she saw him – seeing him, as she now found, being the only solution to the terror unleashed by the calling card – and she was not yet inclined to let Miss Jeffries in on the secret.

'Look here, Edie,' she said. 'Perhaps you could go and ask Maslin to show this gentleman up. No – you needn't stay yourself. It's a particular bit of business that I know about. And Edie – tell Maslin that after twenty minutes, not more, he's to come and tell me that the car's waiting. Not that the car will be waiting, but as if it were, you see.'

Presently there was a sound of footsteps on the staircase, the butler opening the door said something – his name, no doubt, but she did not register it – and there he was advancing across the room towards her.

She knew that she would have recognised him in any case, even without the card or the butler's introduction. There was something about the line of his forehead, the set of his jaw against his collar, that she knew instantly to be his alone. This startled her and in a curious way even predisposed him in her favour, for she liked the familiarity of it. She found herself remembering the last evening she had spent with him in De Smet, in the timber-board house in the snow, and the vividness of her memories rather surprised her, but the fact that he had certainly deserted her, or had intended to, blazed up in her mind and altogether cancelled out the memory of De Smet and the timber-board house in the snow.

'Well, now,' he said, in that easy way she remembered – it was as familiar to her as the line of his forehead and the slant of his jaw – 'this is a great thing.'

There was a mildness in his tone that she did not recall, which might have been assumed, but which she did not dislike. She found herself shaking his hand and offering a chair, which he took in a matter-of-fact way, as if his absence had spanned the previous twenty-five days rather than the previous twenty-five years.

'Well,' he said again, lifting his eyes up and around the room, seeing the mirror, the mantelpiece, the Lalique glass and Mr Priestley's novel in a succession of bold little glances. 'It's certainly good of you to see me, Alice.' The 'Alice', she saw, was put there self-consciously and designed to draw attention to itself. She could not help staring at him. Mentally she was matching her own impressions to those Miss Jeffries had brought up from the dining room. His suit was certainly bad: it had come from a fifty-shilling tailor and did not trouble to disguise the fact. But he was wearing patent leather shoes and a jaunty little gardenia in his buttonhole. Drouett, meanwhile, was drinking in impressions of the room in which he sat. He was not a connoisseur of luxury – what little he had seen of it had been at second hand or even third – but he was shrewd enough to know that practically everything he saw was symbolic of a very great wealth. The Lalique glass seemed to him very wonderful and ornate – and very curious and impractical – but he knew that it was the kind of thing that stuffed shirts had about them. There were tea things lying on a tray – bone china cups of impossible slenderness, a silver sugar bowl with Lilliputian tongs – and he remembered magazine articles about the English at tea. As for Alice herself, he thought that he could not quite make her out. He did not know exactly what he had expected of her, but he was conscious that his expectations had not been entirely fulfilled. He did not – quite – recognise her voice. There was a little of the Kansas twang in it, he thought, but it had been overlaid with other things that had the effect not of disappointing him but intriguing him.

'What brings you to London, then?' she wondered. Again, he admired her coolness. Just as if she were some friend he knocked into every now and then: he liked that.

'Oh, I guess I fancied the trip,' he said, smiling as he did so. 'I never came here before.'

'You are enjoying yourself, I hope? Where are you staying?'

He was sharp enough to realise that this was politeness rather than interrogation, and that it released him from any obligation to be particular.

'Oh, I like it fine. Just now I'm putting up in Bloomsbury, at the Criterion. Maybe you know it?'

He was aware as he said the name that she would definitely not know the Criterion Hotel in Bloomsbury, and that even Bloomsbury itself was probably beyond the range of her experience, but he was unembarrassed. She had asked him where he was staying. Well, he would tell her. It was all very strange. He had an idea that, given what had once passed between them, they should not be talking pleasantries about hotels and how he liked London, but he could not conceive how the wall of this other realm of conversation might be breached, or what he might find there if it should be. On the other hand he could see that the look on her face as she stared at him had changed. He found the look unnerving.

'I thought,' she said unexpectedly, 'I thought . . .'

He knew instinctively that she was referring to his adventure in the snow and the blizzard that had nearly killed him a quarter of a century before. Wondering how much he ought to tell her, he smiled genially. 'Oh, it wasn't so very bad. I got out of it, you know.'

He had spent twenty-five years telling the story of his escape from the storm and had noticed that listeners preferred it in its unvarnished form. And so, in a few sentences, he explained about the drift into which the buggy had tumbled, the haystack that had loomed up behind it and into whose depths he had burrowed, the farm wagon that had found him two days later, and taken him to Allington.

'What about the poor horses?' she asked.

'Oh, I think they froze. No one ever saw them again.'

He knew, as he told his tale, that the greater question of why he should have been on his way to Allington hung unanswered in the air between them and this made him nervous. He got up from his chair and wandered around the room a little, looking at a row of framed photographs and the line of invitations on the mantelpiece with the vague stare of the impressionable tourist. He found that as she asked him other questions, he began to reveal certain details of his life. They were the kind of questions she used to ask him in the past, he thought, and this rather irritated him, for they seemed to draw attention to the chasm that now stretched between them.

'Anyhow,' he said at the close of one of these enquiries, almost blusteringly, 'that's how I've spent my days, and if you'd have given me the chance again I don't expect I'd have spent them any differently.'

She realised, watching him as he roamed around the room, that this was her cue to tell him about her own life, how it was that she came to be sitting in a mansion in Lowndes Square with an invitation card from the Honourable Gerald Claridge glaring at her from the mantelpiece, but she knew also that she did not wish to take it. She was aware – little hints he had dropped had shown her this – that he knew more about her than he had yet revealed, that there were certain incidental details of her existence to hand that could not have been come by easily, or rather could not have been come by easily in America. The thought of his making a study of her life, of burrowing into a core that she kept hidden from the world, alarmed her, for it was something she could not control, and that might take on all kinds of unexpected shapes and forms without her sanction. Looking at him now as he stood by the mantelpiece – he was talking very modestly, making some deferential gesture as he did so – she decided that he looked too comfortable, that the position he had taken up required a decisive check.

'George,' she said. It was the first time she had called him George. 'What is it you want?'

But he was equal to this. 'I don't know that there's anything I want,' he said, and went on looking at the covers of the Society magazines on their shelf and the reflection of his face in the Lalique glass. Somewhere down in the body of the house a door slammed shut. Immediately she felt annoyed with herself, thinking that he had said the right thing and she had not. In a moment, she knew, Maslin would knock at the door and tell her that the car was waiting. She would be grateful for this.

'How long do you suppose you will be in London?' she wondered.

Drouett was equal to this too. 'Oh well. I guess that depends. There are one or two things I might look into while I'm here.' Something occurred to him and he said, 'What happened to the child?'

'There was no child,' she said, blushing scarlet. 'At least – there was, but . . .'

'I'm sorry to hear that,' he said, with what might have been a faint look of scepticism in his eye. 'That's a great shame.'

And then he was gone, under Maslin's supervision – the last thing she saw of him was his patent-leather shoes disappearing out of the door – leaving her to think about his visit. She was aware, even as she smiled over the gardenia buttonhole and the creased red face, that she was horribly disconcerted. Apart from the reference to the child, he had said nothing seriously to alarm her. A part of him – the part that had talked about his life in America – she found almost pathetic, for the realities of that life – its vagrancy and its solitary pleasurings – were all too familiar to her. As for what might happen now, she could scarcely comprehend it. She had said they must see each other again, but what did this mean? She had a vision of him sitting at her dinner table in his fifty-shilling suit and telling the story of how he had hidden in the haystack and been taken to Allington in the farmer's wagon. This, perhaps, was tolerable, but it was the unknown conversations that lay beyond it which she feared, for she suspected that he had not said all he meant to say. She did not know what these things might be, but she knew that they frightened her. She had a wild impulse to fetch her chequebook from her desk, write a cheque for – a thousand pounds? Two thousand pounds? – and have it sent round to the Criterion Hotel, with a note wishing Mr Drouett well and a clear implication that Mr Drouett might now take himself back to New York at the earliest opportunity, but no sooner was the idea in her mind than its foolishness became clear. Drouett had not said he wanted money, was staying in apparent comfort in central London and was wearing a pair of shoes that must have cost five guineas. Why not give him the benefit of the doubt?

'My *dear*,' said Miss Jeffries, who had been conferring with Maslin on the stairs, as she came into the room. 'This is monstrous!'

'What is monstrous?'

'This Mr Drouett! To think of it! A man that you last set eyes upon more than twenty years ago. What on earth can he want from you?'

'Now then, Edie, don't take on,' said Alice, seeing that Miss Jeffries was really upset. 'I don't think he means much harm.'

'Means much harm indeed! You should see the Home Secretary – Mr Hicks that used to come here – and have him sent home.'

'Mr Hicks is out now. It is that Labour man. Don't be silly, Edie. Why should the Home Secretary take the slightest interest in Mr Drouett?'

Miss Jeffries calmed down and allowed herself to be revived with tea out of one of the bone china cups that Drouett had so admired.

'But I cannot understand. Or rather I can – seeing the position you are in. I suppose he wants money.'

'He didn't say he wanted anything.'

'As for that' – Miss Jeffries made a melodramatic gesture with her fingers, which cast doubt upon the judgment of all those actor-managers who, twenty years before, had questioned her abilities. 'Where are you going, dear?'

'I think I shall get dressed and go to Mrs Antrobus's after all. Where does she live?'

'Belgrave Square, I believe,' said Miss Jeffries.

'Gracious! Then no wonder Mr Antrobus is so keen to see the bills.'

Mrs Antrobus's party was full of people in fancy dress whom Alice did not recognise, and the card room, in which she sought refuge, was occupied by some elderly Jewish ladies playing bridge, so in the end she went and sat in a chair in the drawing room and talked to a man in a made-up tie who said he had once met Clara Bow. Through the half-open door the noise of a negro orchestra boomed through the smoky air. It was very hot and the champagne tasted odd. Mrs Antrobus came up to her and said, 'My dear, I just wanted you to know how sorry I was about the dreadful things they wrote about us in the newspapers' and Alice said, 'My dear, it's not of the least consequence. And isn't this a splendid party.' 'Mr Gossip' of the *Daily Sketch* saw her and wrote:

> *Also among the guests was Mrs Keach, from under whose eyelids eternal sophistication looked out a little wearily, and whose mouth, smiling as enigmatically as the Gioconda, can utter all knowledge and all wisdom.*

Mrs Antrobus, who had inclined towards bitterness, was unexpectedly impressed. 'So that is Alice Keach?' she said. 'We must have her one afternoon when there are fewer people and more time to talk.' Shortly after this she was called away to the drawing room to remonstrate with her husband, who was making a nuisance of himself by talking to some of the more important guests.

After he had left the house in Lowndes Square, Drouett wandered north across Knightsbridge into the park. Here there were nursemaids wheeling their charges in perambulators and stiff-shouldered old men tending the ducks. A bay horse came trotting along the Row, ridden by a man in jodhpurs and a hacking jacket, and Drouett watched the little spurts of sand fly up in its wake. Reassembling in his mind the events of the past half-hour, he was conscious of having proved a point, without being entirely certain what that point was. Unquestionably, he told himself, he had not been patronised. The butler in his black coat, the row of invitation cards on the mantelpiece, the sideboards full of glass – all this, he imagined, he had taken in his stride. He had not quite liked the question about what he wanted, but he thought he could understand why it had been asked. On the other hand he had liked the question about how long he intended to stay in London, because it implied that he had not simply come to London to see her.

As for Alice herself, he was not quite certain what he thought. For a woman of forty-five she was certainly very good-looking, and there were even traces of the girl he remembered from the supper table at De Smet, but he knew that a part of him was intimidated, if not by her then by the things that surrounded her. Another part of him had hoped that she might refer, if not directly then obliquely, to what had passed between them, but he saw now that this would have been too much to expect. The bay horse was a hundred yards away now. It was queer, he thought, that Alice should have asked him what he wanted, for he was not altogether sure what he did want. One thing he did want, he told himself, was another half-hour in the drawing room at Lowndes Square, but he was not quite sure how he could arrange this, or if he did it what he might say when he got there. But he was intrigued by what he had seen, not so much its grandeur and solidity, of which he was keenly aware, but its incidentals. The bay horse had disappeared now, to be replaced by a pair of carriages and a small boy on a pony with a groom trotting at his side. Reckoning up the remainder of the day's arrangements, Drouett found that they consisted of an early dinner at the Criterion and a visit to the cinema with Joyce. Then the vision of Alice in her drawing room beneath the wide mirror flew up to trouble him again, and he stood for a moment amid the perambulators and the stiff-shouldered old men, considering it. There was a man selling newspapers in the road beyond the park and he bought one and folded it under his arm in the way he had seen English people do. Later he took a bus back to Bloomsbury and sat on the upper deck reading, with bewildered gratification, the cricket reports and a column that explained why it was that the younger son of a marquess took precedence over the elder daughter of an earl.

18

Twitches on the Thread

In Knightsbridge, the daily routines have begun to assert themselves. It is eleven o'clock in the morning – early for Lowndes Square – but already there are freshly cut flowers arranged in the half-dozen Lalique vases and a little heap of invitation cards and tradesmen's bills laid out on the occasional table next to the fire. Miss Jeffries, who is responsible for these adustments, is somewhere in the lower part of the house, bullying the cook or sitting at her desk in the morning room briskly composing letters. Reaching forward in her chair Alice finds further evidence of Miss Jeffries's administrative zeal in a sheet of notepaper with a series of headings in bright blue ink. *Mrs K. Car theatrical comm. Tea Dorch. LS?!* This Alice takes to mean that she is lunching with Mrs Keigwin, is then being driven to a meeting of a theatrical charity on whose committee she sits, taking tea with the Duchess of Sutherland at the Dorchester Hotel and possibly proceeding to a further social event whose details Miss Jeffries has not yet wrested from a less efficient version of herself in Pont Street or Eaton Square.

Sitting back in her chair, Alice puts the larger thought that is oppressing her to one side and ponders the pattern of the day. It was in this precise attitude – one hand under her chin, the other pinioning Miss Jeffries's list to the arm of her chair – that Miss Helen McKie, the celebrated Society portraitist, took her off for the *Bystander*, but that was a fortnight ago and Miss McKie and her easel and her little tray of coloured inks is long gone, and there is only Mr Nichols seated in the big armchair on the fireplace's further side with one leg crossed over the other to display the suspenders keeping up his socks. Alice does not quite know how she acquired Mr Nichols as one of the ornaments of her drawing room along with the mirror and the Lalique glass, but still – there he is. He is a pink-cheeked, impossibly juvenile-looking but, she thinks, rather calculating man in his early thirties who writes for the newspapers, and for Mr Cochran's revues, is unmarried and known to specialise in Society ladies. Just now Mr Nichols, who knows everyone and goes everywhere, is talking about the parties he attended on the previous night. 'You'll scarcely credit it,' he says engagingly, 'but it seems that Sophie Huntercombe's idea of a ball supper is an omelette and a glass of Vichy water. Really, you know, there's a coffee stall man that sets up on the corner of Berners Street and they say it's because her guests are ready to faint with hunger when they come out.'

'You don't say, Twenty-Five?' Alice absently responds. Mr Nichols is known as 'Twenty-Five' to his Society ladies on account of an autobiography he once wrote maintaining that significant human life ceases beyond this age. Privately, Alice thinks this is a pose, like the photographs that appear every so often in the illustrated papers of him pretending to garden in the grounds of his cottage. But still, it is considered something to have Mr Nichols in one's drawing room, grinning his juvenile grin – he cannot be less than thirty-three – and volunteering a little mild scandal, so she goes along with it.

'They say HRH was at Lavinia Sutherland's,' Mr Nichols now declares, 'but that he found the noise simply intolerable.' To this Alice offers no reply. She is remembering Drouett, sitting in the chair that Mr Nichols now occupies, and what his presence in her life might be thought to imply. Why has he come here? What does he want? She wonders what Mr Nichols would say if she told him about the shadow that lies on her mind? Would he think it an amusing reminder of a bygone life, or be dutifully alarmed on her behalf? It is difficult to tell with English people, she thinks. Sometimes their respectability runs only skin deep. At other times the least deviation from the track has them writhing with embarrassment. Mrs Corrigan, who comes from Wisconsin and whose father was a farmer, is said to live in fear of any mention of her upbringing on the potato patch. But does Mrs Corrigan have a Drouett sending in his card and coming to sit in her drawing room? Alice thinks not. She wonders – Mr Nichols is saying something about the young Guinesses, and their house in Buckingham Street – exactly what harm Drouett could do her if he chose, and decides that it is not very much.

It is a quarter past the hour now – there is a clock striking in the church tower at the corner of the square – and Mr Nichols stirs uneasily in his seat. He is conscious – this fact has stolen up on him almost since the moment of his arrival – that he has failed to shine in Mrs Keach's presence, but aware, too, that not all Society ladies are alike and that stalemate in Lowndes Square may be followed by triumph in Eaton

Terrace. The crucial thing, he thinks, is to keep one's wits about one. Miss Jeffries glides into the room and he stands up and gives another of his bright grins, altogether beautiful in its execution, and insists on shaking her hand. Miss Jeffries, who returns the handshake cordially, dislikes Mr Nichols and has been known to call him a 'viper'. From her chair Alice sees this charade and is amused by it. One day Edie will forget herself with Mr Nichols, she thinks, and there will be trouble. She feels that it is not the proud author of *Twenty-Five* sitting opposite, twisting his fingers in his hand and wondering whether to call for his hat, but Drouett. It is the shock of seeing him, she thinks, that has discountenanced her, nothing more than that. It would have been easier, she realises, if he had metamorphosed into something entirely new, carrying no hint about him of the person he had been. The problem, she decides, is that so much of him – his way of talking, the turn of his head – is as she remembered it. But this does not solve the problem he has set her. What is it that he said about his stay in London? She tries to recall the words, but they have disappeared along with Mr Nichols's smile as he realises that Miss Jeffries's sortie into the room has been conducted with the express intention of driving him out of it.

'My dear,' Miss Jeffries says now, giving the nearest of the Lalique vases a little pat and conveying a little pile of letters requiring signature to the occasional table, 'Mrs Keigwin distinctly asked you for twelve, you know, so that you could talk about . . .' Whatever it is that Mrs Keigwin wished to talk about disappears into a clatter of Miss Jeffries's heels against the fender and a fit of simulated coughing: this is not a subject fit for Mr Nichols. 'It's only Chester Square, surely, Edie?' Alice counters mildly and Miss Jeffries casts an anxious look back, anxious lest her gesture has been misinterpreted. When it comes down to it, Alice thinks, Drouett will want money. That is what most of them want. In the past few years there have been other, lesser Drouetts, people with claims on her goodwill, ghosts from out of the dim beginnings of her English life fallen on evil days. Somehow they have all been dealt with. The only one who has never wanted money is Edie, on whom twenty pound notes have to be pressed and who regards her five hundred a year as a scandal. Remembering them, Alice assures herself that she can deal with Drouett, who has only the fact of their association in his quiver and no other weapon that she can think of except the child – an avenue of exploration, Alice thinks, which is altogether closed off. Mr Nichols is on his feet now and taking his leave, while Miss Jeffries hovers behind him like a malignant sybil and gives the vase such a tap with her forefinger that it nearly smashes on to the carpet. 'My dear,' says Miss Jeffries, before Mr Nichols is halfway down the stairs, 'that man is *using* you. Truly he is. Do you know, he got himself invited to the Sutherlands and then wrote a piece in some dreadful newspaper saying that he had danced with a duchess.'

'Oh, don't take on, Edie,' Alice retorts, rising out of her chair and, in her haste, scattering the pile of tradesmen's bills over the floor. 'Everyone uses me. Why, I believe you would if you knew how.'

'My dear,' Miss Jeffries says in a passion, 'I would *not*' and Alice sees her once again in the bedroom of the Bolton lodging house with her face white from Mr Armitage's rebukes and feels a terrible, magnanimous pity.

Somehow Mr Nichols's departure consoles her. It is as if, with his going, Drouett's spectre has vanished too. 'And I can't believe Mrs Keigwin expects me for twelve,' she says to Miss Jeffries as the two of them momentarily confer. The tradesmen's bills are left on the floor for the footman to retrieve. Outside the leaves are gently descending from the plane trees in the square and Alice's Armstrong-Siddeley limousine, brought round from a mews garage a quarter of a mile away, stands idling at the kerb.

Mrs Keigwin's house is full of noise – it is always rowdy here – with couples lounging on the staircase and a throng of younger people cluttering up the entrance hall, but Alice knows how to comport herself on these occasions. She has a butler escort her through the crowd to the dining room, where the buffet is laid out, and a footman bring her a glass of champagne. By three o'clock the champagne has gone flat and at least half the people present are playing an absurd game that involves rolling half-pennies into an upturned cigarette packet, so she has the butler summon her car and is driven away through the wet Belgravia squares in the direction of Chelsea.

The charity meeting is a decline. When it is over and they are being served tea by the parlourmaid, one of the younger women smokes a cigarette and touches up her lipstick with the aid of a compact mirror, to the silent disgust of her elders. Outside the drawing-room window the afternoon is running out in a sea of blue-grey light; there are flakes of soot, Alice sees, falling over the rain-soaked pavements. At the Dorchester the Duchess of Sutherland has collected Prince Michael of Serbia, Lady Birkenhead, Maurice Baring and a woman supposed to have written an indecent novel, 'not a bad crowd for the time of the year' as someone truly remarks when the Duchess is out of earshot. The Dorchester, too, is noisy, gathered up in some late-afternoon revelry that no one seems to know the meaning of. Alice thinks of Drouett's five-guinea shoes, his heavy jowls, the grey pouches beneath his oyster eyes. Already, she thinks, she cannot quite believe in him or gauge their relationship. London is vagrant and insubstantial, she thinks, threatening to dissolve altogether before her eyes. There is a newspaper lying on the white tabletop, stirring a little beneath the winnowing fans, and she glances at the topmost page, which is about a curious kind of new hairstyle halfway between a shingle and an Eton Crop. This, too, Alice cannot quite believe. She has a feeling that things are running away from her, subtly evading her net.

The gathering breaks up at six, with a prospect of cocktail parties, dinners, nightclubs extending before it. The woman who has written the indecent novel says she will be lucky if she gets to bed before three. The Duchess intends to sleep two hours before the rigours of the night unfold. Alice thinks about Drouett in his hotel, how he passes his time, whom he speaks to. Her alarm has been replaced by a mild anxiety. But he will not come again, she thinks. He will sail back to America and that will be that. Mr Baring says that she looks pensive and offers a penny for her thoughts, and she laughs and says that a woman's thoughts are her own or where would the world be? Outside the air is unexpectedly chill and there are flocks of cinema-goers in the streets. Back at Lowndes Square – very quiet and mournful despite the glinting chandeliers and the butler's familiar tread – there is a letter for her lying on the salver. It is from Drouett, a brisk and respectful letter signalling his delight at the renewal of their acquaintance and his hope that he may see her again, and dark terror sweeps out of a little reservoir whose lid she had thought wedged firmly into place, to mingle with the inky blackness of the night.

Alice did not, as Miss Jeffries had advised, take her troubles to the Home Secretary, but she did think that she might pay a visit to her lawyer. Accordingly, on the next morning she astonished her housekeeper by appearing in the breakfast room at eight o'clock – the toast had yet to be carried to the table, and the *Morning Post* was still in Mr Maslin's pantry being ironed – with a request that the car should be brought round half an hour later for an excursion to Aberconway and Mather's chambers at Lincoln's Inn. There were already a couple of pale young women seated on cane chairs in the vestibule – Aberconway and Mather specialised in

Society divorce cases – but the clerk, who knew that her business was worth at least fifteen hundred a year to his employers, sent her up on the instant. But once arrived in Mr Aberconway's room, which looked out over the wet grass and the dripping trees, and was very unlike a lawyer's chambers, having no shelves of law books but a mantelpiece full of invitation cards, she found herself struggling to explain the purpose of her visit.

She knew that Drouett's arrival in Lowndes Square had greatly upset her; she knew that his letter – those three or four sentences about his delight in renewing their acquaintance – was simple torture, but she could not find the words with which to convey this to Mr Aberconway. Consequently she shuffled her hands in her lap, ran her eye over Mr Aberconway's line of invitations, asked a question or two, made several remarks that mystified Mr Aberconway by their obliquity and lapsed into silence. For his own part Mr Aberconway, who sat watching her from behind his roll-top desk, making occasional indentations in his sheet of blotting paper, was intrigued. He had known Mrs Keach for the best part of a decade, esteemed her, found her shrewd, businesslike and decisive, and commended her to his colleagues as a woman who knew what she wanted. But what she wanted now, apparently, was to sit by his fireplace twisting the fastenings of her handbag and asking him if he would be at Lady Cunard's supper party next Thursday fortnight. It was all very puzzling and he could not make it out.

'I have had a letter,' Alice said at last, pushing Drouett's envelope gingerly across the surface of the roll-top desk. 'I thought you might advise me.'

Mr Aberconway picked up the envelope, read its contents, which seemed to him highly innocuous, noted that the stationery was of the cheapest kind and put it down on the blotting paper. Several questions occurred to him, but he decided to begin with the most obvious. 'This Mr Drouett is a friend of yours?'

Mr Aberconway had once or twice seen his client annoyed, and several times thought her irritated or cast down, but he had never seen her embarrassed.

'I suppose he could be called that.'

'Well – one is either a friend or one is not, surely?'

'There was an – association.'

'An association?' Mr Aberconway rolled the word around his tongue.

He knew at once that it meant something discreditable and this intrigued him quite as much as Mrs Keach's confusion. Having waited for a prompt, which eluded him, he went on, 'And how long ago was this? A fairly long time, I take it?'

'A very long time ago. Before I came to England.'

'And now this person has' – Mr Aberconway stirred the letter again with his thumbnail – 'come to see you?'

'He called at my house yesterday.'

'Did he say what brought him to London?'

'He said he was on holiday.'

Again Mr Aberconway looked at the letter. It really was very innocuous. Yet it seemed to him that the situation was perhaps more complex than it appeared. Had Drouett been staying at Claridge's, he would not have given it a second thought. Never having heard of the Criterion Hotel, Bloomsbury, he was immediately suspicious. But still he wanted to know more about Alice's dealings with Drouett and he suspected that the way to obtain this information was to feign an inability to help.

'You will forgive me for saying so, Mrs Keach,' he said now, 'but I hardly see that this is a matter for the law.'

'Isn't it?' He was surprised by the force of her tone. 'I think it is.'

'Certainly people can be very tedious in renewing old connections, but I don't think you can stop a man whom you once knew knocking on your door. If you find him objectionable, simply send him away. I take it that's the gravamen of the case?' But something in Mrs Keach's eye told him that this was not the gravamen of the case. Mr Aberconway was aware, as he made this judgment, of how much he disliked mystery. He liked divorce cases involving barmaids with yellow hair and co-respondents with black-and-white shoes who did not prevaricate in the witness box.

Gallantly – Mr Aberconway was always gallant – he pressed on. 'Have you any obligation to him?'

'None. If anything, the obligation is the other way round.'

Mr Aberconway let that pass. He would have recoiled at the suggestion of blackmail, but he would also have known how to deal with it. And he did not think, having seen several such items in the course of his career, that this was a blackmailer's letter.

'Did he' – Mr Aberconway did not like to enquire if Drouett had asked for money – 'did he seem in want of anything?'

'He was wearing a pair of patent leather shoes.'

He looked to see if she was joking, but saw in a moment that she was not. Still, he knew, there was information to which he had not been made party. Cautiously, he tried to sum up what he had been told: 'A man whom you knew many years ago in the United States, to whom you are under no obligation, and who has not asked you for assistance of any kind, but has called at your house. Why is that so very troublesome, Mrs Keach?'

What Alice wanted to say to Mr Aberconway was that she had a vision of Drouett reminiscing about those days in De Smet and asking her about the child – a question she knew it would terrify her to be asked – but she did not think that she could tell him that. Instead, she said rather hastily, 'I . . . I suspect his motives.'

Mr Aberconway sighed. He suspected all kinds of people's motives: his clients'; his wife's; and the editor of the *Legal Gazette*'s, but he could not for that reason bring them to court. He decided to temporise: 'If it would make you any happier in your mind, we could have him . . . watched. Naturally in our line of work' – he meant divorce cases – 'this kind of surveillance is sometimes necessary. There is a . . . gentleman' – he did not like to say 'private detective' – 'I could engage if you wished it.'

'I do wish it.'

'It will be rather expensive, I dare say.'

'That doesn't matter in the least.'

'Well, no – perhaps not,' said Mr Aberconway, who remembered that it never did with her. 'Now, where is this fellow staying? The Criterion Hotel, Bloomsbury, is it? And what does he look like? I can't imagine he goes anywhere very much, but one never knows . . .'

19

Changes of Address

In Middlesbrough, Scunthorpe, Rhyll – places Drouett has not yet visited – the sun continues to shine. Here in London, though, the summer is turning into autumn. The station platforms at Euston and King's Cross are full of horsey gentlemen in tweed jackets and bowler hats, with field glasses slung over their shoulders, bound for Uttoxeter, Towcester and Market Rasen. The dark squares are full of strewn leaves and the gardens left to moulder. At dawn the light has a particular eerie, translucent quality that turns the high buildings, the rows of houses rising up the hill towards Hampstead, pale and ghostly in its shadow. The Society magazines, which for the past two months have consoled themselves with charity tennis tournaments and the promenade at Cannes, break out into a riot of fancy-dress parties and *fêtes champêtres*. In Liverpool the skeleton of a baby is discovered in the basement of a derelict house by a workman. There are bonfires burning in the public parks and football results on the wireless. A nursery maid is run over by a carriage in Hyde Park and an unemployed man who claims in court that he has not tasted meat for a fortnight charged with stealing a duck from the Serpentine.

All this Drouett sees from the window of his Baker Street apartment. Or rather, reads about. He still finds the London evening newspapers inexhaustibly fascinating. Fatstock prices, diplomatic receptions, domestic hints, profit warnings – Drouett swallows it down as regularly as the weak English coffee of the Corner Houses. He is getting the measure of England, he thinks, taking its pulse. It is this feeling that has taken him from the Bloomsbury hotel to the Baker Street apartment – this and the need for further economy, and the fact that Joyce likes her privacy. Drouett is puzzled by Joyce, whose dress, demeanour and background suggest a respectability she does not in fact exhibit. An American girl of Joyce's upbringing, he reckons, would want to know where she stood. But Joyce seems untroubled by their relationship. She has a habit of arriving at the apartment early in the evening after work. Some nights they go out to a movie or a café. Mostly, though, Joyce is content to stay at home. There is something proprietorial about her, Drouett thinks, but also something vaguely detached, as if she does not quite see him, know who he is. She calls him 'darling' in the kind of strangulated way he has heard English movie stars talk: Drouett cannot get over that 'darling'. He has even been to see her parents in one of the outer suburbs – Purley? Cheam? He cannot remember. Joyce's father is about the same age as himself, a stuffed shirt who works in a bank, but not unfriendly. Joyce, he notes, turns meek and attentive in their presence, doesn't smoke and leaves conversation to the older people.

Joyce. Wood smoke. Newspapers. Alice. The apartment is small by Philadelphia standards and costs two pounds a week. There is supposed to be a porter living somewhere in the basement who will take out the trash and mend fuses, but Drouett has never seen him. A hundred pounds remains from the money he brought from America, kept in a pocket-book. Instinct tells him to conserve it, although Joyce has her own ideas. Her talk about money is nearly always in code. 'Expensive' in this occluded vocabulary means 'dangerously ostentatious'. Joyce likes things to be 'civilised'. A ride in a taxi is civilised, as is supper in a restaurant. Sometimes, lying in bed in the apartment early in the mornings after Joyce has gone to work, Drouett wonders what he is doing here in London, what exactly he hopes to achieve. Back from his visit to Lowndes Square – he was still at the Bloomsbury hotel then, with the dog lying in its basket and the taxis roaring in the distance – he wrote her a letter. Her reply, in handwriting, was non-committal. Since then she has been away, he thinks, at her country house, or abroad: the newspapers give occasional details. But it is autumn now and the vacationers are sailing home. That kind of life is beginning again. Only the other day he saw her name in a list of guests at some luncheon party: Lady Colefax, Mr Harold Nicolson, Mrs Keach. Several times he has tried to recall the conversation they had in the big drawing room with its profusion of glass and its chain of invitation cards dancing over the mantelpiece, but its precise nuances always escape him. This is worrying, for it seems somehow to erase him from the scene of which he was a part, leaving only the glass and the damask carpets. The autumn wears on. The lights in the square begin to go on at six, then at five-thirty. The Prince of Wales departs by air for Paris. At the Duchess of Sutherland's ball the Hon. Stephen Tennant creates a sensation by arriving as Taglioni in the role of La Sylphide. The River Ouse bursts its banks near King's Lynn and kills three people.

Seeing out the fall, high up in the Baker Street apartment, Drouett became aware that his inaction had begun to oppress him. There were things that he wanted to say to Alice – to Mrs Keach – but he was not altogether sure what they were. At the same time he knew that the life he was living here in London was not indefinitely sustainable. The other half of his liner ticket lay in his pocketbook beneath a handful of dollar bills not yet changed into Sterling, hidden from sight but disagreeably present in his mind. Once about this time, opening the drawer where he kept his money, he found that his resources were down to sixty pounds. This surprised him – he could not recall spending the money, did not know where it had gone – but he knew that London was an expensive place and accordingly he made one or two little economies in his dress and expenditure. He could not do without his newspapers – there were three of these, generally bought in the morning, at noon and in the early evening – but he would perhaps not renew his suit, just for the moment.

Joyce noticed this new regime and remarked upon it. 'George,' she said, 'it seems to me that you're getting frightfully mean.'

'What makes you say that?' he wondered.

'Well – you could at least get that dreadful pair of shoes you go about in resoled.'

'There's no harm in being careful, I suppose,' he said, flaring up in spite of himself. But secretly he was ashamed about the shoes.

All this led him to a decision that was unusual for him. Until now he had represented himself to Joyce as a tourist, a prosperous visitor over to see the sights. Increasingly, though, he found himself wanting to ask her advice. Several times lately, while she chatted to him about her day at work or how they might amuse themselves in the evening, he had caught himself thinking of Alice and the drawing room in Lowndes Square, and his inability to separate these two parts of his life pressed on his mind.

'Say,' he began once, 'you ever hear of someone called Alice Keach?'

'Isn't she that woman the papers are always going on about? One of those Society people.'

He could not, of course, tell her everything about Alice. But he thought that he might tell her – something. And so, choosing his words with what seemed to Joyce an unusual hesitation, he explained that he and Alice – Mrs Keach – were, if not old friends, then people who had known each other well at an early point in their lives.

Watching him as he spoke, and noting the hesitation, Joyce understood that he was not telling the whole truth, but she was impressed by the connection. 'Isn't she supposed to be awfully rich?'

'It certainly looks that way,' Drouett admitted.

'If she's an old friend of yours, George, you ought to go round and say hello.'

'Maybe I'll do that,' Drouett conceded.

He did nothing about it for two days. But on the third he put on the suit that needed renewing and set off for Lowndes Square. It was an afternoon near Christmas, with fine rain falling over the wet streets – grey and melancholy they seemed to him – and the lamps in the Knightsbridge thoroughfares blazed out against the advancing twilight. Surely she would be there, Drouett thought, crossing the square from the northern side and spying an automobile or two drawn up at the kerb, but the superior butler who opened the door, with perhaps a glint of recognition in his eye, said that, no, his mistress was not at home. Drouett did not like that glint. 'She could at least have seen me,' he said to himself as he made his way back across the square, thinking that the butler had orders not to admit him. Then he told himself that he was being foolish, that it would take more than the butler to keep him out of the big drawing room with the shining glass. 'Anyhow, I shall see her,' he said to himself.

A few days later, having dressed himself with exemplary care once more, he called at the house again. This time he was in luck. The door was half open, there were people coming in and out, a tradesman was delivering a carpet and a parlourmaid – there was no sign of the superior butler – thinking him one of Mrs Keach's regular visitors, happily accepted his card. Reaching the door of the great drawing room – he could see the light shining off the glass as he approached – he had a little speech ready on his lips and found that all kinds of stray thoughts had taken a coherent shape in his mind. But the room was full of people – a dozen at least collected by the mantelpiece, another three or four moving up the staircase behind him – and his courage failed him. He took a cup of tea and went and sat in a chair, far away from the conversing throng, and the people moving in and out of the room – it was one of Mrs Keach's Thursday 'teas' – looked at him as they passed and wondered who he was. Only once did her eye fall on him. He had been there half an hour when he found that a little knot of talkers with Alice at their midst had moved to within a yard of the chair where he sat and he rose hurriedly to his feet.

'Why, Mr Drouett,' she said. 'How are you?'

'I'm keeping well,' Drouett told her. Still he might have said something, might have drawn her to one side, requested an interview in another room, but there were people crowded around and more light shining off the glass, and his courage failed him. For a moment he tried to attend to the conversation in which Alice was engaged – something about a race meeting, the Attorney General, he could not quite make it out – then the absurdity of his situation struck him and he went downstairs, took his hat and coat from the parlourmaid and made his way back across the square to the Underground station. Still he was not displeased – not quite. He had proved something, he thought. That butler had not made a fool of him. He would go to Lowndes Square again on a Thursday and not be kept out. He bought another paper from a street vendor and carried it down the station steps into the blackness beyond.

When he got back to the apartment he found Joyce putting on an expensive-looking, or rather 'civilised', dress he had not seen before. 'You promised to take me to that new place by the river at Staines,' she said. 'Don't you remember?'

He did remember.

'I was thinking that we could stay here tonight,' he said awkwardly.

'But George, you distinctly said.' She was very close to tears. Drouett did not like the way she looked at these times – vivid and ghastly, with her skin showing its age under the harsh electric light. He relented and they went to the supper club by the river at Staines, and that was three more guineas gone from the pile of notes in the bedroom drawer.

He had another occupation to add to his thinking, his seeing Joyce and his newspapers. He had taken to walking. They had begun some building works down by the docks at Poplar, and it was his habit on fine mornings to walk down through the City and the East End to see how it was progressing. It had none of the magnificence of New York or Philadelphia, he thought, but the sight of the cranes and the walls of brick that grew daily more immense interested him. It connected him to some part of his youth that he could not quite remember – some sojourn in a big city that was rapidly extending its bounds – and this, too, absorbed him, made him believe that in his journey across the Atlantic and his pursuit of Alice he had not travelled so very far after all. One morning, coming out of the vestibule of the Baker Street apartment at the start of one of these walks, his gaze shifted to the further side of the street, where he saw a man in a trilby hat and a pair of spectacles staring at him. The man was gone in a moment, and Drouett, thinking nothing of it, continued on his stroll. The work on the docks had been temporarily suspended so he amused himself by walking through Canning Town and the labyrinth of little streets around it. Then, stepping off a bus somewhere on the fringes of the City and in search of the second bus that would take him back to Baker Street, he was sure that he saw another man – if not the same man, then remarkably like him – looking at him fixedly from the street corner. This alarmed him and instead of following his customary route to the bus stop at the end of Threadneedle Street he plunged off into a side alley, thinking that in this way he might throw a possible pursuer off the scent. Continually, on the remainder of his journey, he found himself looking back over his shoulder, anxious that once again he would find the man staring at him, but there was no one there and by the time he reached the Baker Street apartment he had almost convinced himself that the whole thing was a figment of his imagination. He was getting a little anxious, he told himself.

That evening he counted his money. A bare forty pounds remained. This startled him, because he could not imagine where it had gone. Then he remembered the evening at the supper club by the river at Staines and cursed himself bitterly for this extravagance. He remembered, too, that the month's rent for the apartment would be due at the end of the week. 'I'll find a way out of this,' he told himself. He stood for a long time in the unlit front room of the apartment, clenching and unclenching his fists. 'Maybe I'll talk to her again,' he said to himself. The evening newspaper lay on the mat and he picked it up and began to read it.

Joyce noticed his depression of spirits. 'You're very glum tonight, George,' she said once around this time.

'I suppose I am a little,' he conceded.

'Shall we go out? Perhaps it would cheer you up.'

'I think I'd sooner stay here,' he said.

He could see that his reluctance irked her and that she was puzzled by it. Although he had no illusions about Joyce, he found that this annoyed him. In the morning, when he had paid the rent for the apartment and made one or two purchases at the grocer's store, he counted his money again. There was a little over thirty-five pounds.

Not long after this an idea occurred to him. From time to time in his wanderings around the block he had found himself nodding familiarly to a man who inhabited an apartment on one of the lower floors. Getting into conversation, the man – he was perhaps twenty years younger than Drouett and worked in the motor trade in Warren Street – had mentioned an address where, if Drouett cared to present himself on a Friday evening, he would find a poker school in progress. Drouett thought that he might make the invitation work to his advantage. He had been a pretty fair player at poker in his youth. Why should he not eke out his resources in this way? Searching for the address, he found it inscribed on the edge of a matchbox. This cheered him. He saw himself coming back with fifteen, twenty pounds, enough to keep him through the winter, while he, while he ... Still his exact aim lay slightly out of view, something he did not altogether care to think of. He spent the afternoon thinking of the poker lore that he had learned back in Kansas forty years ago.

The poker school was held in a room above a public house in Camden – a poor part of London, Drouett assured himself, who had not been there before, as he walked up from the Underground station. There was no sign of his friend from the apartment block and the game they were to play, he learned from the four or five men assembled, was not poker but vingt-et-un. For a moment he thought of making some excuse and escaping into the street, but by this time he was already seated at the rough wooden table – the men looked to him to be small-time clerks or casual labourers – and it would have made him look foolish to retreat. Accordingly he placed a pound note in the pot held out by the banker – he was quite surprised by the stakes – and allowed himself to be dealt the first of his cards. For half an hour or so the luck was with him: calculating his gains he found that he was six pounds to the good. Then came a passage in the game where the cards fell out badly on all sides and fifteen pounds lay in the pot. The four cards Drouett held in his hand amounted to seventeen. Trusting to his judgment, and noting the expressions of the men seated on either side of him, he sat back in his chair and said, 'Twist, I guess.'

Affecting a nonchalance he did not possess, Drouett turned over the card. It was the deuce of spades.

'Stick,' he said. Surely, he thought, nineteen would be sufficient to win. But no, the banker's cards, now produced, amounted to twenty.

'Damnation!' he said, letting his cards fall to the table and giving a little mock-smile lest anyone should suppose he was badly put out. 'I thought I had you there.'

'What say we double the stakes?' someone suggested.

'I'll live with that,' Drouett heard himself saying. He lost five games in succession, won half his money back and then settled into a losing streak that lasted until the moment he retrieved his hat and descended on to the pavement below. So that was another ten pounds gone from his store.

Going back to the Baker Street apartment he affected a bravado that, like the nonchalance he had displayed at the card table, he did not feel. He would find some way of adding to his resources, he thought. There was no need for him to worry. He remembered the liner ticket lying in his pocketbook. But no, he would not give up just yet. By chance, the Society column of the newspaper he had in his pocket contained an account of a Caledonian party held at a house in Belgrave Square: Alice's name was among the guests. He read it in the kitchenette, waiting for his coffee to boil. No, he thought again, he would not give up just yet.

The loss of his money coincided with a crisis in his personal affairs. It was a Friday. Joyce was spending the weekend with her parents. On the Monday evening, waiting for her knock at the door of the Baker Street apartment, he found that it did not come. This surprised him, but he remembered that there had been other occasions when something had caused her to postpone her visit. Doubtless on the next morning there would be a letter. But there was no letter and no knock on the apartment door that evening. On the next afternoon – the Wednesday – he decided that he would take a little stroll down to the legal chambers at Holborn and wait for her to emerge from her work. It was a grey, cold day, with fine rain falling and the position he took up on the street corner made him feel conspicuous. If there was a reason why she did not want to see him, he thought rather crossly, then it was up to her. But still he waited, smoking a cheroot that he found in his pocket – he would have to stop smoking those cheroots! – and pacing in and out of the arc of the street lamp. It seemed to him, when he saw her, that she moved rather hurriedly out of the office door – she was opening her umbrella as she walked – but he moved gratefully across the pavement towards her as if his waiting for her on the Holborn street corner were the most natural thing in the world.

'I was just wondering how you were,' he said. 'I figured you must be ill or something.'

'Oh, I'm perfectly well,' she said, it seemed to him a trifle awkwardly. 'That is' – she gave a little laugh – 'I'm fairly sure I am.'

'It's awful wet, isn't it?' he ventured. 'Why don't we have something to eat somewhere?'

'Actually,' she said – she was still unfurling her umbrella – 'I don't think I want anything to eat just at the moment.'

He saw then how it was. 'She needn't have said that,' he thought to himself. 'She could have said something better than that.'

'I guess I'll see you some time, then,' he said, still wondering if there were some way to retrieve the situation.

'That would be nice,' she said.

Murmuring something by way of farewell – he could not afterwards remember what he said – he began to walk disconsolately back in the direction of Baker Street. After he had gone a block or two, he found that his depression had begun to leave him. Really, he thought, perhaps he was better out of that. He was conscious, too, that Joyce's absence would enable him to pursue a plan he had recently settled on to live more cheaply. It was absurd, he thought, to occupy four rooms when there was only himself to consider. Reaching the apartment he picked up the evening newspaper from the mat and began to examine the column that advertised 'Accommodation to let'. As he did so one or two of the items that Joyce had left behind her – a women's magazine, a chiffon scarf in bright hogpen – caught his eye and he swept them up and hid them from view.

There were nineteen pounds now left in his store. The cheapest rooms in the immediate vicinity he discovered to be in King's Cross and Somers Town. In the end he settled on a thoroughfare called Rosamond Street at ten shillings a week. He was not much put out by its shabbiness – he had endured far worse in American cities thirty years ago – but even so, he thought, making an inspection of the place with the landlord at his elbow, maybe he would burn sulphur against the bugs. Besides, he had almost decided now that he would ask Alice for money. He had not yet made up his mind how he would do this, or what the consequences might be, but the thought of it cheered him and he went back to Baker Street to pack up his possessions less anxious than he had been for many weeks. The apartment was dim and gloomy in the late-afternoon shadow – he did not trouble to put on the electric light – and he moved quickly from room to room collecting his belongings. His head was alive with memories from twenty or even thirty years ago. Drouett remembered being in a hotel in New York the morning after the *Titanic* went down, and going out and breakfasting very comfortably off ham and eggs; standing on a street corner in Philadelphia – he was wearing a tall hat for some reason, now how had that come about? – and watching soldiers marching off to the war. Above all he found himself thinking about a widow-woman who lived in Baltimore in a big timber-board house, with cherry trees growing in the yard, with whom he had eaten his supper many times in a lilac-panelled dining room with a picture of her dead husband staring from the wall above his chair. He wondered why he had not married the woman and how his life would have turned out if he had. He was sixty years old now, he thought, and he wondered what he had to show for it.

He was standing in the darkened hallway – his travelling cases lay a yard or so behind him in the entrance to the kitchenette – when there came a noise of footsteps on the staircase and an envelope fell suddenly through the letter box. Drouett picked it up and examined it curiously. His first thought was that it was from Joyce – he thought Joyce was the only person who knew his address – but he saw that it had been forwarded from the hotel in Bloomsbury. Tearing it open he found that it was an invitation to dinner at Lowndes Square a week hence. He stood for several moments in the hallway with the invitation card in his hand, pondering its exact significance. It seemed to him that this was a good omen. 'I'll be damned,' he said to himself once or twice. Inspecting the card again – his first glance had been of a very cursory kind – he found it to be a very superior production, the lettering embossed on stiff white paperboard with a thin gold band round the margin. This set him thinking again about other such cards he had received at earlier stages in his life. He put the card in the inner pocket of his coat and went out exultantly into the night.

In his first few days at Rosamond Street the invitation dominated his mind. It was with him when he read his newspaper and while he burned sulphur against the bugs – they had come out and marched across the ceiling on his first night there in a long trail, like a ragged army – and when he went out on his walk. He had taken to walking two or three times a week now – to the docks, but also further afield to Hampstead and St John's Wood. Having raised his spirits at first, the invitation – it sat on the mantelpiece together with his picture postcards – now subtly depressed him. He knew that to take advantage of it he would need to be properly dressed. Accordingly, having looked up some addresses in a commercial directory, he went to a tailor in Marylebone High Street and spent half a guinea on the hire of an evening suit. A tall hat he thought he could get by without – no one would see him come or go except the servant who opened the door – but his patent leather shoes were things of horror. Regretting the expense, he bought a pair of cheap shoes for seven shillings and sixpence. All in all the paraphernalia for Alice's dinner party cost him nearly thirty shillings, but he reasoned to himself that the money was well spent. Who knew where it might end? All this time he was thinking about what he now conceived to be Alice's obligation to him. They had been partners once, he told himself. Certainly he had behaved badly – he knew that she had convicted him of this failing. On the other hand he believed – the conversation he had had with Hanson in Duluth burned in his mind – that she had not been quite straight with him. He would like to know what had happened to the child. Weighing the matter up, he decided that, in these circumstances, she could not very well refuse to help him if he asked and that the party – which was clearly evidence of her softening attitude – was a good place at which to commence these operations.

The dinner was at eight. He thought he might set out at seven, to give himself plenty of time. There was a square of mirror on the corner of the mantelpiece in the room in Rosamond Street, next to the line of picture postcards, and before he went out he inspected himself in it. It was a cheap suit, badly made, but he thought he did not look so bad. He took his razor and made various adjustments to his moustache. There! No one could say that he had not made an effort. He had a vision of himself sitting next to Alice on her sofa in the wide drawing room, talking comfortably to her as the other guests stood respectfully to one side and wondered what they had to say to each other.

There were two dozen guests at the dinner. One of them Drouett thought he recognised from his last visit. They ate in the big dining room where the butler had kept him waiting that time, at a long mahogany table dominated by a monstrous silver epergne in the shape of an eagle. Soup, fish, cutlets, game, savoury, ices passed in quick succession. At first Drouett barely noticed what he was eating. His gaze was fixed on Alice as she sat at the head of the table, six or seven places to his right. She was wearing a scarlet bandeau round her head and smoked cigarettes between courses out of a long holder. Then, after a little while, he found that he was able to pay more attention to his surroundings. The other guests seemed very grand to him. On his right-hand side sat a young woman – no more than a girl – who did not speak a single sentence to him during the entire course of the evening, but there was a friendly old lady on his left-hand side who asked various questions of him. Only once did he venture a comment beyond the range of his immediate neighbours. Two men were talking further down the table.

'Of course the Cottesloe's not what it was.'

'The Belvoir's not much better.'

'What do you expect if the farmers won't preserve?'

He realised – these were dim echoes of something he had once read – that they were talking about hunting, which interested him, for he had once, long years ago, hunted wolves in the Indiana backwoods. Something in his eye must have declared this interest, for the old woman said, 'Do you hunt, Mr Drouett?' and, greatly to his surprise, he found himself launching into a little description of this activity while servants cleared away the plates and a young man with a bald head on the further side of the table looked at him very curiously.

After dinner they went upstairs to the drawing room, where a negro in a dinner jacket played jazz tunes on the piano. He took his coffee and sat on a chair thinking that Alice would come and talk to him. Again the mirror and the profusion of glass rather scared him. An hour passed in which he assured himself that presently he would get up, make his way over to the group of people by the fireplace in whose midst she stood and say some of the thoughts he had in his head, but somehow the moment never came. The clock struck eleven, the guests began to drift away and he found himself shaking hands with her in the wide hall. The young man with the bald head could be glimpsed in a side room talking quietly into a telephone.

'Well, George,' she said, half amused and half serious. 'Are you still enjoying your holiday?'

'Oh, I don't know,' he heard himself saying. 'I suppose I'll be heading back home pretty soon.'

And then he was outside in the square once more, looking up at the high, lighted windows and hearing the noise of the automobile doors being slammed shut.

The next day he found a description of the dinner in his morning newspaper, and a sentence that read:

Also among the guests was Mr George Drouett, of Chicago, who entertained the company with a picturesque account of the field sports of his native land.

Drouett felt he had made a mistake. 'I shouldn't have said that,' he told himself. He thought of Alice reading the paper as she sat in the grand drawing room at Lowndes Square until the noise of his coffee coming to the boil returned him to Rosamond Street. It was a grey spring morning and he wandered northwards over the heath, pulling a stick out of the hedge and slashing at the bracken as he went. He would write a letter, he decided, as he stood on one of the grassy promontories with the city's smoke rising beneath him – he could see the dome of St Paul's looming out of the mist far away – and tell her how he was situated. The thought of what he would say in the letter occupied him for the best part of an hour, but then, rather to his surprise he found himself thinking of the old days back in Kansas City and a particular social club he had attended, full of purposeful young men like himself, and a man named Sheridan – he could see him now, standing with his back to the saloon's mirrored surround – saying 'You're a dandy, Drouett' and himself smiling in return while in the supper room beyond the gaudy dresses of the women gleamed under the light. 'Anyway, I'll be out of this soon,' he told himself. He bought another paper at a kiosk and walked home through the dreary streets.

In Rosamond Street the day was fading and a cat's-meat man with a reeking barrow was making his way along the pavement selling horse liver at threepence the bag; the sky threatened snow.

He took out his pocketbook and counted the money. There was a little over thirteen pounds. He would write the letter tonight. But he did not write the letter. He took a long time over his paper – it was very pleasant to him, reading that paper – drank his coffee and looked out of the window at the first flakes of snow falling at a slant over the Rosamond Street rooftops, and somehow the anxieties of his situation left him. Things would fix themselves, he thought: he wasn't beat yet. And he would write that letter. In the morning he woke to find an inch of snow on the window ledge and a blizzard raging in the street.

Boiling his coffee again, and eating the pieces of bread and butter that served as his breakfast, he found himself thinking of Alice. All the complacency of the previous night had left him. He took the notes out of his pocketbook again and counted them, and was horrified by his profligacy. Thirteen pounds! And after that thirteen pounds was gone – then what? He would write that letter now – that is, when he had drunk his coffee and read his newspaper. But in the end the letter did get written. It said what was more or less the truth, that having spent several months in London and exhausted his capital, he wondered whether in the light of their former association she would care to advance him a loan. He wondered for a long time what sum might be appropriate and settled on fifty pounds. Fifty pounds was nothing, he assured himself. The dinner in Lowndes Square alone would have cost that. Surely she would give him fifty pounds. He would ask for fifty pounds for old times' sake and she might give it to him or she might not. He put the letter in an envelope, garnished it with three half-penny stamps and went out to post it in the box on the corner of Rosamond Street.

'Well,' Mr Aberconway said. 'I have had my man follow him about and I can tell you where he goes.'

'Where does he go?' Alice asked.

They were sitting in Mr Aberconway's chambers in Lincoln's Inn, looking out over the wet grass and, such was the degree of leisurely confidence that Aberconway and Mather encouraged in its clients, smoking cigarettes, which Mr Aberconway had procured from a japanned box.

'Where does he go?' Mr Aberconway repeated. He was tired from a late evening spent playing bridge, and wished that the business before him was something that could be quickly expedited and just as quickly forgotten. 'In a word – nowhere. Just now he is living in a – well, a slum almost, in Somers Town. When he goes out he walks through the City or down to the docks. Poplar. Canning Town. That kind of place.'

'Does he see anyone?'

'My man tells me there is a woman with whom he has some sort of – association.'

He meant nothing by the word, but the memory of its former use hung uncomfortably in the air above them. Looking at his client, Mr Aberconway saw that her face was set in an expression of extreme thoughtfulness, as if a succession of scenes and images were passing before her eyes of which he was entirely unaware.

'I have seen him,' she said.

'What? Has he come to the house again?'

Alice explained about the dinner party, and the conversation about hunting and the report that had appeared in the newspaper. As she did so she was struck once more by the pathos of the situation. She acknowledged that Drouett's presence at her dinner table did not so much alarm her as sadden her. It was as if his shadow had stolen in and eaten her savouries and ices rather than the man himself.

'He will certainly think you mean to help him,' Mr Aberconway said, with a faint hint of peevishness. 'If you don't mind my saying, I think you have been rather unwise. He can't be in a very prosperous state, I should say. What will you do if he applies to you for money?'

'What would you advise me to do?'

'We might get him to sign a paper.' Again Mr Aberconway wished he had not stayed so late playing bridge. He was used to his clients deciding to tell him things that he did not perhaps wish to hear, and he fancied that she stood on the brink of one of these revelations and wondered what he should say when it came. The cigarette was all smoked up now, and he extinguished the butt in a little pewter tray that had the arms of an Oxford college emblazoned on its rim, wondered whether to smoke another one and then thought better of it.

'Do you know,' Alice said, 'he was the first man I ever saw?'

'Was he indeed?'

'I was nineteen and I had never been out of Kansas before. I had never seen anything like him. Never. And then . . .' Whatever she had been about to say was lost somewhere in the space between them and Mr Aberconway gaped.

'If he wants money, I think I shall give it to him,' she said. 'Not very much, perhaps, but – something.'

All that day and the next Drouett was gripped by a curious excitement. Postmen were infrequent visitors to Rosamond Street, but he grew accustomed to the sound of their tread. Such mail as arrived at the house was left on a threadbare mat inside the front door and he found himself contriving half a dozen reasons for passing through this door each morning in the hope that there would be a letter awaiting his return. A week went by, yet nothing came. But finally, on a day when he had almost given up hope, there did come – something. Not a letter from Alice but a request from her solicitors in Lincoln's Inn to call upon them at any time that might be convenient. Drouett's first reaction to this was one of deep misgiving. He had written privately to a woman with whom he had been on terms of greatest intimacy and she had referred him to her lawyer. Then, thinking things over, he decided that where money was concerned there was no harm in having a legal representative to hand. So the next morning he put on his shabby suit, buffed up his shoes and made his way to Mr Aberconway's chambers in Lincoln's Inn.

Mr Aberconway, looking up from his desk as Drouett was ushered into his room, did not quite know what to make of him. Precedent had told him to expect a middle-aged adventurer with a knowing grin and co-respondent's shoes, and here was a well-nigh elderly man in a threadbare coat with an expression on his face that was almost apologetic. The little speech that Mr Aberconway had prepared – had in fact scrawled on the margin of the letter – went spiralling away into nowhere. But still, he thought that he ought to be vigilant.

'So you are Mr Drouett, are you?'

'Certainly,' Drouett said. He was not frightened by the lawyer or indeed by his grand chambers, which looked out over the wet grass.

'An American gentleman, I believe?'

'That's right.'

Again Mr Aberconway hesitated. Part of him was amused by Drouett's nondescript appearance. Another part was intrigued by Mrs Keach's association with him. A third part wondered exactly what he wanted, apart from his fifty pounds, and what steps he might take to obtain it.

'Well, now, Mr Drouett,' he said. He was remembering what Mrs Keach had told him. 'This letter of yours to my client, to Mrs Keach. What did you expect to gain by it?'

'A man can write to an old friend of his, I think,' Drouett volunteered.

'No doubt he can. You have not seen Mrs Keach for – twenty-five years, I believe? Yet here you are in London pressing claims of friendship on her. I don't wish to seem discourteous, Mr Drouett, but it is all rather odd. Now, let us be frank with each other. How long do you intend to remain in London?'

'I rather think that's my business,' Drouett said. What he took to be the lawyer's hostility had given him some of his old fire back. 'Don't you?'

Mr Aberconway tried again. 'But my client – Mrs Keach – is especially anxious to know your intentions.'

'I was at her house, you know, this last Wednesday week,' Drouett returned. 'She might have asked me herself.'

'She might very well. I agree. But the fact remains that she has asked me to . . .' – Mr Aberconway decided to try a different tack – 'I believe I am right in saying that there was some . . . association between you?'

'I suppose you could call living together as man and wife an association.'

'Nevertheless, you would agree that this does not give you any legal claim on Mrs Keach. In fact, quite the reverse could be argued.'

'Maybe it could.' Drouett was calculating exactly how much he might tell the lawyer and what exactly might be gained by telling it. The lawyer might not believe what he was told, he thought, but it might disconcert him and he realised that this was something gained. He said conversationally, 'There was a child, you know.'

'Was there indeed?'

'A boy, I believe. I never heard about him until just lately. But that's my information.'

'Again, if there were, it could be argued that any claim was on you, not Mrs Keach.'

Mr Aberconway was thinking furiously. He had no idea whether Drouett's statement about the child was true. On the other hand he suspected that his intimacy with Mrs Keach had supplied him with all kinds of information about her that it was better he should not know, or, failing that, should certainly not be revealed to anyone else. What exactly did he know, and what did he intend to do with the knowledge? Mr Aberconway's instinct was to suspect blackmail, but something told him that an out-and-out blackmailer would not have proceeded by such a circuitous course. Could it be that Drouett wanted nothing beyond his fifty pounds? Mr Aberconway told himself that he ought to find out.

'Well, now,' Drouett said quite affably, knowing that what he had to say would be news to the lawyer. 'She told me the boy was dead. I don't think that amounts to much of a claim.'

Mr Aberconway continued to think furiously. There was an invitation card on his mantelpiece from the Countess of Kinnoull, a reward for confidential advice in one of Mrs Meyrick's cases, and he looked at it, thinking that he would sooner have a dozen Mrs Meyricks and a dozen Home Secretaries pressing down on their necks, than a single Mrs Keach. A secretary came into the room with a message to say that the Honourable Mrs Jamieson was anxious to see him, but Mr Aberconway waved her away. The Honourable Mrs Jamieson would have to wait.

'If I might ask,' he said, 'and quite between ourselves, where did you come by this information about the child?'

'Why,' said Drouett, thinking that a little mystery might not go amiss, 'I went to see Hanson in Duluth.'

'Hanson? Duluth?'

'Hanson was the preacher she took up with after . . .' – Drouett did not like to say after he had left her – 'around that time.'

'And what did this Mr Hanson have to say?'

In answer Drouett opened his pocketbook and extracted the press clipping Hanson had given him in the Duluth mission house and which he had taken the precaution of having jellygraphed. Mr Aberconway held it up in front of his spectacles, put it down on his desk and stared again at the Countess of Kinnoull's invitation. Although he did not necessarily believe that the clipping referred to Mrs Keach he was alarmed by it, for he saw that it was something concrete, something whose source could, if necessary, be investigated and proved to be true or false.

'You must realise, Mr Drouett,' he said, 'that there is nothing at all to identify my client with this affair. Nothing at all.'

'There's Hanson's word,' Drouett said mildly. 'A preacher's word.'

Again Mr Aberconway hesitated. Beyond the window the weak sun was raising little sparkles from the dew on the wet grass. The Countess of Kinnoull's card winked at him from the mantelpiece. The Honourable Mrs Jamieson was in the reception room waiting to consult him about her divorce. He could connect none of this with what Drouett had told him. It was altogether beyond his experience. He went over again in his mind what the past ten minutes had yielded up. He was not quite sure that he believed it all, but at the same time he rather doubted that Drouett's powers of invention could have extended so far. And whether the information was true or not, its only significance, he told himself, lay in what Drouett intended to do with it.

'Mr Drouett,' he now found himself saying, 'what do you want?'

Drouett inclined his head to the question, which puzzled him. He remembered that Alice had asked it. He was not sure what he wanted. He needed the fifty pounds. He would have liked to talk to Alice in her great drawing room beneath the profusion of glass – there were things he wanted to say to her about the old days and the snow falling over the hills beyond De Smet on the day he had left her. He had seen the look of alarm on the lawyer's face when he had told his tale of Hanson and Duluth and flicked the press clipping on to the desk, and knew very well what the lawyer expected: that he would want his silence to be paid for. But still he did not know if that was what he did want.

Mr Aberconway, meanwhile, was calculating. He had almost decided, having been given a free hand by his client, that he would offer Drouett a sum of money, but he was not sure what the sum should be. Too little or too much would probably produce the same result. He wondered whether, in fact, he was getting out of his depth here, and whether it would be better to resign the work altogether, have someone else look at Drouett's press clipping so he could apply himself to the Honourable Mrs Jamieson's divorce. But then he remembered that the legal fees extracted by his firm from Mrs Keach with regard to various conveyancings, trust documents and contractual arrangements had very nearly paid his salary and decided that he could put up with Drouett.

'Mr Drouett,' he said again, with slightly greater force – after all, it was nothing to him, in the end, what Drouett did with what he knew – 'what do you want?'

Drouett looked at him warily. 'Why, I should like to talk to Alice – to Mrs Keach.'

'I'm afraid that is quite impossible. Really it is. See here, Mr Drouett. I am instructed by my client' – Mr Aberconway was improvising, but he thought the cause was a good one – 'to tell you that she is very mindful of your former association. I understand that when she last spoke to you, you mentioned that you were shortly to return to America. Knowing this, she would be delighted to contribute to the expenses of your voyage.'

Drouett blinked. He was thinking of the mission house in Duluth and the look on Hanson's face as he had handed him the press clipping.

'Mrs Keach suggested to me that the sum of one thousand pounds might be acceptable.'

'One thousand pounds!'

'Needless to say' – Mr Aberconway hesitated again, realising that the really difficult part of the conversation still lay before him – 'we should need your assurance that you really did intend to return to America. Otherwise, naturally, there would be no reason for Mrs Keach to contribute to your expenses.'

Drouett nodded his head. One thousand pounds was a lot of money. Nearly five thousand dollars. He was still not sure what he wanted, but he thought that he would be a fool to turn down one thousand pounds. As for giving an assurance, well, he would sign it of course. Giving an assurance never hurt anybody. But still he knew that he wanted to see Alice.

'I think I could see my way to that,' he said.

And Mr Aberconway, who had heard a door slamming sharply beneath him and feared that the Honourable Mrs Jamieson had taken her business elsewhere, said that he was delighted to hear it.

20

Feeding the Sharks

'Dear me,' said Miss Jeffries, coming into the breakfast room one morning with a copy of the *Morning Post* and a heap of letters tucked under her arm, 'it is already the second week in September.'

'It's only last week, surely, that I came back from Biarritz?'

'No, my dear.' Miss Jeffries put the newspaper and the letters on the table among the breakfast things and settled herself in a chair. 'It was three weeks ago that you came back from Biarritz.' Miss Jeffries had spent August in Lowndes Square with the cook and two housemaids on board wages, but bore no grudge. 'Really, those invitations cannot be left much longer. It is only at this time of the year that people's engagement books get so dreadfully full up. It is not like the old days, when Mr Melville used to say that he never dined at home between May Day and Goodwood.'

It was Mrs Keach's custom, born of immemorial habit, to throw open her country house in Sussex at the end of October for a weekend party. The company invited to these entertainments was varied. There were people who were friends of Mrs Keach's and people who were not quite friends but with whom it was supposed – not least by themselves – that Mrs Keach wanted to keep in. A politician or two might be seen there, and the Governor of the Bank of England. Mr George Robey had once come, and Mr Wells. There were people who were indisputably in the public eye and people who shivered lest the public eye were turned upon them. Royalty was not unknown, but mostly of the foreign sort. Beneath this panorama of celebrity, to whom Mrs Keach had for one reason or another chosen to extend the hand of friendship, moved an equal number of guests, not necessarily distinguished in any way, whom she asked because she liked them. All this had a stimulating effect on the proceedings. People sometimes said that the trouble with Alice Keach's was that you never quite knew whom you were going to meet there, but these were the kind of people who also complained about 'sneak guests' and gatecrashers and young men who hadn't been to Eton; and Mrs Keach, luxuriating in her wealth and position, knew that she could ignore them.

'Is there a list?' she said now, turning over the copy of the *Post* and looking at the picture of Mr Norman that adorned its inner cover.

There was a list. Miss Jeffries had taken last year's sheet and added to and subtracted from it in bright red ink. Alice examined it shrewdly, the summer's gossip weighing heavily on her mind.

'The political people won't come. Not with the financial crisis. Nor Mr Norman. We'll send cards, of course . . . Princess Eloise told me she was in America . . . Who's this Mr Acton?'

'I believe he writes poetry. You met him at Mrs Harry Brown's.'

'Did I? Well, put him down then. And Constance Henderson. She needs cheering up. Who's Mr Carstairs?'

'Mr Maltravers's friend, who edits the *Blue Bugloss*.'

'Did I ever see him?'

Miss Jeffries looked hard at the sheet of paper. 'I don't think you did.'

'Never mind. Put him down. And Mr Schmiegelow. We must have Mr Schmiegelow.'

And so they went on. The unmarried daughters of aristocracy living in Belgrave Square, because the gentlemen must be entertained. A commercial friend or two of the late Mr Keach. A cross-talk comedian from the variety halls . . .

'Do you think we can have Mr Burnage?'

'Mrs Corrigan says he is not nearly so vulgar in company. He was in the guards, you know, before he went on the stage.'

. . . Unmarried gentlemen living in mews flats in Pimlico, because the ladies, too, must be entertained. A friend or two of Miss Jeffries, squeezed in on charitable grounds. A liberal-minded clergyman, who it was thought might add gravity to the proceedings . . .

'He won't mind card playing in the evening? Or Mrs Reginald Heber, who is just on her third divorce?'

'Mrs Corrigan says he is the life and soul of the party.'

So everything was agreed and Miss Jeffries, on whom the serious organisation of the event depended, went off to take the rubric of the invitation card to the printer, while Alice sat in her chair in the big, gloomy drawing room and fed her dissatisfaction. She did not quite know why the prospect of the weekend produced in her a feeling of slight unease, but she knew that it did. She went over in her mind the routines of the forthcoming three days at Castlemaine Court – the Friday dinner, the excursion somewhere or other around the countryside in shooting brakes, the Saturday dinner, the rapt exhaustion of Sunday afternoon – and knew that it bored her, that it was very tiring and that the guests meant nothing to her. The gap between her present and her past life seemed very great. For a moment or two she found herself thinking of the Kansas prairie, the wheat fields gleaming in the sun, the country roads that led nowhere. The morning drifted on and one or two people came to lunch – bright, middle-aged ladies back from Venice or Menton, an actor who wanted her to patronise his charity matinée – but still she could not forget the wheat fields and the country roads running on to nowhere. She wondered if they were still there, and if the people she had once known still walked along them. Outside the rain fell over the grey square and the lunch guests, tripping out to their cars beneath the footmen's umbrellas, said that Alice Keach was getting very preoccupied these days.

A few days after this the replies began to trickle in. Miss Jeffries carried them off to her private sanctum at the back of the house and ticked off the names with a blue pencil. The politicians could not come and Mr Norman sent his regards – things were really very pressing – but Mr Schmiegelow, Mr Burnage and Mrs Reginald Heber would all be present. Mrs Keach found that this news further contributed to her gloom. She liked to have people of consequence in her house, for whom telegrams arrived at odd hours of the day and night; to feel, as unexpected news was brought to the dinner table, that she sat at the centre of great events. But the politicians and Mr Norman were not coming, and she was left with Mr Burnage and his comic songs, and Mrs Reginald Heber and her divorces.

Miss Jeffries, who had noted this depression, thought she had an explanation for it. 'My dear,' she said one morning by way of a preliminary. 'Here is another letter from Mr Bullivant.'

'What does he say?'

'I don't know that he says very much. But he apologises very much for the inconvenience and the things should be returned next week . . .' Seeing that Alice was not in the least interested in the subject of her jewellery, Miss Jeffries changed tack. 'My dear,' she said, 'I trust you are not still alarming yourself about that Mr Drouett?'

'Why should I be alarming myself about Mr Drouett?'

'You did not like it when he came to dinner that time.'

'Perhaps I didn't. Anyhow, it doesn't matter. Mr Aberconway says he has gone back to America.'

In fact, this was not quite true, as Alice had discovered on her last visit to Mr Aberconway's chambers, earlier in the summer before she departed to Biarritz. 'He has taken the money all right,' Mr Aberconway explained, 'and moved out of Rosamond Street, but that's as far as it goes. My man says that he has gone back to that hotel in Bloomsbury and hardly ever leaves it. Has he tried to contact you?'

'Not at all.'

'Well, there is not a great deal we can do,' said Mr Aberconway, who had the Honourable Mrs Jamieson in the vestibule again, wanting to see him about her divorce. 'In a week or so perhaps I might write to him once more and remind him of the agreement. But if he is not harassing you, perhaps we ought to leave him be.'

'Perhaps we ought.'

Turning the conversation over in her mind, and remembering the evening on which he had come to dinner, Alice decided that she was not at all alarmed by Drouett and that if he wished to squander her money by living in a hotel rather than taking it back to America, that was his affair. Still, though, he had a habit of intruding into her vision of the Kansas wheat fields and she resented this.

'Well, that is a mercy,' said Miss Jeffries, who perhaps suspected that she had not been told the whole truth, shuffling Mr Bullivant's letter down to the bottom of her pile. 'Now, here is a letter from Mr Schmiegelow asking if he can bring his secretary with him – he is very busy, apparently. And do you think we really ought to have Mr Macpherson?'

'Is that Lord Islay's son?'

'I believe it is,' said Miss Jeffries, who was a walking *Debrett*.

'These people are sharks,' said Alice crossly but with a glint of humour, so that Miss Jeffries, one eye fixed on her employer's face, the other regarding the crocodile of schoolgirls in the square, could not tell if she were joking or not.

21

The Toad Beneath the Harrow

The road down which the bus was travelling was lined with plane trees, which meant that the evening sunlight falling across the seat backs was broken up by a series of angular shadows, like grey fence posts. The seat backs were covered in a red, furry material, but were on the whole more interesting to look at than the advertisement, repeated six or seven times along the bus's interior, for holidays in Skegness. Apart from herself there was no one on it except for a vaguely imbecilic-looking small boy whom the conductor, who appeared to be under some unspecified obligation to him, every so often asked if he wanted to get off.

The party was in Ealing and was being given by some people called Moriarty, who were supposed to have made their money in soft furnishings, although this was something they preferred to keep quiet about. Sometimes these kind of parties were the best. The bus dropped her at an inconvenient point halfway along the high street and she walked past the taxi rank and a pub where men in their shirtsleeves stood taking the air, thinking, despite the fact that it was still quite warm, that it would have been a good idea to have put on a mackintosh over her pierrot costume.

The Moriartys' house was in a kind of lopsided square, set apart from its neighbours and quite big. Several passers-by with nothing better to do lounged by the area railings staring at the new arrivals, but there were no press cameramen. It just went to show, Constance thought. Mrs Moriarty stood inside the open front door smoking a cigarette in an amber holder. She was wearing a cap shaped rather like a lampshade and a shapeless white robe, and looked thoroughly exhausted. When she saw Constance she said, 'Darling, how wonderful of you to come all this way, but isn't it a shame about Patrick?' and Constance said, 'Yes, isn't it?' Patrick had flatly refused to go to the party. He had said, 'I have my reputation to think of. If it got out that I'd been to the Moriartys, what would people say?' She moved on briskly into the interior of the house past a hired waiter in a tailcoat serving glasses of champagne and some cross-looking people who had not been told that it was a fancy-dress party and had come in evening clothes. A man whom Constance had supposed to be the butler shook her hand and said mysteriously, 'Parties aren't what they used to be, don't you think?'

'I'm sure you're right.'

It was not much of a party. The hock cup, which soon replaced the champagne, tasted like boiled sweets melted in tooth water, the mayonnaise had come out of a jar and a man who attempted to sing negro spirituals was drowned out by the noise of people talking about the Gold Standard. Constance took a plate of lobster salad and went and ate it in the kitchen, which was empty except for a youngish man with fair hair – better-looking than the man she had mistaken for the butler – who was making notes with a pencil on the back of a packet of de Reszke cigarettes. After a moment, when the man showed no sign of speaking to her, she said, 'It's frightfully rude of you to stare at me like that.'

'I was just wondering where we might have met. Was it at Alice Keach's?'

'It could have been. She's rather a pal of mine.'

'Or that thing of Brenda's where somebody poisoned the punch?'

'Possibly.'

'Didn't you used to be rather a chum of Ralph Bentley's?'

'That was simply ages ago,' said Constance, who was not impressed by this sort of talk. 'But you seem to know an awful lot of my friends.'

'I'm afraid it's my job.'

'Heavens!' said Constance, on whom recognition had belatedly dawned. 'You're "Mr Gossip", aren't you? How terribly funny.'

After this they got on much better and 'Mr Gossip', whose real name was Simon Macpherson, put the de Reszke packet away and talked about the parties he had been to in the past week. Occasionally Constance corrected him on abstruse points of detail.

'It was quite wrong of you, you know, to say that Ronnie was having a walkout with Betty Fitzclarence. She was only doing it to spite Gavin.'

'Was she? I saw them at the Bat and thought that they seemed to be getting on frightfully well together.'

'Well, Betty's a particular friend of mind and she was jolly upset . . . But what are you going to say about tonight?'

'I don't know. It's rather dull. My editor sent me. Aren't the people called Moriarty? I think they must know him or something.'

'I was at school with Myra Moriarty. None of us liked her. She had rather a crush on the gym mistress.'

'Is she the one in the cap?'

'Yes, that's her.'

After a bit they went and stood in the main room, where the party flowed around them and a man in a dressing gown was doing conjuring tricks with some cutlery. The people in evening dress had disappeared and a woman in a bright hogpen-and-blue bathing costume had gone to sleep on the sofa. Several of the guests came up to Simon and asked him how he was, and Simon said he was very well only his editor was getting on his nerves. Once or twice the telephone rang, but it was only the people in the next house asking that the noise should be kept down. Mr Moriarty stood uneasily by the door, smoking cigarettes and trying not to give the impression that the party had been his wife's idea. In this way an hour passed. 'Gracious,' said Simon as the clock struck eleven. 'I'm supposed to be in Kensington in half an hour. Look, why don't you come and have lunch with me tomorrow?' Constance thought: Sophie won't miss me just this once; in any case she'll probably be out herself. So she nodded her head and said yes, she would. 'I don't suppose there's somewhere I can telephone?' Simon was asking Mr Moriarty. She thought that close up he was not quite as good-looking as she had imagined. The people in the next house had stopped telephoning and were sending servants round instead. Constance decided that it was time to go home. She wandered out into the hallway and through the open front door, where the hired waiter who had previously handed out the glasses of champagne was sitting on the step with his collar undone and drinking soda water out of a bottle. When he saw Constance he said, 'Nice evening for it' and Constance said that she supposed it was. Above the houses in the lopsided square the sky was an odd purple colour, like a bruise, and the air had grown cooler.

There was a bus chugging at the stand in the high street and by waving very hard she managed to make it wait for her. The conductor was an elderly man with iron-grey hair who, when he came to take her money, looked ironically at the pierrot costume and said, 'Any more for the Skylark?'

'Actually,' Constance told him, 'I don't think that's very funny.'

Outside, the debauched streets of Ealing gave way to thoroughfares and parklands that were easier on the eye. She realised that she was extremely tired, but she knew that if she went to sleep on the bus she would feel even worse when she woke up. The advertisement on the space above the window was a different one, not canvassing holidays in Skegness but the beauties of the Hertfordshire countryside, so she looked at that for a while as the bus bowled through the dark streets, past pubs disgorging their clientele on to the grey pavements and little taxi offices and fish-and-chip shops closing up their shutters for the night. Another girl, new to the metropolis, would have extracted a certain romance from these sights, but Constance, who had been in London six years, was unmoved.

It was nearly midnight when she got back to the flat and Patrick had already gone to sleep. There was some post lying on the table by the door – bills, invitations, a letter from her mother – and she sifted through it for a moment, rubbing the toes of her right foot against the ankle of her left, which had begun to ache after the walk back from the bus stop. In the end she had not had too bad an evening, she thought. Outside she could see the taxis surging round the corner of the square. Something was irritating her about the party and, thinking about it for a while, she supposed that it was Simon. He didn't even remember that he'd written about me before, she thought. She ran a bath and sat in it for quite a long time with the light turned off, thinking how odd the top half of her body looked in the pale gleam of the mirror. Outside the window the taxis continued to surge.

Next morning she almost forgot about the invitation to luncheon and was only reminded of it by the sight of the pierrot costume hanging over the radiator pipes in the bedroom. There was a dull red stain on one of the arms and as she drank her coffee she sponged it with a flannel moistened in hot water. Patrick had already left for work at the gramophone shop. At the kiosk at the corner of the square she bought a copy of the *Sketch* and turned to the Society column, where there was a story about some people who had held their engagement party in the reptile house at the zoo, a picture of a woman who had had a porthole sunk into the front door of her flat and a paragraph that read:

Yesterday evening I attended a most spirited party given by Mr and Mrs John Moriarty at their charming house in Ealing. It is not generally known that Mrs Myra Moriarty in her schooldays was an accomplished sportswoman.

This, at least, was the opinion of her old school friend, the vivacious Hon.
Mrs Constance Henderson, with whom I enjoyed a lively conversation.

So he did know who I was, Constance thought to herself as she traipsed into the mouth of the Underground. The penny bun she had bought at the baker's shop next to the station made her feel sick, and after putting it on the empty seat next to her for a while she hid it in her handbag. Like the people at the party the night before, the newspaper was going on about the Gold Standard, but she discovered an article on one of the inside pages which said that social life had become degenerate and read that instead.

In South Audley Street there was trouble brewing. Sophie said, 'Really, Constance, you might have shut the shop up properly on Friday. When I got here this morning the door was wide open and there was an old lady looking for someone to buy a hat from.'

'I'm terribly sorry, Sophie,' Constance said, putting her arms on the counter and thinking how tiresome Sophie could be sometimes, 'really I am. Would it be all right for me to lunch out today?'

'No,' Sophie said, 'you just *can't*. I'm seeing Norman at twelve about those new designs and you know he always takes an age.' I'll go anyway, Constance thought rebelliously. I'll come back in a taxi and she'll never know. 'Oh, has Norman done some new designs?' she asked, thinking to throw Sophie off the scent.

'Yes, he has. They're rather good, I think. Oh and darling, I did ask you to put those cushions away out of the sunlight.' It was a mark of Sophie's bad temper that she would not answer questions about her weekend and rather pointedly went down to the basement to type out some invoices.

The morning passed with painful slowness. An American woman came in and paid thirty guineas for a hideous antimacassar that had lain on the display table for a whole year. At twelve Sophie put on a hat out of the stock and went off to Bruton Street. At half past Constance put a pencilled sign in the window that read BACK SHORTLY, locked the door behind her and went off to the restaurant in Kensington where she had arranged to meet Simon. When she got there she found him sitting at a table just inside the door reading 'The Dragoman's' column in the *Express*.

'Did you know Brenda had a party at her flat last night?' he asked as she sat down.

'Nobody said anything about it.'

'Well, I think it's too bad of her not to ask me after all I've done for her. And now there's this piece of Tom's saying it represented the height of Mayfair *ton* and my editor wants to know why I wasn't there . . . Did you have any trouble getting away?'

'Not really. I just shut up the shop and came.'

The restaurant was half empty, but one or two people came and said hello to Simon and he made a note of their names on the menu card. It was very hot and the fans revolving in the ceiling blew a constant stream of hot air in their faces. Constance began to wonder whether the lunch had been a mistake. She ate a bowl of vichyssoise, from which most of the vital ingredients seemed to have been removed, while Simon wrote more names on the back of the menu card.

'It's a wonder to me how this place keeps going,' he said, 'but people seem to like it and I suppose they wouldn't come if they didn't.'

'I'm afraid I'm hopelessly married,' Constance said, as it seemed a good idea to establish first principles.

'How is Patrick? It is Patrick, isn't it?'

'I've never known him so quiet. He goes off to his job, and comes back and never says anything.'

'Was he always like that?'

'No, not really. Who was that woman who just waved to you?'

'I think it was Princess Bibesco. Perhaps not. It's a terrible strain, you know, having to remember people's names all the time, don't you think?'

'I expect it must be.'

Presently Simon went away to telephone. It was still very hot and somebody had turned the fan up to its highest setting, so that the menu cards were frequently blown off the tables on to the floor. Constance ordered a cocktail and thought that she was enjoying herself rather better. 'Oh dear,' Simon said when he came back from the telephone, 'apparently there's an exhibition I have to go to in Tavistock Square. Would you like to come?'

'I must get back to the shop,' Constance said, who would have liked nothing better than to go to the exhibition. 'But thank you for lunch.'

'He does decorations in seaweed or something. I expect it will be very boring.'

'I expect it will.'

By the time Constance got back to the shop it was half past two, but there was no sign of Sophie and by making a great fuss of a woman who had come to buy a bandeau for her daughter's wedding and charging her an extra half-guinea for a yard of cerise ribbon, she felt that she had satisfactorily concealed her absence. However, when Sophie returned at ten past three it was clear that all this subterfuge had been in vain. '*Darling*,' Sophie said, 'don't tell me you didn't go out because I saw Anthea Carew in Regent Street and she said she'd seen you at the Esperanza, and it really is too bad of you.'

'I'm sorry, Sophie,' she said. 'I'll make it up to you. Really I will.'

The telephone number Simon had given her turned out to be for the *Sketch*'s switchboard, but by pretending to be somebody else she managed to have herself put through to his office.

'Simon, it's Constance Henderson. How was the exhibition?'

'Even worse than I thought. Not even seaweed pictures, but these kind of cat's-cradle things in darning wool. Are you at the shop?'

'Yes. Look, would you do something for me? Say something nice about Sophie, will you? Something really complimentary.'

'Darling,' Sophie said, emerging unexpectedly from the basement with a pile of empty hatboxes in her outstretched arms, 'if you don't put that telephone down and attend to the customers I shall just *scream*.'

Next morning 'Mr Gossip' had a paragraph that read:

Lunching at the Esperanza, I happened upon the ever-elegant Mrs Courtney Wilson, whose stunning costume, discreet enquiry revealed, was obtained at Lady Sophie Huntercombe's fashionable emporium in South Audley Street.

'Constance, darling,' Sophie said. 'I take it all back. Dear old Simon. He's terribly sweet, isn't he?'

'I suppose he is, rather.'

Constance had always prided herself on having definite views about men. When she was sixteen and at boarding school she had admired a riding instructor named Captain Hance who worked at some stables that the girls were allowed to visit on Sunday afternoons. Shortly after this she had cultivated a passion for a cousin who was adjutant to a regiment of the Territorial Army. But then someone had taken her to a party at a studio in Mallord Street and she had decided that the future lay in Art, and before she met Patrick she had been almost engaged to a man who wrote reviews of poetry books for the *New Statesman & Nation*. This, too, she had been forced to concede, had had its disadvantages. Sometimes she thought it would be nice to be married to a man who had a house in the country and would take her to point-to-points, and at other times she thought that it would be nice to live a bohemian life in Chelsea. Generally speaking she liked men who did not make a fuss over her, but hinted quietly that this not making a fuss was a kind of fascination by default. All this, she acknowledged, made her life very difficult and frequently caused her to lie awake after Patrick had gone to sleep thinking of people she had met at parties. She did not necessarily like the people, but she enjoyed thinking about them.

For a fortnight nothing happened. One or two people who had read about the evening at the Moriartys said, 'My dear, you must be very thick with Simon these days' and she replied, 'Oh, I don't know about that.' It was late August now and there were not so many parties because most of the people who gave them were away. Postcards came from Toulon, Nice, Biarritz, Vienna, places even further afield, each with their bright, confiding messages. *Old B. was here with the sweetest little German boy he brought back from Munich . . . And then in the morning there was a terrible stink on the staircase and Poppet said she was sure it was opium . . . Mary said to say hello . . . Harold said to say hello . . . Bliss at the Lido, but heat simply too much . . .* No part of Europe seemed free of their rapt, incriminating spoor. She put the postcards on the mantelpiece next to the Peter Jones bill – there was always a Peter Jones bill – and the diamond clip she was always meaning to have mended when there were a couple of guineas spare, and looked at them in the morning when she brushed her hair. 'Why can't we at least go to Toulon for a week?' she asked Patrick. 'It's frightfully cheap and Daisy says Ed and Billy are there, and everyone's having the most marvellous time.' Patrick said they couldn't afford it, but if she liked they could have a weekend in the country somewhere, so Constance thought of country hotels in summer with the bars full of red-faced men talking about fishing and the church bells waking one up on Sunday morning, and resolved to stay in London. Then her mother decided to pay one of her visits – these were biannual and coincided with her father's sailing holidays – which was worse even than there being no parties or staying at a hotel in the country for the weekend, as her mother rather liked to be taken about, have gossip explained to her and comment rather freely on Constance and Patrick's affairs. And so they went to tea at Fortnum's and to an exhibition of Fabergé eggs that Lady Glenalmond had read about in *The Lady* and, as Constance was in a bad mood to begin with, got thoroughly cross and had a titanic quarrel on the bus going back to Bayswater, after which Lady Glenalmond said, rather tearfully, 'I do think you might make more of an effort when I come to see you. I know things are rather difficult at the moment, but even so . . .' And Constance, not understanding the reference to things being rather difficult, thought: Poor Mums, she does have rather a time of it, what with Dad off at Cape Finisterre or somewhere and Erica breaking off her engagement to that boy in the Foreign Office; and so, resolving to make things up to her mother, she borrowed three guineas from a notecase Patrick had left lying around and took Lady Glenalmond to the most fashionable restaurant she could think of. Lady Glenalmond did not altogether enjoy herself, for there was a black man playing the piano not ten feet from her elbow. Nevertheless, as she sat in the cramped and comfortless cellar, where the flowers drooped in the penetrating heat and the ice in the cocktails melted before it reached the table, she appreciated that a gesture had been made.

'Who is that young man with the red hair?'

'That's Archie Callingham. He came to the hunt ball once years ago . . . Hullo, Archie.'

'And who is that lady?'

'Mrs Keach, mother. You must have heard of her.'

'Is she that American woman who pushes herself forward so much?' But secretly, head lowered above her plate, knife and fork at work upon her underdone cutlets, Lady Glenalmond was impressed.

It was early September now and the stream of Continental postcards had dried up. Peter Jones sent a letter of such unambiguously menacing intent about their account that Constance used the ten-pound note her mother had given her on her return to Basingstoke to pay some of it off. There had been no rain for three weeks and the grass in the parks was a dusty brown colour, and the men in the streets walked with their hats held in their hands, fanning themselves as they went along. Then one afternoon in South Audley Street, when there had been no customers for two hours and Sophie was wondering whether to shut the shop early, she answered the telephone and a voice said, 'I don't suppose you're free to come to a party tonight?'

'What sort of a party?' Constance wondered. Sophie was taking a hat with a garish hogpen band out of the window. She looked pale and tired, and had recently complained that black men could be rather erratic.

'Oh, it's nothing very much. Just a little thing at Brian and Eddie's place in Maddox Street. I thought you might like it.'

'I should like it very much.'

'Darling,' Sophie said. 'It would be wonderful if your chum could say something about us in his column again, because today's takings are exactly a guinea.'

The flat in Maddox Street was on the first floor of a rackety house with a wooden staircase that seemed to have fungus growing over the stair rods. It was even less of a party than the one in Ealing, as the drink ran out and they had to supplement it from the pub round the corner, and the guests seemed mostly to be tough young men, one of whom told Constance that he was shortly emigrating to America and could she lend him a fiver to be going on with? Afterwards, when they were walking back in the direction of Knightsbridge, Simon, who seemed to think she was owed some explanation for the party's awfulness, said, 'Isn't it extraordinary the people one knows? I mean from school and the university and places like that?'

'I suppose it is, rather.'

'My flat's not very far. Would you like to come in for a drink?'

'I really ought to be getting back.'

Simon's flat was in a mews not far from Harrods. As they walked through the darkening streets there was a rattle of thunder in the air and it began to rain in odd little staccato bursts.

'Isn't that extraordinary? It seems to be raining on one side of the street and not the other.'

'Look. If you stay here I'll run and open the door and you can just dash in after me.'

When they got to the flat, which was on the first floor looking out over some wild little gardens, Simon went off to telephone the paper. She could hear him talking through the wall, and the pauses as the copy taker asked him to spell out people's names. There was a decanter with some sherry in it on the sideboard and as she helped herself to this she examined the sitting room, which had clearly been arranged by someone who liked the colour blue, and counted the invitations on the mantelpiece. When he came back, she said, 'Do you know twenty-three people have invited you to things next week?'

'Have they? Twenty-three? That seems rather a lot.'

'Who is Mrs Firbank, who wants you to help celebrate her daughter Myrtle's twenty-first birthday?'

'I've no idea. They come to the office and the secretary sends them on.'

'I expect the secretary has a secret passion for you.'

'Darling.'

A bit later she said, 'You can do what you like with me. I don't mind.'

Afterwards she lay on her back with the sheets of the divan drawn up to her chin. There was a crack in the ceiling that made it look oddly like the map of Australia, and she stared at this for several minutes while the last of the light faded and somewhere above her head what sounded like the noise of a child running in circles pattered on into nothingness. She wondered what she ought to say to him when he woke up and she decided that something about not making a habit of doing this might be suitable. The back of her throat was unaccountably dry, so she decided to go and find some water. When she came back from the kitchen with the half-empty glass in her hand, he was sitting up in bed lighting a cigarette.

'Gracious! You're not wearing anything.'

'Is that very shocking?'

'I shall try and show my appreciation.'

'I don't usually make a habit of this, you know.'

'Nor me.'

'That's not what I heard.'

'What ill-natured friends you must have.'

The telephone rang in the other room and he got up to answer it, and she lay down and looked at the ceiling again from another angle so that the crack now suggested the coast of Norway. She had a habit of dramatising and even romanticising her love affairs but, having not yet thought about it at any length, she was not certain how these techniques might be applied to her present situation. She would see how things panned out. That was the best thing to do.

When he came back from answering the telephone, he said, 'Do you know Alice Keach?'

'You know I do.'

'Of course. How silly. What is she like?'

'Why do you need to know?'

'Oh, just something for the paper.'

'Isn't that rather selling one's friends?'

'You might tell me.'

Their bodies made curious elongated shadows against the lamplit wall as they talked.

It was nearly midnight when she got back to Bayswater and Patrick was sitting on the sofa reading the 'Situations vacant' column in *The Lady*. When he saw her he said, 'How did you get on at Brian and Eddie's?'

'Terrible. Even more pansies than usual.'

'Would I have enjoyed it?'

'Probably not.'

She wondered what Patrick would say if he knew. She had decided that although she was very fond of Patrick there were some aspects of their life together in which he was quite hopeless.

Next morning 'Mr Gossip' had a paragraph that read:

Here in the dark days of September, where so many of the Smart Younger Set are out of town, the earnest seeker after entertainment may have to travel far for his pleasure. So it is gratifying to report that I had to journey only as far as Maddox Street where those confirmed young bachelors Mr Brian Howard and the Hon. Edward Gathorne-Hardy hosted an amusing small party for a select circle of their intimates. The Hon. Mrs Constance Henderson looked altogether charming in green, but complained of the disparity between the sexes of those present. 'A girl needs someone to gossip with,' she remarked.

'I don't say I'm not delighted for you, darling,' Sophie said at the shop, 'but really Simon can be a menace sometimes.'

'What sort of a menace?'

'Oh, just boring things. Robert used to tell stories about him at Eton that would make your hair curl.'

After a while they settled into a routine. Two or three times a week they would meet early in the evening at the Ritz bar or somewhere in Soho, which Simon thought he ought to test out for the sake of the paper. Then, later in the evening, they would go to parties. They went to a great many parties. They went to a party in Pont Street where the food was either red or white and ate lobster, strawberries, chicken and mayonnaise. They went to one in a remote suburb that was held in an airship. They went to parties in Chelsea lofts, where artists' models clinked by in high heels and people wondered whether John would be coming, only he never did. They went to parties in the Bloomsbury squares where elderly ladies in pince-nez picked over the sandwiches and guardsmen in red tunics stared at each other uneasily over the heads of the throng. Sometimes they talked about Patrick, about whom she had begun to feel surprisingly guilty.

'Isn't everyone serious?' she exclaimed one night. They were at a party in Bruton Street where you were supposed to come as a hero or heroine from history, and she was standing next to a man dressed as Napoleon who was talking to a woman who might have been Florence Nightingale or Edith Cavell.

'It's the crisis,' he said. 'You must have seen it in the papers.'

'What crisis?' It had been a mistake to come as Salome, Constance thought. At least three other people had had the same idea.

'Oh, something to do with the Gold Standard . . . Come to think of it, I saw the Chancellor lunching at Simpson's . . .'

Next morning 'Mr Gossip' had a paragraph that read:

In these days of gathering economic gloom, where even the balmiest retreats of the social world are filled with spreading whispers of unease, it was heartening to witness the Chancellor of the Exchequer absenting himself from the cares of officialdom to lunch with a select party at Simpson's. I am told by his companion, Lady Mary Darby, that the Chancellor would not comment on the financial crisis but pronounced the venison pie 'very good'.

She discovered that Simon was quite a serious man in his way. He had read several novels by J. B. Priestley and was making notes for a study of social life in the post-war era. Politically he had detached himself from ancestral ties and made savage remarks about the Liberal Party.

Once she said, 'Did you know Alice Keach used to be on the stage?'

'How extraordinarily interesting. When was that?'

'I don't know. She was rather vague. Before the war, I should think.'

Two days later 'Mr Gossip' printed a photograph of Mrs Keach as Glenda in *The Cab Stands Waiting* which, he informed his readers, had been quite the hit of the summer of 1910. Constance felt secretly ashamed of herself. That's the last time I tell him anything about Alice, she thought. She was cross because Sophie had just had an order from a friend whose three daughters were going away to boarding school and she had had to stay late the previous evening sewing black-and-white ribbons on to a succession of hat brims.

It was early October and the gardens in the London squares were full of smoke from the burning leaves. Sometimes when she made her way to the Underground station rain fell across the grey streets. At other times mist hung low over the tops of the houses, and she remembered the riding stables near her school and the ribbons of breath that rose from the horses' mouths as Captain Hance put them through their paces. She wondered what the autumn would be like and whether she would get invited anywhere decent at the weekends, and what the chances were of Sophie giving her a rise. Mostly she thought about Simon but the results, she realised, were not always very satisfactory, for she had no context for him other than the world she knew. Occasionally she tried to imagine what it might be like to live with him in a house in the country, or to go with him on a holiday abroad, but it was never any good; she could only picture him in the flat at Knightsbridge, or shaking hands with someone in the hallway of a house while the butler took their coats, making notes on a menu card or telling the copy taker how you spelt 'The Honourable'. And besides, she had got used to living in the flat at Bayswater with Patrick and thought that she would miss him if she went away.

One day she surprised Sophie by unexpectedly bursting into tears at the shop.

'Darling, are you sure you're all right?'

'Perfectly, thanks.'

'You can take the afternoon off if you like. I shan't mind.'

'Actually I'm all right, thanks.'

That evening she went to the Ritz bar. It was almost empty apart from some South American people who kept ordering drinks, which the barman claimed never to have heard of. There were lamps shining softly on the tabletops and this, combined with the rain falling over the wet streets and the voice of the barman explaining that he had never heard of a drink called *bombe parisienne*, made her even more depressed than she had been in the shop with Sophie. When Simon arrived he was wearing a mackintosh over his evening suit and carried half a dozen newspapers pressed together under his arm.

'Hullo,' she said with an effort. 'What's happening in the world?'

'Nothing much ... We had a cross letter from that Huntley woman about the party at the Gargoyle. Apparently Doris has patched it up with Valentine. Oh, and I saw Emma in Manchester Square and she said she and Malcolm are going to Cape Ferrat for the winter. What about you?'

'Actually,' she said, 'I might be going to have a baby.'

'Are you sure?'

'Not absolutely. But I might be.'

They talked about this in subdued voices for a bit, while the South

American people tried to teach the barman the recipe for *bombe parisienne*. Later they went to a party in Golden Square given by a man with a cleft palate who painted pictures of birds and said he had known Simon at their private school, which Simon said could not be possible.

Two days later, when she saw him again, she said, 'Actually I was wrong about the baby.'

'You must be rather relieved.'

'I am, rather.' But curiously she spent the next day thinking about the baby that had never been. Her sister Marjorie had had a baby, which had kicked furiously against the walls of her abdomen and she wondered if hers would have done the same.

It was the oddest of autumns. The newspapers were full of dull articles about the crisis, about Mr Macdonald and Mr Snowden and Mr Norman. None of the people who usually gave parties seemed to be giving them any more. Her mother wrote to say that her father was so worried he was thinking of selling the field behind the house to a syndicate who would probably build bungalows on it, to the great annoyance of their neighbours, and some friends of hers in the next square said that they were giving up their lease and moving to Lincolnshire. All over the country, it seemed, life was in flux and ancient citadels flung into ruin.

Personal traffic was equally disturbing. One afternoon she was having tea at Lowndes Square and Alice said, 'I'd offer you all a cigarette, but there are no matches. Maslin never brings any. I don't know why. Look in that sideboard would you, Constance, dear, and see if you can find them.' And Constance, misinterpreting the directions, opened a remote drawer far away from the one indicated, out of which fell a cracked sepia photograph.

'Gracious, Alice, is that you?'

'Certainly it is.'

'What? Sitting in the buggy?'

'Good heavens, no. Look. By the tree.'

'You look terribly young. Where was it taken?'

'Kansas City.'

She had seen a picture of Kansas City once in a book. It did not look like this dreary backyard with trees drooping in the middle distance and children with parched faces playing in the dirt. When she got back to the flat there was another letter from her mother, which said that her father had almost decided to sell the field behind the house to the syndicate, and for some reason this moved her to fury and she sat down and wrote a letter that began: *Tell Father it would be simply monstrous of him to sell the field*, and went out and posted it in the box at the corner of the square.

The next day Sophie closed the shop for the afternoon as the men were putting in new cupboards, and as the exhibition Simon was going to attend had been cancelled owing to a fire and the weather was unexpectedly fine they met by the Round Pond. He said, 'I'm quite exhausted. We were up until two at Lavinia Sutherland's and then I had to give somebody a lift back to Earls Court . . . Darling, can you do me a tiny favour?'

'What is it?'

'Well, it seems Alice Keach is giving a house party down at the Court in a fortnight's time.'

'I know. She asked me.'

'You are clever, being such a chum of hers. My editor's desperate for me to go.'

'Ring her up and ask.'

'Darling . . .'

There was a breeze blowing across the lake that sent the small children who had been playing by the water's edge back to the detachment of nursemaids and governesses beneath the trees. That afternoon they did not go back to Simon's flat but had tea in a nasty little shop in the Brompton Road where the tables were so close to the window that people walking along the pavement made faces as they passed.

Some time later Constance said, 'Well, I've fixed you up with Alice. It took some doing, I can tell you. I don't think she likes Society columnists. You'd better write her a letter.'

'Thanks awfully. Why don't we have dinner tomorrow?'

'I thought we might have dinner tonight.'

'Can't. Terribly boring reception at Mrs Harry Brown's. She rang up and the editor's simply ordered me to go.'

Next morning 'Mr Gossip' had a paragraph that read:

In these days of change and uncertainty, it is a pleasure to report that some of the eternal social verities hold firm. At Mrs Harry Brown's yesterday I chanced upon possibly the most elegant gathering that this autumn's Mayfair round has so far afforded. The Hon. Amelia Sheepshanks, with whom I enjoyed a lively conversation, wore a cocktail dress of quite startling chic. Miss Sheepshanks, whose father Lord Sheepshanks's antirrhinums took a prize at this summer's Chelsea Show, lives in Earls Court with her sister Evangeline and professes an interest in music — 'basically Bach' as she alliteratively put it.

'I don't think I know Amelia Sheepshanks.'

'Oh, I thought you did. She's very thick with Mrs Harry Brown.'

They were at the flat in Yeoman's Row. It was about seven o'clock in the evening and outside the rain drummed on the window. Constance got up from the divan, wrapped herself in a dressing gown and went to the kitchen to make a cup of tea. There were some biscuits lying in a tin and she began to eat them, only stopping when she saw that the third one had a mouse dropping on it. Clasping the teacup in both hands, as if she were bringing some votive offering to an altar, she went back into the bedroom.

'This place is getting awfully squalid. There are mouse droppings on the biscuits.'

'Are there? How frightful. By the way, I did say, didn't I, that I shan't be here next week?'

'No. Where are you going?'

'That place in Devon. The editor's given me a week off and I thought I'd try getting some of my notes in order.'

'I see.'

'I was sure I'd told you. You're not cross, are you?'

'No.'

'It's only for a week and then we'll see each other at Alice Keach's.'

'Yes.'

The rain drummed on the window and she thought, He might have told me.

Several days passed. The cupboards in the shop turned out to have been put in the wrong place and they had to close for another afternoon while the men rearranged them. In Simon's absence 'Mr Gossip' broke out into unexpected lines of enquiry and turned his attention to people and places that Constance seemed never to have heard of. There were no parties, but one evening someone invited her to an exhibition of some surrealist photographs at a gallery in Ebury Street. The gallery owner was a woman who wore a man's pinstripe suit and a monocle. When she saw Constance she said, 'It's good of you to come. We've got quite a crowd. Only Amelia Sheepshanks rang to say she couldn't make it.'

'Oh dear.'

'That's right. Gone off to Devon for some reason. And I was counting on her to buy something too.'

It was not late when Constance got back to the flat, but Patrick had already gone to bed. There was some post lying on the occasional table in the hall – bills, a postcard from her cousin in Kenya and the Peter Jones account – and she flicked through them idly while the sound of the bathwater fizzed in her ears. Afterwards she lay in the bath until the water turned cold, looking at the reflection that her torso made in the mirror, and twisting a strand of hair that lay on the back of her neck with her forefinger. Outside the taxis surged unappeasably round the corner of the square.

Next morning there was a letter from her mother to say that her father was very sorry but the field was sold.

22

The Face Behind the Glass

At Sandringham the King, tweed-suited against the paralysing late-summer heat, is pictured mounting his infant granddaughters on a pair of miniature ponies. The little girls wear tiny berets and, like their grandfather, are unseasonably dressed in woollen coats and scarves. Despite their youth, they look indisputably royal, imperious even. The old man smiles grimly: grooms, governesses, ladies-in-waiting – all the scene-swelling paraphernalia England seems to love – stand deferentially by. At Rochester a hump-back whale is seen swimming eagerly up the Medway. The animal seems susceptible to external influence. If a boat draws up alongside it slows its pace and makes what are interpreted as overtures of friendship. It is supposed to be lonely. All this Drouett reads in his newspaper, high up in the bedroom of the Bloomsbury hotel to which he has now returned himself, decoding nuance, rooting out insinuation. Having observed whales in the Atlantic, he does not quite believe in these accounts of cetacean misery. It is another newspaper stunt, he thinks.

Like the whale, Drouett is susceptible to external influence. It is several months now since the lawyers sent their cheque. Drouett had supposed that Alice would sign it, but no, the name on the line was Mr Aberconway's. The money is safe in the bank, where he draws upon it twice weekly. As for the obligation it imposes, Drouett is not quite sure what he means to do. He has an idea that the document to which he put his signature is not legally enforceable. But one thousand pounds is a lot of money. Why give it to someone who is likely to refuse your bidding? Drouett is not sure about this. There are times, coming round the lip of the square from the newspaper kiosk in Gower Street, taking a bus into the West End, when he thinks he is being followed. Things have turned out pretty well, he feels, while leaving him discontented. Money can buy you Bloomsbury hotels and the company of the American tourists who continue to infest it – there are fewer of these now that the Depression is beginning to bite – but it cannot guarantee you entry to the drawing room at Lowndes

Square. Nevertheless, if Drouett has no immediate strategy in mind, his tactical sense is still strong. He has a set of new suits hanging in the wardrobe and a row of florid ties. No one shall say that he is unprepared.

There are other signs of external influence. In particular, Drouett has reacquainted himself with Joyce. He cannot quite say whether this was premeditated or not, why he had happened to be in a street not far from her place of work at about the hour at which the City closes down, looked up and saw her walking towards him. Luckily he was wearing one of the new suits. The ease with which they seem to have renewed their relationship rather startles him. Like their meeting in the first place, he is not quite sure what to think about it. Joyce, it seems, has taken the opportunity to quietly transform herself in the months they have spent apart. Her hair is shorter; her skirts stop slightly above her knee rather than slightly below it; there is less mention of her parents in Purley. In his absence, there has probably been another man. There are other manifestations, too, of the new Joyce. She is more inquisitive, more restless. There is vague talk of 'going abroad', of a brother in Kenya. Drouett has seen a photograph of this man, standing by the body of a dead python borne aloft by half a dozen native servants to confirm its length. Drouett wonders whether there will be very much for Joyce in Kenya. Meanwhile she seems happy enough in his company, even consenting – this is another new thing – to be smuggled out of the hotel early in the morning.

The dog has also resumed his old place on the travelling rug beneath the casement window that looks out on to the square. Drouett is glad to see the dog, whose presence suggests continuity, the ability to pick up ancient threads in one's life and successfully disentangle them. He brings it biscuits from the plates that are laid out each afternoon in the hotel lounge and has been known to convey scraps of meat from the dinner table upstairs concealed in a handkerchief. Like Joyce, though, the dog has changed. If the woman has turned restless and enquiring, the dog has lost its neurotic quality, grown placid and inert. A rubber ball rolled across the floor stirs no interest. The biscuits, crumbled in their saucer, lie gathering dust.

The new Joyce, he discovered, did not appeal to him as much as the old. There was something about her – something about her look, something about her behaviour when they were together – that demanded continual assertions of his status. He found himself telling her things: about the thousand pounds; about his old life in America; about his meeting with Mr Aberconway. He did not tell her quite everything, but he thought that he had revealed enough for her to be able to infer the rest. At first this alarmed him, for he imagined that the information would lose something in the telling, that these mysteries were part of his attraction to her and were better not exploded.

There were other things, too. Sitting in the room watching her as she moved about it – naked except for a towel wrapped round her waist – he once said, 'You ought to put something on.'

'Why should I put something on?'

'I don't like to see you like that.'

'As if you hadn't seen me like this twenty times! Don't be ridiculous.'

When he thought about it he realised that it was ridiculous. In the course of his adult life he had seen countless women in varying conditions of nakedness. He could never quite think of Alice without remembering her once stepping out of a tub. That had been quite a sight. There had been a dozen other Joyces, at least, with whom he had lived in the closest intimacy. All the same, there was something about Joyce dressed in her towel that he did not quite like, something which did not quite conform to the view he took of her and which, accordingly, he resented. It was the same with the other great matter that pressed on his mind.

Once Joyce said, 'You know, you could make a very good thing out of your Mrs Keach.'

He did not quite know how to respond. A part of him fancied that what she said was true and was secretly emboldened by it. Another part of him was outraged. It was what some cheap little girl from Philadelphia would have said, some little seamstress or store assistant picked up in the course of his wanderings, watching from the divan as he put on his salesman's suit, with a tray bearing the remains of the lodging-house breakfast lying on the coverlet, wondering how much he would give her. Drouett did not care to be reminded of cheap little girls from Philadelphia.

'I don't know what you mean. I don't like to hear you talk like that.'

'I call one thousand pounds a very good thing, George, even if you don't.'

All this disturbed him. He would be reading his newspaper, lost in some account of a grand Society function or a vagrant found dead in the street, and suddenly look up to find himself standing in the drawing room at Lowndes Square. What did he mean to do? He asked himself this question a hundred times. Still the return half of his liner ticket lay in his wallet. He took it out once or twice and examined it. Joyce sometimes talked about coming to see America. She read magazines about spring in Central Park and the latest Manhattan restaurants. Drouett knew that if he returned to America it would not be with Joyce. He found himself rehearsing conversations in his mind with Alice about why he had taken her money but broken his agreement. He fancied that if he could speak to her he would be able to explain something of the feelings that burned up in his chest. He had a vision of himself calmly and reasonably discussing these things with her, just as they had done in De Smet with the light fading over the prairie and the snow gathering in the darkening sky. He tried to remember what they had talked about in De Smet and supposed that it must have been the things you talked about with women, but he knew that Alice had not been like those cheap little girls from Philadelphia, that cheap little girls from Philadelphia did not go on to occupy grand mansions and country estates. He thought about this for a long time. The boys' school had resumed its crocodiles round the square. There were leaves lying piled up in the Bloomsbury gardens and mist hanging over the trees in the dawn. One afternoon, casually, but knowing in his heart it was a Thursday, he took a bus down to Knightsbridge, walked rapidly across Lowndes Square, leapt smartly up the steps and rapped on the door with his umbrella. A glance at the house, in which only a light or two shone and whose area gate was locked up, would have told Drouett that there was no one much at home, but such was his excitement that he did not take it in. The door was opened not by the butler but by a shy parlourmaid.

'Is Mrs Keach at home?' he wondered, coat half open to reveal the glory of his suit.

Knowing that Thursday was her employer's receiving day and assuming that Drouett was one of her regular guests, the girl was more forthcoming than she might otherwise have been: 'No, sir. They're all away in the country. At the Court.'

'The Court?'

'That's right sir. Castlemaine Court. Down in Sussex.'

Drouett thanked her and walked briskly off across the square.

23

The Rocket Descends

'So after I'd rung the third time and the secretary said he wasn't there,' my uncle reported, 'I reckoned I'd go round to his house.'

'The place in Hyde Park Gate?'

'That's the one,' he said, appreciative despite his unease. 'Got up like a blessed hotel. Walk through the front door into a kind of Palm Court. Like the Dorchester. Six footmen if there was one. Billiard room the size of a barn. Never saw a feller so free with his money.'

'It said in the *Mail* that his butler worked for Lord Rosebery.'

'Tall chap as looks like a duke? Wouldn't be surprised,' my uncle said. The silver coffee pot he had picked up at the start of the conversation was still stuck fast in his left hand. 'Anyway, there was a lot of palaver about being called away – urgent meeting in Lothbury and that kind of thing – you know what Atry's like – but I took him off to the billiard room and had it out with him. Said I didn't care who was waiting.'

We were sitting in the morning room of the big house in Eaton Square, which my uncle now favoured for his London operations, beneath the portrait of him by Isbister RA in the flowing robes of the University of Glasgow, which had awarded him an honorary degree. Five years old now, it was beginning to show its age. Reluctantly, as if it were a weapon whose significance was as much symbolic as military, my uncle put down the silver coffee pot and began to sift through a pile of papers from the Louis XVI escritoire, purchased the previous month at a Sotheby's sale. It occurred to me that there were other fellows equally free with their money.

'Did you talk to him about the steel business?'

The papers were not arranging themselves to my uncle's satisfaction. Picking up the pile, he began to deal out the individual sheets one by one, like an outsize pack of cards, on to the tabletop.

'Consolidated Steel Industries of Great Britain he wants to call it. Flotation in the spring. Rationalise sixty per cent of the business, he says.

Reckons that Norman's keen on it in Threadneedle Street. Tiarks at Schroders knows about it.'

'Not a good time to be consolidating anything,' I suggested. 'Let alone the steel industry.'

'You think I don't know that?' my uncle said. He gave a fond, protective glance at the coffee pot, looked as if he might be about to pick it up again but instead took a cigar out of the box on the sideboard and rolled it between his fingers. 'No point in thinking your securities'll fetch anything much in a market like this. That's what I told him.'

Like the Isbister portrait – a rather terrifying thing in fiery reds and purples, out of which my uncle's face loomed pale and incongruous – he, too, was beginning to show his age. In fact, the contrast between them was instructive. Bulky and purposeful five years ago – Isbister had posed him before a table containing various pieces of chemical apparatus – he now looked simultaneously bloated and wasted. There was a little twitch in the nerve above his left eye that sometimes manifested itself when the going got tough.

'Anyhow,' he went on. 'After that I went back to Cornhill. Thought I'd see Sparkes [Sparkes was his broker] and look at some figures. Of course Austin Trades is well down and there's precious little to be got out of that motor business, what with the slump in Birmingham and the h.p. going.'

'We could sell and cut our losses.'

'And send Atry into Queer Street most likely. No, can't stop supporting him. Leastways, not yet. But see here Ralph' – it was a measure of my uncle's gravity that he called me 'Ralph' – 'just like it was a bit of fun, for he doesn't know where all the money is, not by a long chalk, I got Sparkes to make a guess at how much Atry was out for.'

'You mean total liabilities?'

'That's right. Total liabilities,' said my uncle, as if this were the name of some new manufacturing concern he had been invited to take an interest in. 'Well, he reckoned it at eight million.'

'How will that help him consolidate the steel industry?'

'I dunno, Ralph.' There was something ghostly about my uncle as he said this, that the expensive suit – my uncle's suits were still things of wonder – the high collar and the unlit cigar could not dispel. 'He was talking big about Tiarks. Now Tiarks won't lend him the money. There was talk about a prospectus for some new scheme he was planning. I dunno.'

Outside a taxi hooted in the street and a couple of men in silk hats stalked past the railings. My uncle followed them for a second with his eyes, put the unlit cigar into his mouth, humbled for a moment, and stared mournfully at the Isbister portrait.

'Going to take that thing down one of these days,' he remarked. 'Never did like it. He did Atry too, you know. Made him look like the head waiter at the Savoy.'

'The head waiter at the Savoy's a very respectable man.'

'And yet he ain't trying to consolidate the steel industry in the middle of a slump. I dunno, Ralph.'

I was never quite sure how we had got in so deep with Atry, but I suspect now that it was to do with my uncle recognising in him a more substantial version of himself. Atry's father had been a stockjobber's clerk from Peckham, whose first employment had been to run messages from a building that his son now owned, or at any rate leased. The newspapers had had something to say about that. There were times, listening to my uncle talk about Atry — Atry's yacht, Atry's assignations at Bank of England Court — when I thought I detected a faint note of envy. My uncle sometimes made minor adjustments to his dress — floral buttonholes, black-and-white shoes, ties denoting membership of obscure City clubs — that reflected the Atry influence. At other times he was censorious. I saw now that the Isbister portrait had left him in two minds. Part of him was flattered by his association with Atry. Another part of him feared the consequences.

After several false starts, the cigar began to burn. Standing before the glass-fronted bookcase, in which a half-decade's worth of selections from the *Times* Book Club lay in unread glory, hands plunged in his trouser pockets, he looked thoroughly put out, almost tearful. I felt a sudden surge of affection for him, mixed with unease at the use to which the affection might be put.

'What about an election?' I wondered. 'Would that help?'

'Bound to,' said my uncle. He had been offered, and declined, a seat somewhere in Lancashire. 'For a while, anyhow. Then the funds'll start falling again. You'll see.'

'Why don't you talk to Tiarks at Schroders?'

'I'd sooner talk to the blessed Archbishop of Canterbury. Tiarks won't want to see me.'

This, too, was unlike my uncle, who relished words in high places, had no fear of the well-born or better-connected and had once loudly advised the Prince of Wales to 'ave a go of this here soup sir at a charity banquet. Defeated in my efforts to cheer him up, I stared out of the window into the square, which was full of its usual mid-morning traffic: domestics loitering by steps; a butler in conversation with a taxi man; a Harrods van delivering orders; Lady Marjoribanks, who inhabited the next-door house, being lifted bodily by a couple of manservants into the back seat of her Daimler. A parlourmaid brought in the post on a tray and I began, mechanically, to fillet the dozen or so envelopes.

'Anything there?' my uncle wondered.

I looked at the row of invitation cards, densely embossed on quarter-inch-thick pasteboard: the charitable schemes my uncles was cordially invited to support, the annual general meetings of City livery companies he was respectfully bidden to attend, the share prospectuses he was politely urged to consider.

'Mrs Keigwin wants you to go to one of her matinées.'

'Lot of nonsense.' My uncle sniffed. 'Damned awful play and you pay five guineas for the pleasure.'

'The Worshipful Company of Dye Sinkers are having an evening reception.'

'Dreadful lot of old dugouts.'

'Mrs Keach has asked us for a weekend in the country.'

'Has she now?' For once my uncle looked faintly animated, serious but also calculating. 'Kind of place Atry gets invited to, ain't it?' As with the Isbister portrait, I could see him being drawn both ways: wanting to be where Atry was, or might conceivably fetch up, but fearful of the consequences. Outside in the square there was a frightful detonation: spasmodically, in a way that suggested each particular spasm would be its last, Lady Marjoribanks's Daimler began to move off into the direction of Knightsbridge.

'Alice Keach,' my uncle ruminated. 'Her husband tried to do me a bad turn once. Blessed if he didn't.'

Somewhere in the back parts of the house a telephone bell rang and then fell silent. Outside the window a telegraph boy was leaning his bicycle against the railings. On the farther side of the square, moving so rapidly that it seemed he would not be able to stop at the pavement's edge and go tumbling head-first into the traffic, Hoskins, my uncle's *chef du cabinet*, was looming into view. It would not be a quiet morning.

'We'll go to that,' my uncle said.

The telegram – something to do with his speculations in shellac – was borne in on a salver. In the distance the telephone rang again. Shortly afterwards Hoskins erupted into the morning room with such force that he collided with the table. I scooped up the post and, with the exception of Mrs Keach's invitation card, flung it into the waste-paper basket. It was September 1931, and all over London men like my uncle were pondering their telegrams while their butlers listened out for the telephone bell and their waste-paper baskets grew full.

When did I first come to hear of Mrs Keach? I have a memory of a party some time in 1927 and a dandified exquisite saying to his friend that their hostess had really brought together quite an elegant collection of people, and his friend, equally dandified and exquisite, saying it couldn't compete with the kind of entertainments sponsored by Mrs Keach, and the conversation dissolving into a riot of laughter and syncopated music. It was the same with Atry, someone I always believed to be incidental in our lives, someone whom we could take or leave as we chose, pick up and then put down again, or even cast aside, only to find that our destinies ran inextricably together. This discovery was a shock to me, but also an education, for it taught me something that I should have grasped already, that the smooth surfaces of my life were deceptive, that there were huge cracks and fissures into which I might fall with no one to pull me out.

My uncle, too, could never quite fathom Atry, and how we came under his spell.

When I think of my uncle in the lead-up to his great trouble, I think of him as I used to see him in the rooms at Eaton Square. Technically my uncle lived in the house – he had a bedroom somewhere among the servants' garrets – but the lower floors were effectively his place of business. Here Hoskins and an accountant could be found at work in the large drawing room, secretaries typewriting in a little annexe to the side, while an assortment of persons waited downstairs in the hall in the hope of claiming a moment or two of my uncle's time. Not all of these petitioners were City people. There might be a clergyman in a soft hat with a charitable prospectus in his hand, an inventor with a box full of chicken wire and electrical gadgetry. To these recognisable categories could be added vague people – old women with secret memoranda, speechless boys with canvas bags whose presence in my uncle's drawing room was absolutely inexplicable. Where he had found them, or where they had found him, old or young, vague or purposeful, gravely clerical or defiantly secular, they were united only by a desperate optimism: something would be done.

I was never present at any of these interviews, never knew what bargains were struck or favours done, but I think that they fulfilled a need for human contact in my uncle that would otherwise have been denied. He was a solitary man amid the splendour and the bustle of the life he led. The old days of the Intwood Road and the fox's bark on the Colney escarpment and the sound of Cringleford weir were long gone now and rarely referred to. Something had changed, too, in the bond between us, that unspoken compact which had begun on the day the Great War broke out and Mrs Custance and I had travelled the length of the Newmarket Road in search of him, had been confirmed on the night I found him crouching behind the hedge and continued through the first epochal days of the selling of hogpen. He was very affable to me, and very generous, and while I appreciated the affability and the generosity I know that they disguised, and were intended to compensate for, a change in the way that he regarded me. Great riches had encouraged his self-sufficiency and I think he sometimes thought me rather futile, insufficiently dynamic for the multitudinous plans that seethed in his head. I saw through him, but I think, too, that he saw through me.

He said to me once about this time, 'Thinking of writin' my auto-biography, Ralph.'

'Where will you find the time?'

'Time? There's always time.' For a moment he looked peevish. 'Thought I'd dictate it into one of those blessed machines, and then have some young chap work it up for me.'

'What will you say in it?'

Again my uncle looked peevish. I saw that in some small, ineluctable way I had let him down.

Against considerable odds – for I had assumed it to be another of my uncle's schemes, taken up on a whim to be abandoned with the same airy caprice – the book appeared. There are still copies of it in the second-hand shops, in bright hogpen bindings with a portrait of my uncle, owlish and wattled behind his spectacles, as a frontispiece. It was a curious production, for it bore no relation to any event that I had witnessed or participated in. The tone was heroic. There was talk of 'Herculean labours' and 'humanity's signal benefit'. The author, while deprecating his efforts, trusted that his exploits would encourage 'fine scientific minds that labour on unregarded'. There was no mention of his life before the discovery of hogpen, which was represented as having taken place in a research laboratory where my uncle, employed in some minor capacity, had shocked his superiors by the tenacity of his vision. Searching the final chapter of the book, which canvassed my uncle's views on theosophy, rearmament, the shingle and Buchmanism, I came across a reference to 'Ralph Bentley, my trusted confidant and honorary nephew, on whom the responsibility for certain of these enterprises devolved'. Such reviews as there were of *Climbing Life's Mountain* diagnosed a bad case of vainglory, others a kind of ceremonious myth making, but it was clear to me, who had at any rate witnessed the raw materials from which my uncle had spun this fanciful confection, that he believed every word.

By this time my uncle's interest in hogpen was no more than incidental. There were half a dozen mills in Lancashire mass-producing articles in hogpen dye, a pottery at Burslem turning out what was known as hogpen-ware – rather bright, it was thought, for domestic use but with quite a vogue among the lower middle classes – Continental franchises spreading the word from Montmartre to the Silesian coalfields. In these my uncle took a benign interest – and his percentage. He was quite a personality in his way, one of the innumerable pieces of flotsam borne aloft on the variegated social tide that I now believe to have been the era's chief contribution to social history: that phantasmagorical world of popular entertainers, nightclub owners, public moralists and dissolute clergymen – Mrs Meyrick, Sir Oswald Mosley and the Bishop of Birmingham – in which the age abounded. The newspapers, it scarcely needs saying, adored him. They called him 'King Alfred', or even 'Alf' and solicited his views on every subject from Free Trade and the Flapper Vote to the novels of Warwick Deeping, and the confident naivety he displayed in meeting these advances was altogether delightful to them.

But I had other things to take an interest in then, beyond the orbit of hogpen and my uncle's fevered, bonhomous but on the whole not unsuccessful career in the City. My old curiosity still burned within me. I paid a man two hundred pounds once to investigate the enigma of Mrs Custance and Loftholdingswood and my mother – all the incriminating detail supposedly contained in the letter my uncle had mislaid in the chaos of the Intwood Road -- and watched as, very apologetically and noting the unpromising nature of the terrain at every turn, he drew a succession of blanks. A small biography of Mrs Custance could have been assembled out of these researches, and a substantial guidebook compiled to Loftholdingswood and its chatelaine Lady Delacave, but there was no place in either of them for me. All this, I knew, made me restive and dissatisfied. I was part of my uncle's world, and yet not part of it. A part of no one's world, if it came to that. Bred up in comparative solitude, I suffered in the company of others, particularly the company my uncle chose for me. There were other divisions, too, that not even my uncle could bridge. The women I met at his table and at the various entertainments to which we were bidden liked me, I think, but they knew that they were not for me. All this threw me back on my own resources. There was a girl I went to see now and again in her room in Shepherd Market, and the money I sometimes gave her at the end of each visit didn't shame me in the least. Compared to some of the transactions my uncle and I had put our names to in the past three years it had a straightforwardness that was deeply attractive. At the same time, mindful of all my uncle had achieved and thinking that more might be achieved in this line, I hired a little laboratory within sight of the common at Ealing where I concentrated on aniline. There was no guarantee that anything would come of these experiments, but it pleased me to make them out there in the decaying suburbs, far away from the obligations of my other life, with the soft west London light gently diffusing around me.

I don't believe, throughout these explorations – chemical and emotional – that I was inattentive to my uncle's interests, or that I could have done more to arrest his decline. Like the arrival of Atry and Mrs Keach into our lives, the descent of the rocket that had been sent soaring into the bright, contemporary air came by degrees. Perhaps there was a moment when the balance of prosperity tipped irrevocably from one side to the other: if so, I never saw it. But I recall an incident or two from that time whose symbolic importance now seems to me far greater than I then imagined. The first involved another of those dandified exquisites one met at parties – vague young men of about my own age, inconsequential in themselves, but whose uncles sat on Stock Exchange committees, whose cousins wrote gossip columns, whose mothers' entertainments were reported in the *Bystander*. 'Atry, now,' this one said as we idled over our supper in some ballroom. 'Tremendous fellow, isn't he?'

'Tremendous,' I agreed. It was nearly midnight and I was wondering whether to hire a taxi to Ealing.

'That place of his ...' my new friend went on, making an impossibly languid gesture to a footman who now appeared at the table with a newly opened bottle of champagne.

'Hyde Park Gardens, you mean?'

'A showroom. A shop window. No.' He took a sip from the fluted glass before him. 'Odd how the champagne at these affairs is never drinkable. They'd do better with cider cup. No, the place down in Sussex. Marbled terrace. Regiment of gardeners. You know the kind of thing. Know old Atry, do you?'

'We've had ... dealings,' I conceded.

'Terrible bounder, I've heard. Clever, I don't doubt. I say.' He took another sip from his glass and listened, one ear half-cocked, to the blare of music that sprayed over the supper table from the ballroom beyond. 'Isn't this band *awful*? I can't think why they didn't get Harry Davenport. The Huntercombes had him last week in Belgrave Square.'

'About Atry ...' I ventured.

'Oh yes. Terrible bounder, my uncle says. Smokes foul cigars all through dinner. There's a dreadful Israelite wife somewhere he keeps quiet about. Anyhow, you know those Swindon and Wakefield concerns of his? Thought you did. Well, I should look out for the share certificates if I were you.'

'The share certificates?'

'That's what my governor says ... Of course, one can never be *sure*,' he said.

I should have liked to hear more about the Swindon and Wakefield share certificates, but at that moment one diner at the supper table joyously upended a canister of sugar over another, half a dozen debutantes in ball gowns joined in the mêlée and by the time the damage had been put right my new friend had disappeared.

The second incident involved the merchant bank of Simpkins and Trescothick.

Quite what had drawn my uncle to the house of Simpkins and Trescothick I do not know. They were not his kind of people, nor he theirs. They were starchy and conservative, undertook government work, underwrote great mercantile adventures and had a sheet of office notepaper on which no fewer than six of the partners' names were prefixed 'The Honourable'. But my uncle saw none of this. He had some scheme whereby money raised in the City could be used to back the drainage of a saltwater marsh on the Kentish coast, the end in view being a container port that would revolutionise cross-channel traffic. It was not the kind of thing that Simpkins and Trescothick generally countenanced, but my uncle persevered. He commissioned a scale model of the port in brightly coloured balsa wood from an architect and had it sent round to Simpkins and Trescothick's office in Lothbury. He had a newspaper photograph taken of him, in wading boots, on the edge of the saltmarsh. He addressed a parliamentary committee on the subject. And finally Simpkins and Trescothick consented to meet him, in one of the dusty chambers at Lothbury, beneath a portrait of the first Lord Trescothick in the robes of a Cinque Port warden. It was a meeting of inconceivable perfunctoriness, over in thirty minutes, the secretary bidden to take minutes barely putting pen to paper, but my uncle seemed pleased by it. He talked of the beauties of Kent while one of the Simpkins and Trescothick partners yawned into his handkerchief and another one surreptitiously did *The Times* crossword. When it was all over and the clock on the wall stood at ten past one, the senior Simpkins and Trescothick partner shuffled the papers on his desk, nodded at the secretary, who scuttled out of the room, and addressed himself to the firm's solicitor, who had joined us to consider some obscure legal point. 'Come and have luncheon, Wilcox,' he remarked. 'They'll only just be starting.' 'They' were the other Simpkins and Trescothick partners in their panelled dining room with the silver cruet that the first Lord Trescothick was supposed to have looted after Waterloo. Then he turned to my uncle. 'Well, I expect you'll be wanting your dinner, Rendall,' he said.

There was a sudden silence in the room. The junior partners stared into space. Wilcox, the solicitor, gave me an odd, quizzical look and then busied himself doing up a non-existent fastening of his briefcase. Six months or a year before, my uncle might have risen to this bait. Now, for some reason, all the fight had gone out of him. There was a meek shaking of hands and then we went out into Lothbury once more, a Lothbury dense with clerks and typists streaming to the Lyons cafés and pavement dining rooms, in which my uncle looked unexpectedly frail and insubstantial, a small, fat man with a gardenia in his buttonhole and a peevish expression on his face, lost upon the vagrant tide spilling out from the City's dark, unwelcoming heart.

Time dragged, punctuated by telegrams.

The first of these came to Eaton Square three days after the ballroom conversation about Atry. It was signed 'Gordiano' and read: THOUGHT

HAD IN YOU A FRIEND NOT AN ENEMY. I took it up to a private study my uncle had on the second floor and here, at a table surrounded by packing cases and curious dark-coloured folders, attempted to decipher its meaning.

'Who's Gordiano?'

'That Italian feller as works for Atry.'

Instead of seeming mystified or annoyed by this presumption of bad faith, my uncle was merely hangdog.

A thought struck me. 'Have you been selling stock?'

'Just a few hundred of Austin Trades. Nothing to speak of.'

'What does Sparkes say?'

'Sparkes is an old woman.'

One of the packing cases was open on my uncle's desk, revealing an assortment of grimy foolscap sheets. Picking up the first of these, I discovered an agreement to lease 27 Intwood Road to A. Rendall Esq. for the sum of twenty guineas per annum, payable in instalments of five guineas each quarter day, dated 13 January 1911. 'What's all this?'

'Had it sent up from the store,' my uncle explained. 'Certificates gone missing.'

It was my uncle's foible, six or seven times a year, to mislay some vital document. At these times a message would be sent to his repository in the City and three or four likely-looking crates brought back for him to plunder at will.

'But this is old stuff. From before the war.'

'You never know,' said my uncle obstinately.

'What are you going to do about the telegram?'

'Blessed if I know, Ralph. I went down to the Exchange yesterday and had a nose around. No sign of Atry. Took a look in the Jungle' – this was the West African market, where my uncle sometimes impressionably browsed – 'and they said he'd been buying mining stock. Now, what does Atry want with mining stock in Liberia, eh? And there's a deuce of a lot of scrip certificates about – Swindon, Wakefield, that kind of thing. They say he's using them for security. I don't like it, Ralph.'

In the end a telegram was sent back to Atry's City office that read: FRIENDSHIP NOT IN DOUBT STOP WHO UNDERWRITES STEEL CONSOLIDATION QUESTION MARK.

'That'll let him know,' my uncle said, hopefully and, it seemed to me, rather naively. 'This way he'll have to give us a straight answer.'

Twenty-four hours later a further telegram was delivered to Eaton Square. It read: FRIENDSHIP APPRECIATED STOP VITAL UNDERWRITER NOT REVEALED.

Among the detritus of the Intwood Road, my uncle had turned up the representation of *The Fighting Temeraire*. Dusted and reframed, this now hung on the study wall, above a table cluttered with share certificates and several additional telegrams – by turns cautious, respectful and scandalised – which other associates of Atry had sent us in the previous forty-eight hours.

'Looks good, don't it, Ralph?' he remarked. 'Way that sail comes up out of the mist. Wish I'd thought to put it up before.'

'Sparkes says that if we're going to sell any more Austin Trades, this is the time to do it.'

'Sparkes is an old woman.'

It was now the Monday before our invitation to Mrs Keach's. Atry's stocks continued to fall. On the following day my uncle went into the City again and called on those joint stock banks that were known to have an interest in Atry's companies. He brought back with him the melancholy but not surprising news that the securities Atry had deposited with them had been frozen until such time as his liabilities might be discharged.

'Ring up Sparkes,' I counselled. 'Tell him to take what we've got in Austin Trades and put it on the market.'

'I can't do that, Ralph. It'll – what's that blessed word? – destabilise him. Every blessed thing'll go over like a row of ninepins.'

He was still entranced by *The Fighting Temeraire*. 'Nice thing to have about the place, Ralph' he said, more than once.

Later that day I went round to Shepherd Market to see Avril. She was a thin, blonde girl with a slight squint in her eye and an oddly refined air, who looked as if she should have been working in a City office. When I got there she was standing by the door stepping into a pair of high-heeled shoes and trying to straighten out the spokes of a broken umbrella.

'I didn't think you were coming,' she said. 'Another minute and a half and you'd have found me out. I was going round to Berkeley Street to look up some of the girls.'

Avril worked alternate evenings in a supper club. There was also talk of a correspondence course she was meant to be taking.

'What happened about that raid?' I asked. There had been trouble at the club the previous week.

'Oh that? In the end they just took people's addresses and let them off with a caution. You look tired, Ralph. Why don't I make you a cup of tea?'

She was a nice, friendly girl, to whose friendliness I occasionally over-reacted, simply because I liked the time that I spent with her and was always at a loss when it ended. What she considered my excessive generosity was sometimes a source of mild alarm to her, and she had once returned a ten-pound note on the grounds that I 'ought to be more careful with my money'.

'These shoes will be the death of me,' she said, stepping out of the high heels. 'But Mr Sampson won't keep you if you're less than five foot four, so there's no helping.'

Twenty minutes later, when she was combing her hair, she said, 'Where you going this weekend, Ralph?'

She took a frank interest in my social life.

'A place called Castlemaine Court. In Sussex.'

'Oh yes,' Avril said. 'Mrs Keach's place. I saw a picture once in the *Sketch*.'

I left her five pounds. I wished I could have left her fifty.

On the Wednesday, quite by chance, when we had both gone out on sepa-rate errands, I met him at Bank station. It was an extraordinary sight. There was a great press of people in the carriage, but for some reason a single seat, by one of the doors, unoccupied. Towards this, just as the doors were closing, a man, head down and blindly oblivious to every-thing around him, started forward and sat himself down. He wore a conventional subfusc suit, but with a curious hat, not quite a bowler and not quite a homburg, and a silk scarf thrown over his shoulder. The effect was oddly romantic, but without ever quite conveying where the romance lay. He might have been anything from a cross-talk comedian to a Ruritanian adventurer. He lay back in the seat looking tense, half drowned. He had a copy of the *Financial News* in his hand and fanned his face with it, although it was not in the least hot. At St Paul's a woman in the seat next to him rose to get off and he stared at her in mock-amazement, dropped the paper on the floor of the carriage and laboriously retrieved it, together with the hat, which had fallen with it. All this time, five yards away among the press of people, I had been making urgent signals which he either failed to see or studiously ignored. Two or three people – the carriage was full of City men off to see their solicitors in Chancery Lane and High Holborn – looked as if they knew who he was, but were content to let the matter rest there. He opened the *Financial News* and looked at it very keenly. He took a fob watch out from his waistcoat pocket amid a jingle of seals and chains, and examined it like a comic actor. Then he sank back again into the seat, legs splayed on either side, eyes wide open, unblinking.

Finally at Oxford Circus the press of people receded and I made my way to the vacant seat next to him. 'Been waving to you like mad, Ralph,' he said mildly. 'Surprised you didn't see me.'

At Eaton Square there was another telegram, this time from Atry himself, which said, SUGGEST LUNCH SATURDAY.

We agreed that I should go to Castlemaine Court on my own.

24

A Weekend in the Country

There were no taxis at the station and in the end Constance had to negotiate a passage in a fishmonger's van. She sat disconsolately in the front
seat with her suitcase knocking against her legs, watching the countryside
dutifully unfold before her and stoutly resisting the van driver's attempts
at conversation. It had begun to rain and the smell grew progressively
worse during the course of the journey.

Patrick had refused to come with her. He had said, 'I can't possibly go
to Alice Keach's. She never has anyone I want to meet, and besides I've
a lot on at the shop, what with the sale and everything.'

'The sale?' Constance had wondered.

'Yes, the sale. It's going terribly well. We've sold thirty-one gramophones in a week. Schmiegelow's very pleased.'

The van moved slowly through lanes choked with head-high clumps
of cow parsley. Constance looked at them without interest. Everything
was going wrong in her life, she thought. First there was the business of
Simon, then Sophie had announced that she intended to shut up the shop.
She had said, 'They want to raise the rent again, darling, and between
you and me it's all becoming rather a strain.'

Sensing an implied criticism, Constance had said, 'I don't mind working
a bit oftener, Sophie, if it would help.'

But Sophie had said, 'That's very sweet of you, darling, and I appreciate it, but my mind's made up.'

The fishmonger's van had to make several calls before it deposited her
at Castlemaine Court and it was nearly half past two by the time she and
her suitcases were set down on the gravel drive. It was too late for lunch,
but they brought her a sandwich and a glass of sherry in the morning room.
Really, Constance thought, sitting in a chair by the unlit fire and feeling
unutterably tired, they could have taken the paper off the chandelier. 'Has
Mr Macpherson arrived yet?' she asked the footman who brought the tray;
he was an agency man and didn't know. The rain had stopped and one or

two of Mrs Keach's guests, clad in mackintoshes and stout boots, could be seen walking in the park, but Constance decided that the last thing she wanted was conversation. So she went up to her room, which might in the circumstances have been worse, and read *Angel Pavement*, which seemed to her a very silly book full of dull people. She could not make up her mind whether she wanted to be in a place where Simon might come in and talk to her or where there was no chance of seeing him at all, and the indecision preyed on her mind and made her feel even more wretched. A maid came and knocked on the door, and said that tea was being served in the drawing room and did she wish to join them, and Constance said no, she didn't. Then she decided that it was ridiculous to be staying in a place like Castlemaine Court and simply moulder in one's room, so she put on a scarlet windcheater that Sophie had once presented to her from the stock and walked out into the park. The avenue was full of dripping trees and the deer stirred nervously at her approach, but she pressed on manfully round the side of the house past a forlorn-looking croquet lawn and an abandoned kitchen garden. She was so engrossed in her thoughts that she did not notice that the figure coming towards her along the narrow path was Simon until she stood to one side to let him pass.

'I was wondering where I might find you,' he said. The turn-ups of his tweed suit were soaked in water.

'Well, here I am.'

'You don't seem very pleased to see me.'

'Don't I? I'm sorry. How was Devon?'

'Very monastic.' He fell in beside her and they continued along the path. There was an ache in her finger that she wished would go away. 'But I managed a couple of chapters of my book.'

'That's good. Was Amelia Sheepshanks there?'

'I don't know what you're talking about.'

'I thought she was supposed to be in Devon too.'

'Constance . . .'

'Don't Constance me,' she said. The pain in her finger was hurting more than ever.

'I just heard an amusing thing. Apparently Ralph Bentley is staying here.'

'Is he? I don't suppose he'll remember me.'

'It really is raining rather hard,' he said. 'Don't you think we'd better go indoors?'

'If you like.'

'It really was extraordinarily kind of you to get me asked here.'

'Yes, wasn't it?'

'That path there ought to take us to the back of the house, don't you think?'

'Yes.'

They walked on silently through the gathering downpour.

By degrees, and using heterodox methods of transport, the other guests began to arrive. Lady Llanstephan and her maid negotiated the winding drive in an ancient Daimler. The Reverend Chatterley drove up on a motor-bicycle with a large, squat object hidden beneath the tarpaulin of his sidecar. Lady Carbury and her niece were brought by a chauffeur-driven Rolls-Royce. Miss Montmorency, who had been staying with a hunting party five miles away, hacked over on her cob. As for Mr Schmiegelow and his secretary, they were simply found on the doorstep with their suitcases, leaving no clue as to how they had been conveyed there. There was no sign of Mrs Keach. 'I don't suppose we shall see Alice until dinner,' said Mrs Reginald Heber, whose first visit to Castlemaine Court this was. In her absence the guests played spillikins in the drawing room, looked at the Society magazines laid out on the table in the hall or kept to their rooms. Nobody minded this dereliction for, as Lady Carbury remarked, Castlemaine Court was not the kind of place where one expected to be constantly amused, nor Alice Keach the kind of woman one expected to find continually at one's elbow telling one what to do.

'Who is that man with the fair hair?'

'I think he's called Mr Schmiegelow, my lady.'

'And the young woman – the young lady – with him is his wife?'

'I think I heard somebody say she was his secretary, my lady.'

Lady Llanstephan let it pass. Instead, she bore down on Mrs Reginald Heber: 'Rowena . . .'

'Bertha . . .'

Lady Llanstephan knew Mrs Reginald Heber of old. She said, 'I was really sorry, Rowena, to hear about your sister, and the dreadful things that were said about her, and I don't for a moment see how anyone could possibly have imagined that it was her fault.'

* * *

Maslin sat at a small table in the corner of the servants' hall, polishing a silver epergne with the end of a duster dipped in Silvo. The dirt had got into some of the embossed trefoils and the work was probably better suited to someone with less inadequate eyesight, but he plugged gamely away. On the other side of the table, not quite in range, but not quite out of it either, Mrs Walters, the housekeeper, was talking about some people named Eldberberry she had once worked for at a house near Chichester. The effect was that of a low, buzzing noise, sometimes straying into the margin of his consciousness, sometimes not. Maslin concentrated on his own thoughts. He liked thinking and he liked polishing the silver, and Mrs Walters was nothing to him.

Presently Mrs Walters said – they did not talk much despite their seniority in the house – 'It's a shame you have to clean that silver, Mr Maslin, when there are all these girls about the place with nothing better to do.'

There were times when Maslin enjoyed his job and times when he did not. He thought that this was one of the times when he did. It just went to show. He had discovered that if you held the epergne a few inches above the tabletop where it caught the light it was possible to get at the discoloured patches under the rim. All that was needed was a bit more Silvo.

Mrs Walters said, 'But the girls they send us today are so heedless, don't you think, Mr Maslin? Never mind taking a pride in their work, as you and I did when we were young. All they think about is going to the cinema with their young men.' Privately Mrs Walters sympathised profoundly with the parlourmaids, but she was aware of the need for solidarity. 'Would you like me to make you a cup of tea, Mr Maslin?'

Maslin looked up from the epergne. He wondered what the old girl was on about now. There were drawbacks in working for Mrs Keach, he thought. On the other hand these were compensated for by distinct advantages. The drawbacks included Mrs Walters and the country air, which he suspected was bad for his health, and the human contacts of the servants' hall. The advantages included Mrs Keach, whom he greatly respected and enjoyed reading about in the newspapers.

'Just say the word, Mr Maslin, and I shall make you a cup of tea.'

It was no good. He would have to say something. But conversation was very difficult. He knew that. Finally he said, 'Cleaning the silver's not an easy business.'

Mrs Walters was thinking about the weekend's guests, whose names had been conveyed to her by the maids. She said, 'They say that clergyman has brought a harmonium with him on his motorbike.'

'The mistress likes it just so. If there's so much as a spot of dirt on that epergne I shall be the one to know about it.'

'And that Mr Burnage is a great disappointment. He doesn't look as if he could say boo to a goose.'

'There's still half the plates to be cleaned before dinner. You can't set a house to rights in a day. It stands to reason.'

Maslin put the epergne down reverently on the tabletop. Mrs Walters knew nothing of his responsibilities. Well, that was her lookout. He glanced at his watch and found to his surprise that it was gone four. Footsteps resounded suddenly above his head, and he thought he would either take his tea into the pantry or go and inspect the morning room. Both prospects appealed to him so forcibly that he took a moment to make up his mind. The morning room, then. His life, he thought, had never been so full of purpose and resolve.

The rain had stopped and the sun come out, and the light was cascading into Alice's sitting room. The room faced south and the light was coming at an angle, so the overall effect was oddly subaqueous, like a torch beam shining into a swimming pool. All this gave the furniture of the room a curious spectral quality, except where the light fell on it and it blazed out into dramatic modernist flourishes. Someone had propped one of the windows half open without bothering to secure the fastening and this rattled irritatingly against the frame.

She sat in an armchair over the unlit fire, looking out across the wet fields. There was not a great deal to see, except the dripping trees and the curve of the river beyond them, but she found the view soothed her. It was about half past four in the afternoon and already a maid had come up, sent by Miss Jeffries, followed half an hour later by a footman, to ask if she would like to come down. To each of these requests she had sent back delaying messages, but she knew that she did not wish to go down. Instead, she sat silent in the armchair and looked out over the wet fields, knowing as she did so that her mind was far away and could not be coaxed back to the business of the day unless it was put back into kilter. A curious thing had happened. Reaching into the drawer of a bookcase that stood by the side of the fireplace she had happened upon the photograph of the house in Kansas, and Aunt Em and Uncle Hi standing before it. It was so long since she had seen it that it took her a second or two to establish what it was, and another second or two to become aware of its effect on her mind. Something told her to put the photograph back in the drawer beneath the fan of papers that had half obscured it, but she discovered that, however great her resolve, she could not do this. The photograph was a matter of consuming interest to her. At any rate, no harm could come to her from looking at a photograph. Like the view from the sitting-room window, there was not so very much to see, simply the front of the building, with the sycamore tree to one side and Uncle Hi's buggy drawn up in front of it, and Uncle Hi and Aunt Em standing in the foreground with their faces half hidden in the glare of the afternoon sun. She thought, calculating rapidly, that if Uncle Hi and Aunt Em were still alive they would be, respectively, seventy-three and sixty-nine, which did not seem so very old, but she realised that the lives they might have pursued were unimaginable to her. Living or dead, they were framed for ever in the photograph: they could have no life beyond it.

A dozen other pictures from that time came into her mind: Asa smiling at her from his cradle in the mission house parlour; Drouett picking his way along the seat backs to sit alongside her on the train; snow falling on the low hills beyond De Smet; Hanson's face receding into the darkness of the little parlour at Van Buren; Grand Central Station. Fragments of conversation, hoarded across the years against such a moment as this, tumbled into her head. She remembered Drouett giving her the money to buy a dress and her saying 'You might not like it' and him replying that he would, so, and the money – it was a ten-dollar bill with Lincoln's face staring from it – dangling between her fingers and then being hidden away in the front of her shirtwaister. All this was very sharp and clear to her, and very painful, and she wished that there were someone with whom she might share these scenes from her past life. But there was no one, only the dripping trees in the park and the empty grate. If Drouett, or Hanson, or half a dozen other people from those days had walked into the room she would have sat them down and plied them with questions, so great was her desire to see them again. She thought that of all the men she had met, Drouett – the Drouett of the train journey and the supper in the little town on the Kansas line – was the one she had liked the best. She wondered what would have happened to her if she had met Drouett in the normal course of things rather than on a train heading west. The words she had spoken to Hanson on the night she left Chicago were so clear to her that she could have written them down. Chicago! At that moment she would have liked nothing better than to go to Chicago and walk by the lake shore and saunter down Van Buren, past the burlesque theatres and on into the grey suburbs and the blue horizons beyond.

All this quite naturally made her think once more of Asa, which was something she knew she dared not do – a quite unaffordable luxury – but, equally, it was impossible for her not to do this. She remembered him in the mission parlour on Van Buren with Hanson dandling him on his knee, and making up the parcel in the high-windowed room at Thurloe Square, and with a final, restless glance she put the photograph back in the drawer beneath the fan of papers and pushed it shut. A further ten minutes, she knew, and another of Miss Jeffries's emissaries, or possibly even that lady herself, would come to see where she was. Well, she would come. But not quite yet. There was a packet of cigarettes on a table by the window and she took one out and smoked it, blowing the smoke carefully away from her face and resting her fingers on the window ledge while she looked out once more at the park. She knew that in the next few hours she would be required to say a great many things to a great many people, and she found herself going over them in her mind. The knowledge that she did not wish to do this, would have sooner sat in her room and brooded over Drouett and Hanson and Chicago and the train rolling on to Grand Central Station, and Asa's face staring up at her, was very troublesome to her, but she knew that she could not resist. Another five minutes passed and she threw the burned-out cigarette stub into the fireplace, examined herself briefly in the mirror that hung by the door and made her way to the great staircase where a maid saw her and ran to carry news of her descent to Miss Jeffries. As she walked into the drawing room there was a little stir – men who had been lounging on sofas with newspapers rose bravely to their feet, the knots of conversing women broke suddenly apart and fell silent – and Miss Jeffries, coming forward with her badgery hair done up in a grotesque arrangement of ribbons and pins, said 'Alice' very loudly, and dropped a teacup, whereupon Mr Burnage, on cue, said that she should be mistress of herself though China fall.

'I tell you, Alice can be quite a tragedy queen,' Mrs Reginald Heber said to Mr Schmiegelow, with whom she had struck up an intimacy. 'You know, there are times when I don't understand her at all.'

After dinner some of the guests played Consequences by the drawing-room fire.

Mr Montagu Norman met Miss Tallulah Bankhead in the Ascot enclosure. He said to her: 'What price the government, old girl?' She said to him: 'If I offered you a cigarette it would be a de Reszke.' The consequence was that the plot thickened.

'Who is Tallulah Bankhead?' asked Lady Llanstephan, who had been trading genealogical details with Mrs Reginald Heber on the sofa.
'An actress.'
'Yes,' Lady Llanstephan said. 'I see.'

Mr Ramsay Macdonald met Loelia, Duchess of Westminster, at the Forty-Three. He said to her: 'Play up the Arsenal!' She said to him: 'I've a husband and children to support.' The consequence was that Mrs Meyrick was let out of Holloway.

'I don't believe I've heard of Mrs Meyrick,' said Miss Jeffries. 'And what is the Forty-Three?'

This weekend I had the great good fortune to be a guest of Mrs Keach's at her country house near Haslemere [Simon dictated into the telephone in the butler's pantry]. Our hostess had, as is her custom, assembled a choice selection of guests, many of whom could be seen after luncheon braving the discomfort of her elegant but somewhat inspissated park. Among them I was pleased to see my old friend Lady Llanstephan who, such is her appreciation of Mrs Keach's hospitality, had come up specially from Carmarthenshire. Mrs Reginald Heber was magnificent in blue and I had an interesting conversation with the Rev. Harold Chatterley about his missionary work in Canning Town . . .

'You never met Lady Llanstephan in your life before,' said Constance, coming up behind him. 'And what does "inspissated" mean?'
'It's to do with the weather. It's the editor's new word. He says it's almost as good as "*démodé*". Is there anything else I should put?'

'Why not' – she paused, trying to think of the cruellest thing she could possibly say – '"Sadly, a longstanding engagement prevented Miss Amelia Sheepshanks from attending. 'We shall all miss her,' Mrs Keach said.'"

'I can't talk to you when you're like this,' Simon said.

Constance burst into tears.

Later they sat in Simon's room drinking gin out of a hip flask he had found in his luggage.

'She's very rich, you know,' said Simon, who liked to be matter-of-fact about these things. 'But no great sense of style.'

'I wouldn't mind her, if only you cared.'

'But I do care,' Simon said. His eyes were glassy from the gin. 'I care a great deal. Did you see your Mr Bentley?'

'I don't want to talk about Mr Bentley. You can't possibly like her,' Constance said.

'I never said I did.'

'But you spent a week with her in Devon.'

'Please don't start that again.'

Later Constance went back to her room, where the fire had been lit and the bedside lamp switched on, turned the key in the door, took off her shoes and stockings and sat cross-legged on the hearthrug. She thought: What I should like is to be back in Bayswater with Patrick, lying in the bath and listening to the taxis in the square. Then she thought: No, what I should really like is to be at home, lying in bed on a summer morning with Vera bringing me a cup of tea and Daddy reading *The Times* in the morning room. Then she thought: No, what I should really like is to be at the Embassy Club having supper and listening to the band, only not feeling tired or worrying about Simon and Patrick and everything. A bit later there was a sound of footsteps in the corridor and a knock at the door.

'Go away,' she said, without looking up.

'But there was something I particularly wanted to ask you.'

'Go away.'

'Constance, please open the door.'

She did not say anything else and presently the footsteps went away.

Mr Schmiegelow was quite at home at Castlemaine Court. One or two of the less socially experienced guests, new to the protocols of the country house weekend, sat nervously in their chairs like actors awaiting their cues, but Mr Schmiegelow was not among them. He roamed purposefully around the house, calibrating his impressions with the photographs he had seen in *Country Life*. He was heard in the servants' hall asking apologetically if he could have the use of a needle and thread. Mr Maslin found him in the billiard room admiring the set of Caroline prints that hung there. A county history from the bookcase in the drawing room was thought to have absorbed him for nearly half an hour.

Mr Schmiegelow's interests were strictly interior. On the Saturday morning, when most of the gentlemen went out into the park, he sat in the drawing room and talked to Mrs Keach about a mullioned window that ran along one side of the house. 'You see,' he said. 'If you extended the frame by only three or four feet you would enhance what is really a very pretty view down to the river.' And Alice thought that he was very good-natured.

In these and other ways Mr Schmiegelow continued to make a good impression. His return of the needle and thread to Mrs Moorehead in the servants' hall caused a sensation. He mended a brooch of Miss Jeffries's, whose fastening had come away, and listened respectfully to the Rev. Chatterley's account of his adventures in the Bow Road. Occasionally he went away to make telephone calls.

On the Saturday afternoon, when an excursion was arranged to a neighbouring estate, Mr Schmiegelow said that he had a headache and retired to his room. Clearly, it was not a very bad headache, for twenty minutes later he could have been seen – had there been anyone to see him, for most of the servants had been given the afternoon off – walking up the back staircase to the upper floors of the house. Here he looked very interestedly at everything that came his way: at the corridor that led away to the west wing, where there was an antique sundial kept under glass; and at a Lely portrait that hung on the wall. Still, anyone who saw Mr Schmiegelow would have said that his interest was not entirely satisfied, that there was something he was in search of, which he did not find. He passed an old, glass-fronted bookcase on one of the landings and stopped to look at the books inside it. He tried a door, found it locked and stared hard at it with his hands in his pockets, turning the tips of his shoes thoughtfully on the grey carpet, and was discovered in this attitude by a maid advancing round the corner with a brush and dustpan.

'Can I help you, sir?'

'Do you know,' said Mr Schmiegelow conversationally and with great affability, 'this is such a big house that I declare I have got lost in it. Would that be the bathroom?'

'No, sir. You'll find the bathroom this way. That's the mistress's sitting room.'

Mr Schmiegelow apologised for his error and continued on his way.

At night the servants' hall lost its air of soft, inconsequential clutter and became angular and remote. The winded sofa and the bent armchair that Mr Maslin sat in to read the newspaper faded away into darkness, the shadows climbed up the walls and the remnant of firelight – not quite extinguished by the pail of water Mrs Walters had thrown on it two hours since – shone off the bar of the fender and the ancient warming pans that lay by the fireplace. Farther back in the house, towards the kitchen and the sculleries and the wide space where the corridor ran round to Mr Maslin's pantry and the storeroom, there were night-lights on the wall brackets, but here the atmosphere was ghostly and unreal. Sidling into the room on shoeless feet, Ella stopped to peer at the clock on the nearside wall and found that it was half past midnight. That was Rose for you, working an eighteen-hour day and then wanting to sit up with Ethel M. Dell's *Silver Wedding*. Catch her doing that, Ella thought, noticing the cold from the stone flags seeping up through her toes and feeling pleasantly superior to Rose, flat-chested Rose whose mother wrote to her twice a week, who thought Max Miller vulgar and hoarded silver joeys in a pink-and-white souvenir mug labelled 'A Present to a Good Girl from Blackpool' against her marriage to an auctioneer's assistant from Haslemere who was allowed to hold her hand on Sunday afternoons off but not a great deal else.

Planting her feet gratefully on the square of carpet, she considered her options. She would have a cigarette – there was one tucked behind her ear in readiness – and then she might wait ten minutes. That was if she didn't fall asleep first. Ten to one Rose would want to go to early service, too, and leave her with the fires to lay. There was generally a box of matches on the table next to Mr Maslin's chair and she grasped for it through the murk to light the cigarette. Twenty yards away, far beyond the pantry and the storeroom, at about the point where the back staircase met the twist in the corridor, there was a faint sound of boots descending and Ella shifted slightly to one side and sat herself down, cigarette still in her mouth, in Mr Maslin's armchair. Fun and games. Well, there were other people up to fun and games on the premises. The tall chap in the bad suit, for example, whom she'd found in the passage outside the mistress's sitting room. Ella kept her eyes open. Not like Rose, who hadn't even noticed that Olwyn, the last kitchen maid, was going to have a baby until the day Mrs Moorehead paid her off. The boots were coming nearer. Ella swung her legs over the side of the chair and took the cigarette out of her mouth, and Paul the footman came into the room.

'You're a one, ain't you?' he said, seeing her through the gloom.

'You can keep your bloody voice down for a start,' Ella said. She realised that she had no idea what she expected of him or he of her. Apart from the obvious thing. There were little beams of light beyond the window, where the road curved round the gates of the park, and she followed them with her eyes.

'There's no one about,' he said. 'Trust me for that.'

'Where you from, then?' she asked. His accent was almost cockney, but overlaid by something else.

'Colchester. Essex. What's it sound like? You going to give me a fag?'

She was still watching the beams of light across the park. 'I might if you can stop pawing me like a bloody animal in the zoo.'

She could see him looking nervously at her through the dark. He said, as if it were something he had been burning to tell her for hours, 'Here. Were you in the drawing room at teatime?'

'No. What happened?'

'That bloke with the dog collar, that sky pilot. Only brings a f*****g harmonium out and starts singing.'

'Singing what?'

''ymns. "Nearer my God to Thee". You never heard anything like it. Old girl I was handing out tea to f*****g near put her cup in my lap.'

'You're from the agency, aren't you?' Ella wondered.

'What if I am?'

'So you'll be off Monday morning. 'Spect you're married as well.'

'Catch me being married.'

'What's that noise?' Ella said.

'What noise?'

She was bored by the footman, she thought. 'That noise. Sounds like it's coming from the hall.'

'One of the guests,' he suggested. His voice had gone sullen. 'Nothing to do with us.'

'I'm going to bed,' she said.

'Not if I know anything about it.'

There was a brisk flurry of movement and the ashtray that had lain on the edge of Mr Maslin's armchair went skittering over the floor.

'You lay a finger on me,' said Ella, 'and I'll scream fit to bring the house down.'

Outside the beams of light had receded into the distance. Rose would have put Ethel M. Dell down on the bedside table and be lying fast asleep, mouth open, with her arms clasped together on either side of her face like a baby. She peered into the gloaming, but the footman had already gone. The agency footmen always took fright at the least hint of trouble. She'd run into him tomorrow when he was doing the silver in any case. Sunday was always a big day in the country. Anything could happen. Feet shivering on the stone flags, hands stretched out to fend off unseen protrusions of wood and metal, Ella set off towards the stairs.

Sitting on the floor of her bedroom, with the decanter she had taken from the drinks tray in the drawing room balanced in her lap, Constance thought that she felt slightly better. Outside the bedroom window, beyond the mullioned glass, there were bats swooping beneath the eaves and she watched them for a moment before swilling a little more of the decanter's contents into the tooth mug. She would just drink a little more of this whisky, then she would go to bed and forget all about Simon, and Patrick, and Amelia Sheepshanks, and Sophie and her shop, and Daddy selling the field, and the sight of Ralph Bentley eating his dinner in Mrs Keach's dining room, and all the other things that oppressed her. That was what she would do. And tomorrow she would get up early and go back to London, and Simon could do what he liked about it. Yes, that was the thing to do. She would drink a little more whisky and go to bed and Simon could . . . She found that she could not remember what it was that Simon could do, so she sat on the carpet, legs splayed out in front of her, arms propped behind her by way of balance, and considered it. Then she thought that this was undignified and the kind of thing that people at parties did who had had too much to drink, so she decided to take off her clothes and go to bed. There was no sign of her nightdress and she hunted for it for a moment under the pillows and beneath the coverlet. Then it occurred to her that, being quite warm, she had no need of a nightdress, and so, placing the decanter and the tooth mug on the bedside table, she got into bed in her underwear.

The important thing, she thought, was not to get really drunk, because that might complicate her plans for the morning. She would just drink a little more whisky and then she would ... It was funny about Amelia Sheepshanks, she thought, being so rich but having no great sense of style. 'No great sense of style,' she said out loud, and then laughed because it seemed such a ridiculous thing. 'No great sense of style, poor girl,' she said again. Looking up – the light was still on and she could see across the room – she saw the reflection of a face in the dressing-table mirror – rather flushed and wide-eyed – which she supposed must be Amelia Sheepshanks. The apparition amused her and she laughed again. Perhaps she ought to get out of bed and switch out the light, she thought, but she was perfectly comfortable where she was. The important thing was not to get too drunk. She would just drink a little more whisky and not think about Simon, and Patrick, and Amelia Sheepshanks, and Sophie and the shop. She caught sight of her hand lying on the coverlet beside her and the silver wedding ring digging into her finger. What an extraordinary fat white thing it was, with no sense of style at all. Hurriedly she pulled her hand out of sight beneath the sheet. Really, she thought, I ought to get out of bed and turn out the light, but the important thing was not to get really drunk, to lie there and drink a little more of this whisky and feel sorry for Amelia Sheepshanks, who although frightfully rich had no great sense of style ... Ten minutes later, as the owls hooted in the trees and the tooth mug rolled over empty on to its side, she fell asleep.

25

Death in the Morning

'There's telegrams . . .' said my uncle vaguely.

We were sitting in the morning room at Eaton Square with the day's post on the table before us: a dozen letters, a packet or two, an enormous brown-paper parcel which, unwrapped, turned out to harbour a birthday cake. Through the half-open door of the adjoining room, Hoskins's head could be seen labouring over a column of figures.

'Who sent you the cake?'

'I dunno, Ralph. Some woman.' He fished for a moment or two in the litter of envelopes and torn wrappings, and re-emerged with a scrap of notepaper. '"*To Mr Alfred Rendall, with every good wish, from one who owes you more than she can say . . .*" Not my birthday, neither. Queer!'

Unsolicited gifts, bizarre representations, unlooked-for intimations of support were a feature of my uncle's public career. Moralists wrote to commend his achievements and disparage his lapses. Bishops asked him to sit on committees. He was the patron of, among other institutions, a boys' club and a ginger group for the preservation of stately homes.

'Anything I really want to tell you,' my uncle went on, 'and I'll ring of course . . .'

'Of course.'

In the next room Hoskins's head kept low over the column of figures, to the point where his nose seemed almost to be touching the table.

'Any sign of Atry?'

'Expected this morning,' my uncle said. 'And Austin Trades were at fifty-seven and a quarter last night. Wouldn't surprise me if they went down to forty by lunchtime.'

The crates of bygone paraphernalia had moved downstairs from the study. Now three or four of them lurked in the corner of the morning room, their tops jemmied off with a crowbar that lay against one of the chair backs. My uncle looked at them covertly. He seemed flustered, anxious, but not unhappy.

'Still searching?'

'Share certificates,' he said. 'Can't find 'em anywhere.' There was something disturbing him, I could see, beyond the missing documents and the vagrant – vagrant but by now horribly menacing – figure of Atry.

'Expect me Monday lunchtime,' I said.

Almost on cue, I saw Hoskins, ear attentively cocked, rule a line under the piece of foolscap beneath his nose, raise his head from the tabletop and turn expectantly towards the doorway.

And so I drove off down the Embankment and over Chelsea Bridge, through grim, rain-drenched streets, and on into the distant countryside, a journey that – though I did not yet know it – would take me not merely to the Surrey heaths and the Sussex weald, but to the farthest shores of past time and the memory that gave them life.

I was on the road to Haslemere when I first heard the ghostly knocking, felt the first faint twitch upon the thread. It was the London road that led down to Brighton and the south-west, and it meant nothing to me beyond its utility and the picturesque arrangement of its fields and hedgerows on either side, except that . . .

It was curious how that road grew upon me, how I looked at the road signs and anticipated the names of the villages that were painted on them. Presently the road veered away beyond a low escarpment of red brick with yew hedges and bunched elms behind, and I turned into the park. Here the drive dipped a little and the house was not immediately visible. A moment later and its turrets and pinnacles, the great bank of azaleas that lay to one side, the distant gleam of the river, the handful of motor vehicles drawn up on its gravel surround, came gradually into view. There was no tremor of instant recognition. I knew only that I had been here before, knew, for example, just how far in one direction the azaleas extended to one side of the house and how far the curve of the river extended in the other.

Even then, true realisation didn't dawn on me. The great hall through which I walked, with a footman carrying my case, and the stairs beyond it stirred no echo. It was only when I stood in my bedroom in the east wing looking down on the kitchen garden and the apple orchard beyond it that a key turned in my head and the door to the past swung open. This was Loftholdingswood. The patch of bare ground thirty feet below was where Edna and Elsie had hung out and battered the carpets. Edna and Elsie! I almost saw them beneath me: Edna with handfuls of lank hair escaping from under her housemaid's cap, face scarlet from her exertions, and Elsie darting sly looks at the kitchen window to see if Mrs Custance's eye was on her. Then I felt a tremor of doubt. Surely that greenhouse hadn't been there? And what about the trees that Edna and Elsie had hung the laundry line across? But then, like the parts in an enormous jigsaw, things fell gradually into place. There was the oak tree that I used to skirmish under by the side of the vegetable garden. That was the path that led away to the estate offices and the gamekeeper's cottage, and the little glade where Mrs Custance and Miss Mort sometimes set out chairs for themselves on Sunday afternoons in the summer. It was Loftholdingswood all right. Everything fitted. I simply gazed at it, at the fields running into the distance and the tops of the trees and the glimpse of the river, half of me exulting in the sight of this long-dead world mysteriously returned to view, the other half rather scared by its immediacy and the vision of past time it brought back to the surface. It was where I'd grown up, where I'd sat listening to Mrs Custance, watched Mr Palmer and Mr Montagu poring over *Debrett*, where I'd been left to make my own way in life and no one had ever returned to claim me. And when I stopped to think about it, there was nothing at all outlandish about what had happened. The estate had been sold off after Lady Delacave's death – I had an odd feeling that the room in which I was standing had actually been hers – someone had renamed it and that was that, Loftholdingswood had become Castlemaine Court.

I sat on the edge of the bed and wondered about this revelation. Who was there to tell? Not even my uncle knew anything about Loftholdingswood as I'd known it. Mrs Keach might be interested, but do you go running downstairs to the drawing room of a country house and start telling anyone who wants to listen that this is where you were brought up? No, there was nothing for it but silence, at any rate until I got back to London. Meanwhile there was a huge fount of curiosity that I wanted to satisfy. All that afternoon, while the other guests continued to arrive – Mrs Keach kept to her room for some reason, leaving Miss Jeffries to play chatelaine – I roamed around the house and its grounds to see what else I remembered and how the place had changed in the seventeen years since I'd been gone. It was outside, though, that someone had really been at work to alter things. They'd grubbed up half the orchard and turned it into a croquet lawn, and the old kitchen garden where the cow parsley had grown up six feet high was now orderly lines of vegetables. Half the outbuildings had been demolished and the forge had been converted into a summer house. The old garden sheds were still there, though, and on one of them I found the initials R.B. carved on the window ledge. That gave me a start, I can tell you, because I couldn't remember carving them. When had I done it? 1913? 1914? There were other odd mementoes of my old life. The corridor that ran away from the hall towards the servants' quarters was still painted an arsenical green, and looking at the books in a glass-fronted case in the billiard room I found a copy of *Lorna Doone* with Miss Mort's signature on the flyleaf.

As the afternoon went on, some of these ghosts receded and I no longer stepped into my room imagining that Mr Montagu's voice would rise up to drive me out of it, or walked out into the kitchen garden supposing I'd see Mrs Custance at the window summoning me in to tea. I spent an hour or so in the dining room meeting the other guests, several of whom I knew. Mrs Reginald Heber had been to dinner at Eaton Square. Mr Chatterley, the clergyman, had once solicited my uncle's interest in a boy's club in Poplar. Burnage the comedian my uncle knew from somewhere.

Mrs Keach came into the room, murmured to Mrs Reginald Heber, attended to something Burnage said without much enthusiasm and then said to me, 'It was good of you to come and see me.'

I made my uncle's apologies and she said, 'I know about that. Mr Atry, isn't it?'

I admitted that it was Mr Atry.

'*I* used to have dealings with Mr Atry,' she said, a bit inconsequently. There was a pause when she might have said more about Atry, but then she gave a little shake of her head, the spell was broken and she said, 'Do you know Miss Montmorency? I believe she's very interested in horses' in a tone that suggested I should be very foolish if I shared Miss Montmorency's interest, and passed on, leaving me to deal with Miss Montmorency as best I could.

There was one final twitch on the thread, just before dinner, when a tall, pale-faced girl with her hair shingled almost into extinction came sulkily into the room. It was indisputably Constance. When a rearrangement in the crowd of people by the mantelpiece brought us together, she said, 'I don't expect you recognise me at all.'

'But I do. I should have known you anywhere.'

I realised, as I had done five years ago, that the sulkiness was not deliberate but merely a part of her personality, like lamplight suddenly blazing into a darkened room, quite indiscriminate in its effects.

'You must introduce me to your wife,' she said.

'But I'm not married.'

'Aren't you?' she said. 'How silly of me. Somebody told me you were. But you must excuse me. I'm being taken in to dinner by Lord Clavering.' And that was that.

Meanwhile there was something else calculated to drive away the ghosts of Mrs Custance, Mr Montagu, Miss Mort and even Constance. Somewhere I still have the pile of telegrams my uncle sent me over the course of the weekend at Castlemaine Court. A footman used to bring them to me as I lingered in the morning room eavesdropping on the increasingly fantastic conversations between Mr Burnage and the Rev. Chatterley. The first one, which arrived on the Friday afternoon, went: ATRY WITH MARQ OF W CHARING X HOTEL STOP TRY SELL AUSTIN STOP TO SPARKES STOP. This was more or less decipherable. The Marquess of Winchester was the chairman of one of Atry's companies. The rest meant that my uncle had gone into the City to attempt to offload his holdings in Austin Trades. Barely had I digested this information than a second telegram joined it: AUSTIN IMPOSSIBLE STOP CRASH STOP SETTLEMENT DELAY QUESTION MARK STOP HOPE ALL WELL STOP. The Austin Trades shares were proving unsaleable. 'Settlement delay' meant that whatever had happened to Atry's account was of such magnitude that the fortnightly settlement date – due on the following Monday – might have to be suspended. Then, shortly before dinner, came a third message: OPEN QUOTES WE ARE ALL CRIMINALS CLOSE QUOTES STOP NOT US NOTE OF EXCLAMATION HIM STOP WAKEFIELD SCRIP NOTE OF EXCLAMATION NO NEED RETURN STOP.

Much of this was made intelligible by the next morning's newspapers. Atry had crashed. 'We are all criminals' was the admission that he and certain associates had made to the investigating accountant. All trading in his shares had been suspended. It was thought, additionally, that the corporation scrip certificates that he had been using for security were counterfeit. The Director of Public Prosecutions was at work. The news did not go unnoticed by Mrs Keach's guests. Mrs Reginald Heber remarked that she hoped her brother had not done anything foolish, went away to telephone and returned reassured. Miss Montmorency said that her father had said that Atry was rather a counter jumper but that it was rotten luck. There was a fourth telegram from my uncle around mid-morning. It said simply: RUINED NOTE OF EXCLAMATION. I read it standing on the terrace, where various of Mrs Keach's guests had assembled, looking up at the big, high windows, and the footman, still holding the empty salver out to me, said – he was growing weary of this – 'Any reply, sir? The boy's waiting in the 'all' and I shook my head and said, 'No, no reply.' And I laughed a little, because I knew that we were not ruined, but only embarrassed, and that there might, in addition to the embarrassment, be an inconvenient question or two to answer. Later I remember sitting in the drawing room amid a crowd of guests all drinking tea and talking about the crisis, making calculations on the back of an envelope and reassuring myself of this. In ordinary circumstances I should have returned to Eaton Square, to my uncle, to Hoskins and the rows of figures and the henge of crates, but these were not ordinary circumstances.

And so I sat and watched. In particular I watched Alice – whose role in this gathering was, it seemed to me, as detached and incidental as my own. I watched her as she stood on the terrace talking to Mrs Reginald Heber and it occurred to me that she was altogether lost somewhere in a world where Mrs Reginald Heber could never follow. During the entire dinner on the Saturday night – soup, *entrées*, cutlet, roast pheasant, sweet, savoury – I watched her as she ate, or did not eat, and I never saw a woman more remote from the scene she surveyed or the people around her. Miss Jeffries, I noticed, was her conduit, drew her out, drew her in, led her into conversations and away from them again. You could not say that she sulked, for she smiled and murmured, and when Mr Burnage told his little joke about the girl who was only a subaltern's daughter but she knew what Reggie meant she gave a little tap of approbation upon her wineglass with a spoon. But it was as if the life of the house flowed around her and she barely saw it. And there was a way, it seemed to me, as she sat there with her hands folded neatly in her lap and her eyes not quite seeing the things that passed before her, that she was somehow connected to the disturbance of the previous twenty-four hours, although I could not understand why.

I could not let the discoveries I had made go altogether unheralded.

'When did Mrs Keach buy this house?' I asked Miss Jeffries.

Miss Jeffries liked questions of this sort. In a ponderous and uncertain world, where countless people clamoured for her employer's attention, they emphasised her own consummate importance. She said, 'When did Mrs Keach buy this house? I think it was Mr Keach that bought it. After they were married.'

'And when were they married?' I enquired, because it seemed a question that Miss Jeffries wished to be asked.

'Let me see. I think it was 1911. Perhaps 1912.'

'You know, I used to live here,' I said. 'Before the war.'

'How very interesting,' Miss Jeffries said rather uncertainly.

'Very odd in some ways,' I said. 'Seeing the place again like this.'

'How very interesting.'

Next morning, just as a party was assembling in the hall with the aim of setting out for church, there was an urgent summons to the telephone. I took the call in a little anteroom whose walls were covered with photographs, one of which turned out to be Mrs Keach in the role of Juliet.

'You got to come back, Ralph,' said my uncle's voice – breathlessly.

'What's the matter? Surely nothing else has happened to Atry?'

There was a pause.

'*Unbelievable* thing to happen . . .' he went on.

It was a long time since he had been in a mood like this, where excitement rendered him inarticulate and the significance of what he had to say hung permanently beyond his grasp.

'Ralph,' he said again, with a long exhalation of breath. 'Ralphie.' There was a crash somewhere in the background. 'Unbelievable thing. Was rooting through them crates, you know, the ones I had sent up from the store. And the thing is. *The-thing-is-Ralph*' – again the words came concertinaed together – 'I found Jane's letter.'

For a second I had no idea what he meant. 'Jane's letter?'

'The one that got lost. All them years ago.' He was calmer now: the flames were dying down. 'Couldn't open it myself, of course.'

'No.'

'You'll have to come.'

I remember certain things about the next hour and a half very vividly: bidding farewell to Miss Jeffries (where was Mrs Keach? Mrs Keach was not to be found. Mrs Keach was indisposed); a taxi that was depositing a grizzled, elderly-looking man in a dark suit on the gravel drive as I set off; a diversion in Battersea, where a circus was making its way to the park, with a couple of elephants tramping the grey streets and the people stopping listlessly to watch as they went by. And then I was standing in the morning room at Eaton Square before a table crammed with trays and half-unfurled newspapers and little bits of cardboard with figures scrawled on them in a variety of coloured inks. Here another circus was noisily under way. My uncle, unshaven, tieless, but in a morning coat with cigar ash all over the lapels, was reading telegrams from a pile on a silver plate. At the farther end of the table Hoskins and a clerk were conferring over an enormous spool of graph paper marked with descending blue and black lines. My uncle was talking to himself, making tiny gulping noises that caught in the back of his throat, and the telegram he was reading danced up and down in his quivering hand.

'So you've come, Ralph,' he said.

There was something petulant about the look he gave me. He felt, I suppose, that his enjoyment of this first crisis might now be threatened by a second.

'You'll want to know what's happened, of course,' he continued. A telephone rang somewhere in the back of the house. 'That'll be Sparkes,' my uncle said. Hoskins and the clerk had already vanished from the room, so silently that I never saw them go. 'D'you know,' my uncle said, 'there's talk of suspendin' the Exchange tomorrow? Can you imagine it? All on account of Atry and them certificates.'

It seemed to me that we were getting away from things.

'The letter,' I said.

'It was like this, Ralph,' my uncle said. 'It was late last night. Hoskins had gone home and I was going through them boxes. Don't know why. Never found what I was looking for in them. Too late now, anyhow. Reckoned it might ease my mind. *You* know – thought I might find another picture, perhaps, I could hang on the blessed wall. And then I found a copy – you'll hardly credit this, Ralph – a copy of the *Pig Breeder's Gazette*. You remember when I took the *Pig Breeder's Gazette*, and Asquith and Churchill and everything, and the smell of the slurry, eh? And I thought to myself, I'll have a read of that – it was past midnight then and I knew I'd never get to sleep. So I did, and just as I started – there's the letter.'

He had it now between finger and thumb: a buff envelope, very creased and dog-eared.

'Have you opened it?'

'No,' said my uncle very quietly and sincerely. 'Left it for you.'

I tore it open. There was not much to read. Half a page on the privations of war. Half a page on Mrs Custance's health. And then . . .

'What name?' my uncle wondered.

'She was called Alice Hanson,' I said. Now I had the information it did not seem so very wonderful. Hanson was a foreign name, as far from Bentley as one could travel.

'Don't mean anything to me,' my uncle confirmed. 'Anything else?'

'From America. An actress.'

'Nothing about where she went? *Circumstances.*'

'Nothing.'

'Odd woman, Jane,' said my uncle breezily. 'Always knew more than she let on. Never said anything. Always. Alice Hanson.' He tried the syllables again. 'You could look her up, you know, Ralph, if she was an actress. Theatrical papers and such. Alice Hanson. Think of it.' He spoke the words again. 'Well, now, that's settled at least.' My uncle had lost interest in the letter. 'Not as if there's anything to be *done* . . .' he murmured, half to himself, half to me.

'What about Atry, then?' I asked.

And so my uncle delivered himself of a picturesque monologue, dramatising it as he went along, playing the part of Atry, associates, banking officials and accountants almost without realising that he had assumed the roles, taking the substance of each of the telegrams he had sent me and extrapolating from them extraordinary scenes of accusation, confession, guilt and remorse. Wondering a little how my uncle had obtained all this information, I followed Atry and his minions to the Charing Cross Hotel, heard his representations to the Marquess of Winchester, went with him to the City and that fatal meeting with Sir Gilbert Canning, skulked with him in the office of the Director of the Public Prosecutions, stood with him as he wrote and signed an affidavit acknowledging his responsibilities.

'They say Norman's in charge,' my uncle announced. 'D'you think he'd see me?'

The vision of my uncle and the Governor of the Bank of England discussing Atry's fall was perhaps the most fantastic of all the mental pictures the day had thrown up.

'Better stay here,' I counselled. 'Take the call if it comes.'

'You're right,' my uncle said. 'There's a deal of work to be got through as it is. You won't mind', he wondered, a bit nervously, 'if I let Hoskins and the boy back in here?'

'No.'

It was about half past twelve. All across Eaton Square servants were opening doors and expensive-looking cars were arriving to deposit equally expensive-looking lunch guests on the kerbside. It occurred to me that there was no one in the whole of London to whom I could take the news of the past half-hour. As I turned and walked out of the morning room my uncle, Hoskins and the clerk were already making a meal out of some sandwiches that the butler had brought in on a tray. Adversity had made them zealous, zealous and resourceful. In the end I left the car in the square and walked through Belgravia and across Green Park to the Ritz where, in the bar, half a dozen people sat rather self-consciously disporting themselves. I knew them from parties, from charity balls, from an entertainment my uncle had once given on one of the pleasure boats moored at Charing Cross pier, and they seemed eager to renew our acquaintance. 'So you've being staying at Castlemaine Court?' they said. 'That must have been fun.' 'Constance Henderson was going,' they said, 'and my dear have you *heard* about her and Simon?' Someone mentioned the crisis. 'Isn't Ramsay Macdonald *such* a poppet?' somebody said. 'You're looking dreadfully *solemn,*' somebody else said.

The party broke up at four. The Bright Young People went happily off down Piccadilly to tea in each other's flats or early cocktails at the Criterion bar, but I knew that there was no point in my following them. A door in my life had shut, while another now lay half open, full of unimaginable hopes and terrors. It was as if a conjuror, bent over a box of random, unclassifiable shapes had, with a flick of his wrist, chosen to turn them into a single, coherent mosaic. At a telephone box near Green Park I called Avril's number, but there was no reply: she would be out somewhere with her friends from the club, or visiting her mother in Leytonstone. In the end I decided to take the Tube down to Ealing. It was a month since I had been to the laboratory, and there was dust all over the mahogany tables and a crack in one of the panes that had not been there before, but the place was oddly congenial to me and I took some aniline and began distilling it, noting the variations in the colour of the dye and recording the changes in a notebook I kept there, thinking all the while of the investigative schemes I would pursue. I saw myself in newspaper libraries, hard at work amid the theatrical agents' files, in the offices of private detectives. I had an image in my mind of what my mother might look like – one of those striking, fine-boned faces that stare from stages to command the people beyond them – and as the twilight rose in the street and soft rain fell against the bleary windows, I kept it exultantly before me. It was midnight before I poured the last flagon of blue-black water into the sink, extinguished the gas burners, turned the key in the lock and went back to Trevor Square.

It was here that my uncle arrived very early after breakfast, still in the morning coat he had worn the day before, with a copy of the *Express,* which he pushed frantically into my face even as I opened the door.

'Look at it!' he said. 'Look at the blessed paper!'

'What is it?' I wondered. 'Have they suspended the Exchange?'

'Exchange be blowed,' said my uncle briskly. He tossed the newspaper down on the mat between us, so that its headline lay revealed. 'Looks to me, boy, as if you left Castlemaine Court just in time.'

The rest you know.

Drouett stood on the gravel forecourt looking back at the retreating taxi. There was another automobile, a low-slung sports model, leaving at the same time, and for a moment he watched as the two vehicles jockeyed for possession of the drive until the sports model suddenly broke away, as it was bound to do, and went careening off in the direction of the park gates. As their outlines receded across the russet-coloured horizon and the noise of the engines faded away, he grew conscious of his solitude, here on the forecourt of the great, high-windowed house, and with a lightness of step that did not at all reflect his deep inner misgivings he skipped up the worn steps and beat hard upon the door with his fist.

He had hired a taxi to Waterloo Station, taken the train to a place called Haslemere and hired a further taxi to bring him to this final destination. It was a curious thing, but he seemed somehow to have detached himself from his body, to be looking down on himself as he stood on the stone steps. He had assumed, sitting on the train and in the taxi as it alternately climbed and then descended the road from Haslemere, that there would be words in his head he would be able to say, but somehow this had not happened, and they hung – like the words Joyce had spoken to him at breakfast – slightly beyond his consciousness, above the point where he could bring them down.

And now here he was at the door of Castlemaine Court. It certainly was a fine place, he thought. He had seen pictures of places like it in magazines, but nothing had quite prepared him for the reality of it, the acre or two of gravel surround, the vista of high, oblong windows, the caryatid on its plinth above the fountain. He had a vision of himself in a buggy with a couple of brown Morgan horses sweeping on to the forecourt from its southern side, where he suspected there were stables, and tearing off again across the park. Suddenly the door was being opened and a housemaid in an apron and a starched white cap stood on the threshold. Although he did not know it, he had picked the best time in the weekend to arrive at Castlemaine Court. It was about half past eleven and a good proportion of Mrs Keach's guests were at church. This, together with the reluctance of certain other of

Mrs Keach's guests to stir from their rooms, meant that the lower parts of the house were almost deserted. The servants, too, had mostly dispersed. The daily life of the great house had hardly begun and there was no one to answer the front door except Ella, who knew nothing of prohibitions or, not having set eyes on him before, of Drouett, and saw nothing amiss with him other than the fact that he had no luggage and was beating the pair of wash-leather gloves he had in his left hand nervously against the jacket cuff of his right.

'Is your mistress at home, I wonder – Mrs Keach, that is?' Drouett began amiably. He handed her a card which said that he was Mr George Drouett of the Criterion Hotel, and Ella, looking at it, could find no fault.

'Is she expecting you, sir?' Ella asked. She assumed that he was a guest, arriving late, and yet he had no luggage, not even a valise or a satchel. On the other hand he was very respectably dressed – Ella had noticed this the moment she opened the door – and had asked for Mrs Keach by name.

'Mrs Keach will know who I am,' he told her, almost confidingly. He had stopped beating the wash-leather gloves against his wrist and instead slapped them against his stomach. 'Maybe you could tell her that I'm here.'

Rather to his surprise, for he had expected to see the stern butler lurking in the corridor, Drouett found himself in a little antechamber beyond the hall where there was a chair or two, an assortment of coats and scarves, and a stag's head staring from the wall. The housemaid was in retreat across the corridor to the staircase. Still shaking a little from the nervous effort of the previous few moments, Drouett sat in the nearest chair. He did not know what he wanted from Alice other than that he wished to see her. There were certain questions that he wished to ask her, but again, he could not think how to put them into words. He fancied he had made a mistake, that he would have been better off staying in the hotel bedroom with Joyce, yet he was aware that the hotel bedroom, Joyce – practically all the life he now led – were hateful to him. He got up from the chair with a start, wiped his hand across his forehead and then sank back into it. He would return to America, he thought. He would tell Alice this. He saw the two of them sitting across a spacious wooden table of the kind they had in houses like this and him gravely explaining matters while she nodded her head.

Alice was shut fast in another little private chamber of hers not far away from the great hall and so near to it that she had even heard the knock at the door and wondered idly who it might be. Just at this moment she was sitting at her rosewood desk looking at a sheaf of letters – nearly a week's accumulation – that swarmed all over the pink blotting pad and the sheet of foolscap on which she made occasional notes for Miss Jeffries, who had the job of writing her replies. She heard the housemaid's footsteps recede across the hall and, a moment or two later, heard them march back and stop before the door.

'Gentleman to see you, mum,' said Ella, as she handed over Drouett's card.

Alice put the paperknife with which she had been slitting her envelopes down upon the desk, picked up the pasteboard card Ella had handed her and looked at it. Seeing Drouett's name on it did not seem so very startling to her. A part of her was not surprised to find him standing on her doorstep sending in his card. Another part of her, flaring up in anger, threatened to sweep this first part away, but somehow it held on and the anger became vexation and then something very close to curiosity. Sitting at the desk and looking at the card with Drouett's name in its curlicued framing, and at the paperknife with its curving scimitar blade, she wondered what she ought to do.

'Is Mr Maslin in the house, Ella?'

'He's still at chapel in the village I believe, mum.'

'What about Miss Jeffries?'

'In her room, I think, mum.'

Alice wondered whether she should send for Miss Jeffries and then thought better of it. After all, what could Miss Jeffries do that she could not do herself? Still, though, she hesitated. Other than asking him what his intentions were, she had no idea what she might say to Drouett, yet she knew that she wanted to see him. Searching for some practical way of soothing her restlessness, she picked up the paperknife, ran the point gently into the palm of her hand, found it to be unexpectedly sharp and carefully put it down.

'Ella.'

'Yes, mum.'

'Ella.' Again Alice paused. She was thinking of events in her past life in which Drouett had not actually featured but in which his influence had been determinedly felt. 'You had better show Mr Drouett in. And Ella' – for the girl had already turned towards the door – 'in a quarter of an hour, please bring me a cup of tea.'

'A quarter of an hour, mum?'

'If Mr Maslin is back, ask him to bring it. If not, come yourself.'

Wondering a little, Ella moved off down the passage, leaving the door half ajar. Alice listened to her footsteps disappearing. Quickly she began to arrange the papers on her desk into some kind of order, a process that took her longer than she imagined, so that when Drouett arrived in the room she felt rather than saw him, heard Ella's pronunciation of his name, the shuffle of his feet and the click of the door catch as Ella departed, before she raised her head and saw him. She was prepared, she thought, for almost anything. What she saw was a rather elderly-looking man, grey hair turning rapidly to white, very well dressed in a dark suit with a tiepin and gleaming black Oxfords, and also, she thought, a kind of hopelessness, as if there were something about him and the situation in which he found himself that he did not quite grasp. Not knowing what in the least to say, and with the white envelopes still strewn about the table before her, she uttered the first words that came into her head. 'I'm surprised to see you here, George.'

Looking back at her across the table, Drouett's eye was caught by the interplay of colours: the russet brown of the desktop, the white of the envelopes, the red of her hair. She was wearing a morning gown, emphatically modern in its design but allowing certain hints of an earlier era in women's fashions, which he remembered and appreciated, and he thought how splendid she looked. He wondered for a moment what would have happened if he had not left her in the wooden house in De Smet.

'Well, now,' he began, again in that old way she remembered. 'It's good to see you, Alice.'

She did not know what to say to this. A part of her wanted to remind him that he had promised – signed a piece of paper, taken money – to disappear entirely from her life, but somehow she could not bring herself to do this.

'You'd better sit down, George,' she said, gesturing to a chair on the further side of the desk. 'How did you get here?'

He explained about the journey to Waterloo, the train ride through Surrey, the taxi from Haslemere, and she stared at the envelopes on her desk, at the paperknife and at his moustache, which moved evenly up and down as he spoke. As on the previous occasions they had met, she realised that she could not divine from his attitude or look what he wanted.

'What do you want?' she asked.

It was the third time he had heard this question. He looked up as she asked it, a little shamefacedly. He was about to answer as he had answered before – that he wanted nothing – when he remembered something that he very much did want, so he said, 'Well, I should like to know about the child.'

He could see her react to this. The fingers of her right hand, which were lying on the rosewood tabletop, moved a little. They pushed at an envelope and moved it the merest fraction away.

'There was no child.'

'I guess there was,' he said, not triumphantly but carrying his point. 'I saw Hanson, you know.'

'You saw Hanson?'

'Sure I did,' he said easily. 'About a year and a half ago. I found Hanson all right. At a mission church in Duluth. We had quite a little talk. He told me all about it.'

She could not answer this. She sat in her chair and pushed at the edge of one of the envelopes again so that it moved a little way further along the table.

'Say,' he said, and he did so quite amiably, without the least hint that there was anything ominous in the words. 'What if that child was mine, not Hanson's. I suppose I have a right to know what became of it?'

'I don't think you have any rights at all, George,' she said.

'Maybe I don't. But a fellow gets curious.'

For his own part, Drouett did not quite know why he laboured the question of the child. Certainly, he told himself, he would have liked to know what had become of it, but he could also see that talk of it distressed Alice and might therefore be disadvantageous to him.

'George,' she said, as if it had only just occurred to her. 'Even if you were to tell anyone about this, they wouldn't believe you.'

He saw now – and the thought had crossed his mind a moment or so before – that she assumed he had come to blackmail her. This irritated him. Couldn't a fellow ask a question about his child without being thought suspect? But another part of him – not the predominant part, but a part nonetheless – thought that another thousand pounds would be very pleasant.

'Hanson's a preacher,' he said. 'The kind of fellow people listen to, I suppose.'

'I cannot believe that you saw Sven,' she said.

'Sure I saw him. Like I said. In a mission shack down in Duluth. Not two years ago. With a Mrs Hanson and a yard full of kids. Duluth!' Drouett paused. 'I suppose there are two Mrs Hansons, isn't that so?'

He did not realise that he was incriminating himself, that what to him was simple information – testimony to his powers of enquiry and dogged resolve – was to her evidence of the harm he meant to do. He thought that he was merely confirming the interest that he had taken in her, but at the same time he was too shrewd not to sense her disquiet and want to play on it.

'George,' she said. She had risen to her feet and was standing behind the rosewood table, turning the paperknife over in her hand. Looking at her watch she saw that in five minutes Ella would return with the tea tray. She thought that if he mentioned the hundred and eighty-seven dollars and her desertion of Hanson she could not bear it. 'George,' she said again, 'what do you want?'

He registered dimly that this was the fourth time that had been asked of him and still he could not answer it.

'What kind of a question is that?' he wondered, and the ghost of the old Drouett of the Kansas railroad and the low hills beyond De Smet wandered up to oppress him. All this time Drouett was darting little glances at her, at the mass of papers on the desk, at the tawny stones of the jewellery round her neck – he had once put his hands on that neck, he thought – at the point of the scimitar paperknife. Not seeing how much he had annoyed her, he was calculating hard how the thing was going and believing that it was not going too badly.

'You may have another thousand pounds. Another two thousand. If only you will . . . give your word.'

'Well now, a fellow might give his word and not act on it,' Drouett said with a ghastly attempt at jauntiness. He did not mean any malice by this. He meant only to convey how frail and imprecise words were, how the turmoil in his mind could not be subdued by them. He laughed a little, jinked a little way nearer to the desk, thinking he might have some effect on the look on her face, which he saw now was a terrible look. He had made a mistake, he thought, coming down here. Joyce had been right and he had been wrong. He had made a bad mistake and he ought to wash his hands of it. Above all, he wished she would not look at him like that.

'Alice,' he began. He put out his hand to touch her arm and thought that he felt the slither of fabric as she twisted away.

There was a whirl of brisk, purposeful movement. The paperknife, with its scimitar tip, still glinted in Alice's hand. At one point Drouett raised his arm. Some of the papers tumbled on to the floor. First Drouett appeared to be on the table's flank, then he seemed to have retreated behind it. In the confusion the paperknife disappeared from view and then re-emerged. Gradually the noise – little snaps and detonations and gasps of breath – gave way to silence. Alice sat feebly in her chair, one hand still clutching the knife, while Drouett, making odd wheezing sounds, hung over the desk, one hand stretched out before him on the wood to break his fall, a word forming on his lips that was never quite uttered, a gesture beginning in his other hand that was never quite made.

And this was how Ella found them, coming into the room through the half-open door with the tea tray balanced against her hip, and dropping the tray instantly on the white carpet, and giving first one scream and then another, then turning and fleeing out along the passage and into the great hall, where the footman put out a hand and tried to stop her and Miss Jeffries, arriving from the staircase, saw her flight, and then out of the drawing room and through its open french windows and on to the terrace, where she collided with Lady Carbury and a tray of crockery and fell on to the grey stone with the fragments of the smashed teacups descending on to the skirt of her black uniform like so much confetti.

'No ladies present, are there?' wondered Mr Burnage. 'Well, here's one, then. *She was only a fishmonger's daughter, but she lay on the slab and said "fillet".* Christ! What was that?'

I wonder where Constance is, thought Simon Macpherson. Because all this business about Amelia Sheepshanks is becoming just the tiniest bit tiresome and I . . . *Heavens!*

'To think', Lady Llanstephan said, 'that I came all the way from Cwmrhyddery for *this* . . . Bilson, what is that noise?'

'I'm sure I don't know, my lady.'

Mr Maslin heard the screams as he toiled through the vegetable garden on his way back from the Wesleyan chapel. Mrs Reginald Heber heard them as she sat before the mirror in her bedroom combing lotion into her black, patent-leather hair. Miss Montmorency heard them as she stood in the stable saddling up her hunter. The Rev. Chatterley heard them as he stepped back into the house with a prayer book in one hand and his hat in the other. Mr Schmiegelow heard them as he came down the back stairs with the brown-paper parcel under his arm. Only Constance, arms flung back across her pillow, careless of the mid-morning sunshine flooding into her room, slept on insensibly as, far below her, footsteps pattered over the terrace and, a little later, there came the sound of motor cars – several motor cars – travelling at speed along the bumpy inclines of the park to grind up the gravel in the drive.

26

Beverley Nichols's Diary

Woke up at 5 a.m. in X's flat near the back of Victoria Station. It really is unbelievably squalid – I was absolutely compelled to wash my face and hands in the sink – and I can't imagine how I was persuaded to go there. Gave X £5, which I suppose he will spend on gin – or something worse. Went back to Stanhope Gate and sat in a cold bath for half an hour to reduce the swelling, put on a suit, ate the excellent breakfast prepared for me by Gaskin, in the way that only Gaskin knows how, and somehow got round to No. 2 Court at the Bailey by half past nine, which I really think is a tribute to my pertinacity. Here there was a huge scrum of people milling on the pavement, practically knocking me off my feet, but a nice usher recognised me and took me into the press gallery. Rather a seedy crew assembled – the man from the *Sunday Despatch* was actually eating sandwiches out of a paper bag – I suppose they are all otherwise employed interviewing burglars on their doorsteps at two guineas per thousand words – but I consider it a feather in my cap to be asked to cover such an important event. I also think the *Sunday Times* is quite right to choose me. I shall probably make a better job of it than any living writer. Hugh Walpole would be too sonorous, Priestley too bluff. Willie Maugham would be distinguished but dull. Also, none of them is a good enough reporter.

Besides, even had Lord Kemsley not asked me, I should have offered my services to some other newspaper group, if only to help poor Alice Keach, who is a noble woman and will no doubt spend the next fortnight having disobliging things written about her by people who would sell their grandmothers for an invitation to Lowndes Square. Does that sound snobbish? Well, it is not meant to be. Perhaps I am allowed to be the tiniest bit snobbish about Alice Keach, who in addition to being a great lady is also a dear friend of mine.

Which is not to say that all this is not terribly shocking. The facts, insofar as they can be established, are quite incontrovertible. An American, Drouett, is found dead on the floor of one of the downstairs rooms at Castlemaine Court, stabbed in the neck with a paperknife. Alice is holding the paperknife when first discovered by the parlourmaid and, later, by the guests. Everyone says that she feared blackmail, but what, one wonders, is there to blackmail her for? Certainly she was brought up in a poor way in America and may have done discreditable things before Guy Keach married her, but Mrs Corrigan is a farmer's daughter from Wisconsin and I know stories of Mrs Harry Brown that would make one's hair curl. Some of the newspapers have stories saying that she and Drouett had a child together, but there is no proof of the child's existence or anyone who knows anything about it.

It is all very mysterious.

Spent an hour or so watching the jury being sworn in. Ten men and two women. All horribly undistinguished: one or two of the men no more than office clerks. Actually, I should be grateful for this imbalance. Women in a jury never see the woman's point of view. They would not see Alice's. They would be either envious or disapproving. The men, on the other hand, will be more worldly. They will say to themselves: 'Here is a distinguished lady goaded beyond reason to commit a crime she did not wish to. Let us be merciful to her.'

While all this was going on – and very tedious it was too – I let my eye rove over the public gallery, thinking it might be useful for my report. The usual crowd of middle-aged women come for a day's entertainment. One or two of Alice's genuine friends at the back, heads bobbing beneath the high ceiling. It is all desperately sad. On any other day they might be lunching with her at the Berkeley. Now they are waiting for some nasty old man to ask her impertinent questions.

During the lunch hour I was very virtuous. When I should have been eating oysters with Noël at Wheeler's, I went instead to the *Sunday Times* office to see my editor. A bumptious little man in an old Blundell's tie, who evidently does not realise that Alice is not just 'some Society woman'. He said to me, 'I suppose you know we are anxious for a conviction?' I replied that I could understand a prosecuting counsel being anxious for a conviction, but I thought it odd in a respectable newspaper. 'Naturally,' he said, 'we should not at all wish to influence what you write.' To this I merely nodded my head. Then he said, 'There is a report come in from America, and they have found a man with whom she definitely had a child.' Then it was not Drouett's, I asked. He said he did not yet know. They have assembled a whole page of photographs from plays in which she took part twenty years ago. Odd, because I saw several of them when I was a boy and did not remember her in the least. Poor Alice! To have Mr Silas in his Old Blundell's tie – I don't believe he ever went anywhere near Blundell's – dropping his cigar ash over her portrait! Anyhow, I said he should have his two thousand words by Saturday morning.

Later. Why is it that judges are always supposed to be cruel monsters who drink tawny port and itch for the hanging cap? Ours is a perfectly nice old gentleman who makes little jokes to the barristers and helps himself to lozenges out of a box when he thinks no one is looking.

At half past four a sensation – everyone had supposed there were still jurors to be sworn in – when Alice is brought into the dock. Everywhere a rustle of clothing and a sharp intake of breath as people pressed forward to see her. The nasty little man from the *Sunday Despatch* actually put down his bag of boiled sweets to get a better look! I had made a special note to myself to write down what she was wearing, but in the excitement almost forgot. I should say that she had on a dress in deep crimson (Hartnell? I shall have to enquire) with a dark wrap round her shoulders and an exceedingly chic, smallish hat. All this, though, overshadowed by the look on her face, which is quite piteous. A woman who went on the stage playing Ophelia with that face would get a round of applause before she ever opened her mouth. She did not move; she *glided.* After the initial murmur, an absolute silence as she takes the stand in the dock. A prison wardress with her looking exactly like Madame Defarge, but a nice, gallant usher who brings her a cushion and asks if she would like a glass of water.

I shall mention the nice usher in my report.

The judge asks her two questions: her name, which she gives, quite loudly; and how does she plead, whereupon she says, in the tiniest voice imaginable, that it is not guilty. The judge, whom I like more and more, smiling and encouraging, as if it is all nonsense and he cannot imagine why they should be here. Then she is taken down again, the court breaks out into a fusillade of whispers and the nasty little man from the *Sunday Despatch* goes back to eating boiled sweets.

It turns out that this is the end of the first day's proceedings.

Later. Dinner with Mary Ridgeley Carter. A tiresome American woman, who is apparently in love with me. The talk, inevitably, of Alice. Mary

C. said she had it on good authority – what is 'good authority', I wonder? – that her weight was down to six stone, and that the prison doctor was injecting her with insulin to ginger up her appetite. Too horrible, if true.

Went to the Criterion bar later and found X with a couple of disreputable young men. East End toughs in wide-brimmed hats. He really is unspeakably sordid in his amours. Home early and to bed.

13 February 1932

In high dudgeon – a rather nice word, which sounds like a fish – at breakfast when Gaskin, together with my coffee, brought me an Income Tax demand for £870. I suppose this will pay for a lot of nasty children to go to school in a charabanc with soft rubber seats. I never went to school in a charabanc. I had to walk.

Arriving at the Bailey I met Peter Spencer-Churchill on the steps. Distrait as ever. Said he had been talking to Winston, who was gloomy. Winston said that his own experience, when at the Home Office, was that jurors always wanted to convict rich defendants in murder cases out of sheer envy. Whatever Drouett had done, there would be sympathy for him. 'She must, at any rate, admit the blow' &c. Got to my seat in the press gallery and found to my inexpressible relief that the man from the *Sunday Despatch* has disappeared. Perhaps he overate himself. Anyway, it will be a blessing not to have to listen to the rustle of his paper bag.

I am getting used to the atmosphere of the court now, I find: the shiny wood of the jurors' box; the gloom of the judge's stall; the pale, prurient faces in the public gallery. Somebody could write a very interesting study of the group psychology on display – the silences broken by a sudden tumult of whispering for no apparent reason. Today, when they brought her in, there was absolute quiet, though you sensed that everyone in the room was on thorns. Then, quite unexpectedly, someone shouted 'Good luck to you!' and was immediately shushed by the judge.

She does not look well. White-faced. Not glancing to either side, as one might expect. Still very elegant. All the newspapers – I have them spread out on the bench in front of me – make this point. No sign of the gallant usher from yesterday, just the grim old wardress.

The judge is about to make a statement. No, he is not. He is merely summoning one of the defence barristers for a conference of whispers. The defence counsel is Mr Samways. Do I know Mr Samways? I think I ought to, but then I am so bad at names. It is considered proper here in the press gallery to call Mr Samways 'Jimmy'. Anyway, the whispered conference is followed by a little stir of movement and the prosecuting counsel, Mr Nixon, stands up to address the court.

For a man who is perhaps five feet four inches tall and meagre to the point of insignificance, Mr Nixon ought not to be so theatrical. Instead, he puffs up his chest like a pouter pigeon and speaks to the jury as if he were a low comedian haranguing the pit at the Hackney Empire. In the course of the next few days, he assures us, he will demonstrate irrefutably that the defendant committed murder, that a visitor to her home, an American gentleman, having no inkling of his fate, was done to death in earshot of her guests. He is aware – at this point he turns his head and looks directly at Alice – that he is dealing with a celebrated figure, that all the world knows Mrs Keach, that lords, earls and duchesses have dined at her table, that she numbers – and here Mr Nixon gives a dramatic little pause – royalty among her friends, but this is no reason why she should not be arraigned for her crime. Undoubtedly there will be excuses made in her defence. Undoubtedly there will be – another dramatic little pause – sympathy for her. But this is not material. He has no brief for the deceased, the unfortunate Mr Drouett – here he pauses not dramatically but respectfully. Mr Drouett may have been a bad man, and his motives in coming to see Mrs Keach on that fateful day questionable. Then again, he may not. But once more, this is immaterial. No, what he intends to prove is that he was wilfully murdered, cut down in cold blood, and that the person – another look at Alice – who committed this crime should be punished with the fullest rigour that the law allows.

All this went on until nearly lunchtime and was rather tedious. But there was a moment when I pricked up my ears. This came when Mr Nixon announced that he intended to present to the jury an explanation of Mrs Keach's motive in murdering Mr Drouett, involving a thorough account of their previous association. Here I saw Mr Samways give an anxious little jerk of his hand and mutter something to his aide-de-camp, but Alice merely looked on into the middle distance. Was she even listening? Who could tell?

Went and had my lunch in a foul little café full of fat men choosing their racing selections in the *Sporting Life*. Fascinating as all this is, one cannot ignore the fact that one has a professional life – not to mention a personal life – to which to attend, and so I went off to the *Chronicle* office to telephone Cochran about the revue numbers he wants, and had the most amusing telephone conversation with Mrs Ronnie Greville's butler, who always has difficulty with his aitches.

SELF: This is Mr Nichols. I wish to speak to Mrs Greville.
BUTLER: I don't believe she's in the 'ouse, sir.
SELF: But it's Mr Nichols. I am to dine with her next month.
BUTLER: Now I think of it, sir, she's in the horangery.

All most exhausting.

Back to the Bailey at 2.15, just as Mr Nixon was getting to his feet again. Impressed, in spite of myself, by his dexterity of manner. When he takes out a handkerchief and flicks it, the people in the public gallery follow the gesture. Important. When he reaches the end of a paragraph, falls silent and takes a glass of water, they wait attentively for him to recommence. Very important. This afternoon he is interrogating the first prosecution witnesses. I say 'interrogating' for there is something a little sinister about Mr Nixon, however bland and insinuating his questions. The witnesses stolid and respectful. The police constable who found Drouett's body and the police surgeon who certified the death (a puncture wound to the carotid artery, it turns out). Burnage, the comedian, who was first to the room, looking to make something of the occasion, but dealt with in a minute or so. A girl in a white hat and too much lipstick – the parlourmaid at Castlemaine Court, I take it – explains how she opened the door to Drouett, thinking him to be one of the guests, and twenty minutes later, bringing a tea tray to her mistress's room, arrived a moment or so after the fatal blow was struck. Mr Nixon, I note, is particularly ingratiating with the parlourmaid, gets her to supply a picturesque account of Drouett lying dead over the desk and Alice with the paperknife in her hand.

This, of course, was Nixon's cue to have the knife brought in. It was beautifully done. An usher carried it in ceremonially on a kind of salver and Nixon stood over it, stepped back from it, picked it up and then held it out in front of him. First he asked the parlourmaid if she recognised it, which she did, then he called the butler, Maslin, to see if he recognised it, which he did too. Then Lightfoot, the police constable, again to confirm that he had retrieved the knife from the floor beneath Alice's chair. All this received in stark silence by the gallery, and the members of the jury nodding their heads like metronomes. Mr Samways, I could see, was itching to break this spell and managed to ask the police constable if anyone else had touched the knife before it was taken away for examination, but Nixon had a fingerprint man in the box to declare that the marks on the knife were nearly all Alice's, with just a dab or two of Drouett's around the blade. Mr Samways up again to sow in the jury's mind the thought that this might indicate nothing more than self-defence against the deceased's assault, but instantly shushed by the judge and the floor returned to Mr Nixon.

Then came one or two of Alice's house guests. Old Lady Llanstephan was very funny. Refused to answer Nixon's question as to where she was when the news first broke – everyone assumed that it was because she was in the lavatory. Simon Macpherson, whom one has come across, had moved heaven and earth not to be called, as otherwise could not make a killing writing it up for the *Sketch*.

Mr Samways, meanwhile, doing his best with the prosecution witnesses. Asks Burnage half a dozen questions about what he saw, but none of them has the slightest effect. Did she say anything? No, Burnage swears she did not. What was the expression on her face? Burnage says that it was 'somewhere in the middle of next week'. Were there signs of a struggle? Burnage can't say, except that there was paper – letters and envelopes – all over the floor.

And that is that for the day.

In the press gallery the reporters from the cheap papers – dreadful crew! – are actually offering odds on Alice's conviction. At lunchtime the price was 3–1, shortening to 2–1 at the adjournment. I took this as a bad omen.

Later. Cocktails at Barbara Back's, a nice woman but less than discreet. Also well-connected. Has heard that Nixon intends tomorrow to produce some absolutely sensational witness who has only just turned up. Like the short odds in the press gallery, all this fills me with foreboding. Thought of Alice eating her dinner in Holloway, where they are keeping her, and nearly wept at the pity of it. Eventually went back to Stanhope Gate, took a letter card and wrote on it: *Alice, darling, this is just to say that all the judges are insane . . . Love from Beverley*, which I then addressed to *Mrs Alice Keach, c/o Holloway Prison, London N7*, and went out and posted. They will not let her see it.

Later. Coming back from posting the letter card I discovered X waiting for me on the doorstep (knowing, presumably, that sensible Gaskin would not have let him in). There followed a dreadful scene in which X accused me of discarding him and I, in turn, accused him of keeping bad company and not caring whom he went to bed with or was seen about with. What the neighbours will think I cannot imagine.

x (*on leaving*): It's not money I want, but friendship.

Really!

14 February 1932

Valentine's Day. Apparently this morning a dozen red roses were delivered – anonymously – to Holloway, which is very nice-minded of someone.

We are all old friends in the press gallery now. The man from the *Sunday Despatch* is only a distant memory. The reporters from the cheap papers call me 'Mr Nichols', which amuses me.

I expect they would all like jobs on the *Sunday Times*.

Several of the papers have got wind of the sensational witness. Great speculation as to who it may be. A little man from the *Mirror* convinced that it would be some blackmailer to whom Alice had paid money. Huge excitement, consequently, as Alice brought in (silent, quite impassive, Gioconda-like) with Mr Nixon sweeping down into his stall like a cat that has just been given the cream. Mr Samways tries a representation to the judge on press reporting of the case, which he thinks unfair and prejudicial, and the judge shakes his head, warns of the danger of contempt of court, but declines to be drawn. Then Nixon is on his feet. It is his intention, he declares, to establish the motive that caused Mrs Keach to do away with the man who arrived at her door at Castlemaine Court. To this end, he has searched very widely – a glance at the jury, whose members are looking at him like rabbits mesmerised by a luxuriating snake – to secure persons who can assist in this endeavour, and he will commence by calling Miss Joyce McKechnie.

Miss McKechnie is a thoroughly nasty piece of work. Nearer forty than thirty, wearing what I believe is known as a 'costume' and a dreadful hat. Represents herself as Drouett's 'fiancée'. 'Mistress' would be nearer the mark. Just the kind of woman one sees hanging round the Criterion bar hoping that someone will buy her a drink. Ugh! Not quite as well informed about Drouett and his designs as I think Nixon believed her to be. Nevertheless, she said that Drouett had told her that he lived with Alice in America when she was quite young, and that he had had £1,000 from Alice's solicitor, Aberconway. A letter read out in court by one of Nixon's young men confirmed this and Mr Samways did not try to disprove it.

All this time Nixon paying her ghastly little compliments, at one point expressing general regret that she should not shortly be standing at the altar as Mrs Drouett. Horrible!

I cannot believe that anyone on the jury benches could be taken in by Miss McKechnie, who positively simpered at the judge and darted ogling little glances at the men who sat drawing portraits of her for the newspapers. Indeed, after several minutes of this Nixon seemed to think that she might not be doing him good and appeared to lose interest. Samways excellent with her, I thought. Had, of course, a copy of Aberconway's letter and noted the passage in which Drouett was requested to return to the United States. Why had he not done this? Miss McKechnie had no answer. Had Miss McKechnie hoped to gain anything from her fiancé's petition to Mrs Keach (an intervention from Nixon, which the judge disallowed)? Again, no answer. What was Miss McKechnie doing now? She was living with her parents at their home in Purley. Was it true that she had been dismissed from her previous employment when discrepancies had been discovered in the petty cash? Here Nixon intervened and had the question struck out, but the damage was done. Certainly everyone in the press gallery agreed that she was a nasty little gold-digger.

A pretty girl sniffing into her handkerchief would, of course, have had the jury on her side. But not Miss McKechnie, with her simpering and her 'costume' and her dreadful hat.

I have been taking care, while all this is going on, to keep my gaze on Alice. In fact, I have decided to make a study of her. Just when everyone's attention is fixed on the witness box, I shall be examining the look on her face, the play of her hands &c. It will be fascinating from the human angle and add substance to my report.

I must remember – it is the court reporter's great obligation – that she is a *real person*. Flesh and blood.

The worst of it is that I can see myself in her dining room discussing the case with her as if we both had nothing to do with it.

She is worth a dozen of Mrs Corrigan, or the Duchess of Sutherland. Well.

At lunchtime a message to go and see Silas at the *Sunday Times*.

Very curious. Began by asking: what did I think was the public mood with regard to Mrs Keach? I said that so far as I could deduce, it was broadly favourable, the roses sent to Holloway Prison &c. Silas disagreed. Said that there had been slogans chalked on the pavement at Lowndes Square saying: SHE SHOULD HANG. Also a Labour paper – I think the *Herald* – had calculated she spent five thousand a year entertaining, and a very queer story – mere gossip, I should say – about a couple of Lelys going missing from the house on the day of the murder. 'What does that have to do with whether or not she murdered Drouett?' I wondered. Silas shook his head and said there was such a thing as public opinion, which it was his duty to reflect &c. All this very ominous. I contented myself by saying that I would consider the facts as I saw them and write what I thought, whereupon he bowed and said he thought we understood each other perfectly, which of course we do not.

Back in court, one could see that something was up. The judge was examining a memorandum, which one of the defence barristers had given him. Mr Nixon was puffing himself up in his stall like a thoroughly disagreeable toad. Then the judge taps with his gavel, the press reporters fall silent, the stenographers pick up their pens and a little sigh goes through the people in the public gallery as they settle down in their seats. I like Mr Nixon less and less. He seizes a fragment of paper, stares at it through his half-moon spectacles, puts it down, looks at the ceiling as if there is another fragment of paper hanging there that he wishes to bring down and interrogate, then says very quietly, for maximal effect, with the people in the public gallery straining to hear him and the old judge swivelling his head, that he proposes to read us a paragraph from the *Chicago-Sun-Tribune* printed some time in 1905.

It is about a Mrs Alice Hanson, the wife of a Lutheran pastor, wanted by the authorities after absconding from her husband's mission church in Chicago with their child and nearly two hundred dollars in cash from the mission fund!

I watch Alice's face as this is read out. It is quite without expression. A blank sheet. If I did not know it was she I should hardly recognise her, so devoid is she of any animating spirit.

Mr Samways jumps up with an objection, but Nixon has already put the paper down and is calling the Rev. Sven Hanson. Absolute sensation in the court. A tall, awkward-looking man with a broad forehead and a greying beard makes his way to the stall, where he stands turning the fingers of his left hand anxiously in the palm of his right. Alice – I am following this in the minutest particulars – gives him one look – bewilderment? Anguish? I cannot tell – and then subsides into her chair. The reporters in the press gallery set up a great whisper and are rebuked by the judge. Then absolute silence.

Nixon has clearly been coaching this Rev. Hanson. Answering questions, he looks nervously at him, opens his mouth a little, nods his head and looks as if he were racking his brains to remember what to say. Pronounced Scandinavian accent. Says 'yas' instead of 'yes'. *Very* uncertain. Agrees that he is the Reverend Hanson and that he is pastor of a mission church in Duluth. Nixon wonders: does he see anyone that he recognises.

HANSON   (*pausing*): It is hard for me to say so, but yas.
NIXON: The defendant? That is, the lady sitting there?
HANSON: That is so . . . Yas.
NIXON: And what is your connection with this lady? With Mrs
         Keach?
HANSON: You must understand that it is hard for me to answer this.
NIXON: I understand perfectly. Let me make it easier for you. I have
         here a piece of paper, issued in the city of Duluth,
         Michigan, in the year 1905 solemnising the marriage between
         the Reverend Sven Hanson and Miss Alice Alden. Are you
         that man?
HANSON: I am, yas.
NIXON: And is this lady that woman?
HANSON: She is . . . That is, I believe her to be so, yas.
NIXON: You have heard me read to the court a paragraph that
         appeared in the *Chicago-Sun-Tribune* newspaper in 1905. Is it
         a true representation of the facts as they are known to you?
HANSON: . . .
NIXON: It would be a great convenience to us, Mr Hanson, if you
         could speak a little louder.
HANSON   (*dramatically raising his voice*): It is all true. Of course it is.
         Would I come all this way if it was not, if it was not my
         duty? Certainly it is true. She was my wife. Mrs Hanson.
         You have heard the marriage lines. Mrs Hanson, yas. We
         lived at the mission at Van Buren, in Chicago. A very poor

place. There was a fund for the poor people who slept in the street. One hundred eighty-seven dollars in a box in my office. On a Sunday after service I go out on business. When I return, she and the money – and our child – are gone.

At this there was a gasp you could have heard in the street, so that even when he went on to give the boy's name – Asa – swear that his mother sat in the dock opposite and wish (I was not entirely sure that he believed this) that God would be merciful to her, he did so amid a torrent of whispering.

There was a great deal more of this. The precise circumstances of their marriage, the routines of the Chicago mission house, with Samways interrupting continually on the grounds that the evidence was prejudicial, had no bearing on the case, and nine times out of ten being slapped down by the judge, who did not, perhaps, seem such a benign old man as he had two days previously. There was a moment – a single, dreadful instant – when I thought that Alice was about to say something, that she intended to stand up in her stall and intervene, but in the end she thought better of it.

Then, with the air of a man who is going to perform some tremendous party piece, Nixon took out Drouett's photograph from his pocket, the photograph that has been used in all the press reports. This, Hanson confirmed, was the man who had come to see him in Duluth wishing to know about Alice.

NIXON: You must forgive me, Mr Hanson, if I ask a question that may cause you pain. The child. Your son. What age was he when the defendant – Mrs Hanson, the lady here – left Chicago?

HANSON: Six months. Seven months.

NIXON: And you were married – let me see, where is the piece of paper? – a year before. How long had you known Mrs Hanson – the lady here – before this date?

HANSON: It was God's will that this should happen. He that sent her to me.

NIXON: I don't doubt that it was. How long?

HANSON: Two weeks.

NIXON: So there is a possibility – you must forgive me for asking this, Mr Hanson, but it is necessary for me to establish the truth – that the child was not yours, but Mr Drouett's?'

Mr Samways, by this stage, was on his feet with a violent objection – what Hanson said was lost in the tumult – but Nixon had already announced that he had no further questions and resumed his seat. Shortly after this the day's business was concluded. I looked at Alice – the Sphinx would have been more forthcoming.

I was supposed to dine with Victor Cazalet at the House, but in the end sent a message to say I had been prevented. Victor has plenty of other friends he can dine with: he will not miss me. Besides, the nonentities who infest the place are depressing. One would hear more elevated debate at the Peckham Working Men's Club. Instead, I went for a long walk, trying to establish in my mind what the day had yielded up. It is all very suggestive and I think Nixon is playing a rather dangerous game. He wishes to give Drouett a motive. Well, that is fair enough. Everyone needs a motive. But the more he reveals about Drouett – his subterfuges &c – the more he risks encouraging sympathy for Alice. Those jurors will go back to their homes in Fulham thinking Drouett was a bad lot. They may think Alice killed him, but they will still think him a bad lot. This can only be a good sign.

Coming back from my walk to eat the delicious late supper Gaskin had prepared, I found a letter from X. A most disagreeable effusion it was. When I think of all I have done for that man – taking him to places where he certainly would not have been admitted on his own, putting up with indelicacies that a less fastidious person would have been revolted by – and now to present me with what is virtually a demand for money with menaces. Well!

I have an awful feeling that X may turn out to be my Mr Drouett.

15 February 1932

It is hard to believe that all this has been going on for only four days. The newspapers have swollen to extraordinary sizes in their coverage of it, with all kinds of people one has never heard of claiming Alice's friend-ship and urging their points of view. This morning when I was having breakfast – Gaskin is very solicitous of me, which is decent of him – Drawbell from the *Chronicle* telephoned to offer thirty guineas for a thousand words on 'Alice Keach as I knew her'. I declined.

Actually, I could write a perfectly excellent piece on this subject, but there is such a thing as selling one's friends. Besides, the *Sunday Times* would be cross.

To the Bailey promptly at nine. We have quite a little club going here in the press gallery now, all conducted with immense courtesy. 'Mr Nichols, will you take this seat?' &c. Rather nice. This morning the shrewd-looking man from the *Mail* brings me a copy of *Twenty-five* to sign, saying 'You seem to be making a profession of eternal youth. What measures are you taking to preserve it?'

I replied, 'No measures, only measurements.'

We began with half an hour of Mr Samways doing his best with the Rev. Hanson, but really there was very little he could do. The man has a story and he sticks to it. He had a wife, who left him, and after a decent interval, having had the first marriage annulled, he married another. It was as simple as that. No point in Samways implying devious motives to him – there was an occasional hint of this – as he clearly has none. Jurors always sympathetic to a poor clergyman, virtue being so much more admirable at one remove. Alice impassive in her box. Mr Nixon all the while champing at the bit, clearly itching to bring on someone yet more disagreeable and conclusive. Really, when all this is over, if it ever is, I shall have to write a sketch of Mr Nixon for one of the magazines. It would be very amusing, as well as allowing one to get a little of one's own back. In the end Nixon announces that he will call Miss Marjorie Hawkins. Barely a whisper in court: no one has the faintest idea who Miss Hawkins is. There emerges a tremulous little woman of what I believe is known as 'a certain age', very humble to anyone who addresses her, but clearly proud and animated by her value to all these great people. Alice looks at her, can't quite make out – so it appears – if she knows her, lowers her face once more.

Miss Hawkins, as I might have guessed from a showy ring or two on her fingers and a rather arch way of speaking, is connected with the theatrical profession. 'Dressed' the defendant when she appeared at the Globe before the war, and at other places, as well as accompanying her on a northern tour in 1910. 'What name did the defendant appear under?' Nixon wonders, and Miss Hawkins gives what is almost a little curtsy and says that it was 'Alice Hanson', at which Nixon nods gravely and makes a tiny note on his sheet, as if this revelation were of any significance at all. This, as I suspected, was the preamble to an investigation of Alice's theatrical days – none of it particularly injurious, continually interrupted by Samways on grounds of impertinence, but defended by Nixon and allowed by the judge as a necessary background to subsequent allegations. I could not decide whether Miss Hawkins, with her glinting fingers and little tosses of her head, was merely saying what she knew or had a score to settle. She has a way of rolling her fingers in her hand as she speaks that reminds me of Ottoline Morrell. Having been encouraged by Nixon to recollect numbers of bygone dramatic productions in which no one present could have taken any conceivable interest, she is then brought sharply up to the mark. Did the defendant – Miss Hanson, as she was then known – appear to have any dependent relatives? Miss Hawkins does a great rolling of her fingers and looks faintly alarmed. No, but . . . But what? Mr Nixon wonders. Well, Miss Hawkins suggests, occasionally Miss Hanson would despatch letters to an address in . . . might it have been Sussex? At least one of them had a banknote in it, as the letter, given to Miss Hawkins to take to the post, had not been properly sealed and the money had all but fallen out. Does Miss Hawkins recollect the name and address? No, Miss Hawkins does not. Did Miss Hanson ever say anything about these letters or the person to whom they were sent? No, she did not.

I could see that Mr Nixon was tired of Miss Hawkins by this point and happy to give her up. Mr Samways, on the other hand, was delighted to get her into his clutches. He had only two questions, he announced, and then Miss Hawkins, for whose presence here today he was sure that everyone was exceedingly grateful – here Miss Hawkins simpered, as if she thought she might be about to be presented with a bouquet – and then she would be at liberty to depart. Had she found Miss Hanson a considerate and generous employer? Why, yes, Miss Hawkins had, she said. And was it true that Miss Hawkins had been dismissed from the Liverpool Empire in the summer before the war when a certain sum of money had vanished from one of the dressing rooms? To this also Miss Hawkins miserably assented and slunk away.

It was thought in the press gallery that 'Jimmy' had handled this superbly. The jury will think Alice betrayed by a cunning little woman who should have been grateful to her &c.

At lunch the men at Wheeler's were saying that Alice would be called directly afterwards. Silas had sent a message from the *Sunday Times* saying that he wished to see me. This I ignored. One cannot all the time be at the beck and call of newspaper editors. Back in court there was a great stir – clerks hurrying this way and that – and it seemed as if the men from Wheeler's were right.

I make a point of looking at Alice directly as she takes the stand and noting down my impressions. She is wearing something in black – I dare say Mr Samways has advised against the least hint of frivolity. She looks, well, 'ghostly' is not quite the right word. Translucent, maybe. The kind of woman of whom, if one saw her on the cinematograph, one would say 'The fates hang over her' &c.

I dare say all this is very melodramatic, but I never saw anyone in a courtroom so detached from the world around her.

When I saw her I wanted to call out to her across the court, but of course one cannot do that sort of thing.

And so Mr Nixon began his cross-examination.

He wished, he said, with a nod to the judge and the jury and the newspaper artists who are taking off his portrait for the umpteenth time, to establish exactly what kind of person the defendant was, the life she had led, the circumstances that had foreshadowed this heinous and very regrettable crime in which a man whose motives might not have been those of unblemished knightly purity – he actually used these words – now lay dead through no fault of his own. That concluded, he would proceed to the event itself, with the aim of demonstrating the defendant's guilt. There followed half an hour of questions that you or I could have answered with no need for Mrs Keach. The number of her establishments. The number of rooms in those establishments. The kind of entertaining she did in London and elsewhere. The kind of people she entertained and was entertained by. All this Alice answered in a low voice, with occasional glances at Mr Samways, the latter burning to intervene but constrained by the fact that Mr Nixon's enquiries were so very innocuous.

All this was very tedious, but as it went on my respect for Mr Nixon increased by the moment. He was clearly building up to something and the realisation of this set the court agog. And then, at the close of a question as to whether Alice had three or four weekend parties a year at Castlemaine Court, he suddenly enquired: when had she first met Mr Drouett? One had an idea of some of this from things that had appeared in the newspapers, but the story, as here laid out, is simply sensational – there is no other word. And here Mr Nixon was playing his dangerous little game once more: withholding sympathy for Drouett – the deceased is never of any account in a murder trial – in pursuit of his motive. So Drouett had absconded from the house in De Smet, had he, Nixon enquired? Presumably this had left her with no very great opinion of him? No, it had not, Alice confirmed. Another Prosecuting Counsel would have hastened forward to Drouett's reappearance, but Mr Nixon was bent upon chronology. He was sorry to pry into personal matters in a way that might be thought indelicate – here a murmur ran round the court and the reporters bent over their notebooks – but there had been a child, had there not? Was that child Drouett's? Did Alice, in fact, know whether it was Drouett's child or not? Here an apoplectic objection from Mr Samways, but Alice's voice rising to say that she thought it was.

And here Mr Nixon very prudently stopped his questions about Drouett and went off in another direction. The boy had come with her to England, had he not, when she had commenced on her theatrical career? What had happened to him? He had been boarded out, Alice replied, at first in London, then in the country, in Sussex. I fancied that all this took an immense effort on her part. Had Alice loved the boy? Alice had. Had the course of Alice's career allowed her to see very much of him? I looked at Alice as this was said: her face was a mask. No doubt this was a painful question (I could happily have cut off Mr Nixon's head with one of the ancient pikestaffs that hang at the back of the court as he said this), Mr Keach having died nearly six years ago, plunging the defendant into the state of widowhood, but when had they married? And surely this was a bigamous marriage? What did Alice think about that? Alice gave the date as 1912. Various other questions about Mr Keach's wealth, habits, inclinations &c. What was Mr Keach's opinion of the boy? Alice could not answer. Had Mr Keach met the boy? Known about the boy? Again, no answer, but Mr Samways protesting furiously. Had it – he was sorry to ask this, truly he was – been a precondition of her relationship with Mr Keach that he had not known about the child? At this point Mr Samways did finally get the judge to intervene, but the damage was done.

16 February 1932

I have a new friend here in the press gallery: Mr Broughton. Mr Broughton reports for the *Star* and comes, I should say from his accent, originally from Wolverhampton.

Mr Broughton and I are extremely intimate. Already I have heard about his son, who is 'in' the motor trade, his daughter, who is a manicurist, and the family home at Croydon.

Actually, I have an ulterior motive in cultivating Mr Broughton's acquaintance. I want to know what the readers of popular newspapers think about the trial. Mr Broughton, after consulting his wife, is adamant that the business of the child is greatly undermining public sympathy, for as he explains, 'the women won't stand for it'. Either some plausible explanation has to be vouchsafed, or Mr Samways will have to find a conclusive way of demonstrating that Alice did not strike the fatal blow, did so by accident or in self-defence. That is what Mr Broughton says.

This morning everyone seems out of sorts. The judge is querulous, Mr Samways subdued. Alice barely raises her head. Mr Nixon, whose voice has already begun to crack, asks her about Drouett's journey to England. Was she surprised to see him? Yes. Astounded, even? Yes. How had he known where to find her? He had apparently seen her picture in a Society paper. Did he say that he had come to England especially to see her? No, he had said that he was on holiday. Did he seem in want of money? No. And yet she had given him a thousand pounds. Why was that? She wished to contribute to the expenses of his return. And that would cost a thousand pounds? No answer. What had been Mrs Keach's reaction to Drouett's appearance at her house? Had she wished to see him? No, she had not. Why not? She had nothing to say to him. Did Drouett speak of the child? Yes. How had she answered? That it was none of his business. She had not wanted to see Drouett, but there had been an occasion when she entertained him to dinner. Why was that? She had felt sorry for him. Had Drouett asked her directly for money? Yes. How much? He had asked her for fifty pounds. But she had given him a thousand? (Objection from Mr Samways, overruled by the judge.) Yes. And then, despite his thousand pounds and his promise to return to America, Drouett had arrived on her doorstep at Castlemaine Court. If she felt such hostility to him, why had she admitted him? Would it not have been simpler to bar the door? Had she not agreed to see him merely to prevent the possibility of scandal among her guests?

One has to admire Mr Nixon for the way he did this. What he is saying is, in effect: 'Here is a base, worthless man, impelled by base, worthless motives to blackmail a woman he seduced when young and then deserted. So base and worthless, in fact, that she is driven to kill him.' The more one sympathises with Alice, consequently, the more one accepts the possibility that she is a murderess.

Significantly, when he comes to the interview in Alice's room at the Court, he has much less to say. It is as if he is signalling to members of the jury that he – and they – already know, or may surmise, enough.

NIXON: The deceased was found with his throat cut, the weapon later identified as a paperknife, found in your hand. Do you deny this?

ALICE: No.

NIXON: Did you strike him with it?

ALICE: No. At least I do not remember doing so.

NIXON: A man is found dead of a wound sustained by a weapon which you are discovered to be holding. How do you account for it?

ALICE: I remember that there was an altercation, but I do not remember striking him.

NIXON: An altercation. Why was there an altercation?

ALICE: It is difficult to explain. I had ... offered him money to go away. He said that this was all very well, but how could I know he would not behave as before?

Why, Nixon then enquires, if he were blackmailing her, should she not have taken the matter to the police? Alice says – she is not looking at Nixon as she does so – that she did not wish to. At which Nixon changes tack. The murder weapon, he reminds us, has been examined by Mr Hurst the forensics man, and found to contain a number of her fingerprints around the blade, but very few of Drouett's. How does she account for that? Alice says that, naturally, she had been using the knife before Drouett's arrival. Nonsense, says Nixon, Drouett's fingerprints were put there as he tried to defend himself, as, roused to a state of fury, she attempted to murder him.

There are no further questions! I can think of a dozen I should like to ask.

19 February 1932

The most annoying weekend imaginable! Really, there are times when one would like to give all this up and retire to the country to cultivate one's garden. But then there is one's public to think of, not to mention certain amenities that only London can offer.

Anyway, I had Gaskin call me at seven on Saturday, breakfasted at eight and devoted the entire morning to my report for the *Sunday Times*. One cannot skimp this kind of work if one is to make a success of it, so I did not. Full descriptions of Mr Nixon and Mr Samways, the public gallery &c. No one in any doubt, of course, as to where one's sympathies lay. Finished by twelve and had it sent round to the paper by messenger, and then out to luncheon with Mrs Reginald Heber in Bryanston Square. And this is where the trouble began. Mrs Reginald Heber excessively moral. Said that if this were true, could not forgive Mrs Keach for abandoning her child, the poor baby &c. This coming from a woman who, to my knowledge, visits her eldest boy at Eton once a year and sends him to his grandmother in Perthshire for the holidays! A woman who, if Alice had not taken her up, would still be married to that absurd Major Earp and living in the Fulham Road! I said merely that when the trial was over and a judgment pronounced, Alice would know who her friends were.

Dreary evening at the Bat, thinking that if one has friends, and those friends know where one is likely to be, then really they should make an effort to come and see one occasionally.

Then on Sunday morning, my report . . . Really! I have been writing for the press for a dozen years, but the treatment I have received on this occasion beggars belief. Of course, Silas could not very well alter what I had written and the descriptions of Alice in court, the nobility of her bearing &c, were there as I had set them down. Everything else, though, had been blatantly geared to suggest that she would be found guilty. A flaring headline that demanded: IS THIS THE FACE OF MURDER? A dreadful photograph, taken at some party, that makes her look foolish and calculating at the same time. And my name barely visible on the margin of the page.

The only consolation is that some of the other papers are worse.

The *Express* has engaged a psychologist from the Roehampton Clinic to cover the trial, who maintains that Alice has a 'classic criminal profile', whatever that means.

Thought about writing to Silas, then thought better of it. I shall write to Lord Kemsley instead.

Finally, to round things off, coming back from a solitary cocktail at the Ritz bar, I discovered X once again loitering on my doorstep. Happily, all the fight had gone out of him. When I asked what he intended to do, he said he thought of going to America, where there might be an opening in publicity work. I said I thought this was an excellent idea.

I decided to give him £50, which would be money well spent if he really does go to America.

On Monday morning, arriving at the court at 8.45 – again, I have Gaskin to thank for this punctuality – I have another little conversation with Mr Broughton. Mr Broughton very sharp and spruce – says he spent Sunday at his mother-in-law's, which always gives him an appetite for the week's work. Of the feeling that Samways has been dug into a pit from which he cannot very easily escape, that Nixon – of whom Broughton has a high opinion – has been very cunning. 'You see, he can work the sympathy vote for all he's worth, Mr Nichols, he can prove that this Drouett was a bad 'un from the off, but what does that do other than give her a reason for killing him? After all, a crime's a crime.' Mr Broughton thinks that Samways's only chance is to strike out on a bold and original new line of his own. 'And he'll have to forget about the child,' Mr Broughton says. 'The child don't explain what happened in that room. Only she can do that.'

My good opinion of Mr Broughton is raised yet higher by the fact that this is exactly what Samways proceeds to do. He begins – all lawyers have to do this – by declaring that never in his experience has a case been so misrepresented, that never has a woman who wished to do good in the face of extreme provocation been so harshly treated, that never has a case been subject to such misguided speculation and base insinuation.

There is a good deal more of this. The public gallery, the press and – it seems to me – Mr Nixon rather puzzled as to what is going on. More puzzlement when Mr Samways starts to bring on his witnesses. He has Lady Carmody to testify to Alice's good nature, her charities, 'her stealthy beneficent acts' as Lady C puts it. He has Miss Jeffries, Alice's *chef du cabinet*, brought up to salute her employer's munificence. He asks her about Drouett, whom Miss Jeffries is clearly itching to disparage, but never gives her the opportunity, wants merely to establish the number of Drouett's visits to the house, his reception and so on. Maslin the butler to confirm this. Did Mrs Keach seem alarmed by Drouett's presence? No, Maslin says, the mistress treated him like any other of her guests. A woman I don't know, present at the dinner Drouett had attended, to remark that he seemed to enjoy himself and contributed to a discussion of hunting.

Still no indication of where this might go. Samways making an elegant little summary of all this to the jury. They may have been led to believe that the deceased was a blackmailer, from whose solicitations the defendant shrank, but here she was inviting him to her home, to dinner, treating him as an equal in orbits where he could not ordinarily have looked to move. All this despite the fact that Drouett had abandoned her many years before and his effrontery – well, many people might consider it that – in presenting himself at her door after so long a time. All this very well done and evincing sympathy for Alice, but, I think, of a different kind.

But of course, Samways continued, his real interest – and the jurors' interest – would be fixed upon what happened in that room at Castlemaine Court, into which Drouett had burst in such an untimely manner. In particular, he wished the jury to know, or if not to know to consider, the deceased's state of mind when he made that fatal interruption. He had stressed the defendant's kindness to Drouett, which he would later have her confirm. But with kindness came prudence and circumspection. He then produced Mr Barnes, a private detective employed by Aberconway to observe Drouett's movements over a period of several weeks. Mr Barnes, who looked as if he should be telling jokes on the halls, confirmed that Drouett had made several changes of address, at one point descending to a slum in Somers Town, only leaving it for long, inconclusive walks to the docks and the eastern part of the City. Nixon, who had been listening to all this with keen interest, bobbed up to ask Mr Barnes if Drouett had been aware of this 'hounding' and was shushed by the judge. Mr Barnes, closely questioned as to the deceased's habits, volunteered that he had seen him once in a café where he appeared to be 'talking to himself'. Samways gave a sharp look at the judge, and had a maidservant who opened the door to Drouett once to attest to his great nervousness and agitation, and suggested that the deceased was perhaps of an excitable and volatile temperament.

Once during all of this I looked at Alice and am certain that she caught my eye.

Later. Bumped into Peter Spencer-Churchill again. More distrait than ever. Says he knows someone who knows Samways, and that she is sunk in gloom, thinks she has no future, even if acquitted. Also that Spilsbury, the Home Office pathologist, has become involved, may be called. This I thought significant. Went to bed more cheerful than for many a day.

Later. Wrote another note to Alice – *This is to say that your friends are cheering you on! Love from Beverley* – and posted it to Holloway. Perhaps some kind wardress will let her see it? I have a feeling that a women's prison must be worse than a men's. I have a horrid vision of bars of carbolic soap and lesbian ladies lurking in the shower cubicles.

20 February 1932

I am thoroughly exhausted, of course, from too much work and worry. Also, neglecting other parts of my life. Messages from Cochran, Ivor, Noël &c all unanswered. But this cannot be helped.

Great excitement in the court, as Spilsbury is indeed to be called. An impressive figure. Stares at Nixon from the box as if daring him to address him. His testimony took nearly all the morning, but quite riveting. Mr Broughton, at my side, lost in admiration, kept making little ticks in the margin of his notebook. Mr Samways's attitude properly humble. They were very grateful to Mr Spilsbury for sparing his time, and for getting up the facts of the case. Mr Spilsbury had visited the scene of the incident and examined the weapon. He had not, unfortunately, been able to examine the deceased, whose body had already been interred, but he had seen the surgeon's report, and the autopsy. Would he care to comment on how the deceased, Mr Drouett, in whom everyone was so interested, had met his unfortunate end?

Mr Spilsbury said that the case exhibited a number of distinct peculiarities and that he had made a special study of it. The deceased had certainly been killed by a single blow to the throat, which had punctured his carotid artery. He would submit that such a blow, to be fatal, need not be delivered with any great force. A glancing, or an accidental, contact at such a vulnerable spot would have the same effect. (Mr Nixon was positively desperate to interrupt, but could find no opportunity. Besides, the judge, interested in what Spilsbury had to say, would not look at him.) He had examined the fingerprints left on the weapon with some care. Their evidence was by no means decisive. Certainly, there was a preponderance of the defendant's and a smaller number of the deceased's, but those of the defendant suggested that the weapon had been grasped very firmly, that the deceased's hand may well have been clasping the defendant's as she held it. Further, he had examined the police surgeon's report of the physical examination of the defendant conducted a few hours later. This had noted an abrasion on the defendant's upper torso, consistent, if not with the blade of the knife itself, then with the mark of a signet ring, or something of that sort. He gathered that such a ring had been removed from the right hand of the deceased. He could not exclude the possibility of the defendant attempting to harm herself and being restrained by the deceased, or an accidental blow delivered by either party. It was, he concluded, impossible to determine the force with which the blow had been delivered. The lack of any ancillary bruising to the throat and windpipe of the deceased suggested that only a small amount of force had been used.

All this was heard with the greatest fascination. Mr Nixon tried a few questions, but was cast aside almost negligently by the force of Spilsbury's expertise. Subsequently – it was by then half an hour or so beyond the lunch hour – some fine legal point arose on which Nixon, Samways and the judge crossly conferred, and proceedings were halted for the afternoon. I took a cab home through the foggy streets and relieved some of my feelings by writing a letter to Silas saying that I could not possibly produce another report under such conditions and that they had better get someone else.

Later. Came home from supper at Doris Castlerosse's to find a package containing a gold cigarette case and a note from X saying that he fears I have misjudged him. The plan to go to America a mistake. May we meet &c. Touched, in spite of myself. If there is one thing I pride myself on, it is an ability to play these situations with a straight bat. And there is such a thing as charm.

21 February 1932

A polite note from Silas, regretting my decision &c, and offering a signed column for the next three weeks at twenty guineas. I expect Lord Kemsley has intervened. I shall write a curt note of refusal to Silas, in the hope that Lord Kemsley will be further annoyed with him.

The newspapers now taking a different line, several addressing themselves to the question of what shall happen to Alice if she is found to be not guilty. What would her place in Society then be? Mrs Lees-Hennessy is quoted as saying that she doubted very much if she could sit down to dinner with a woman who had killed somebody, even by accident. As Mrs Lees-Hennessy is the kind of woman who would run across Lowndes Square barefoot with a pack of wild beasts snapping at her heels if the result was an invitation to dinner, this must be one of the most hypocritical remarks I have ever encountered.

Apparently yesterday's adjournment touched upon a request – I am not sure from whom – that the jury should be allowed to see the scene of the crime. This was agreed, hence the suspension of the proceedings for a further day.

I am not sure whether I approve of this. A mean-spirited juror, examining Alice's home, would be confirmed in his prejudices – unconscionable luxury &c. Even those disposed in her favour may be taken aback. How hard Alice worked for her position, the constant pressures to which a great hostess is subject, quite beyond this kind of person, I always find.

Spent the day writing odds and ends, and making notes for my new book, which I really think will be excellent.

22 February 1932

As expected, Alice takes the stand. She does not merely look tired. She looks *ill*. It is really quite intolerable that she should be treated in this way, but apparently a request from Samways for a further adjournment on medical grounds was refused. And this when a coster woman accused of petty theft would be allowed to stay comfortably in bed until she felt better. Monstrous!

Today she is dressed in grey, with what looks like one of Sophie Huntercombe's hats. It is a very elegant hat, as I shall tell Sophie when I see her.

Mr Broughton very excited. Says his wife 'has a feeling' that all will be well. When I contest this, he names half a dozen murder trials in which his wife's instinct has been proved right.

A nasty man who wrote a very savage piece in today's *News Chronicle* is given the cold shoulder in the press gallery, which I take as a good omen.

Alice: mournful, resigned, chic, submissive, *ethereal*.

Everyone agog to see how Mr Samways would commence his interrogation. He began by announcing that there were certain matters relating to Alice's former career that had been misrepresented and the truth of which would be vital to the jury in their understanding of the case (the judge, I think, has decided that he likes Mr Samways and does not like Mr Nixon – certainly, Mr Nixon's star seems to be in the descendant and the judge loses no opportunity of shushing him). Consequently, Mr Samways spends the best part of an hour taking

Alice, with infinite courtesy and good manners, through her early life: the meeting with Drouett, her marriage to Hanson, her flight, first years in England. To nearly every misdemeanour that has been imputed – short of the murder – she readily admits: the taking of the money, for example, which she represents as the only means of escaping a situation hateful to her. Mr Samways helps in this by painting a sentimental picture of a young woman 'cast out into the wilderness and far from the bosom of her family'. I am not sure I quite agree with this: what strikes me is Alice's resourcefulness, audacity &c. The business of the child is sketched over in a manner not very satisfactory to anyone. I confess I could not make out whether Alice had kept it from her for reasons connected to her profession, her marriage, or both, or whether some other agency had supervened.

Alice looking so fatigued and unwell that at one point a chair is brought.

And then, the heart of the matter. What had been Alice's reaction when Drouett had first arrived at her door in Lowndes Square? She had been very shocked. She could not imagine why he might want to see her. That being the case, why had she not simply refused? She did not think that she could do that. Why not? Because of their former association. Did he at any point say what his motive was? No. Did he ask for money? At one point he had asked for £50. Why then had she given him twenty times that? She thought that it might encourage him to return to America. Did she regard this as blackmail? No. That is, she could not understand what it was that Drouett wanted. He seemed to wish to be in her company. That was the best she could say.

Mr Samways's face at this point really ought to have been photographed and shown to the young men trying for jobs at Elstree as an example of how *not* to assume a sardonic expression. How had she felt when she learned of his presence at Castlemaine Court? That he had no business to visit her there. And yet she did not refuse to see him? There were guests present. It was easier than to send him away. How did he appear? He seemed frightened of something? Frightened! (Another tremendous sardonic glance.) What of? He kept looking about him. As if he thought she would not be pleased to see him. And was she not? No, she was angry. There was a quarrel? She had offered him more money. To leave England and not return. He had said: what would happen if he took the money and did not go?

SAMWAYS: Why were you so anxious that he should go? You say that he did not seem to know what he wanted.

ALICE: There were things he said that made me believe that he meant me harm.

SAMWAYS: But what harm could he do to you? You feared that he might attempt to discredit you?

ALICE: Yes, I suppose so. Yes.

SAMWAYS: And this altercation that began between you, how did this come about?

ALICE: I was holding the paperknife. I suppose he thought I meant to strike him with it.

SAMWAYS: And did you?

ALICE: I never hurt anyone in my life. I did not mean to strike him.

SAMWAYS: And yet he was found dead in your room. Can you account for what happened?

ALICE: I remember him pulling at the knife. I think I feared he would strike me with it.

SAMWAYS: Mr Spilsbury has suggested that you may have tried to harm yourself.

ALICE: Mr Spilsbury is wrong.

SAMWAYS: What was your reaction when you saw Drouett fall to the ground?

ALICE: I could not imagine why he had fallen. I could not see that it was anything to do with me.

SAMWAYS: Were you aware that you had the knife in your hand?

ALICE: No. I remember looking at it and wondering how it had come to be there.

SAMWAYS: You do not regard yourself as responsible for his death?

ALICE: No, not at all. No.

SAMWAYS: Thank you. That concludes my defence, Your Honour.

---

23 February 1932

The *Sunday Times*, I discover, has employed Gilbert Frankau to write about the trial in my place. He will write an unctuous piece, full of the most ghastly sentimentalities and misrepresentations. Really, Silas will make himself the laughing stock of Fleet Street if he goes on like this.

Yesterday I went to supper in Bloomsbury – *not* a place one is generally found – and there, of all people, was H. G. Wells. I do not think Wells likes me. But he was interesting about the trial, which he has followed avidly. Says that only four things could logically have happened: one, that Alice killed Drouett meaning to do it; two, that she killed him not meaning to do it either in self-defence or by accident; three (unlikely) that he killed himself; four (even more unlikely) that some unknown person did it. However, as Wells pointed out, this allows for a variety of judgments, ranging from manslaughter to outright acquittal.

The newspapers, I notice, markedly more sympathetic. Alice's charitable work made much of. Disgreeable stories of Drouett – mention of a woman who bore an illegitimate child of his and whom he then abandoned – imported from America.

Naturally, wild horses could not have dragged me away from the Bailey this morning. But imagine my horror to find, when I arrived there, that the most spiteful and vindictive trick had been played on me, and that Silas has had my pass to the press gallery revoked! He is, of course, perfectly within his rights to do, but as an example of mean-spiritedness this beggars belief. The public gallery was by this time packed to the rafters. Nice Mr Broughton, coming up the gallery steps as I was arguing with the usher, offered to convey messages, which was very decent of him, but I said no, clearly I was fated to follow these final throes in the newspapers just like everyone else.

And so, when one of my dearest friends was anxiously awaiting her fate and I should have been there to support her, I found myself at home making more notes for my wretched book, which I am sure now has no hope of success, and nervously listening out for the telephone.

At lunchtime Peter Spencer-Churchill rang. Said situation not too bad. Closing speeches on both sides dull. Mr Nixon cold and insistent. Samways playing the self-defence card for all it was worth. Alice gloomy in the dock. The judge, as I had anticipated, offering the jury the three options of murder, manslaughter or acquittal on grounds of self-defence.

I do not know how I got through that afternoon. Twice I decided I would take a walk around the park, put on hat, coat and gloves and reached the corner of the street, only to turn back. I was terrified to use the telephone lest Peter should ring again, as he had kindly promised to do. In the end I drank three whiskies and soda, thus breaking a rule about drinking in the afternoons, but could see from the look Gaskin gave me as he brought in the siphons that it was the only thing to do in the circumstances.

Finally, at 5.30, when I had given up hope, Peter rang again to say that they had brought in a manslaughter verdict. The judge allowed the provocation she had suffered and the unusual circumstances, and has sent her to prison for five years.

I suppose I should be grateful that she has been spared death. But another part of me weeps to think of this brave and noble woman stitching blankets, or whatever it is that female prisoners are compelled to do, in the company of a lot of costerwomen from the Mile End Road who have poisoned their husbands.

And yet I am grateful. Very.

Later. Woke up at 6 a.m. in a foul hotel where I went with X somewhere near Waterloo. Why does one do these things, I wonder? Even at this hour the foyer was awash with Levantine-looking gentlemen busily ordering taxis. Slunk back to Stanhope Gate – Gaskin, opening the door, pointedly avoided my eye – and found the newspapers lying on the table saying that Alice is seriously ill, has been taken from the prison infirmary to the Middlesex and that the gravest fears have been expressed for her health.

27

Flights

Out in the middle channels the waves were not so choppy, and it was possible to stand on deck looking out above the rail and the green swell that rose vertiginously beyond. In the distance long, indeterminate islands, looking curiously like pieces of papier mâché, lay set out beneath the brooding sky. Mr Schmiegelow had discovered that the back part of the boat smelt of diesel from the engine and the front part of the boat of cocoanut oil from the hold. Accordingly he was standing at the back of the boat with his hat pulled down over his head, smoking a Russian cigarette and shooing the smoke away with his hand when it threatened to blow back into his eyes. His secretary, rather extravagantly dressed in a fur coat, with her hair drawn up under a gay little cap, came picking her way through the wasteland of loose spars and coiled rope ends that lay across the upper deck towards him.

'It's nearly dinner time. You ought to come down.'

'Why should I want to have dinner?'

'You can't sit staring at those pictures all evening. Even if they are rather lovely. Anyway, the captain's promised to sing.'

'In which language, I wonder?'

'I think he's a White Russian. That's what the waiter told me the other night.'

Mr Schmiegelow smiled and took the cigarette out of his mouth. 'Really, it was a mistake to smoke this. It is not a preventative against seasickness at all.'

'That Swede who said he was a whisky salesman told me how nice my coat was again. That makes three times.'

Mr Schmiegelow thought about the whisky salesman and the fur coat. Then something else struck him and he said, 'I felt sorry for Mrs Keach. I liked her. I am sure she did not mean to do what she did. There must have been some mistake.'

'You ought to come,' she said, taking his arm. 'Or the captain will be disappointed.'

'England . . .' Mr Schmiegelow began mildly, but whatever he said was lost in a roar of surf that beat against the side of the boat. In another moment or two they went below.

'Good evening?'

'So-so.'

'See anyone interesting?'

'Just the usual people . . . Brenda was at the Kit-Kat. She said to say hello.'

'Stout girl, Brenda. Was she with David?'

'All that's been over for nearly a month, I thought you knew . . . Patrick, that policeman came round again this morning.'

'I thought we'd agreed that I'd told them everything I knew. About the gramophones and so on.'

'I think he wants you to make another statement.'

'This is ridiculous. I'm a chartered accountant. I can't be expected to know the proper price to sell a gramophone for.'

'Apparently there's three thousand pounds owing or something to the banks Mr Schmiegelow was borrowing money from.'

'Is there?'

'Yes.'

'And then nobody has the least idea where he went.'

'Don't they?'

The Hendersons regarded each other uncertainly. In the last month their lives had not run on an entirely satisfactory course. At least one Society column had taken to referring to Constance as the 'Gin and It Girl'. Just now they were living on some money Patrick had borrowed from his cousin.

'Damn!' Constance said, beginning to open the post. 'The Peter Jones bill is £32.16s. I was sure we gave them some money last month.'

'I've been thinking,' Patrick said. 'Mummy said that Uncle Hector was looking for someone to help him manage the estate. You know, pay the ghillies and so on. Why don't we go up there for a bit and stay in one of the cottages?'

'Isn't it absolutely miles from anywhere?'

'Well, they say Perth is rather nice, at least if it isn't raining. And it's not far from Nina's castle . . . But would you mind, not being in London?'

'Actually, darling, London's begun to get rather on my nerves. What with all this business about Alice, and Mr Schmiegelow and everything.'

'Has it? Well, I'll write to Uncle Hector then ... Oh, and Simon Macpherson rang for you.'

'Did he ... ? How far did you say it was from Nina's castle?'

'About forty miles.'

Outside the taxis surged round the corner of the square.

*

As the train bore south through the declining afternoon, and the Spanish frontier grew nearer, a curious thing happened. There was nothing to indicate who we were, or our eventual destiny, but almost by a kind of osmosis something of our purpose seemed to have communicated itself to the world beyond the dirt-smeared window. At Perpignan, where we halted for a while and hawkers went up and down the carriages selling fruit and stale patisserie, I saw a middle-aged woman staring at me from the platform. It was a look of absolute contempt, as if she knew very well what I was doing and why I was here, and hated me for it. Then, as the train pulled out into the open country beyond the town, there came a different kind of recognition. Half a dozen times a labourer working in the fields, his outline silhouetted in the fading light, would stand stiff-backed against the orange sun and, clenching his fist, give the anti-Fascist salute. The dark-haired man with the Birmingham accent on the far side of the carriage, with whom I had several times got into conversation in the twelve hours since we had left Paris, watched these signals with interest. 'Solidarity,' he said more than once.

There was a kitbag lying on the floor between us, from which during the course of the journey he had produced bars of chocolate and packets of sandwiches. Now he reached into it and took out a bottle of beer, so dark-coloured that the contents looked like ink, jerked off the cap on the metal edge of the seat and waved it in front of me. 'To Spain,' he said. It was the last week of 1936. Franco's army had reached Zaragoza and I was bound for the Aragon Front.

To Spain.

After the great days of hogpen were over, of all things, I took up politics. There was a little money remaining to me after the crash – a thousand or so a year – and with this I determined that I would make myself useful.

335

I had an idea that the Labour Party, if it meant business, should ally itself with Science, that what went on in a laboratory was at least as important to human progress as what went on in the Houses of Parliament, and to this end I sat on committees with Arthur Ponsonby and Mrs Webb, addressed meetings of the Socialist Science Society and, as I now think, did no good to anyone at all, least of all myself, a person whom – I must be honest about this – I very much wanted to help.

My uncle was amused by these affiliations. 'Sittin' about in people's drawing rooms that ought to know better [he meant the people, not the drawing rooms] talking a lot of hot air,' he sniffed. I took the hint. To him the exploitation of hogpen was much more of a symbol of human advancement than the pamphlets issued by the Socialist Science Society. 'Put a man in a decent suit, give him ten bob to spend and tell him he ought to be proud because his house has two rooms more than the one next door,' he once told me. 'That's progress, Ralph.'

He lived in the north in those days, somewhere near Thirsk, and I rarely saw him. When I did it was to detect an optimism that, blighted by circumstance, had now become narrowly fantastic. He sat on the boards of three or four companies that swam in and out of solvency, and made frequent fruitless applications to the Patent Office. Sometimes a friend made in the great days of the selling of hogpen and the house in Eaton Square would look him up. While he luxuriated in these attentions, my uncle was also saddened by them, for they reminded him of the person he had once been and – this in spite of the optimism – could never be again.

He was, I think, slightly disapproving of me and the path I had taken, while allowing that the special circumstances of my case demanded a good deal of indulgence.

I had not told him I was going to Spain.

I cannot remember the precise moment during the trial – five years ago now, but still very vivid to me, like a cinema reel endlessly replaying in my head – when I found out the truth about myself and this annoys me. It's odd that I should recall Elsie and Edna banging out the carpets in the square beyond the kitchen garden, and Mrs Custance's face as she got into the cab at Norwich station, but not the vital juncture when, as it were, the final pieces of the jigsaw of my life fell into place. It was as if – then and for some weeks later – I were walking through a series of grand, high-ceilinged rooms, full of noise and confusion, with people running towards me to say words that I could not understand, and the thing that I really wanted bobbing out of reach before me through the throng and never quite allowing itself to be pinned down.

I could think of no one to tell except my uncle – and Avril.

'Gracious,' she said. 'You *have* had a shock. Think of it. Your ma – your mother . . .' – Avril became less refined when she was excited – 'being Alice Keach. What on earth must it feel like?'

'I don't know. It's as if . . . as if you'd been searching for something for years and all the time it was standing on your sideboard waiting for you to pick it up.'

'Do you remember anything about her at all?'

'I don't know. If I try very hard I can remember being in a park. Somewhere here – in London, that is. With a woman in a pink dress. A blue dress. Who knows what kind of a dress it was?'

'Gracious,' Avril said.

'But she might hang,' Avril said at one point in the conversation.

'You shouldn't say things like that.'

'No, I shouldn't, should I?' She was a nice, friendly girl and I felt better for talking to her.

Not long after this Avril told me that she was going to get married to a man who owned a repair garage in Mortimer Street.

My uncle, when the news was brought to him, was incredulous but not, I thought, particularly inquisitive nor taken aback. 'Alice Keach!' he said. 'Who'd have thought it?' It was the week in which he signed away his last, lingering interest in hogpen. 'Explains a lot,' he said, a little later. What it explained I could never get out of him. He was still negotiating with one of the many banks to which he and Atry had owed money, and could perhaps be forgiven his self-absorption.

In the absence of anyone else, I took my deductions to Miss Jeffries. It was a curious interview, conducted in the drawing room at Lowndes Square, on the sixth or seventh day of the trial – the morning newspapers lay on the table between us – in which Miss Jeffries wavered, in a way that was wonderful to see, between what she knew were her obligations to me and what she imagined was her duty to her employer, without ever, or so it seemed to me, connecting the two in her mind. She knew – not every-thing, but a great deal. She knew of Mrs Custance and the transaction that had taken me to Loftholdingswood, and even produced from somewhere a letter from that lady. She advanced the theory that it must have been Mrs

Custance, on her own initiave, who had given me the name Ralph Bentley. She did not believe that Guy Keach had ever heard of my existence. What she did not know were the circumstances that had led to my transfer, unilaterally and without explanation, to the cottage on the Intwood Road. Had my mother simply ceased to support me? Given Mrs Custance a free hand? Had she, when it came to it, been just as discountenanced by Mrs Custance's death as I had? None of these questions could Miss Jeffries answer and, although I believe that there were certain things she did not tell me, I do not think that she deceived me.

It was my uncle, still able even in his decline to bring off feats of this kind, who arranged, through some highly placed sympathiser, for me to see her. Alice was by that time – it was a fortnight after the trial – very ill, lying in a room at the Middlesex Hospital with a nurse in permanent attendance, but lucid and able to greet me with a gesture of her hand. They had told her who I was, but the look that she gave me as I sat by her bedside was quite inscrutable. Her face was altogether wasted, but it struck me that I resembled her, and that an onlooker would have known that we were mother and son, and this thought gave me the oddest sensation. Once or twice the nurse administered oxygen through a mask.

'So you're here, Ralph . . .' she said and I nodded.

'Odd you should have been called Ralph. Why should they have called you that?'

'Perhaps they thought Asa wasn't English enough.'

'There was a clergyman came before,' she said. 'Wanted to say a prayer.'

'Mr Chatterley?' I wondered, remembering the mission in Canning Town.

'No, not him. A bishop, this one was.'

The nurse said, unsentimentally, 'You'll not get much sense out of her, I'm afraid. The poor gentleman who came this morning said he couldn't make out a thing.'

All the time I kept my eyes fixed on her. Her face had lost its texture, turned gaunt and weather-beaten, so that her eyes became conspicuous by virtue of their brightness. They were blue eyes, like cornflowers.

'Edie said you were coming,' she said, and I wondered for a moment if she really did know who I was and the nature of the bridge between us.

'Edie's been good to me. Did you know, I've known her twenty-five years? And she might have hated me once.' She was not quite coherent, but it seemed to me that the gaps between her words were caused by sheer bafflement. 'Edie couldn't act, you see, and I took her place from her. There's many people wouldn't forgive that.

'Somebody will have to take care of Edie,' she said.

It occurred to me that she saw things I could not see and that in all probability she believed Miss Jeffries was there in the room between us.

'Do you know' she said suddenly, 'the last time I saw you? Before now, I mean. It was in a park – Hyde Park or St James's – and you were about five years old. I had you up for the day to show you about. And now you're what – twenty-seven? What *must* you think of it all?'

'I remember the day in the park,' I said. 'I can't remember you – or not much – but I can remember the day.' Something else stirred in the recesses of memory and I knew that the picture on the mantelpiece of the Loftholdingswood parlour had been hers.

'I was always going to find you . . . Ralph,' she said, and I realised that in her confusion she had been about to call me by my baptismal name. 'And now I have. Or you've found me. What are we to do about it, eh?'

'I don't know that there's anything we can do.'

'You look like him – a little,' she said.

'Like my father?'

'Like George. Do you know,' she said, with unexpected fierceness, 'he was the first man I ever saw? The very first.' I saw that whatever hatred she had felt for him had been anaesthetised by long-dormant memory.

'What was he like?' I asked.

'What was he like? What is anyone like? Now I think of it, he was the only one I ever cared for. He had a way with him, you see. He made you feel that you were worth the trouble he'd taken with you. Not that he was worth anything. But still . . .'

'Poor precious thing,' said the nurse affably. 'I don't suppose she knows who she is. You'll be wanting a cup of tea, I expect.'

She rambled a little about her life. It was like looking down upon a great, shadowy concourse of people and seeing an individual head every so often illuminated by a dazzling flash of light. Sometimes I think the people baffled her and she stared at them through dense, obscuring clouds, trying to puzzle out their exact significance.

She pronounced Guy Keach's name half a dozen times, but whether in sorrow or reproach I could not tell.

Eventually her voice settled itself into a low, indistinct monologue, from which occasional phrases rose ominously to the surface. 'Not to be pitied, Ralph, not to be pitied,' she said more than once.

'Why not?'

'He could never understand,' she said and I supposed that the 'he' meant Drouett. 'How one never wants to be reminded . . . One never wants to be reminded . . . I don't suppose he meant any harm, but one never . . . wants . . .'

What she did not want to be reminded of I could not persuade her to tell me.

'You mustn't mind me when I'm gone,' she said once, with painful clarity. 'For I never minded you when I ought to have done.

'You've a *life* ahead of you,' she said, with a very clear indication that she had not. And I suppose that this was the moment when I wished that she should live.

You will think it very foolish, but a part of me had planned a future for the two of us, five years on. I am not sure, at this remove, what it consisted of, but I think I saw a house somewhere in the country, entirely detached from the corroding influence of the past, where some of the interior damage of our lives might have been repaired. And curiously, this thought persisted, so that, even after she died, a week later, I was still afflicted by these odd dreams of a sunlit terrace, a pillar or two of Cotswold stone and a female figure rising from the table to greet me.

When she had been dead for a week, Miss Jeffries sent a brown-paper package. It contained a photograph taken in the backyard of a small house in the American Midwest, where she stood among a group of people gathered around a horse-drawn buggy, a pendant bracelet, which Miss Jeffries believed had come with her from America, and a bundle of letters, sent to her at an address in Northumberland and mostly dating from the early 1920s, from individuals, institutions and government bodies disclaiming all knowledge of my existence and whereabouts.

That is all, really.

By this time the train had reached Banyuls-sur-mer, the last halt before the frontier. The fields had gone; on the left was a view of the Mediterranean – grey and untidy in the fading light – and there was the sound of gulls skirling above the telephone wires. I sat back on my haunches, unlit cigarette between my fingers, looking at the pair of boots

– hobnailed, with huge khaki tongues and already blistering my feet – I had bought in Paris two days before, relishing the odd feeling of displacement.

The dark-haired man with the Birmingham accent looked suddenly less hopeful, as if he doubted the value of what he was doing, feared exposure, humiliation and disgrace. One foot perched uneasily on his kitbag, he said, 'Think they'll let us through?'

'Bound to. There's that letter from Pollitt, remember, not to mention what they told us in Paris.'

'After all,' he said, 'we're here to help.'

It was true: we were there to help.

The train was gathering speed now, coasting on, moving through the unmistakable landscapes of the south, on towards a world laid out in half a hundred newspaper articles and magazine features: olive groves debauched by tank treads; *pieta* in black raiment, ragged columns of marching men; flags borne aloft in torchlit squares; makeshift field hospitals; the rattle of gunfire.

And all the years beyond shall be my hell on earth.

Note

I should like to acknowledge the influence of Simon Garfield's *Mauve: How One Man Invented a Colour that Changed the World* (2000), David Kynaston's *The City of London, Volume III: Illusions of Gold, 1914–1945* (1999), and Leonard Merrick's wonderful – and wonderfully underrated – novel of Edwardian theatre life, *The Position of Peggy Harper* (1909). The career of Beverley Nichols, which this account in no way travesties, can be further explored in Brian Connon's biography *Beverley Nichols* (1991). And thanks to CC for Loftholdingswood.

Every effort has been made to trace the copyright holders whose material is included in this book, but some have not proved possible at the time of going to press. The editor and publisher apologise for any material included without permission or without the appropriate acknowledgement, and would be pleased to rectify any omissions in future editions.